JOURNEY OF ASHES
A Boyhood in the Holocaust

Anna Ray-Jones and Roman Ferber

Journey of Ashes: A Boyhood in the Holocaust
© Anna Ray-Jones and © Roman Ferber, 2014

ISBN-13: 978-1496150288
ISBN-10: 1496150287

First Edition, August 2014

Production, Cover and Text Design: Richard Knight
Cover illustration: *The Fireside Angel* by Max Ernst, 1937
Private Collection. Courtesy of the Max Ernst Estate.
© 2014 Artists Rights Society (ARS), New York/ADAGP, Paris

All rights reserved. No part of this publication may be reproduced or transmitted in any form or by any means, electronic or mechanical, including photocopying or recording, or by any information storage and retrieval system without written permission from the authors. Exceptions are brief quotations in any reviews for inclusion in a magazine, newspaper, website or broadcast.

For information, contact Anna Ray-Jones via

    Email: **arjones@donleycomm.com**

    Website: **www.journeyofashes.com**

*This book is dedicated with love and reverence
to the memory of Leon and Manek Ferber
and to the numerous members of the Ferber family
who lost their lives in the Shoah.*

DISCLAIMER

Many names, characters, places and incidents in this book are products of the authors' imagination, or, if present in history, are used in a fictitious context. Any resemblance to actual occurrences, locales or persons, living or dead, is coincidental. The content is inspired by the personal history of Roman Ferber and should be considered as a literary interpretation of events he experienced in WWII.

Acknowledgments

Much gratitude and deep appreciation are due to the following friends, colleagues and institutions that were instrumental in the development and birth of this book. First and foremost is Maxine Ferber who read every page and their multiple revisions with diligence and patience and who was an endless source of guidance and insight.

Other dedicated readers who also gave their time and wisdom to the journey of the manuscript include: Marion Osmun, Ian J. Coates, Joyce Berry, and literary agent Peter Prescott. The authors are likewise much indebted to copy editor, Vicki Cameron and website designer and online publishing consultant, Richard Knight. Research in the USA, the UK and in Poland was generously helped by Newton W. Lamson, Llion Roberts, Professor Viktoria Hertling of Touro College, Berlin, Miriam and Will Shnycer, the late Chris Schwarz, Founder and Director of the Galicia Jewish Museum, Krakow, Miroslaw Obstarcyzk and Wanda Hutny and the archival staff of the Auschwitz-Birkenau State Museum, and by the Holocaust resources of the British Library, the Imperial War Museum, and the United States Holocaust Memorial Museum.

The Authors

HOLOCAUST SURVIVOR ROMAN FERBER was born in Poland in 1933. He spent his childhood confined by the Nazis in the Krakow Ghetto, and in the camps of Plaszow, Gross Rosen, Brinnlitz, and Auschwitz. After the liberation, he was rehabilitated in what had become the Displaced Persons camp of Bergen Belsen in northwestern Gemany. In 1949, at the age of 16, he immigrated with his mother to the USA and settled in New Jersey. For over three decades, he served under several mayors and held key positions in the city government of New York including: Special Assistant to the Deputy Mayor for Business & Community Development, Director of Manufacturing & Wholesaling, Director of Business Development, and Director of Job Development & Treasurer of the NYC Job Development Loan Program.

ANNA RAY-JONES is the author of *Sustainable Architecture* in Japan published by John Wiley & Sons, 2000. She has also written several screenplays including *The Haunting of Rachel Gottlieb*, a semi-finalist in the Nicholl's Screenwriting Fellowships of 2005, and *There Might be Angels*, a finalist for the Kairos Screenwriting Prize of 2009. Her short story, *Him Woolly*, was a winner of the new fiction prize of 2009 awarded by the Journal of Arts and the Environment. Her next book, a work in progress, is called *Loom Song*, a novel about Irish linen weavers shipped out as felons to Australia in 1828. She is currently a Senior Vice-President at the PR agency of Donley Communications in New York City.

Contents

PART I: 1939 ~ 1941
Introduction: Burning Amber...5
Krakow in Winter...11
Life under the Invaders...24
The Night Gardener..38
Encroaching Dangers and Safe Departures.................................49
Borek Falecki..58
Leaving Borek Falecki...73

PART II: 1941 ~ 1943
The Krakow Ghetto..89
Taken...105
Bitter Hours...120
Betrayals...135
Blood Will Have Blood...151
The Narrowing...167
Streets of Fire...181

PART III: 1943 ~ 1944
The Traveler from Vienna..199
Plaszow Spring..211
Dodging the Devil..223
A Murderous Shade of Blue...235
The Journey from Plaszow...251
Shifts of Fate..265

PART IV: 1944 ~ 1946
The Camp at the End of the World..275
A Bitter Liberation..297
The House on Dluga Street..311
The Secrets of Rabka Zdroj..323
Graveyard Days and Reunions...336
The Journey to My Mother...349
Epilogue: Bergen Belsen...362
Postscript...364

*"Earth, do not cover my blood.
Let there be no resting place for my outcry."*

JOB 16:18

Preface

THE LITERATURE OF WAR is a deeply varied landscape populated by writers of all stripes, some willing soldiers and heroic rebels, others luckless civilians, many of them witnesses with seared memories. In acts of resistance, imprisonment, brave escapes and schemes for defiant survival, storytelling takes on a whole set of authorial functions other than the conventional.

Holocaust literature in particular carries the weight of conserving a painful past with many works bringing the power of direct evidence to the war crimes courtroom. It also creates a legacy of revelation and memory bequeathed to the descendants of victims, and serves as a haven on paper for survivors to mourn and honor their losses. Such accounts come in diverse models: final letters, journals, documentary narratives, detailed histories, memoirs and more.

The importance of the genre is even more relevant since the *New York Times* reported on March 1, 2013, on a thirteen-year old research project at the United States Holocaust Memorial Museum which uncovered evidence "...that so far has shocked even scholars steeped in the history of the Holocaust." New investigations now reveal that the scale of destruction was much more extensive than was previously known. Researchers have cataloged a staggering 42,500 Nazi ghettos and camps throughout Europe, spanning German-controlled areas from France to Russia and in Germany from 1933 to 1945.

A good number of authors who are also survivors have given urgent voice to this terrible seam of history. Others managed to write before the conflagration consumed them. While monstrous in its origins and impact, the Holocaust or the "Shoah" (the Hebrew term translated as "catastrophic upheaval") has become a singular arena in American letters, influencing many prominent Jewish and Gentile writers alike. It has also created a complex and thorny relationship with literature, including off the beaten track hybrids such as the elegantly fused *Schindler's List* that, although carefully based on fact, technically and emotionally offers the experience of a finely honed novel.

Non-fiction narratives abound in this corridor of the world's library. Indeed, literary and historically minded purists have exalted the first-person eyewitness accounts as the foremost politically acceptable form by which to represent this profound human experience. Such testimonies and wartime autobiographies have a solid truth-value, a resolute stand and proof against the ludicrous arguments of deniers. However, like all good books, clarity, relevance, and literary merit depend on who is doing the telling. The archives of Holocaust writing are sadly rife with many great stories badly told. Works that soar above mere documentation are rendered with a sense that the poetics of the heart are still alive in a hounded people emerging from the darkest places on earth.

When one considers Holocaust non-fiction that is deeply affecting, the essential classics come to mind: Eli Wiesel's *Night*, Aharon Appelfeld's *The Story of a Life,* and the powerful works of Primo Levi that describe his survival in Auschwitz. Other authors command more subtle power in commonplace memoirs, poetry, and diaries, as in the graceful detailing of Anne Frank's young life in confinement.

Fiction and the Shoah present a different approach. Novels dare to investigate this dark matter with artistic license and engage hearts and minds in seeking understanding and meaning via creative synthesis. It is a form that fares expansively in its artistic reach and often breaks the boundaries of the imagination. This is evidenced in Martin Amis's *Time's Arrow* that makes skilful use of a reverse chronology and in *The Book Thief* by Markus Zusak, where Death itself narrates a tale of intersecting lives and survival.

Holocaust fiction frequently offers philosophical and psychological elements not always present in purely testimonial narratives. In this literary sector, writers take up the daunting task of bringing the reader deep inside the skin of survivors, perpetrators and observers. They quest for truth and significance through interpretation and command all the bells and whistles of fiction's toolbox. These include visualization, symbolism, universal themes, dramatic invention, pathos, humor, layered action and meaning, shifting time structures, and so forth.

This approach requires the writer to knit together fact and fiction to communicate the harsh realities of a tumultuous and dangerous existence. It's a device that has been successfully utilized in such novels as *Pilgrim among the Shadows* by Slovenian writer Boris Pahor, in Piotr Rawicz's *Blood from the Sky*, and in Fred Wander's *The Seventh Well.* Irene Nemirovsky, whose best-selling book *Suite Française* was discovered some fifty years after her death in Auschwitz, is the resurrected subject of her daughter's "mémoires rêvé", a brilliant imaginative chronicle called *The Mirador*. Élisabeth Gille was five years old when the Gestapo took her mother away. However, this lyrical "dreamed' biography is her attempt to reach across time to formulate some identity and presence of the gifted parent she never knew.

Journey of Ashes: A Boyhood in the Holocaust claims a small corner in this literary modality filled with variegated constructs of Holocaust storytelling. The authors have also produced a literary fusion: a book woven from true narrative, imagination, memory and fiction.

The work arises out of a creative collaboration between a Holocaust survivor from Poland, Roman Ferber, and British author and screenwriter, Anna Ray-Jones, who both found in the shaping of the manuscript that much history is under constant reconstruction, and that veracity is not the only road to channeling Roman's boyhood experiences onto the printed page. To endure a period of living in daily terror of annihilation when one is young and most impressionable (as Roman was) makes severe demands in old age on clear recall and the fragility of thoughts.

Journey of Ashes traverses a fine line between humor and tragedy, and presents a fascinating interpretation of a boy's recollections of growing up in Krakow surrounded by the encroaching Nazi invasion. It also depicts his family's striving for normalcy in the face of the unimaginable. Many people, especially children, in the context of being terrorized by the Nazi regime, still maintained a strong semblance of what it meant to be ordinarily human. They laughed, argued, fought, loved and feasted, and nurtured each other, even as their world was eroding.

For most Holocaust survivors, memory is a shifting force, hammered and reshaped by the healing mechanisms of time, distance and circumstance. This is both a challenge and a gift to a writer. The authors here are expositing the visceral wartime experiences of a boy from the age of six to thirteen, yet it's important to note that the actual story was awakened some sixty years later.

In its telling, the book creates a point of view that combines a child's acute observations with the verbal and psychological deft of an adult fictionalized memoir. This allows the reader to journey with Roman the younger, seeing the world fractured and ablaze with destruction just as he witnessed it. Along the route one is also engaged in intimate commentary with the elderly survivor (now a man in his eighth decade) looking back at the boy who charted a living road through the maelstrom. Where memory fails, the authors have fused fiction and interpretation with historic circumstance and constructed characters (some of them archetypes that surrounded Roman and the Ferber family) and have integrated them into the story.

Nazi policies defined the apprehended *kinder* (children) of their enemies as "useless eaters", a hideous validation in sending an estimated 1.5 million children (both Jewish and Gentile) to an early death. Given their contemptible program of slaughter, that a young boy should survive multiple incarcerations in the camps despite his raw vulnerability is a startling miracle in itself. In some instances, Roman won the aid and protection of kindly adults; in other moments, he suffered the depredations of those who had long since lost their humanity to Hitler's regime. However, it was his humor, courage, and sturdy sense of self that served as his lifeline, even in the darkest hours of deprivation and loss.

Journey of Ashes

PART I: 1939 ~ 1941

Introduction

Burning Amber

IN A SECRET COMPARTMENT of my mother's jewelry box, she kept a rare amber brooch mounted in laurel leaves made of Russian silver. The surface of the lid presented a landscape in marquetry of two herons dancing by a river. If I pressed a panel on the underside of the box, out shot a hidden drawer revealing the amber treasure. Of all her finery that gave me much delight to ferret around in when I was seven, the amber brooch held my fascination most. My mother would stoop before me so I could fasten it to her collar.

"Don't stick me with the pin, Romek," she'd caution.

"Mama, I know how to do it!" I'd whine, puncturing holes in the silk of her dinner dress. The translucent gem always cast a golden light on her cheek. I'd caress her face softly and the illumination would gild me too. When the brooch rested on her dressing table, I would hold it up to the lamp to see fragments of ancient conifer needles and delicate ferns suspended in the honey-colored stone.

"It comes from the Narew River," lectured my older brother, Manek, who at sixteen knew everything. "They've been pulling amber out of the shallows there since the fifteenth century."

"Do they net it like fish?" I asked.

"No, you pinhead, men rake for it in the riverbed. You should read more books."

Ever hungry to impress him, I spent hours roaming through my father's old encyclopedias to discover that ancient people on the Baltic coast believed that amber had magical properties; lynxes rested in caves drawn by the scent of its congealed resins, and that when polished, the gem manifested buried desires in the wearer with its subtle magnetic fields. Burn it and it smells like a distant forest ablaze, its flaming sap tarry and pungent, the reason many Poles call it "*Burstyn*" or "burnt stone".

In the afternoon quiet of the bedroom I shared with Manek, I rested on my quilt and twirled the amber brooch between my fingers, watching the sunburst patterns it made on the ceiling. When I held it up to my eyes, the furniture became suspended in a flaxen haze. Up close, I imagined merging into the yellow stone to drift among its tiny fronds.

In my reverie, I swim the Narew riverbed, diving through blankets of green algae; I glide along the amber trench, beneath the tumultuous waters that carve a route into the far reaches of Byelorussia.

Introduction

Now in my eighth decade, I still see the small boy of those afternoons, dreaming through the facets of a gemstone. My old man's memories spin on it, pulling up filaments from the past. Some recollections are tremulous accountings, untrustworthy in detail, others faded and passing shadows. However, there are episodes so real to me that I can walk beside that child of more than sixty years ago. I stare up at the faces he encountered, hear the words he spoke and sense his responses. Of all his reactions, fear and affection are the most magnified.

I want to lean down and ask him how was it possible, Romek, that you once walked with demons who used to be men? Each hour swayed between a potential bullet in the ear and the shock of finding yourself still standing very much alive in your worn boots.

How did you conjure such moments of survival when death repeatedly brushed against you but hurried on to claim his next prey?

How was it that you lived at all?

The German invasion of Poland in 1939 washed over my father, Leon Ferber, with no chance of wearing him down. He was a man of audacious optimism, a quality that endowed him with an awesome innocence so easy for others to betray. Despite a German decree that eventually took away his job as a traveling salesman for the Pelikan Pen Company, this undefeatable stripe in his character always made my mother uneasy.

"We don't need the money yet, Mala," was his gentle protest during the crucifying winter of 1941. My mother protested angrily, saying he might bury her yet in her diamond wedding jewelry along with the corpses of her starving children, but no. Send the amber brooch along with the sapphire earrings to Boris Pinski, an infamous black marketer whose trading ground was the Krakow Ghetto. I recall the booty earned us a good supply of bread, beef sausages and several oranges, (the latter a fragrant luxury in that era).

My father entertained me with many stories during the years of our wartime confinements; gripping tales of night fishermen in their flat-bottomed vessels called "pychowkas", who trawled the Narew River for trout and amber deposits loosened by the upstream rapids. The amber catchers, terrified of the German patrols, would enter the water silently and fill their nets with fish and their sacks with the gemstone's matrix, harvesting just enough of both to avoid sinking their craft. The dense alder swamps near Chelmno sheltered a universe of wildlife and often the splash of an oar awakened nesting bitterns, warblers and marsh harriers. The men would freeze, waiting for the plaintive birds to calm down before punting away from the avian alarms that could so easily expose them.

"Papa, can we go fishing there one day?" I asked my father.

"One day, Romek, when all this trouble is over," he assured me.

I recall it was the early 1940's when the country relatives of my father's colleague, Jakob Hershkowitz, fell into silence. Papa had the story in detail. Jakob's family had been farmers in the Kolo district for several generations, and of the thirty-nine people in his clan, nothing had been heard from them for several months. A message arrived saying that their houses were abandoned, farm animals stolen, and their crops weed-choked. Because of his pale eyes and a forged identity card, Jakob obtained a travel pass as an Aryan and went to Chelmno to search, especially for his beloved younger sister, Sossia.

He never returned.

Today, the Narew River that meanders around Chelmno is ambitiously deemed by some as the Polish Amazon. It braids itself into several tributaries, flowing through boggy swamps and verdant forests, creating countless oxbows and lush water meadows dotted with wild flowers. Beavers churn across peat ponds and white-tailed eagles feed their own nestlings on the hunted chicks of lapwings and redshanks. Travel brochures, in breezy phrasing, now advertise the pleasures of the vast national park in the region, *Special weekend packages include kayaking, nature walks, and full accommodation at an agro-tourist farm. Family discounts available.*

The giant oaks and black alders of the Rzuchowski forest are topped with storks' nests the size of washtubs. Wolves shadow their way along birch-lined tracks only they know. The dense trees create great avenues of gloom and stone quiet, a green dusk that extends for several kilometers along the surge of the river. The branches permit little sun and even the concerts of birds are absorbed in bark and leaves. Certainly, no shouts would have been heard here in 1941, not even from the open rail cars or the secret gas vans of the experimental *Waldelager* (Forest Camp).

Sossia Hershkowitz, my father once explained, possessed a solitary genius. She would hide in the barn to read the Talmud and skillfully argued points of theology with Yeshiva scholars. Her parents so admired her religious acuity they would have offered her to the Rabbinate if she had been born a son.

I met Sossia only once. She came to my family's apartment in Krakow with Jakob, in 1938, just before she was married to Herschel Kovacs, a husky landsman with skin the color of toasted grain. My mother had a sly notion to match her with my brother, but Sossia was five years older than he, her body and face already settled into a woman's form with all its embedded powers. Manek, whose head was muddled with political theory and impetuous idealism, was not what she needed. I thought her lovely with her broad smooth face and heavy-lidded eyes. She had a way of raising her head slowly to meet the gaze of another with an intense directness, speaking her thoughts with care and precision.

Introduction

In the deserted farmhouse kitchen, a cone of notepaper is concealed in a jar of flour. It lies among the invading mealy bugs but neither Jakob nor his enemies will ever find it. In the *Briefaktion* (Operation Mail), you must write, the detained were advised, a postcard, a short letter—we wouldn't want your relatives to worry about you. We have orders. You *must* write. The mail was always sent to Berlin for special processing and post-marked at the city's postal depots. Replies were permitted only through the Association of Jews in Germany, letters that floated into nothingness.

A whole team of dedicated censors will pick over the words of the correspondents, nervous that the most innocent greeting will be coded with revelations. Write, Pani (Mrs.) Kovacs, while you still have time. Sossia appears adamant. The Polish police officer, new at the job, is crude and uncertain before the calm will of the young woman. He pushes her down into the kitchen chair and thrusts the notepaper at her. A spike of fear is in the motion, quelled violence. Sossia lifts the pen.

Dearest Jakob,

The Polish police have orders that we are to be resettled temporarily. They say it is because the communists want to take the farms. The sergeant has promised us the fields will be harvested for the war effort, and if all goes well, we shall be able to return home very soon. I took a little soil from the upper meadow and tied it in a napkin. I think that holding it close to me wherever we go will draw us back here, that our ground will not forget us. The children are in good spirits but miss their favorite uncle.

I kiss your face, my dear brother, and wait for the time I shall embrace you again.

My unending love,

Sossia.

The real facts do not appear on the page except for the last few lines that were as true as steel. The letter will never reach Berlin. She signs her name as she hears the sound of military trucks thundering down her mud-choked lane. She scrawls a quick postscript and thrusts the page into the flour jar. The police corporal, in his shame, totally forgets the missive he's supposed to retrieve. "Call your children!" he barks urgently. He hurries to Sossia's window to have his authority shriveled by the sudden arrival of the neighborhood collaborator and the *Einsatgruppen* (SS killing squads).

The sediment strata of the Narew's swamps is a bone library for those who seek the fossils of early European rhinos, who would pry open the secrets of coiled ammonites and shells so ancient they are beautifully opalized. However, the layers of the riverbed, like the ploughed fields around Chelmno, have new content now upheld by the ochre veins of amber. Seamed into the earth, and above the remains of creatures that walked out of coral lagoons millions of years ago, lie the ashes of over a hundred and fifty thousand Jews. Flowing downstream above the amber matrix are the powdered frames of Sossia Kovacs, age twenty-seven, her husband Herschel, thirty, their twin sons, Reuben and Natan, both not yet six, and pretty Hanna, aged two.

It was my father, in his search for Jakob, who would open the flour jar to discover Sossia's holy lies and her postscript from the divine sufferer, Job, *"Earth, do not cover my blood. Let there be no resting place for my outcry."*

❦

Cities age not unlike people.

Wood and stone give way to desiccation just as the human frame is bent and betrayed by time. Memory colludes with the deceits of longing and the places I recall as fresh and vital in my early years are weathered and malformed in reality.

In 1984, I stood outside our old apartment house on Waska Street for the first time in over forty-four years.

It was no more than a crumbling deserted slum, the front door covered in flayed paint. Boarded up windows gaped open where a few planks have been wrenched away, as if someone had just departed in anger. The battered front door hung askew and the walls facing the back alley were patterned with spray can commentaries on the unraveling powers of communism, sexual mockeries and fierce notations of decline in my former neighborhood of the Kazimierz, corroded as it was in the 1980's with drugs, poverty and casual violence. One scrawl read, *"Na Co Czakamy?"* (What are we waiting for?) Another in bright red paint called out in letters a meter high, *"Solidarnosc!"* (Solidarity!)

I don't seek to enter the place but stare up at the empty building and listen to the loose roof slates rattled by the breeze, the slam of decaying shutters two floors above. I feel cheated by the awful cravings for my lost family that drew me back to this address. How foolish is the need that compels people to do this? No resonance of my former existence remains here. These ruined wind-blasted rooms held only the yawning immensity of all that was erased. Even the ghosts have left.

I hurried away down the street and into the brilliant air of a September afternoon.

I crossed the Vistula by the Pilsudskiego Bridge, into the district of Podgorze, (once the site of the Krakow Ghetto). The pavements there were saturated with lament, courage and rebellion; witness to a never-ending theater of deportations, the clop and roll of horse-drawn wagons balancing the depleted belongings of families relocating yet again, as the Ghetto was reduced once more. The enclosing walls cemented with the bitterness of men commanded to board up the windows that faced the Aryan side of the streets.

Introduction

It was a short distance to the *Plac Bohaterow Getta*, (the Square of the Ghetto Heroes), once named the *Plac Zgody* (Peace Square). On one side of this cobbled rectangle still sat the *"Apteka Pod Orlem"*, the Eagle Pharmacy of Tadeusz Pankiewicz, a Catholic pharmacist who helped so many with free medicines during the waves of atrocities. From this plaza, my grandparents, aunts, uncles and cousins were transported to the killing factories of Belzec and Treblinka. In those exiling days, many of the deported hastily scratched messages on walls and cobblestones with keys or hairpins, urgent faded inscriptions from parents to children, from wives to husbands. *"Dear Krystof, we are ordered to the railway station, look for me, Anna."*

You can still find such places in many sections of the former Ghetto. The killing grounds on Targowa Street, and on Wita Stowsza, where the Germans shot a group of elderly women, and at the corner of Nadwislanska and Solna Streets, where Jewish orphans from the *Kinderheim* (the Children's Home) were executed on one June morning. Some were once my playmates and their faces rise so clearly from my trapped memories.

The children look more surprised than afraid, bewildered by the sudden march from their playground. They stare at their executioners quizzically. The soldiers sup long pulls of vodka to guard against the wind playing at the curls of a six-year old girl; such a thing could undo a man. The youngest kids ask if they should cover their eyes against their forearms, as they did when playing hide and seek. Their nurse, who had chosen not to abandon them, answers serenely, yes, my lambs, hold my hand tightly, and do not look at the men. Keep your eyes closed.

These are the walls of a thousand sorrows without names.

Stones that still echo from outrage, bricks filled with the last murmurs of the slain. I run my fingers over their pebbled surfaces and add the words of the Kaddish to all that they have heard.

1

Krakow in Winter

MY STORY TRULY BEGINS on a bitter cold afternoon in November of 1939, when my best friend, Moniek Hocherman, a boy whose family lived down the hall, conned me into lying to my mother.

"They're here!" he whispered through the sliver of our apartment door. His reddish hair is skewed upright, a rooster's comb above eyes alight with expectation. "You have to come with me…now!"

"I can't. She'll skin me if I leave the house!" I hissed back.

The kitchen door was also ajar but only my mother's swift hands were visible, working a steady chop, dicing turnips for her soup. I saw my head joining the roots on her cutting board but Moniek is waiting and I'm scrambling for excuses.

There were all kinds of restrictions on my movements in those winter weeks of long ago. Ice skating was certainly forbidden as rumors flourished of ice floes as big as houses surging up out of the Vistula to split open a boat's hull. The screech of crushed timbers could be heard as far as Wawel Castle. I gawked in fascination when my father told Mama of the tough job of recovering the drowned sailors, their faces upturned, surprised in death, hands pressed against the lid of solid water several meters thick from bank to bank.

There were other dangers beyond the river. More cautious father-talk spoken over our heads; Papa and Mr. Hocherman complaining about the city being turned into military wolf runs, curfews and checkpoints to avoid, along with the vulture gaze of informers. I was forbidden to look out of the window during the day, and not to be on the streets alone, or even to play outside with other kids. However, this particular afternoon is ripe for adventure. Moniek is shoving his pale moon-face into mine and campaigning. "*Idiota*! Tell her you're just coming over to our place."

I called back the lie to my mother, grabbed my coat, and slid out of the apartment into his persuasive intrigues.

"Are you sure it's them?" I asked. "Do they have horses and swords like the *Ulani*?" (Polish cavalry units.)

"Swords, yes. Horses, no!" barked my friend impatiently, towing me by the sleeve. "Get a move on or they'll be gone!"

Moniek, who collected toy soldiers by the hundreds representing several eras, was obsessed with a stirring vision of the Knights Templar from a children's illustrated history much frayed from his thumbing. For a Jewish kid of an observant family, he was on fire about Jerusalem being saved by the Christian platoons of the Virgin. He swore to me the bold knights had now arrived in Krakow, having left their fine horses and embossed armor at their castle in Marienburg.

Our concierge at the time, Gisela Zaluski, guarded the lobby of our building from the doorway of her apartment like a vigilant official at a frontier post. She kept watch seated beneath a tattered reproduction of Our Lady of Czestochowa, speed clicking through her rosary as if to infer some divine appointment. I remember her as a heavy, loose-skinned woman with a face the texture of cold lard. Her immense bosom had tides of its own, cresting against the black apron and the neckline of the gaudy chintz dresses she always wore.

My mother complained that her piety assumed major sin in others. Jew sin burned Gisela the most. She crossed herself every time she passed a synagogue, (an act that in our Jewish neighborhood, the *Kazimierz*, would make her a human windmill). Once an elderly rabbi with the light of the prophets in his eyes ascended the stairs to visit my father and raised his hat graciously to the woman. After he passed by, she searched for the hoof prints of the Goat in the dust. She frequently grumbled to Mama that the blood of Jesus flowed in rivers for such non-believers as those who lived above her, that she's wearing her knees out every night praying for our salvation. My mother gently advised she should get a thicker carpet.

Gisela monitored all human traffic that transited the hallway, noting what the residents were wearing, the times of their coming and going. When tenants' mail was delivered, she rattled their packages carelessly and held their envelopes up against the sun, hungry to discern their secrets. Getting by her unnoticed required extravagant cunning.

Eager for the streets, Moniek and I halt at the half-open window on the second-floor landing and drop marbles into the courtyard. The clatter causes the concierge to lumber from her chair and stump forth into the iced weeds to investigate. We exit the lobby unseen and out into the cutting frosty weather.

The afternoon sky held a pale anemic light as we headed toward Wawrzynca Street, past Moszczynska's, the kosher butcher, closed by last week's decree, next Leon Budowski's tailoring shop, boarded up since he and his family emigrated to Canada. We halted to a sedate walk and hid in the doorway of the tobacconist's because I spied Mr. Plonska, a pen-purchasing client of my father's, striding along the sidewalk, and, as Moniek had ordered, our mission was to be daring but invisible. Just before we reached the Plac Wolnica, we heard the bass murmur of a male encampment.

The square's fountain was surrounded by a platoon of rugged men dressed in polished black boots and dark green uniforms covered with glittering insignias. Rifles with silver bayonets are propped against benches while many of the warriors stripped to the waist to wash in the frigid waters, unperturbed by the November winds.

Moniek and I were mesmerized at the sight of them and tried to conceal ourselves behind a plane tree. Thick slabs of ice floated in the fountain's basin, frozen spume hung from mouths of stone dolphins. Using their rounded helmets, the soldiers scooped and poured the freezing water over their heads. Others played aggressively, dousing their companions.

One man had his back to us, his skin streaked red from scrubbing among the icicles. He stood up to dry himself, caught us gawking at him, grinned and beckoned. Moniek dragged me from our hiding place. The soldier towered above us, smiling through a grill of perfect teeth to reveal incisors of gold. Water glossed his carved muscles, all corded veins and sinews. He was a physically splendid Colossus with yellow hair and eyes of pale steel who regarded us with amused indifference. By now, Moniek and I had lost our bravado and continued to gaze in awe at the warrior. I mustered a shy, "Good afternoon, Sir."

The half-naked "Knight" smiled and responded in German, *"Grüßt euch, kleine Männer. Ihr müsst bald nach Hause gehen. Die Sperrstunde ist um fünf und die Stadt wird sehr gefährlich für kleine Kinder."* ("Hello there, little men. You must go home very soon. The curfew is at dusk and the city becomes dangerous for small children.")

Although not understanding a word he said, Moniek and I glowed with privilege that so lordly a presence had deigned to address us at all. The soldier made a gentle "shoo-off" motion with his hand and said something to other men who laughed loudly in our direction. We retreated respectfully.

We dawdled along Piekarska Street to devour with longing the expensive chocolate and cream pastries in the windows of the bakeries, some already shuttered. A plump kitchen girl, with one eye turned and flour up to her elbows, stood in the doorway of Ruzany's patisserie pulling hard on a cigarette.

"Don't you boys have any parents?" she jibed.

"Two each," said Moniek sweetly.

"Then why, for the love of Jesus, aren't you home with them?"

"Thought we'd take a stroll," I answered.

"You'll be strolling right to hell if you don't get off the sidewalks," she sneered, flicking her cigarette butt over our heads. She's on cue for the rumble of military trucks a few streets away and the tramp of boots assembling into divisions—its curfew and the evening patrols were about to start their rounds.

"We'll have to take the alleys," announced Moniek.

We turned into the Jadwiga Passage, a dark, foul-smelling tunnel connecting a back street to a secure route home. A small circle of fading daylight was visible at its eastern end. Water dripped on us as we slid along its mold-lined walls and the center of the passage enveloped us in total gloom. I stumbled against what felt like a bundle of rags that gave off a blistering stench of urine. The rags spoke.

"Out at this hour? You're too stupid to live!" jeered a male presence. A grabbing motion came at my ankles but I leapt aside from whatever creature was slumped there against the wall.

"You have money?" the voice demanded. "I'm very hungry!"

"No, Sir," answered Moniek.

"Just kids are you?" wheedled the speaker.

The voice had a teetering edgy threat. The sudden tightness in my stomach rewarded the bakery girl's words, but nothing in her sarcastic prophecy had prepared me for the cold terror gnawing at me now. I was very frightened and my fear made me feel stupid and babyish.

"They say that there's famine in Warsaw and cannibalism is back in fashion. I hear the haunch of a well-fed young boy tastes like suckling pig, mm?" The ragged thing gave out a hideous chuckle. "But I think you two are kosher-approved, eh?"

In the darkness, we could barely discern the man rise up against the bricks, but I heard his obscene laugh, and the metallic rasp of steel striking flint. A crest of blue flame ignited from a cigarette lighter died away in deep-pitched eyes, set in a gaunt face whose cheeks were striped with deep cuts and dried blood.

Moniek gasped, pulling me slowly backwards by my jacket. His hands were trembling. "Romek, let's go...now," he whispered to me.

"No!" ordered the rag demon. "You leave when I say! Maybe you'll leave never!"

"Run, Monny!" I shouted.

We hurtled toward the cameo of fading day at the end of the passage. The awful rustle of fabric and the piss-scent of our pursuer followed us for several minutes. His wolfish grunts demanding "Get me some food. You will, or I'll geld you both!"

Emerging from Jadwiga, we darted down a long narrow lane to encounter...the impassable red bricks of a very high wall! I could hear the wounded shout of our crazed assailant coming ever closer. We stared at the stubborn bricks as if to melt them.

"OK, give me a leg-up," said Moniek, "I'll pull you up after me."

I cupped my hands into a stirrup under my friend's right foot and groaned as I threw his full weight skyward. He was on the wall's rim in an instant and reached back for me but my arms were short of his grasp.

At the far end of the street, the monstrous figure of the limping rags suddenly appeared bellowing, "Pig meat! Pig meat!"

He was god-awful tall and moving fast!

"Jump, Roman, jump high!" encouraged Moniek.

I ran at the bricks, leapt, fell, and leapt again. Fueled by terror and sheer adrenalin, I finally grabbed on to my friend's wrists. He hauled me up just as the scarred man started to pelt us with stones. On the other side, we both dropped swiftly into the soft earth of an expansive well-kept garden where we hid beneath dense shrubs, the maniacal chant still cursing us from the cul-de-sac.

"Think you're safe? Think you'll live to be men? Those days are over! Soon you'll be grateful to eat rat shit!"

The house that belonged to the garden was deadened from human absence. Through its cobwebbed windows, we could see rooms devoid of furniture and pale squares of timbered floor lightened from where carpets had once lain. The tradesmen's gate of the residence led us out into the beginning of Waska Street and to the safety of our apartment building.

※

We climbed the stairs, much chastened. Moniek went back to his collection of toy soldiers, his sketches of medieval knights and battle maps of the Crusades pinned to his bedroom wall and me to the potential wrath of my mother. A woman frequently provoked by my high-risk sin of charging around the streets of Krakow during these baneful days, where people disappeared inexplicably and our nights were taunted with anguished shouts and distant gunfire--in the time when the devil first arrived among us.

I took off my coat and gave it to Moniek to hide under his bed to prove I had been at his place all afternoon. I rolled up my sleeves and strolled nonchalantly into our apartment. My mother was in the living room, having tea with the career gossip from next door; an unhappy viper named Eva Twardowska. Mama nodded to me as I crossed the room but resumed her polite engrossment of Eva's bitter narratives.

Heading for my bedroom, I lay down to ruminate on murderous beggars and their dangerous powers. The reedy pitch of conversation from the two women washed across the doorframe as they contested disasters back and forth.

"Andrzej Goldberg, the dentist on Florianska Street? No one has seen him in weeks," bleated Eva.

"And Emmanuel Glinka, the Yeshiva librarian, innocent as a lamb," opined my mother, "apprehended for not surrendering books to be burnt, can you imagine?"

Eva followed with, "The same thing befell Erela and Zofia Klimitz, the dressmakers from Vlavoska Street, and Chaim Drevnovitz. You remember him, don't you? The upholsterer who liked boys too much?"

Mama pitched in next, "You must recall Golda Natanski who used to perm my hair, the one who had three husbands of blessed memory. Her shop's totally closed up and pad-locked."

Eva whined again, "Then there's Milosz Czielski, that nutty philosophy student, never well equipped for this world and too learned for the next. His sister has searched for him everywhere, but no great loss there!"

"And the *Tzaddik*, (the holy man), Jakov Mojsiewsky," declared Mama, "My Leon says he used to wander the graveyard of the Remuh Temple, making mitzvahs for the newly buried and praying to ensure that no unhappy dead pestered the living."

"But Jakov was not taken," I heard Eva explain. "It was his wife, Fania, and their two daughters. She offered herself to the German sergeant in exchange for freeing her children. The soldier, a disgusting brute, forced the *Tzaddik* to watch while he made indecent with his wife. Can you imagine, and in front of those young girls? Fania loosened that long braid of hers and tried to hide her nakedness. All three were put on the transport anyway."

A short silence, then my mother murmured, "Poor Jakov, his mind fractured from such obscenities."

"Of course, he divorced that whore, Fania, the very next day," said Eva in sour tones. "I knew the Rebbe that wrote up the *Get* (a rabbinical writ of divorce). Jakov could no longer remain in their home. You know what they say about a nest fouled. He burnt all their possessions and willed G-d to numb him against the beauty of any woman. Now he lives by night, raiding garbage from the best hotels so he can eat. His grief torches him without mercy and he does penance for Fania's shame by cutting his flesh with a razor; one pain to suffer that might erase all others. In the daylight hours, he conceals himself from accusing eyes in the darkness of the Jadwiga Passage."

⁂

I hear other echoes from that time, not all of them fraught with loss. I carry within my old man's memory many images and reach for those that bring with them the unforgettable charge of love that renders each detail bright and new again. I rest once more in the muscular curve of my father's arm as he proudly shows me a sterling silver pen—the Pelikan 100N.

"While simple in its design," he says, "this small barrel of ink, Romeczku, can move mountains."

I stare at its heart-shaped nib skeptically.

"Don't give me the face like a withered pickle," laughs Papa. "I'm telling you the truth."

On the desk before us is his leather briefcase open to displayed rows of expensive fountain pens resting in their green velvet beds. The outside of the case bears a sterling silver crest of a pelican feeding her chicks.

"Look at this one," he declares and lifts out a staunchly built black and green striped model. "This is a classic, the "Stresemann", one of my best sellers since 1929. And see here, this one is called the "Toledo" because of its Spanish-style sleeve and the gold filigree; a beautiful writing instrument for my more discriminating clients."

I take the Toledo pen from him; it feels heavy and luxurious in my hand.

"Who buys these things, Papa," I ask him, inscribing my name badly with the fine gold nib all over his desk blotter. I am learning to write under the martial tuition of my Catholic nanny, Bronka, and vainly believe that I have great penmanship. However, my signature appears to have been scrawled by a lame chicken on the run from the *Shochet's* (kosher butcher) blade. I form the letter "R" well enough but the rest of my name falls over in a blurred storm of ink.

"Romek, my customers are all types, from forgers to dentists, from bank clerks to judges," answers Papa. "But you must understand what it means to be able to use the written word and learn to express yourself well."

He pulls me up onto his lap and places his broad fingers over my ink-stained paw. "Your *Belfer* (the Cheder teacher) tells me you're studying the book of Genesis in class. Come, we will write a verse together."

He slides a tablet of notepaper toward us. The handsome Toledo pen glides easily over the smooth blank sheet guided by my father's hand over mine as we recite together and write in slow, careful script: *"In the Beginning…G-d formed man…of the dust of the ground…breathed into his nostrils the breath of life; and man became a living soul."*

The paragraph looks good except where I have pressed too hard on the end of a line, giving it a blobby kick with the nib.

"The scholar who first wrote those words did so thousands of years ago," lectures Papa, "passing the deeds of the prophets down to us. Words are the natural music of the hidden worlds. They can speak of love, condemn a man to death, or be the voice of heaven. Write your name again for me."

He releases my hand and the Toledo and I go on signing alone. Biting my lower lip in concentration, I scribe in shaky but distinct letters, *Roman… Ferber.*

In the Polish census of 1978, barely a few hundred names were recorded of those Jews remaining in the ancient quarter of Krakow known as the Kazimierz. A Rabbi complained to the local newspapers that it was hard in such times to organize enough men of faith to form a minyan. However, when I was a boy, my neighborhood held over sixty thousand Jews and a great number of gentiles. Many of both groups were my father's clients. Before the Second World War, the two communities intermingled with each other in relative civility and the narrow lanes and byways echoed daily with the melding of Polish and Yiddish.

Krakow in Winter

My family had lived on Waska Street since the day of my parent's marriage, in a quarter once the oldest and most thriving Semitic settlement in Poland, equally elegant to the civic and architectural grace of my city. King Casimir the Great built the Kazimierz around 1335 especially for Jews. His benevolence towards them was reportedly based on his fiery love for a Jewish woman named Esther, whom he installed in a fine mansion at 46 Krakowska Street (now a museum). Esther bore him two daughters, both baptized as Catholics, and a son who was left to his Jewish fate and forbidden any claim to his royal heritage.

We were a very close family, knit by tradition, complex affections, benign conflicts, and a sense that our happiness was durable and deeply rooted. My father, a naturally serene man, was the core of these bonds, honing his calm nature from having grown up in a chaotic household with eight siblings. He never wore a yarmulke or hat, except in Shul and was fond of saying, "What is to G-d is to G-d and what is to *Menschen* (mankind) is to Menschen."

My mother was one of seven and our clan on both sides reached to thirty or more. In the early years of WWII, Papa still traveled throughout the country selling Pelikan pen products. However, he always made sure he returned home for the lighting of the candles on Friday evenings and share Shabbas with us. He was pious (but not a zealot) who believed that, "Religion is to spirituality what agriculture is to nature."

"Leon, don't blaspheme in front of the boy," Mama chastised.

"Not in the least, my darling. I want Romek to understand that a farmer can plough and sow a field but in time, the earth will return it to its wild, original state. Similarly, if left to their own devices, man and the Divine would still find each other in kinship."

My mother was a strong-willed woman with a mercurial nature, brought up in a household without much religion. She flaunted convention by delivering my brother and sister in a hospital when it was the customary for the midwife to come and birth a child at home. (I was home-born to the great delight of my father who met me barely minutes after my birth.) My indelible image of Mama is one of a natural, discreet elegance, always clothed in some wonderful fabric of subtle color, an antique brooch gleaming on one shoulder, a trail of perfume drifting after her.

My older brother, Manek, at sixteen, had movie-star looks and exemplified the character of my father, patient, good-natured, with a ready sense of humor. An active member of Dr. Thon's Zionist organization, he dreamed of entering the political life and believed that a civic career was his destiny.

Eight years my senior, my sister Hanka was a petite pretty girl with lustrous brown eyes and an outgoing aggressive personality. I recall my mother telling me that soon after I was born my sister decided to murder me. She simply had no need of another brother. Fascinated that I'd led such a dangerous life as an infant, I was curious to know what methods Hanka had devised for my assassination.

"There was the time she hid you naked in the chicken coop," said Mama, "during a rainstorm but the hens kept you warm. We heard you yell over the clucking. She tried putting you outside the front door but Mrs. Hocherman came to your rescue, even though Hanka told her you were an orphan left by bad women. She even proposed that we sell you but Papa thought we'd never get much money for such a small baby."

Somewhere in this tale, I sensed my mother had done some gilding of the facts. She had a wicked glint in her eye, and seeing the stumped look on my face, gave me a bone-crushing hug, "It seemed less trouble to keep you," she said. "And when Hanka decided to stop killing you, she really came to love you very much."

Possibly, due to these early plots of fratricide, I never had quite the same closeness with Hanka that I had with Manek. He was a solid hero of mine, and I always sought to emulate him.

※

Friday night dinner at our apartment was a festive, boisterous affair. My father loved to play the gracious host and our home was a regular haven for clients, friends, and relations (sometimes of dubious or brief connection). This was not always to my mother's liking but Papa would nudge her affectionately, saying, "Come now, Mala, where's the harm? We should be grateful, we have much to share."

"*Borie pri ha gafen*," Papa would recite as he raised the Kiddush cup to welcome Shabbas, then we would all sit down to feast on gefilte fish, homemade chicken soup with flanken covered in the required half-inch of fat, a freshly baked challah and always potatoes, amazing in any form. Often we had a roast goose or chicken from the small nation of testy poultry that lived on our back terrace. For desert there would be compote made from prunes and apricots and a cake with fresh cooked apples, washed down with a dark bitter tea.

One Shabbat evening Papa announced, "I've invited Elezar to dinner. The poor fellow is having his fur business knocked sideways by the Germans."

"Oh, please, Daddy, not him. He's such a pompous bore," groaned Hanka.

"Hanka, he's a lonely man. For a few hours, he can be in the warmth of this family. Besides, your mother and I find him amiable company."

According to my know-it-all sister, Elezar Zelek, a well-heeled furrier from Warsaw, was an egomaniacal lecher given to bouts of sudden melancholia brought on by too much vodka. He wore the skins of his profession, even in summer, and possessed a pale linen suit with a fine trim of blond mink. He was known for misusing penniless street women, susceptible waitresses and the jaded wives of wealthy men. He would flatter the wife with luscious displays of ocelot skins and photos of elegant American women in furs he'd never made, persuading the lady to wring yet another expensive coat from her spouse.

Krakow in Winter

In winter, Elezar would climb our stairs, leaving fuzz balls of beaver fur drifting behind him. He smelt perpetually of forest beasts and the badger grease his maid combed through his fur coats to give them luster. His hair shone with same oily patina. With his plump, pink face sunk well into his shoulders, he looked like some misbegotten crossbreed of nature, with the exception of his small, fussy hands immaculately manicured and weighed down with onyx and diamond rings.

On this particular evening, I sat next to Elezar at dinner, trying to ignore his bestial odors while he grumbled bitterly to my father that ever since Warsaw surrendered to the Germans, he had to conduct his business from his country manse outside Radom.

"I'm telling you, Leon, I have a fur vault out at the house worth millions of zlotys, but who can buy in this economy?" Elezar complained. "Pass the latkes, please, Hanka."

The man ate like a tiger. My sister, who disliked the furrier intensely, handed him the steaming dish and he piled up his plate for the third time.

"My suppliers in the Ukraine," he continued, masticating his words, "can't get their mink pelts across the border without having some SS *diebische verbrecher* (thieving criminal) pilfer the shipment. And you'd be hard pressed to find a tailor alive who still knows how to block skins a high quality coat requires."

"I understand," said my father, meaning to comfort, "it's not a time for luxury goods."

"Easy for you to say," declared the furrier. "You're lucky that people can still afford your pens."

"Writing is a necessity and pens an essential," Hanka commented tersely. "My father's right about furs, and who wants to dress in an animal's terror anyway?"

"Hanka, apologize at once!" rebuked my mother. "I won't have you being rude to our guests."

Manek gawked at Hanka with pride while our father, looking very pained, pressed his hand over his mouth as if he was about to hurl his supper.

I feared Mama, whose eyes were incandescent with rage, was going to drag my sister away to the kitchen and slap her senseless. Instead she recovered herself and said calmly, "Hanka, dear, there are several fur coats in my closet, loving gifts from your father to me via Elezar, which I'm happy to possess."

"Wear them in good health!" Hanka shot back and stormed out of the room.

"You must excuse my daughter," murmured Papa humbly. "At her age she instinctively rebels at everything."

Instead of being chagrined, Elezar beamed, wiping the gravy from his several chins. His lips were wet and his eyes lit with a kind of queasy longing. "What a firebrand! Lucky is the man who gets that wild mare in harness," he said.

Elezar was inordinately fond of my mother and frequently advised her on how to maintain her furs. I remember a time when he had all her coats stacked up on my parent's bed, examining them for split seams in a cloud of farm minks, blue fox, and chinchillas. Among them was a garment Hanka had deemed *Mama's cape of horrors*, a wild Siberian lynx jacket with a detachable collar fashioned from an entire animal, complete with the paws and head intact bearing black tufted ears and yellow glass eyes that would never sight prey on the tundra. I dove into the pile of coats and rolled around in their perfumed softness while the fur merchant droned on at Mama.

"Mala, my angel, Russian sable cannot be kept in a box, it will age too quickly. Moreover, never dry your furs by the stove when they are wet, the skins will contract and shed. Before you know it, your coat will be as bald as an egg."

I watched him as he leaned in very close to my mother to light her cigarette, his knuckles caressed her chin lightly and his eyes glinted with that same hunger the evening Hanka had insulted him. I felt a flash of jealousy and a need to distract her. I pulled on her dark mink and went traipsing grandly around the bedroom, "Look at me, Mama. I'm a black bear."

"Romek, you're ruining my coat," said my mother.

Elezar became the reason that fear took up residence in my mother's closet. At least, I blamed him for it. He had his pattern cutter send Mama a parcel of silk garment sacks to house each of her furs. One evening when my parents were being entertained over at the Hocherman's apartment, Moniek and I snuck into the master bedroom, hoping for some sport with the bagged zoo of my mother's. I slid the closet door open. The lynx collar hung down to expose the clawed feet and the beautiful spotted head of the skinned cat; the yellow glass eyes stared out at us.

"Don't open the sacks," said Moniek timorously. "What sort of animals were they?"

I scrambled a tale that took me away with it. "This one here is a Russian bear that fat Elezar murdered in a knife fight." I poked a finger into the silk coverings. "The one behind it is a herd of white foxes that turned silver and blue after they were killed. Mama's favorite is a mink trimmed with the skin of an African lion who broke out of a leg trap and was shot twenty times before he would give up his life."

Moniek's eyes grew as big as moons. "That's awful!" he disdained, "poor lion. Aren't you afraid that he'll come back and haunt your mother?"

"I think he does. When Mama wears the coat to card games at Aunt Cyla's house, she swears she has no luck at all."

From somewhere down in the street came a sudden scream of brakes, car doors slamming, someone running, then popping sounds, more feet echoing on cobbles and loud yells of protest. A bullhorn was announcing some prohibition in German. Next, I heard my brother's urgent footsteps in the hallway and opened the bedroom door to see him hurrying through the apartment, heading for the bathroom, a sheaf of newspapers held up to his face, his hat pulled down low.

"Stay where you are, Romek!" he ordered savagely.

The bathroom door slammed hard. I felt like crying at his dismissal of me. Moniek grabbed my arm and nervously pointed at the closet. Every one of the fur bags were swaying to the mournful pleas and arguments coming from a block away.

※

Later that night I smuggled the lynx collar away from the whole jacket, secretly brought it into bed and laid it on the pillow beside me. I turned out the lamp and cuddled against the big cat form. It smelt of my mother's perfume but removed from its tailored realm, the animal looked noble and alive again. I fell asleep with it in my arms, but later awoke to whispering coming from our darkened living room.

"You must never mention this to your mother, ever!" I heard my father command. His voice sounded thick and constrained; water running, drawers opening and closing, and my father's footsteps returning hurriedly from the kitchen.

"Keep very still, you should have had this washed and bandaged earlier, we have to stem the bleeding," he was saying to Manek. "Where are the others?"

"At a safe house in Olsza, they took the printing plates with them. Three of us left the cellar first, as decoys." My brother's voice was labored and nasal, "We had the platoon out distanced until I looked back and found myself alone."

"So much trouble for a one-sheet newspaper, what the hell were you thinking?" my father demanded.

"I was thinking like you, Papa," whispered Manek hoarsely. "You've always said make a difference where you can, when you can; that such actions hold the world together."

A gap of silence fell between them and it seemed to fill up quickly by a small ocean of my father's confusion and pain.

"Manek, only a fool dies for nothing. What about Lukas and Chaim?" he sighed.

A wedge of candlelight spilled across the floor illuminating a vision that sickened me. My brother staggered past the open gap of the bedroom door and for a few seconds, I could see his face, bloated and purple, his left eye closed, his forehead heavily bandaged with a dark island of fresh blood already seeping through the gauze. He hesitated to answer our father.

"Lukas hid in the sewer. Chaim is in the military jail in Grzegorzki. He tried to outrun them, but they cornered him on Dajwór Street. His legs are all shot up."

"Dear G-d! He won't see the light of day for months, if ever," my father declared.

"Papa, I'm nauseous, I need to lie down."

"You need to rest. In the morning, we'll explain to your mother about your 'biking' accident, understood?"

My brother staggered on Papa's arm and moaned as he is helped into the bed across from me. I saw the sheen of tears on my father's cheeks as he draped the covers tenderly over Manek and sat by him for some time, smoothing the quilt, his face full of disbelief and sorrow. I lay very still and pulled my lynx closer to me. The cat collar is devoid of bones but his glazed eyes comforted me, they have a wise amber light reflected by the candle my father forgets to blow out.

I fell into a dream, moving at high speed through a light snowfall; on either side of me, I see a thick forest where spotted hides glide through ill-lit shadows. Unseen animals growl defiance. My feet have grown claws and webbed fur tufts that skid along icy crystal trails. I am exhilarated that I can change my speed just by thinking of its increase. Then a hideous screeching occurred, the spring bolt shot of a leg trap pitched me forward and I found myself in a vast free fall, a babble of menacing argument through a bullhorn mocking my descent into an endlessly dark pit.

I awake shouting in terror but am instantly enfolded in the arms of my nanny, Bronka. My brother across from me remains in a heavy sleep, wheezing uncomfortably. Bronka strokes my hair and coaxes, "Shush, Romeczku, shush, everything is fine. Go back to sleep."

2

Life under the Invaders

MY FATHER WAS A DEVOTED PATRON of the Rebbe of Belz named Aharon Rokeach, a mystic of formidable powers who was descended from a celebrated Hasidic dynasty. (In our war days, Rabbi Aharon also topped the Nazi's most-wanted list of influential Jewish clerics and his safety was under constant threat.) The Rebbe's followers had endless stories about his transcendent holiness, how the *Ruach Hakodesh* (the Holy Spirit) shielded him from danger, and how he could actually see into heaven to discern the thoughts of G-d and direct his devotees accordingly. (I never knew if he ever foretold of the satanic terrors soon to be visited on Poland's Jews.)

Funds needed to be raised to sustain the Rebbe's court that my father would personally deliver to him. Donations were collected from friends and colleagues of my parents through the many card games conducted at our apartment, where those not in good standing with their Maker would deliberately lose hand after hand, that the Rebbe might intercede on their behalf for their not-so-secret sacrifice. On these evenings, our doorbell shrilled repeatedly from visitors bearing written solicitations for prayerful help from the Holy One.

It was my task to sit in the hallway and call out to my mother whenever I heard a petitioner coming up the stairs. I listened in fascination to requests for the success of a business, the fertility of a barren bride, or protection for a son fighting with the consistently defeated Polish army. After opening the front door for the umpteenth time, my mother's patience was in shreds, "This home is not a psychiatric clinic!" she protested to the depressed man seeking his wife who had fled with his bank account.

A retired major, Elisha Haim, arrived next and suggested to Papa that the Belzer Rebbe could counter the German invasion by causing all their generals to die in their sleep.

"You couldn't really call it the sin of murder, Leon," he said to my stupefied parent. "It'd be like the first born of Egypt slain. Let these Krauts take their war to the afterlife, and leave the living to their rightful days."

"The Rebbe's gifts are not for death-making!" chastised my father.

I listened as Elisha made some bitter retort of how the Germans had tried to firestorm the great Synagogue, built in 1843 by the founding Rabbi of Belz. "For that alone, they should be wiped out like the vermin they are!"

"G-d is the cement of his own house," answered Papa calmly.

"Not when the Reich's commandant drafted a team of local Jews," countered Elisha, "to deconstruct the building brick by brick."

Journey of Ashes

My father allowed himself a half-smile and said with quiet assurance, "The temple was taken apart, it's true, but by hands that cherished every stone. It's an edifice in transition. The Rebbe has it from the most hallowed authority that we shall see it arise again, not in Belz but in Jerusalem."

Elisha patted my father's arm in sympathy, as if to calm such wild fantasies. Still shaking his head in disbelief, he allowed Hanka to lead him away into our living room.

Papa grinned and lifted me up to his shoulder. "Your eyes, my boy, will be witness to such things, when you are a man."

(I was to remember his words some fifty years later. They echoed as I prayed for him in the Belz Beis HaMedrash HaGadol, the magnificent Synagogue envisioned by Rebbe Aharon during the years of his exile in Jerusalem but actually built in the 1980's by Rabbi Yissachar Dov Rokeach, the fifth Belzer Rebbe.)

Visiting Belz entailed a train ride into the Galician countryside where Papa would point out various villages along the route. He instructed me that once we got to our destination, I should watch my manners—since the Holy One personally had G-d's ear and would report to the Almighty any infractions made by a small boy. Legends of the Belz Rabbis were famous, from hiding a sick baby from the Angel of Death to sealing night demons up in brick pits. I stared from the train at the chestnut hides of cows drinking from ponds and mangled my father's words with visions of the demons and me together, peering out of the closing wall as the last stone is laid in place. However, no chastising angels could ever take away the sweet pleasure of riding the train with my father.

At the prayer house in Belz, we found the receiving hall full of men wearing black gabardines and fur hats, and serious-faced boys, newly minted by their bar mitzvahs, holding prayer books to their lips. The Rebbe, a dramatic-looking figure dressed in embossed silks, appeared very regal but thin from his many fasts, with a full beard and long payess. He sat on a high cushioned bed, ready to offer advice and blessings. A nervous-looking man plaintively beseeched the Holy One for help. His family's business is in ruins. How shall we live with such difficulties?

"Your despair makes G-d grieve," advised the Rebbe. "Human lives are beloved of his heart but they are also fleeting shadows, little minutes on legs. You have struggle. You have pain. You're a lucky man to be so considered by your Creator. How can you know the grace of heaven unless there's trouble that illuminates the mercy and power that enfolds you?"

I float in hot water made fragrant with dried linden flowers that my mother claims has a pacifying effect on the bather. She has slim hopes this folk remedy will reduce my daily inclinations to mischief. My skinny right leg is hoisted over the side of the bathtub and held by my own personal Venus, Bronka, who is sponging my limb with the same gusto she used to scrub our kitchen floor. She is a muscular, golden-haired beauty of twenty-six who'd served as our live-in maid and my nanny for the last seven years.

"Your friend Moniek", she says, a sly glint in her eyes, "told me you two were out after curfew."

"He wouldn't say that!" I am hurt that she, of all people, would corner me.

"Little liar! Do you think life is the way it used to be?"

Bronka thrusts my leg back under the foaming bubbles and scours my arms. "Romek, people are becoming mean from fear," she explains, "from not having enough to eat, and from the war making a prison of their every waking hour. A person needs a hundred eyes to see the dangers around them, especially on the streets. Promise me you'll stay indoors after curfew?"

"I promise. Are you mad at me?"

"No, my sweet darling, I'm not mad. I just don't want to be without you, ever."

She grabs my face and kisses it fiercely, getting suds in her hair. "Stand up now. It's time to dry off." She hands me a huge white towel and questions, "What lessons do we learn in the bathtub?"

"To be careful of very hot water, not ever to bathe alone, and not to show off my pee-pee in front of ladies." I answer with contrite importance. "So please turn your back now, Pani (Madam) Bronka."

Bronka grins and turns away, covering her eyes with both hands. I leap out of the tub, swath myself in the towel and plot wickedness. I partially open the door to the kitchen then lean over the foaming bathwater.

"Hurry up, Romek, we need to get you dressed," she urges.

"OK. You can look now."

The minute she turns, I bring my hand across the water's surface and heave up a great shower, completely drenching her. She squeals and threatens to kill me but I am already through the open door in a second.

"You little turd, I'll hang you by your heels!" she splutters, her face covered in soap bubbles. "Come here this instant!"

I go hollering in glee through our apartment with Bronka in hot pursuit. We do several laps around the living room; she is fast but was not as maneuverable as a soap-slicked boy. I duck under the dining table. She makes a grab for me and captures the towel instead. I shoot out from under the table and headed for the front hall where Manek was just entering the apartment. He is so astonished at finding me naked with this lovely woman breathlessly speeding after me that he drops his books.

"Hey, Romek!" he says, grinning, "ten years from now this will be a situation you'll thank heaven for."

"Maybe not, I may murder him before his next birthday," answers Bronka. She rolls me in the towel, lifts me bodily on to her right hip like a sack of grain and we head for the bedroom. She unfurls me gently onto my bed, places a pile of clean clothes on the pillow, and kisses my damp cheek. "Hanka was right. We should have pawned you at birth. I want you dressed in five minutes."

Although my nanny, Bronka is a Catholic, she is a well-loved member of our family, an adoring third parent to me and holds my mother's authority in the house whenever Mama needs to travel with my father.

She sleeps in a former pantry cum bedroom next to our large kitchen. On cold nights, or whenever I feel lonely in my own sheets, I drift over to her bed to rest in the shelter of her broad back. It is Bronka who taught me how to read from children's storybooks such as *The Glass Mountain, The Old Man's Son,* and *The Prince and the Foundling.* My joy is to nestle against her soft shoulder and let her melodious voice spirit me away into yarns about captive princesses, a miracle-working horse, and a witch who took on the shape of a hawk.

My memory of Bronka is inseparable from the first ham sandwich I ever ate. Sunday was her day off and she would take me strolling through the Planty, the lush municipal gardens that encircled the inner core of Krakow. If I whined that I was tired and hungry, she'd coyly suggest, "Come on, Romek. Let's go eat some pig," and haul me to the nearest delicatessen for a ham roll and a soda. She made me promise that this would be our secret, explaining that pork was good for children because it prevented whooping cough. Years later, my mother admitted that she knew all about this kosher violation and even gave Bronka the money to buy the offending item. (Since those Sundays, I've never lost the taste for ham.)

※

Early in the New Year, currents of nameless fears and rumors coil through the snow-choked streets of Krakow. From the throne room of Wawel Castle, Commandant Hans Frank, head of the new general government of Poland installed by the Reich, decrees that our synagogues are to be shut. His squads make temple raids, taking away the silver and gold censers, candelabras and gilded scrolls. His intention is well discerned. Cut at the roots, break the vital cornerstone and create an urban desert for our coming exile.

My father and brother retire much too frequently to the front hall and argue in frantic whispers. Their secrecy is so ominous, so provocative that my ears ache from the strain of listening. I drag my wooden train across the living room carpet, making sure I edged closer to their conversations. It takes me days of eavesdropping and not-so-subtle questioning of my mother and Manek to knit together the innumerable violations against religious practices that cause my father to lock himself in his study and narrate loudly to himself in the warning letters he writes to various relatives.

I press my ear against the door's oak panel, listening to snippets of his solitary discourse. I pull a chair forward so I can reach the keyhole, and to this day, I regret the sight of Papa's shoulders heaving in dry sobs as he reads a message received from Hassidic cousins in Nowy Sacz. Their missives are full of how the ancient synagogues of Bedzin, Sosnowiec and Dabrowa have been burnt to the ground. Sacred texts are plowed as fertilizer into fields and the words of the Prophets leached into potato roots. Papa's reply laments the destroyer's raids against the famous Talmudic Library, the Yeshivot Chachmei Lublin (Academy of the Sages of Lublin), and the spiritual light of Polish Jewry and learning, who's *Tzadikks* (holy men) were the intermediaries between humankind and the powers of heaven.

"What grossness arises in men's hearts," my father recites above his pen, "that they should desecrate so sacred a place? Don't these Germans heed their Catholic heritage? How can they worship their Christ and disregard his Father who sustained Abraham and his people? Holiness is not something one can cut on the tailor's bench, so much for today and less for tomorrow."

My spying is undone by Hanka—her sharp fingers hooked under my armpits plucked me off the chair instantly. I go and pester Mama and my brother for more details but they dismiss me with smiles of affection. I read about chameleons in my book on lizards and take to covering myself in straw, hiding beside the chicken coop on the balcony where the hens mutter and fix me with their stony glare. If I leave the terrace door ajar, I can hear everything being said in the living room. Manek is telling my mother that the illuminated manuscripts and rare testaments of the Talmudic Library were carted to the central marketplace. It took twenty hours to burn the scholarship of several centuries; that the weeping of the Lublin Hassidim was so loud the Germans ordered the military band to play robustly to drown out their keening. After the blaze had subsided, Rabbis and Yeshiva students alike knelt down in the embers to rub the ashes into their clothes and hair, as if sacred knowledge cremated might rise to permeate the prayer shawls of so many mourners.

In the coming weeks, I discover that G-d is highly portable. My father, brother and men from the Remuh Temple and other synagogues spirit Torahs across rooftops and through basements to various secret repositories. The Word is ferried under a pyramid of turnips on the cart of Leon Sulkowski the root farmer, its sacred scrolls to be hidden behind the walls of the projection booth of the Poteckimenag. The contents of prayer houses are carried away and concealed beneath the tiled floor of the Mikvah on Szeroka Street and in the hollow columns of fake Italian marble holding up the lobby of the Warszawa ballroom where German officers often danced with indifferent Polish girls.

JOURNEY OF ASHES

My sister describes to me a magnificent Torah whose binding shimmered with gold leaf, its cover is inlaid with sapphires and pearls and portraits of Old Testament saints skillfully enameled in each corner.

"It was made long ago by Sephardim goldsmiths in Lvov," says Hanka.

"Can I see it?" I plead.

"Oh, you think I have it in my back pocket?"

Later, I hear Hanka telling Mama that the five-centuries-old volume was wrapped in cowhides and transported in an empty wine cask to the Cistercian monastery outside Kielce where it will remain respectfully hidden by the monks throughout the war.

※

By the time I had been enrolled in the *Cheder* (a religious school) three blocks from our home, I could read and write in both Polish and Yiddish. Our classroom is a plain arrangement with rows of rough-hewn wooden benches and a creaky stove that gives out misery heat in one corner. Directly before us is a wide desk, the demarcation zone of our *Belfer*, (our religion teacher), Itzhak Lovitz, a humorless dried stick of a man, semi-shaven with narrow eyes beneath a black hat. He always wears the same threadbare gray suit, white shirts faded to a bilious yellow and he looks perpetually undernourished, but becomes an energetic tyrant when provoked. He will routinely glide along behind rows of his pupils, intoning a lesson, easily seizing on any slacker like a hawk on a gosling. Lovitz offers stories of rabbinical saints as paragons of the purity and single-minded virtues we should aspire to, but as he observes, we are so hopelessly inadequate that the Creator himself would be hard pressed to find a purpose for our existence.

"You boys should learn from the moral example of Rabbi Yisrael Ben Eliezer, the Master of the Good Name," he commands and explains how many legends are also attributed to the senior Eliezer, the revered father of Rabbi Yisrael, who advised his son to, *"Fear nothing in this world other than G-d."*

During one of these paralyzing homilies, I am forced to hide the crude drawing of a naked girl Moniek has just passed to me, concealing it with my sleeve seconds before there was a menacing hiss in my left ear. "Now, Roman Ferber, who is the one that the good Besht was advised to fear?"

I catch the buzz of my teacher's voice but barely the question. My mind turns into a total landslide, so I blurt out, "The Angels of Satan, Sir." I hear a loud crack followed by a shattering pain in the back of my head; the lights in the room seem to dance and brighten.

Next, the Belfer's hiss is in my other ear. "Ferber, you are a smart aleck of a boy but you suffer vast chasms of amazing ignorance, entire valleys of mental ineptitude, which, with G-d's might, we will expunge from you!"

Life under the Invaders

Before my ignorance or my person can be erased, I make sure I knew the life of the Baal Shem Tov better than the Saint himself did. Under the Belfer's program of teaching by terror, I study hard and am soon able to recite, word for word, from the scripture that makes my father so proud, he calls me *Kaddishel*.(Little scholar).

The Belfer often scares the wits out of me but I have come to appreciate him as a living repository of the holy screeds. I strive to reach Olympian levels at recitation and am finally enjoying some limelight and warm approval from my teacher around the time he receives an edict from the high command at Wawel Castle: close the Cheder or suffer arrest. The next day, school was out —forever.

At first, Moniek and I are overjoyed at this odd liberation until we discover that no other schools in the city will take us. The last time I ever see Belfer Lovitz, he is shuffling away with a heavy sack of religious books he was taking to the Rabbi of the Alte Shul for safekeeping. We never heard of him again.

❋

I soon learn there are certain kinds of courage that have to be acquired gradually and that fearing G-d or any number of wonder Rabbis won't save you from bitterness or loss. I come home one day to find that Bronka is missing from our lives. She had packed up and left without a word, except the mutual tears and the regrets she and my mother expressed. It feels as if someone has died. I stand in the middle of our living room full of pleading questions. *How could Bronka go? Why did you let her leave? Why didn't she wait to say goodbye to me? Will I see her soon? Will I see her ever?* My mother kneels beside me, taking my hands in hers. Tears have made dry rivulets through her face powder, although she remains pretty in her sadness.

"It's not because she didn't love you, Romek", Mama says softly. "There were orders, a notice from the Reich's office."

"I can't go and visit her?" I ask, sobbing freely now.

"Maybe, when matters improve and the peace comes."

I feel swallowed up in a gigantic and useless misery. Then, my mother is in the misery bubble with me, both of us drenched in loss. That night, my parents allow me to sleep in Bronka's cot. I find one perfect golden hair on the pillow that trigger a howling for hours at my nanny's absence until my grief exhausts me. (I later learned Bronka had to stop working for us because the Germans forbade Polish citizens to be employed by Jews, especially Christian females under the age of forty-five.) I have a faint suspicion that the prohibition had something to do with men being with attractive women but I am ignorant of the mechanics of the situation.

In the early months of the German occupation of my city, different groups of military being to arrive daily: first the Wehrmacht, the front line soldiers, and then German police followed by the *Die Sturmabteilung*, (Storm

Troopers), and the *Die Sicherheitsdienst*, (the Security Service) who often patrol the streets undercover, plus the SS elite and their political arm, the Gestapo.

Our illicit radio reports that the Luftwaffe is bombing *shetls* (Jewish villages) in the provinces. Fearing it would be our turn soon, Manek tapes up our windows so the glass will not become a death tool. Our radio days are short-lived as the Germans soon make ownership of all such devices illegal but my brother decides to hide ours for future use. I see my father's face in the lamplight, his expression still full of hope and assurance. "Don't worry so much about this war, it will be over soon." he cajoles. "No matter who's invading, we will shelter under G-d's protection."

However, G-d must be busy elsewhere and is certainly absent from the office of the *Judenrat* (the Jewish Council) who are ordered to implement increasingly odious sanctions. Jews cannot study, teach, or conduct business and our bank accounts and assets are confiscated. In several areas of the city, we are compelled to walk only along the gutter beside the rolling traffic. By their new decrees, the Germans drive out the *Shochets* and their *Bodeks*, the kosher butchers and their assistants and close down the market in the Plac Zydowski that sells kosher food.

I am not the only scholastic dropout in our family. Hanka and Manek, both excellent students, are dismissed from their high schools. My father argues for defiance to take the place of restriction and disappointment. During one such heated discussion in our kitchen, I hang off the back of his chair to just to feel the charge of his energy as he tried to put things right. "They can shut down the schools," he declaims to my brother and sister. "But they can't close your minds! There are books in this house and good teachers out of work all over the neighborhood. We will bring the education home and you will continue with your studies. That goes for you too, Romek."

"But, Papa, who's going to teach me," I ask, coyly eyeing my acid-tongued sister and willing to the angels, *please don't let it be her!*

"Mama can help with your reading and grammar. Manek will work with you on your math and science and I will be the Belfer for your religious lessons."

"I get a reprieve from this toad of a boy?" Hanka queries.

"You can spend some time entertaining him," advises my father. "He's a child, not a lifeless rock. He needs some fun now and then, even more so because of what's happening out there." He gestures to the open window.

A piece of simple cloth is issued also to contain us, a cotton band with a star emblem embroidered in blue. That October, an order had gone out from Wawel Castle requiring all Jews in Poland over the age of 12 to wear this signifier. The item looks as if was designed by some constipated Nazi committee who must have squabbled with tailors and guild embroiderers over the quintessence of this insidious little rag. What shade of white should the ground weave be? How deep the blue of the star? Is it necessary to have "Juden" appliquéd in the center (like the French version in yellow that bore the word "Juif")? The item comes in a two-piece kit composed of a pale strip of cloth plus the blue square of David's star, and it falls to the women in our community to sew one part on to the other. My mother reads the instructions aloud to us.

"It says here that the armband has to be exactly ten centimeters wide and the star must be correctly positioned eight centimeters in the center of it. There will be a severe penalty if this rule is violated. I wonder if they have a patrol just for measuring the correct spacing on the thing."

To add insult to injury, the Reich required all wearers to purchase the item for ten zlotys through the Judenrat. Looking back at that time, I'm chagrined at how easily I would perceive the most inappropriate things as a novelty, until I learned their real meaning. I didn't think wearing the blue star was such a big deal, because at my age I wasn't required to. Mama sewed extra armbands to be pinned inside coats and hats as life insurance against the disasters that would befall Papa and my siblings if they were caught on the streets without one. Hanka and Manek colluded in a smoldering rebellion at having to consider the band at all; that they could argue with my parents like adults was to me a delicious, soaring wickedness.

"I'm not going to wear that damn thing and be branded like a beef cow!" explodes Hanka. "They can wipe their German arses on it!"

"I don't want to hear this toilet talk!" barks Mama. "No young girl should speak so coarsely!"

Oh, terrific! The war has come into our house! Scenes like this are usually good for at least an hour of mother/daughter barbed fighting. Trying to appear nonchalant, I roll my toy truck along the sofa arm, always an excellent ringside seat for such blow-ups.

"Hanka's right, Mama," declares Manek. "I'm not wearing it either. It's a target sight for any Jew-beater to come and kick the crap out of me."

Our father put a different spin on the matter. "You will both wear it, if you want to live," he insists sternly. "And you will do so with pride!"

I immediately back him up. "If Papa wears the Star, I'll wear the Star. I wanna wear the Star!" I chant loudly.

"Shut up, you poisonous little fink!" orders Manek.

"Don't bully the poor child," chides our mother.

Papa's jacket is slung over a kitchen chair. I grabbed his band from the sleeve, pulled it up over my arm, scrawny and blanched as a length of butcher's string. It's way too loose; I fit it around my bird-bone shoulder, the star uppermost, and fancy that I look like a recently promoted general. My father smiles broadly. He comes over to me, kneels down and cups my hands in his.

"Romek, my feisty little cub," he says. "The new law says this is not necessary for small boys."

"I want to wear it, Papa! I will!" I screech priggishly, trying to steal the show from my smart-ass siblings who are grinning at each other. I am losing some serious ground here and can't think of anything smart to say to trump them.

"Look, Romek, if you want to wear the band," says Papa, "Mama will make one up especially for you. However, I want you to understand what it means. When I was young, my Rabbi called the star the Shield of the Ages, the "Magen David", because it brings much protection to the one who wears it. See, right here, the points of the star symbolize G-d's rule over his universe in all six directions. Such things are the jewels of faith, to be cherished always."

My father takes the armband off my shoulder and raises the blue star reverently to his lips. The gesture is light and quick but watching him do this with such sublime authority makes my heart spin with pleasure.

"Remember the lines I taught you?" he asks. "After we finish reading the Haftorah on Shabbat? Blessed are you, Oh, Lord our G-d, the Shield of David."

✡

I wear my personal star armband for about a week, ramming it on my head so I can go gliding, in a bad imitation of a kingly stride, down the corridors of our apartment house. Moniek gives me the devious eye and negotiates a new arrangement. We can enact all the wars of King David using his set of toy soldiers (which he had collected by the hundreds since he was four) if he can wear the armband as a crown for one of the battles. I remember his mother once telling mine that Moniek had been a premature birth and his angular head, egg-shaped from him hurrying his way into the world, has the form of a badly-made loaf collapsed in the baking, so the band settles right above his eyes, making him look downright furtive. Still, it is an excellent plan. I argue to play David in his early years as a shepherd lad.

"I don't think so," teases Manek. "The Book of Kings says that the young David was *beautiful to behold and of a comely face*. You have more of a going face. He was a good musician too and sang psalms. You sing like a hinge."

"Go wet yourself," I sneer. "You're not in the game."

Moniek and I rework the shepherd boy's battle against Goliath of Geth. He wins the regal role in a coin toss and I am left to play the wicked overgrown villain. To be that tall a giant, I stand on a chair at the head of our stairs with a mop as my lance and the garbage pail lid for a shield. Moniek takes up a position in his apartment doorway some ten yards from Goliath's camp. Using parent-prohibited marbles as ammunition, he fires off several rounds with his slingshot that miss me but carom smartly off the wallpaper, making a pitted mess of the chintzy painted roses.

"Are you blind?" I say mockingly. "You're supposed to kill me!"

"Hey, dog-face, I'm the King here!" he yells, lining up my head in his sights. "Get ready to die!"

Life under the Invaders

His next shot flies through my hair and slams off our front door post. The terror of it is so startling that the chair spins out from beneath me and I come crashing down on dozens of his soldiers, each one four inches of brittle lead. His troops are immediately reduced to filings but their miniature swords and lances pierce the front of my pullover. Moniek cackles in triumph and I squeal in agony at the sharp points impaling my stomach. Our racket causes the ancient Pani (Mrs.) Mirowski who lives on the floor below to come bellowing out of her apartment.

"Degenerates!" she screams up the stairs, her loose teeth clacking in a dancing rage. "Who brings such devil's spawn into the world to disturb the peace of respectable people?" Her cat, a sleek gray lathe of a creature, appears from behind her thick varicose ankles, his eyes darting a villainous green at us. It is time for a retreat.

Moniek and I quickly gather up the armies of Israel and relocate to the far end of the corridor. We wait an eternity for Widow Mirowski's frenzy to run out of steam and finally hear her door slam before we line up King David's militia against the Philistines in the desert of Engaddi. "David had about four hundred men on his side," I declare, putting on the star crown. "But I could beat the pants off you with less."

"I can let you have about two hundred infantry soldiers and six cannons," bargains Moniek, tumbling more of the lead figures out of an old hatbox. "But we're going to ambush your guys first, OK?"

He positions his attack platoons in clusters of thirty hidden between the banister rails. I have the Israelite legions arrayed on two flanks along the linoleum when I caught an odd muffled wail coming from down in the lobby and the haltered step of someone laboring up the stairs. Moniek is busy fiddling with his archery units, but still I heard a low growling sob and a heavy footfall, coming closer. I grab my friend by the arm. "Shush, listen."

"Not Ma Mirowski again?" he whispers.

Moniek faces me with his back to the stairwell but I can see well enough over his shoulder at what looked, at first glance, like the head of a hideous skinned beast emerging from below. A flayed, red-meat thing in a ripped overcoat staggers up the last stair tread...to turn into our corridor! For some seconds, I have lost the reality of the day. The lines of little tin men around my knees become a blur. I stand up slowly and grip the oak banister. My whole focus is drawn to the sibilance of a terrible grief issuing from a blood-drenched figure now slumped against the wall. Moniek stares up at me, tracking my glance then turns and gives out a wrenching scream. "*O Boze! Tatus! Tatus!*" ("Oh G-d! Papa! Papa!")

The ear-splitting cry unfroze me and I run to Mr. Hocherman. His arms are rigid and he is staring down in awful wonderment at his open fingers aimlessly sifting the blood issuing from his wounds. Several of his teeth are missing and his head and face are split open in many places. I feel at such a loss to help him that all I can do is pat the man's arm and yell for help. In the same minute, my mother and brother came running out of our apartment. Manek, ever cool-headed, reads the scene instantly, darts back in and returns with a large towel.

"Sit, Issac, please," urges my mother to the battered man. She puts her arms around his quaking shoulders and she and Manek gently lower him down. They sit all together on the top stair with the two of them blotting his wounds.

"Romek," Mama orders me, "go to the kitchen at once! Bring a pail of warm water, more towels, and disinfectant and bandages from the bathroom cabinet, and some cognac from the dresser. Run, now!"

I fly through our place, dragging the heavy bucket and spilling the contents on Mama's fine Persian carpets. I make a ten-second stop for the brandy, the antiseptic, clean dressings, the towels and am back out on the landing again, my heart in my throat. Manek takes the pail and he and Mama set to washing Mr. Hocherman's face.

"Better see to your friend," says my brother soberly, nodding at Moniek who has stayed rooted to the same spot in the corridor shaking and sobbing, afraid to approach his father. I crunch on some of the tin soldiers as I reach for him.

"It's OK, Monny," I say. "It's OK."

He lets me lead him to where he can squat down and embrace Mr. Hocherman from behind. Issac takes a long draught of brandy and comforts the terrified boy clinging to him. "Don't cry, son, I'll live. Is your mother home yet?"

The story soon comes out that, on this particular afternoon, Issac Hocherman had encountered a group of German soldiers on Starowislna Street. They had grabbed him by the starred armband and slapped him around, trying to force him to expose himself on the sidewalk so they could mock his circumcision. He'd made the grave mistake of protesting, "This is outrageous! I am a Polish citizen!"

The assertion had earned him several vicious kicks and rifle butts in the face. The soldiers had made a pitiful carnival of him, dragging him roughly by the heels like a butchered carcass along the pavement with onlookers fearfully ignoring his cries.

I have never before seen a human being so badly hurt. It is not so much the harrowing gashes on Mr. Hocherman's face that make the pit of my stomach drop, more the look of unfathomable despair in his eyes. As he later would say, it was as if he had awoken to some other plane of existence where everyday kindness and civility had dropped away.

Mrs. Hocherman finally arrives home and is white-faced to see her husband so badly abused. She and my mother lead him into their apartment while Manek hurries off to get Dr. Borowski to come and stitch up his head.

Life under the Invaders

I gather all the tin soldiers and shut them up in the box. Moniek remains inconsolable so we sit close together on the top of the stairs for quite some time. He finally stops weeping and both of us fall silent. We don't speak of the incident ever again. The next day I take my armband with the Shield of David and throw it in the trash.

※

There are now many such bad occurrences in our streets. The German soldiers have a childish bullying mentality where they will let loose violently at any Jew anytime; they have no sense of restraint, no pity at all. They hurl sexual insults at young Jewish women and accost religious Jews to spit on them and cut off their *payess* (side locks) as souvenirs, or shave their beards with their bayonets. All a man could do was stand there, send his mind away to heaven and pray that the blade would cut only hair. Such horrors have Mama constantly forbidding me to be on the streets alone.

Another crucial prohibition is not looking out of the window. I learn this to my terror the morning that I was almost taken out of the world, just before lunch. Hanka and Manek are out and my father is visiting the black marketer, Boris Pinski, to barter more of Mama's jewelry for food. (I plead to go with Papa ever since Manek had mentioned that Boris was missing several fingers of his right hand. Lost, so my brother claimed, while delivering grenades to a resistance mission that leveled an SS warehouse down by the river. It is rumored that he had replacement digits fashioned from gold forcefully acquired from Hungarian gypsies.

Mama, however, has forbidden such a trip for me to gawk at the gilt-handed Pinski and I am trapped with her, bored rigid and watching a light rain trace rivulets through the grime of our living room windows. My mother is clanging about among her pots in the kitchen, trying to revamp last night's soup. I was gazing aimlessly through the window at the school across Waska Street when I see several military motorcyclists park their bikes at the corner and pull out their cigarettes. Someone else has seen them too. A window shade is raised up at the school and a pretty fresh-faced girl of about fourteen is suddenly waving at me. I grinned and waved back. Then I realized she is actually signaling to a handsome soldier astride his bike down in the street. He smiles up at her but quickly raises his rifle and inexplicably...fires!

The shots crack the peace of the street as thunder trapped in a box. When the ringing in my ears stops, the window where the girl had been standing was a jagged mess, terrible screams and shouts issue from within the school. I look down at the soldier who was laughing heartily with his companions. The men applaud his marksmanship and buff his shoulder with their fists, some pointing their fingers up at the houses around them. I see him reload his weapon and raise it again.

"Romek, what was that awful noise?" Mama calls out from the kitchen.

She hurries into the living room carrying a large bowl filled with a kugel mix she was stirring. I have my face pressed hard to the glass, hoping to see the girl from the school appear again. My mother comes to the window too. By some innate maternal compass, she hurls her mixing bowl to the ceiling and grabs me by my shirt collar yelling, "Get down!"

I remember the pleasant sensation of flying horizontally over an armchair at great speed. The thundering noise bellows again. Then, Mama and I are falling forever through an endless cascade of almonds, flour, rain and tiny diamonds of glass. When the mess settles, I am buried beneath her soft body, nose down in the carpet, with the dining table sheltering us. I look up to see her face covered in white, like the clown on stilts at the Gorski circus. The downpour is now in our living room, wafting in sheets through the fractured casement and spattering the polished wood floor. A circle of small holes dots the ceiling, leaking shreds of plaster.

My mother drags both of us on our knees into the kitchen where she undresses me to the waist to pick small splinters of glass and wood out of my shoulders. I feel her hands shaking as she plucks away at me.

"Mama, are you OK?" I ask carefully.

"Yes, I'm fine, Romek," she lies. "But if you ever go near the window again, I will throw you out of it or disown you!"

My right shoulder is suddenly wet, first from her brief tears, and then from her light kiss. She turns me around, strokes my cheeks as flour falls out of her hair and all over us. I giggle, and she smiles most beautifully at me. "You're a very brave mensch, Romek," she says.

"You too, Mama ," I reply, with a deliberate case of the cutes because it suddenly occurs to me that we will have to explain the shattered window to my father and why there are bullet holes in the ceiling.

"What do we tell Papa?" I ask her.

"The truth, Romeczku, the truth," she says.

My father mentions nothing about the damage in our living room when he comes home. I am not put on trial for window gazing or provoking gunfire and Papa spends a long time caressing my hair, seemingly grateful that his youngest son is still attached to it. That night, he and Manek board up the destroyed window frame to shut out any further harm.

We later hear from neighbors that the wounded girl has survived, but her face is now tattooed with bullet fragments and of her nose, only her nostrils remain. Her lips eventually heal into a tight snarl—she cannot close her mouth on one side and walks with a shawl pulled down over her freakish appearance. Her father eventually sends her to live with farm relatives near the great forest of Białowieża where she can be hidden from human scrutiny. There she would herd goats and other field beasts that would trot beside her in their innocence. I never saw her again but her ruined gaze would arise before me for many nights to come.

3

The Night Gardener

HUNGER KNOWS NO DECORUM.

The early spring of 1940 brings another season of food shortages that make nimble and inventive thieves out of honest people. Among them is Yehuda Lipnicki, a renowned Cantor, a Ba'alei T'filos, (an accomplished exponent of musical prayers sung in orthodox Synagogues). Manek winks and says to me that Yehuda is a committed "agriculturalist." The moniker sounds so grand; I think it must have something to do with my brother's Zionist group that meets at odd hours in damp cellars all over town. The Cantor owns no land, yet others in our community have also dubbed him "Yehuda the Gardener."

It's a Monday evening and I sit alone before a splendid tureen of soup cooked up by Mama from chicken bones, anise bulbs and a huge sack of carrots about my height that had been mysteriously deposited outside our front door during the night. I am first at the table and stare at my empty plate, inhaling the fragrant vapors from the tureen and willing Yehuda to get himself up our stairs so we can eat. From the kitchen came the yeasty counterpoint of fresh challah baked by Hanka. The twin aromas are like a raw steak to a street dog. My father enters to sit down by me but before he can, there's a sonorous voice in the hallway and a striking looking, barrel-chested man bursts into our living room to embrace him. "Leon, my good friend, you look so well!" he booms.

Yehuda Lipnicki wears a heavy beard and the black furze on his chin melds into a wild arrangement of even blacker curls on his head, a dense cape of dark to settle around his shoulders. His lips are red and full and his voice resonates as if he were declaiming under an archway. It has a rich and many-layered tenor, seasoned from ringing off the vaulted ceiling of the Miodowa Street Temple where young women wept indiscreetly at his trebled notes that carried such a yearning sensuality beneath the sacred phrasing. Mama says he is known to be magnanimous with his affections, declaring fidelity an unnatural state, the barb of the unloved and the root cause of withered devotion.

Gossips from our Shul claim that women drying up from longing and the indifference of cloddish husbands can depend on having their souls and bodies revitalized by the gilded chords of the Cantor. He also sang several of his children into the world, all by various mothers but all of whom he cared for equally with a tender and energetic passion.

To my naïve ears, conversation for Yehuda seems just another form of chant at a lighter timbre. The deep brown tones of his speech make me forget my shrunken stomach and I remember my father saying that G-d had pulled Yehuda's soul up into his tongue for the sheer delight of having his creation praise him. Everyone finally sits down and Hanka pours the rust-colored soup into the bowls. The Cantor's glittering eyes fall on me but he addresses my father.

"I'm moving house," he declares.

"Where are you moving to?" asks my mother.

"Wherever Hans Frank decrees that I should go."

"Are you under some suspicion?" my father questions.

Yehuda gave a bass chuckle that vibrates the water in the crystal tumblers.

"Not in the least! And soon, Leon, you and this lovely family will also relocate."

"So, Yehuda, you're giving up singing for fortune telling," says Manek. "What about your night gardening?"

"Why would anyone garden at night?" I pipe up.

"Romek, eat your soup," Mama orders.

The Cantor reaches across the table and raises my chin to his face. His touch gives me a jolt of fear—the back of his broad palm is gloved in the same dark hair as his beard, springing in curls from his knuckles. He has the hands of a centaur.

"First the relocating, Romek, and then the gardening."

For the next hour, Yehuda explains how the German occupiers are now in the people-moving business. Just that morning, Governor Frank had issued an edict for all Jews to surrender their apartments in the next two weeks so that Poles could move into them. The Germans would set up house in the more select quarters of former Catholic residences.

"They've already driven the intellectuals and academics from their homes and sent them to hell, G-d knows where," says Yehuda.

"This is intolerable!" explodes my mother. "This apartment is where Leon and I began our lives together. No one can deprive us of it, no one!"

Yehuda takes her hand graciously. "Pani Ferber, fate doesn't always allow us a choice. Survival makes beggars and gypsies of some men, of others, thieves. I serenade G-d in his tabernacle but at night, I break his commandments so that my friends, my children, and I may eat. I'm convinced that heaven is not too bothered by this. As for losing my house, I'd rather live under the sky than die for real estate. A home is any place where peace dwells and danger does not."

My father listens to the Cantor intently, tracing his fingers along the table linen in an abstract fashion—something he did when formulating some weighty decision. "One's attitudes cannot be fixed, given our current situation," he says.

The Night Gardener

"You have some time, Leon. The relocation arrangements are not without their flaws," Yehuda advises, "which is unusual for these Nazi administrators. They make a religion out of paperwork and everything in fine print. Not all the Poles have fancy places and, in fact, because there appear to be more Jews living in well-appointed dwellings, this exodus and resettlement, I promise you, is already totally *farmisht* (disordered)!"

"To evict every one of us makes no sense. It screws up the labor pool in the city. Who's going to fill all jobs we'll vacate?" asks Manek.

Yehuda rakes his cloud of dark hair with his fingers and bits of hay cascade down around him, revealing shirt cuffs streaked with grass stains. He assures my brother, "Don't worry. It's rumored that a thousand or more Jews with certain skills will stay, drafted into unpaid work to support the war effort. The rest of us have to clear out, on pain of arrest."

My mother takes the bread knife and saws away at the challah in high temper.

"Do they expect us to live in the streets of some faraway place, among strangers? Both Leon and I have elderly parents. Are they to be uprooted too and made refugees in their own city?"

"Any place where peace dwells and danger does not." My father echoes Yehuda's words.

"Papa, where are we going?" I insist, imagining us already in some splendid new setting.

"I know the Horowitz's own a country residence in Borek Falecki," he explains. "I'll speak to them about renting part of the house. I'm sure they'll agree."

My mother's eyes have a frantic light in them. She knots her napkin into umpteen different modes and scrapes invisible crumbs nervously into her palm. The Cantor pushes back his chair and says to her kindly, "You know, Pani Mala, I carry with me a medicine for all kinds of worries? It never fails, I promise you!"

"I'm afraid to ask what it is," answers Mama, forcing a smile.

"Ah!" he grins, "let me convince you."

Yehuda stood up and broke into the grace usually sung after meals, the *Birkat HaMazon*. An ocean of glorious noise sweeps through our dining room, curling back off the walls. I can feel the vibration of his singing transmit through the floorboards. He delivers his song to my mother, and it seems to me that he draws out of her the noxious powers of a sharp sorrow provoked by the dinner conversation. Her face relaxes and the fear that tightened her delicate jaw gives way to an astonished radiance. Yehuda dovetails into Solomon's song, bringing the vibrato down low, sustained on certain lines, and expanding them passionately where the king burnishes his devotion to his Shulamite bride. "Set me as a seal upon thine heart, as a seal upon thine arm: for love is stronger than death."

The final notes die away, leaving a deep stillness defined by the soft breath of my family. No one speaks for a several minutes. Yehuda stands with his eyes closed, his body gently swaying, respectfully permitting the waves of song to depart from him. I don't want it to end. Without his rousing voice, the room seems dim and ordinary.

"Please, please, can you sing some more for us?" I ask with grave politeness.

"I could open the piano," offers Hanka, "if you wish?"

The Cantor raises his eyes, his gaze fiery and full of merriment. His black-furred hands seize me by the waist, hauling me up into the dark of his beard. It smells of soil, incense and anise.

"Little Romek, what is the next best thing to singing?" he declares, laughing. "It's a smart boy who is a connoisseur of music and a pretty girl who can caress a piano as keenly as she would her sweetheart! Hanele, play for me!"

Although no one could comprehend it at the time, Yehuda's impromptu recital was to be the last musical evening we would ever spend in our apartment. However, for the next two hours, we danced and sang as loud and long as any tavern drinkers. Hanka hit the keys of our ancient Bechstein with verve, putting her own individual riffs on many traditional tunes while Manek and my father alternately waltzed my mother across the carpet. Yehuda sat me down on his wide shoulders and leapt and skipped as he belted out a polka song in Yiddish, *Sis Der Step Shoyn Opgeshorn*, a ditty about a randy farmer that had a lot of references to fruit, "Your eyes are as black as cherries...my love is as ripe as plums...come, enough already with waiting."

The bass of his voice thundered through my small frame and he whirled me around at a stomach-churning speed, making me squeal with delight. Down the channels of dark places that I would soon travel from this time forth, no brute force or fearsome condition could ever erase from me the exhilaration of this night.

From my vantage point high up near the ceiling, I filed forever the shining memory of my mother dancing with my father in the manner of young lovers, with Mama blowing me kisses from across the room. I recall Hanka looking like a French chanteuse at the piano, glamorous and sultry in her ivory lace blouse, her light contralto racing to keep up with Yehuda's quick Klezmer variations, and my brother, Manek, smiling and clapping his hands in time to the music. As the heat of the evening wound down, my father served schnapps and black tea. I nodded off in the arms of the Cantor, barely aware of being passed to Manek, who carried me to my bed, put my nightshirt on backwards and rolled me into warm quilts.

"I'm not tired," I slur.

"Go to sleep, you little wolf, or you'll be a dishrag in the morning."

The Night Gardener

"Manek, why does Yehuda garden at night?" I pester.

My brother snuffs out the bedside lamp, his face carved by the streetlight outside our window.

"Yehuda doesn't so much as garden as harvest," whispers Manek softly.

※

The Cantor's tale, as explained to me by my brother, drifts into my consciousness like bits of interesting debris borne ashore on the incoming tide of sleep. Yehuda stores a rusty bicycle in the cellar of Grushinka Belowitz, a tanner's daughter who, despite her constant perfume of uric acid and pungent cowhides, is now heavy with their second child. Down among the reeds of the Vistula, another of his lovers, Ravina Krasnik, has persuaded her father to keep a small rowboat tethered to his coal barge for Yehuda's night depredations.

By land and water, the Cantor would defy any curfew or patrol, biking like a shadow across Krakow then rowing up the river until he reaches the outlying farms beyond the city. Yehuda knows every field and orchard between Pychowice and Kostrze and could dig or pluck carefully at their perimeters, raking up potatoes and turnips, pruning at strawberry beds or gathering apples, two or three from every tree, in numbers adequate for his needs and some to trade. His raids were gentle enough never to leave the farmers at a disadvantage. The one time he risked capture was the night he delayed until dawn and was so entranced by the stars falling into the sun's ascent, he started to chant his morning prayers.

His resonant song soared across meadows and forests, piercing the semi-darkness, startling a young fox in his kills and causing the sheep to rise up from their grass beds. It reached the sleepless ears of a woolgrower named Radek Pieninsky. Radek was Catholic enough to think that some saint was abroad in his fields and calling out to him for his many sins until he discovered the larcenous silhouette of Yehuda on his bicycle, swerving through his flock with a sack of contraband vegetables balanced on the crossbar. Pieninsky took down his hunting rifle and fired off several rounds, murdering an old ram and rousing his hens to poultry hysteria but Yehuda escaped, still singing, and survived to divide the spoils of the night between his two paramours and the children he'd sired on both of them.

※

I am soundly napping in my bedroom one afternoon when a conversation brings me to a half-wakened state. It is like listening to people talking on the trolley car when the metal shanks hit a relay on the tracks and drowns out every other sentence.

"Mala, it's beyond my control," comes my father's pressing whisper. "The law has to be obeyed."

A low angry gasp from my mother answers him. Then he utters what was to become, for an upright man, the lie of the century.

"No, no, my love, don't be afraid, we will be alright. I promise you."

"How will that be possible?" my mother hisses angrily. She sounded like a choking snake. "Do you expect me to feed your children with stones?"

I slide off the bed and try to listen to them through the partially open door, fearful of what is hidden in the words that barely reach me.

"One has to be resourceful," Papa cajoles.

"Have you lost your mind?" Mama's voice is a glissando of rage. "The only thing to make this better is to get our lives back the way they were!"

There is deadly silence for a minute or two. Next, I hear them sputtering at each other until Manek walks out of the kitchen and ushers them both into the living room. I hear the sound of wine being poured into glasses and Papa saying the job he has held for over fifteen years with the German-owned Pelikan Pen Company is no more; he had been fired that very day.

Still, the narrowing draws tighter. In late April, the Germans enact a confiscation decree on Krakow's Jews, 2,000 zlotys minimum to be paid out per household, plus all valuables are to be surrendered. The enforcers close off streets and commence searches from house to house. My father appears in the living room one morning prior to the raids with a clutch of fat, sealed envelopes and other small packages.

"Mala, please take these." He hands my mother a bunch of the envelopes. "Put them under the hen house shingles, use old nails and hammer them well, then baffle the space with straw. I don't think they'll be searching out on the balcony. Roman and Manek, come with me."

For the next two hours, my brother and father use my scrawny frame and fingers as a pincer delivery system. They thrust me underneath the electrical heating units where, being small enough to fit, I unscrew valves to stuff rolls of zlotys, the many parts of silver candelabras, and some of my mother's jewelry inside the vacant spaces between the coils.

"Work slowly and carefully, son," encourages Papa, who knelt beside me to hand me the small velvet bags of Mama's trinkets.

"Hope the heat's switched off," jokes my brother. "You could come out of there, Romek, with the perm of the century."

I start to giggle. My head and upper body are wedged tight beneath the radiator and I can't stop laughing. I am trying to push Mama's three-strand Tahitian pearls into a cavity but the necklace catches on the sleeping coils and breaks, sending the luminous beads spinning out into the living room. I hear Manek guffaw and my father moan, "Dear G-d! Is there no end to these aggravations? Romek, don't move!"

I lay there in the gloom with my feet sticking out from under the radiator like a dead man while they scoop up the wayward pearls. Manek ties them up in a sock of Hanka's and I pull it up into a hollow pipe of the heater via a string.

The Night Gardener

I do better at our next hiding place.

At one end of our living room, we had a large, traditional, marble-tiled stove we used for supplemental heating during Krakow's punishing winters. It was constructed with a tall chimney flue and a lower interior just wide enough for a small boy's head and shoulders. Manek and my father have the dangerous idea of taping envelopes containing several thousand US dollars and Polish zlotys inside the flue and sealing the space up again. I hear Papa say this is our future 'traveling' money, which pleases me, since it sounds like a vacation in the offing.

"Just use the inside top of the flue. We'll loosen a few tiles and cement them back in place," suggests Manek.

"Isn't it going to be hard to see what we're doing?" asks Papa.

"Not with Romek as our front man," says Manek with a grin. I stick my head in the grate and find that there was just enough space for me to see way up into the flue. My father, standing high on a ladder outside, pries away the top layer of tiles so we can look at each other through the tall gap.

"Now, Roman, you have to guide me, watch for any envelopes sticking out from the holes, OK? They shouldn't be visible at all."

Through this opening, he packs a small fortune in string-tied envelopes and tapes them behind the tiles by feeling about the cast-iron ledge of the flue's interior, driving down on to me fine clouds of soot. Papa calls me his little warrior as he fumbles about gluing the tiles back in place, as I shout up to him, "A little to the left, no, now go right, put the cement there."

When I clamber out into our living room, I am as black as basalt but swollen with pride at being a key part of this adventure. I take a step and a sinister fog of soot rose out of my clothes. My mother comes back in from the balcony and yells at Papa and Manek that they were both dolts; hiding cash in stoves is not a fit job for a child. *Just look at the state of him!*

"We can scrub him down, Mala," pleads my father. "Dirt he always survives."

"Try not to move or inhale, Romek," she commands and goes to fetch an old sheet. Manek, who is enjoying the whole escapade immensely, lifts a hand mirror to my face. The boy in the glass is unrecognizable, black curls merge into my carbon-coated skin, the whites of my eyes and teeth blaze out like bleached laundry from this dusky visage. My mother wraps me from head to foot in the sheet and carried me out to the poultry terrace where she strips off my clothes. A relay of rinsing buckets progresses from the kitchen via Papa and Manek. Mama scrubs me back to my normal pale self in the chilly air among the hens that peck viscously at my ankles, annoyed that their smooth brown eggs were speckled with soot. Mama washes the eggs off too, removing any suspicious traces.

That night, there was a family confab about Mama's furs and other placatory objects high on the list of items to be confiscated. Diamonds and money, not withstanding, I have no wish for the lynx head on Mama's coat to be hunted a second time. She has let me play with it all these weeks as if it had been a real pet, the fine spotted profile with the ear tufts has taken on a wonderful aliveness, appearing to me as an animal in a suspended rest from which he would one day awaken. I go out onto the balcony and catapult my lynx on to the roof. There he would not be discovered, but his feral gaze can look down from the chimneys on the snub-nosed German jeeps trolling through the Kazimierz

⁂

The next morning, the time comes for our apartment to be searched. At 6:00 a.m., we hear the aggressive stomp of boots on the stairs and knocking at apartments at the far end of the corridor. We sit tensely in our living room, all eyes on my father.

"Everyone is to stay very calm and be polite. I will talk to them. No one is to give them any argument. The less said the better."

An imperious pounding on our front door and Papa leaps up at once to answer it. Two German police officers in leather trench coats and arm insignias with swastikas enter, followed by a bespectacled Polish official with a few strands of hair plastered across a balding dome of pink skin. He carries a clipboard and bears the skittish manner of an oppressed bank clerk. Behind him is the group's informer, Elezar Zelek! A sallow-skinned heavy-set officer, who seems to own the authority among them, barked at us.

"Get up, all of you! Stand by the window. No one is to leave this room."

We obey and watch the ravishment of our home unfold.

"Well, hello there, Elezar, always a good friend to man or beast," Hanka greets the furrier caustically.

From the kitchen and the bedrooms comes the sound of closets opening and crashing shut, drawers yanked from their wooden runners and hurled to the floor. A police officer returns to the living room staggering under the weight of my mother's black mink, the silver foxes and a Persian lamb cape. The second man follows, carrying a candelabrum, a set of silver Passover cups, some cheap jewelry and the 2,000 zlotys—each item deliberately left in my mother's dresser and closet.

Elezar counts the money in a breezy acquisitive manner, as if friendly extortion was a normal everyday occurrence. He looks directly at Papa without any embarrassment and says, "It's nothing personal, Leon. In time, I will be able to explain this."

"Don't shame yourself further, Elezar. A man is known by his actions, no matter the circumstances," answers my father.

"Please, believe me. It's for your own good."

"I imagine that you and goodness would be a bad fit," Manek interjects. The furrier gives my brother a look of raw hatred but is pulled aside by one of the searchers who harangues him in a ludicrous stage whisper.

"You said they had more furs, Cartier watches and American dollars!"

"They had, her husband bought from me regularly and often paid cash," hisses Elezar.

I stand in the shelter of my mother's skirts, her arm around me, watching these interlopers stab at cushions with their fingers and tip the contents of my father's roll-top desk onto the floor. They scoop books from the shelves, throwing them in loud cascades of pages across the room and kick the carpets over. There was a screech and ping of agonized piano chords as they opened the tiger-walnut lid of Hanka's baby grand and slammed it against the wall. The Polish official had found my mother's kitchen scissors and was about to snip away at the strings and felt hammers when my sister speaks up.

"If you damage it, it will bring you no value," she declares calmly. "It's a rare Bechstein, a wedding present of my grandparents, from 1902."

"Beware of this one," warns Elezar, "she has some cunning traits."

"Stupidity isn't one of them," argues Hanka. "That piano is worth over seventy thousand zlotys at least. Only a fool would ruin it."

"She's right. I'll put it on the list," says the Polish official. "We'll see if we can get the army engineers to move it. Do you have any other valuables?"

"Whatever we had we sold for food," my father lies.

The barrel-sized officer begins tapping on the radiators with his reddened knuckles. The echo returned would vary according to the density of valuables hidden in the coils. Manek shoots me a warning glance and I press closer to my mother. For endless minutes, the policeman drums along the radiator's ridges, each hit beat a thrum of terror in my chest. Manek has tightened the valves so hard as to be a nuisance to remove. Still, the German is showing a hungry interest.

"They must give off a good heat," our inquisitor says.

"Not anymore. We can't afford the fuel. They're beginning to rust from lack of use," explains my mother plainly.

The other policeman is standing by the tiled tower of a stove. He opened the door to the range at the bottom. Daylight flooded in and revealed the small square of piled soot and the very visible impress of a child's hands!

"You, boy, come here," the interrogator orders, pointing to me. My mother clutches me back but then loosens her grip at a quick eye signal from my father.

"Are these your hand prints?" asks the man.

"Yes, sir," I say in a low voice.

"How come they're in the stove?"

I look into his face, at his broad jaw and thick lips, at how his mouth can command so much disaster. My thoughts went running in twenty different directions, and then cleared to plain reason. Blessed days of rain—just a week ago when Moniek and I had the best time jumping into deep puddles in the fractured concrete of our courtyard. My mother had complained then about a place to dry my sodden boots.

One quick mental rehearsal and I explain, "When my boots are wet, Sir, my mother has me set them in the stove to dry."

The policeman lowers his face to mine; so close, I can smell the stench of stale beer and onions on his breath. "If you're not telling me the truth," he threatens in a solicitous tone. "I'll thrash you until you do, do you understand?"

Before I have time for this hazard to register, a great yell rises up behind me and I am yanked back to the safety of my brother's side.

"Want someone to flog that's worth the stress on your whipping arm, instead of a defenseless child?" Manek shouts at the top of his lungs. "Wouldn't you like to hit the jackpot without too much digging, huh?"

The room is suspended in the power of his voice. He turned to the shocked Elezar and points, "Here's your prize! Try the basement of his house in Radom, a black marketer's bazaar, foreign currency, jewelry, and more furs than can be seen in any jungle. Bank accounts in six different names and a fortune in cash under the floorboards from the women he pimps. Beat on this!"

Manek grabs the furrier and thrusts him hard into the chest of the policeman. Both men stumble ignominiously against the stove. My brother then turns and pushes me close to my stunned mother, whispering, "Don't be afraid, Romek."

I heard Elezar screeching loudly, "You lying prick! Arrest this bastard! Arrest him!"

In the next instant, everyone is shouting with a hundred voices. I drift somewhere above the mayhem while my body remains sheltered in the folds of my mother's skirts. My father is trying to explain to the officers and Elezar how his oldest son is overwrought and just trying to defend his younger brother. Hanka closes ranks with Mama and me while the Polish official sits down on our sofa to write details on his clipboard, seemingly oblivious to the dangerous clamor in the room.

One of the policemen swears and slams Manek in the face with a gloved fist, knocking him to the carpet. My mother screams and my anguished father pleads for reason. Manek tries to rise but the officer hits him in the ribs with his pistol butt and then stubs it down hard on his left hand. I, too, yell out something incoherent when I see my brother coil up in agony and the blood spring from his swollen fingers. Into this widening seam of violence steps the milquetoast Polish official, screeching in parliamentary tones, "Stop this at once! We can't afford such incidents. Take what you have and leave!"

Elezar Zelek, pale from how order has so easily fallen away from their might, also coaxes the police to leave. They holster their guns and stagger out, carrying our goods with them.

A paralyzing quiet washes over our living room. My parents help my brother carefully onto the sofa. My mother is weeping in halting sobs and my father holds my brother close in his arms, telling him how courage and foolishness are sides of the same coin, not always good for transaction. Hanka, shaking and somber-faced, gently binds her brother's broken hand. I cannot see for my tears but I approach the hero of all my days, sick at heart that he is hurt on my account. He is smiling at me, full of painful triumph.

"So, Romek," grinned my brother through gritted teeth, "Now you know what it's like to look the devil in the eye. You were great, kiddo, my brave little man."

I weep harder at his twisted face. Not wishing to press against his injuries, but needing so much to touch him, I hang on lightly to his bludgeoned frame, still sturdy and full of fire, and cry repeatedly, "I'm sorry, I'm sorry!"

4

Encroaching Dangers and Safe Departures

THE CANTOR WAS RIGHT about the Nazi plan to exile Jews from the city and the chaos it provoked. The Judenrat assist the German administration, informing them as to what type of Jews live where. However, many Christian Poles, formerly living in grubby tenements, who thought they were about to move into a well-kept home, actually find themselves being shuttled into the shabby attics and basements of poorer Jews while the SS billet themselves in the elegant residencies of rabbis, doctors and other professionals. Many Nazis are not that keen on being garrisoned in the Kazimierz since Hans Frank, head of the German Government in Poland, has deemed it, "That foul nest of Semitic persistence." The occupiers prefer the green core of the city around the Planty with its wide lawns and lush gardens. It is mostly Poles that are shunted unhappily into our neighborhood.

By early autumn, much of the city's population had become nomads overnight. Hordes of people crisscross the bridges and avenues with their furniture and household chattels piled on anything that has wheels. In Krakow's town hall, now the German Office for urban control, bureaucratic fever is at an all-time high as disgruntled Polish Gentiles protest at being put out of their homes. They have been ordered to pack up and are being whipsawed between one address and another, blaming the Jews for all these relocation antics.

For their part, Jewish families take to the roads of the countryside, often putting themselves in mortal danger of arrest, or exploitation by collaborators who might just as easily murder them for money as betray them.

Several family members, my uncles, their wives, cousins and grandparents, have already scattered to wherever they could. My mother's parents are still in Krakow; their bakery has been confiscated, and they have been forcibly moved to a grubby slum. Other relatives sought the obscurity of nearby towns like Wieliczka (famous for its salt mines where one could descend into the briny gloom by the same elevator built for the visit of Kaiser Wilhelm). By the end of January, the Stadthauptmann (Town Commander) Schmied has proclaimed that the number of Jews in the city is too large, and Jews not employed on services of importance to the Reich would have to leave.

❋

It is on a Wednesday when a rain-sodden member of the *Ordungdienst* (the Jewish Police) appears at our door with a notice bearing an official stamp. It decrees we have one day to vacate our apartment. Mama flies into a torrential rage and abuses the OD loudly, calling him a heathen and a treacherous *gonef* (thief).

Encroaching Dangers and Safe Departures

"Have you no shame!" she screeches at him, "What kind of Jew turns against his own?"

"A Jew who wants to continue living," whines the caller in apologetic tones.

Manek and I have taken up eavesdropping in the shadows of the hallway, secretly enjoying the confrontation with glee. Mama is on a full volcanic blow out.

"You should have died in your mother's womb!" she rants. "And not be a living curse, a disgrace to your family and your Rabbi."

From our hiding place, I can clearly see the pallid face of the OD man; his eyes had the numbed gaze of a dead sheep. He is dressed in a raincoat too big for his emaciated frame and the gaunt wattles of his neck rises nakedly above the collar. He stands impassively before my mother's tirade, dropping the soggy order at her feet and saying to her dryly, "You have twenty-four hours to leave. You can move out voluntarily or depart in your coffin. It's your choice."

My father declares the same afternoon that we should pack immediately and prepare to travel to Borek Falecki, a bucolic area of woods and streams at the end of the trolley line some ten kilometers beyond Krakow. He arranges for us to live with the Horowitz family, friends of my parents for many years, who'd already relocated to their large country house outside Borek. We are only allowed to take clothes and whatever else we can carry. My parents make a tense determination of needful items: bedspreads, pillows, blankets, and as many garments as possible.

Papa goes over the piles of stuff in the living room, approving this and nixing that, only to have his decisions reversed by Mama. Things fly in and out of sacks and back in again, as he counters, "Mala, we can't take it all!"

Hanka, Manek and I must have boxed up the china and silver cutlery three times before we get the selection right. We empty the hiding places behind the tiles of the marble stove and take small valuables that can be easily stuffed into suitcases along with a few holy books and my father's tallit. My mother hastily stitches the bundles of paper money and her left over jewelry deep inside the lining of our coats. With our remaining wealth hidden, we are, so to speak, quite expensively dressed!

"One quilt, one blanket per person," announces Hanka.

"Two extra for Romek," counters Mama.

"Why?" demanded Hanka.

"A small boy doesn't have a woman's body fat."

"He should be so lucky."

Hanka layers me in multiple shirts and sweaters and I roll around the room like a small, inflated Golem, only able to move my arms with difficulty.

"So many outfits: the poor boy will suffocate," complains my mother.

"Another sweater, Romek, darling?" says Hanka with a wicked grin.

"Mama, let me dress him," offers Manek. He peels some layers off me and puts the garments in my backpack. "You look like a badly-stuffed chair," he teases.

"I don't care, I'm going on vacation," I declare smugly.

"Don't you boys argue", says Mama. "We need to organize food for the journey."

My mother has spent part of the spring canning fruits and other delicacies and she is damned, she declares, if she is going to leave them for any German schnorrer. My brother walks me into the kitchen, stands me on the counter and we begin emptying the pantry shelves.

"Right, midget man," says Manek, "Hand me down only what I ask for, OK?

I reach up and gingerly haul out jars and cans while Manek makes a count of the goods. "Flour, dried beans, lentils, crocks of goose fat, goose legs, pickled eggs, pickled cucumbers, leave the borsht, the jars are too heavy, ditto the fruits in brandy. Let me have the dried fruits, the jam, the tea, and the matzo meal. Give me the saltbox next and the smoked chicken."

At the time, I think the flurry of packing and our leaving is a great adventure. We are about to head off into the wild blue wherever. (It doesn't occur to me that we are experiencing the last hours we would ever have in our apartment.)

That night no one slept much. My parents grow more fearful of overstaying the appointed "get-out" time. My canny brother, who could always mysteriously acquire the most unlikely items in an emergency, has purchased a sturdy wagon from the closed lumberyard of Eli Zelberger—its owner, now imprisoned in the Montelupich jail for overpricing a timber contract in the construction of the Reich's barracks at Piasek.

To my utter delight, the vehicle comes with an elderly rheumatic horse that Mama says should have been made into glue long ago. Nevertheless, to me this spindle-legged creature is magical, despite the sharp ribs pressing through his splotched hide. He has a gurgling cough that sounds startlingly human and a habit of swallowing snappishly at the air, as if each breath is a hurried effort against the time he might never stand again. To me, he is a noble mount and he is ours! The adventure is getting better! Here is a steed that, once we got to Borek Falecki, no doubt shall be mine to ride through verdant forests on daring quests that all boys know how to invent. I name him "Moses" because he is taking us to promised safety.

The timing of our departure is crucial. Too early in the still-shadowy dawn may leave us vulnerable to the German patrols. Too late in the morning might also bring disaster, since we would be caught up with all kinds of human flotsam trying to get out of town. Crowds and German soldiers are a lethal mix; rills of molten aggression and fear contaged them. One protest, one loud insult can easily spark an avalanche of rifle fire.

Encroaching Dangers and Safe Departures

Manek pulls Moses and the cart into the alley behind our building and waited outside while the rest of us stand for the last time in our living room. My father gathers his arms around Hanka, Mama and me and says a short prayer for the journey. Mama's eyes are wet. Her fingers reach out and caress the beautiful oak credenza that had been a wedding gift.

"We should go quickly, without any regret," says Papa. He grabs my hand and herds us through the front door. It slams behind us…forever.

It is still far from daylight when we meet up with Manek down in the alley. Onto the wagon's flat bed go the blankets, quilts, pots, pans, sacks of food, a few small crates, and each person's small suitcase. I stay by Moses, feeding him the remains of my breakfast kugel. The horse has very few teeth left. My hand inside his slavering jaws is like sticking your fingers up the warm innards of a cooked chicken. As I fuss with the animal, Mr. Hocherman, a frayed coat over his pajamas, comes hurrying around the corner of the alley with Moniek.

"We came to wish you all G-d-speed," he whispers, embracing my parents.

Moniek, who is wearing second-hand glasses so thick they enlarged his eyes to a freakish scale, does not look at me. He seems shrunken and dejected.

"Hey, Monny, look, we bought a horse. Isn't he great?" I say.

My friend hangs his head, a palpable misery rising out of his shoulders.

"You can pet him if you want," I offer cheerfully, already knowing that there is no rousing him from this gloom. I take his hand and place it on the graying muzzle of Moses. The old-man horse rolls a hoof forward and gently cribs at Moniek's sweater. My friend hides his face in the tangled mane and mutters accusingly, "You're not coming back, are you? You're not coming back ever?"

Hanka, who always had a soft spot for Moniek, pats his shoulder.

"We're only down the road, a few kilometers away," she says sweetly. "You can come and visit us whenever you like."

The two fathers gather about us, with Mr. Hocherman explaining to Papa over the horse's neck that they are moving to a cousin's farm outside of Wieliczka. From the other side of Moses, I can hear a faint snuffling then Moniek raises his head, strands of horse mane hang from his eyeglasses that are now steamed up by his tears. He walks over to me with something in his hand.

"Here, take these with you," he says and hands me a crumpled brown paper bag. Inside, are two dozen or more of his lead soldiers from his armored knights' collection, several are astride tiny metal horses, finely painted in every detail.

"Some are mounted, the rest are infantry."

"Thanks a lot," I say awkwardly.

Then, his father gently tugs him away from me, saying, "We should let these good people begin their journey."

Moniek becomes sullen and frozen. Hanka lifts me up into the cart to conceal me between two boxes. Mama gets up next beside me. The two fathers made their goodbyes as well but suddenly Moniek runs, sobbing loudly, back into our building. Mr. Hocherman blows air through his cheeks and looks embarrassed, as if he is somehow to blame for his son's wailing desolation echoing off the cobbles. I cling to the bag of lead warriors; a great nagging sadness and an urgency to be gone buzzes through my head; all competing for my reason.

On that frosty morning in 1940, my boyhood friendship with Moniek Hocherman was closed out forever. I didn't know it at the time but I would never see my partner at arms again. Monny had always fascinated me because his mother had insisted that he'd been born "out of his time" and was already a quirky, solidified eccentric with a heady imagination, pulled to wandering in the ancient mists of Arthurian legends, Templar knights and deeds of valor. No one imagined then that he would never live beyond the age of eight. (It was decades later, when I encountered his sister, Renia, on the streets of New York City that I discovered Moniek was rounded up in a kinder transport in 1941 and sent to a sure death in Treblinka.)

Had Moniek persisted in the step of time with me, I'm sure we both would have been old men together. Maybe it's fortunate that I will never have an image of him as an aged face. Whenever he comes to mind, I still see a boy with a quirky sideways grin, too much static in his carrot-colored hair, lining up his regiments of tin soldiers in strategic battle formations worthy of Napoleon.

At the hour of our departure, the dark is giving way to the morning but a rousing wind blows about us with a biting chill. Manek puts a gray blanket over the meager shoulders of my horse to keep him warm and somewhat camouflaged. I am about to utter a shout of wonder when Mama shushes me sternly. All I can do was to point at Moses' feet, at his "boots". My brother has carefully clothed his hoofs in sacking to silence his clop and to ensure he doesn't slip on the frost-rimed cobbles. "One broken leg from this old nag," he declares, "and we'll be taking his place between the shafts."

We set off.

My father walks ahead while Manek and Hanka stride beside the wagon, leading the animal gently along. The plan is to move like phantoms, as discreetly as possible so as not to draw attention. We speak in hand signals to each other. Papa hesitates at each cross street and checks both ways in anticipation of any dangers. At one point, he brings us to a dead halt and we wait a fearful eternity, hidden in the gloom of an ancient arch. Up ahead, German police on motorcycles roar back and forth across the Plac Wolnica.

Encroaching Dangers and Safe Departures

They stop, chat to each other and to our relief, ride off together in the opposite direction to our route.

We have to get to one of the Vistula's bridges. I put my hand on Moses' bald rump and send him a thought that he is a brave horse and that I will reward him later with slavish love and some warm oat mash. Hanka speaks softly to him as Manek turns both beast and cart into a narrow deserted lane with high fences. Up ahead, I hear the light rush of the river beneath a cacophony of other sounds, faint voices, shouts, honking horns and tramping feet. Moses senses the water too and hurries his pace, a light plume of mist issuing from his nostrils. He snorts and pulls hard on the wagon with Manek and Hanka's arms laid across his companionable shoulders.

Emerging from the lane, we find ourselves in what could have passed for the rush hour except it is the Krakow evacuation. Cars, trucks, wagons—vehicles of all description and size congest the streets that access the bridge. Weaving in and out of this clamorous traffic are hundreds of pedestrians with suitcases. On either side of the bridge's entrance, German platoons yell through bullhorns for people to keep moving. The heavily armed guards are conducting spot checks and pulling people over. Several travelers are lined up with their hands on their heads beside the military trucks.

"I don't like this," warns my father. "They're making random searches."

"And their morning quota of arrests," says Manek anxiously, "we'd be safer if we split up, made our group smaller."

"Manek's right," Papa answers. "Hanka, take Mama and Romek and some of the bags—start walking across the bridge but make sure you conceal yourselves in the center of the crowd. Keep your heads low. Don't talk with anyone. Don't look at anyone. Just keep moving. G-d willing, we'll meet on the other side."

He has us wait for the moment when the platoons on the access ramp are looting people's suitcases. On the south flank, the patrol has stopped a man dragging a large cabin trunk and opened it to find it packed with hams, sausages and smoked goose meat, all now spilled out on the sidewalk. One soldier skewers a string of Kielbasa with his bayonet and waved it merrily around as the apprehended protests that he is not a Jew but a good Catholic, a delicatessen mensch off to deliver his goods to his clients in the country. He then begins to sell the soldiers on the merits of his curing methods that did not impress them at all. A German sergeant handcuffs him to the bridge rail for later interrogation.

On the north perimeter, the platoon there is arguing flirtatiously with six attractive women who were pulling spangled dance costumes out of their luggage. Their manager, a bloated heavy-set man with a garish purple waistcoat was not smiling. He was already under arrest and sporting a bloody gash on his forehead. My father watches the timing in these scenarios and edges us around the smoked meat confrontation.

"Go! Now!" he hisses to Mama, Hanka and me. My legs kick the air as the two women haul me off my feet into the flood of people. Papa and Manek take the wagon and Moses and find a place for him between two buses crawling laboriously across the span. I look back to see my father up on the buckboard of the cart with Manek who has the reins in hand. The blanket that covered Moses now lay over our belongings. Both men and horse disappear into the morass of hooting vehicles.

"Walk quickly, Romek," urges Mama. "We must keep up."

She lets go of my fingers to change her heavy suitcase to her other hand. Two young men in front of us drag a travois on which they're hauling a grizzled old woman who looks dazed and distracted. A family with several small children follow with the youngest packed in amongst household goods borne along in a wheelbarrow. They also have a large yellow dog that is towing a little girl tied to its leash. The dog grins proudly at me but growls a warning when I reach out to pet him.

"He won't eat you," says the child's pretty mother, "but he's very protective of little Nechama."

"Where are your parents?" says Nechama's father.

"Just back there," I answer confidently.

"May you be safe on your journey," offers the mother with a sweet smile.

The family walks on before me and I turn around expecting to see Mama and Hanka but instead meet a broad wall of oncoming strangers. Some people order me roughly out of the way. My eyes devour every face, I call for Mama and Hanka desperately at the top of my lungs but my shouts are eaten up in the noisy crowd. Panic and dread overtake me.

"Sir, have you seen my mother and sister?" I plead of a fat old man dressed in an expensive mohair overcoat and carrying a velvet carpetbag.

"Maybe you no longer have such relatives," he sneers.

"Please," I beg. "My mother, my sister, I've lost them."

"Then you are a careless schlemiel. Quite a waste of family to misplace in one morning," he says, brushing me aside roughly.

I run up and down the edge of the crowd dragging my rucksack, my voice breaking from the urge to weep. I begin to yell my father's and Manek's name loudly.

A male voice shouts back from the passing crowd. "I am Manek!"

"Manek Ferber?" I call with fervent hope.

"No, Manek Blumstein, from Szeroka Street."

The tears are pouring down my cheeks when a firm hand grips my shoulder and a crisp accented voice asks me in perfect Polish.

Encroaching Dangers and Safe Departures

"Boy? Where are your people?"

Through my blubbering, I gaze up into the chiseled features of Captain Heinrich Von Brandt of the Wehrmacht dressed in an immaculately tailored uniform. (His title I note from a clear scrawl atop a sheaf of orders listing Polish names that he's clutching.) An iron cross hangs from his collar, a pair of well-cured leather gloves are tucked into his belt and in his highly polished boots my own wretchedness is reflected. His pale skinned face sits regally above this finery with eyes the color of green water staring down at me. Now I feel doubly cursed and have the crazy idea I will confess that I'm an orphan so he'll never be able to apprehend my family. The Captain takes a linen kerchief from his breast pocket and dabs at my eyes.

"I know a lost child when I see one," he says.

"Sir, are you going to arrest me?" I ask fearfully.

"*Nein, mein kind, nein,*" (No, my child, no), he laughed uproariously at the idea. "Being lost is not yet on my mandate of Jewish crimes. Come with me. We will find your family."

He makes an imperious signal with his gloves and a military Daimler with the top down weaves its way through the crowds to stop before us. I am placed in the back. Von Brandt takes a seat in front and orders his driver to scout the never-ending line of humanity crossing the bridge. "Boy," the Captain orders, "stand up so your parents might see you among all these wanderers."

I do as he asks but feel like a complete nudnik, a Jewish kid riding behind a high-ranking Nazi officer in a Reich staff car with the little swastika flags blowing merrily above the front bumpers. Many people in the crowd give me dark looks, from others came glances of pity, assuming I am already a prisoner. However, all these concerns melt away when I hear joyous shouts of "Romek! Romek!" from the passing line and see my mother and Hanka come hurtling toward the car. They stop abruptly as the officer leaps out of his seat. I see a wave of fear cross their faces. Von Brandt salutes them and takes off his cap with an elegant deference.

"*Hier, mein Damen* (Here, my ladies)," he announces pleasantly. "I'm happy to deliver you what appears to be a stray boy. He is yours, is he not?"

"Yes, sir, he is," my mother answers warily.

He lifts me down from the vehicle and chimes, "Reunited and all is well."

"Thank you so much, Sir," says Hanka, her brilliant smile laying on the charm. "We're very grateful."

He makes a swift bow to her, a restrained courtesy but leans down to me and says softly, "I have a son your age in Germany. I have not seen him for over a year. Stay close to your mother and don't ever wander away from the people who love you."

"No, sir, I won't, I promise." I vow. He stares at me with a mixture of sadness and tender interest, then climbs back into the Daimler and it roars away. My mother gathers me up in her arms and showers me with kisses. Hanka pats my shoulders and says, "You scared us half to death. I've never been so glad to see you."

"Are you going to tell Papa about this?" I ask my mother between her lips smacking off my cheeks.

"Maybe, when you're grownup."

The three of us make it to the far side of the bridge that is not so heavily guarded. Just half dozen sentries are marching there, looking bored and more interested in who was entering the city than the Jewish detritus leaving it. We walk with our suitcases further on to a small stand of oaks where we had arranged to meet up with Papa and Manek.

There is no sign of them. Car after car passes us. My mother falls silent, an edgy anxiety in her eyes as she stares at the swirl of exhaust fumes and dust raised by the escaping refugees. I track where my mother's gaze rests, scanning every group that passes us. Four people on bicycles come toiling by harnessed to a small Citroen that had no engine and no doors but was full of luggage. The cyclists seem like they were dying under their struggle to haul it. Beyond this motorless contraption, I hear a whooshing explosive snort, the asthmatic arrival of Moses!

"Mama! It's them, it's them!" I yell.

Beyond the heads of the marching travelers there's the cart with my father and brother waving. Moses clops along dutifully, his hooves now free of their wrappings. Papa jumps down and runs to embrace us all. My mother kisses him many times too, leaving rosettes of her red lipstick all over his face. I lunge at the horse joyously and hug his bony neck. Moses reaches down to nibble at my hair. Manek laughs and swings me up on to the horse's back.

"Roman, get off that moth-eaten animal at once before you break your neck," orders my mother.

"It's OK, Mama," assures Manek. "I'll keep him safe. Now, Romek, you can ride the rest of the way like a prince!"

5

Borek Falecki

ONE IS GRANTED ONLY SO MANY CHILDHOOD SUMMERS.

Idyllic sunlit times such as the June mornings of 1940 in Borek Falecki when I would jump out of bed, eager for all freewheeling adventures in the offing, including afternoons spent swimming in the Wilga River, and staying up late to watch the longest days broaden into silken heated nights. However, I'm getting ahead of the story.

It is almost noon when we arrive at a sizable gabled dwelling in a huge meadow patched with snow. Manek turns the cart and Moses off the winding drive into this front field. The door of the house flies open and Israel Horowitz, his wife, Luisia, and all their kids came tromping eagerly across the winter grass to greet us. Behind the parents are two eye-catching daughters, Salka and Gizia, long-limbed and very pretty, acorns of breasts pressed against their shirt fronts. A boy about my age follows, their brother, Tadek. The adults shout boisterous hellos and run at each other enthusiastically; there is much hugging, *kvelling* (gushing) and hand shaking.

I sit for minute on Moses, feeling very important but not knowing how to dismount easily. Turning sideways, I attempt to bring my right leg over his neck and leap from my mount with a movie hero's flourish. Instead, I jump awkwardly and fall flat underneath the animal's belly. Moses skitters a step back, gentle enough not to step on me with his splintered hooves. Tadek guffaws and calls out, "Who's that stupid kid?"

We become firm friends from that moment on.

Despite the winter's grip loosening too slowly, my sojourn at Borek Falecki feels more like life should be. Each day is made for adventuring with Tadek. He is an outgoing, confident boy, full of moxie and ready for any escapade. His siblings too are already teenagers and he frequently competes with his wickedly smart sisters to assure his place in the family. The Horowitz family had established a serene country life long before the German banishments took effect. They feel hidden and sheltered beneath the lush hills. When I ask my father if we can stay here, in this peace, until the war was over, he offers a half-truth, saying, "I don't see why not. Since we've been ordered to this place, we should strive to be happy here."

We are discouraged from visiting the nearby village of Borek because of the substantial military presence there, or to any of the farms to seek the company of local kids who are predominantly Christian. For Tadek and me, the double-edged rule is: be safe and you will be lonely, but we have each other and that's enough.

However, one is not necessarily out of harm's way in these outlying communities, where the residents had known each other for generations. There was a thriving business in Jew-baiting and paid betrayals. German staff assigned to such rural backwaters was usually former bank clerks or civil servants always eager to score points with the Governor General in Krakow by keeping up the quotas of arrests.

A main highway from the city curves around the south side of Borek Falecki and is a busy artery for troop movements on their way to plague the smaller villages of Southern Galicia. However, the house in the meadow is in a secluded bend of the Wilga River, set back off a seldom-used road and shielded on three sides by a barrier of dense pine forests. Here, for the first time in months, I can play outside again without fear of sharp-toothed dangers, but the slow drag of winter brings its own special problems.

On one eventful night, I am just falling asleep in the attic bedroom assigned to Manek, Tadek and me when more than the weather disturbs me. Outside, old snow cover, frozen smooth, has lacquered the fields and the pines, causing tree branches to snap under its weight. During the night, there came a sluice of blizzards, and snow light casting a milky glow throughout the room. I awake at the patter of hailstones to see this luminance flicker in pale swirls along the floral wallpaper.

I get out of bed and pad to the window. The surrounding evergreens are a ridge of pointed shadows rising above the blanched spindrifts that scud across the front field. The level of snow rises ever higher, promising good snowshoeing for Tadek and me tomorrow. I track my gaze from one stand of pines across the field to the next but my eyes never make it past the ruined fence beside the lane.

Someone is standing there on the drive in the white maelstrom!

The tall silhouette is not moving but just staring up at the house. I looked at this dark form for a full minute to be sure it is real. It has to be an advance man from Borek's German garrison waiting for the armed truck to turn into the gate—we are being targeted for a sweep! I pull back from the window in a surge of terror and practically leap onto Manek, who has been snoring like a generator in his bed under the eaves.

"Get up, they're coming for us! Manek, wake up. Please!"

My brother is alert instantly, grabbing me by my throat as if I was the arresting force. He leaps to his feet and lifts me off mine for a strangling second, and then lowers me. "You dumb kid! Don't ever surprise me like that!"

"Manek, there's a strange man outside! He's watching the house!"

"There's no man, and they're not coming for us."

"How do you know?" I persist, still terrified.

"Because we'd have been warned, that's how."

Borek Falecki

"You're dead wrong! Come and see!" I plead.

I drag him to the window and pointed through the curtains. Manek throws open the casement, letting the blizzard rush in. He grabs me by the shoulders and thrusts my head out into the bitter cold. "Take a good look, little brother," he orders. The snow spattered my face but I stared down…at an empty drive. The dark figure is gone. "If you're going to spend the rest of the night hell-bent on seeing ghosts come out of the forest," he says, "you'd better come and sleep next to me. I don't want the parents up here having hysterics."

Manek pulls me into his bed, my nightshirt soaked and my hair littered with snow. There is no safer place than to shelter against my brother's muscular chest. I pull the covers over my head and glue myself to him.

"Manek" I whisper, "I'm scared."

"Don't worry. I'll tell you when to be scared. Settle down, you'll wake Tadek."

I watch the snow-lit shadows of our room for a long time, listening for the return of the interloper. There is nothing to be heard but the three of us breathing in unison and the wind's answering lament.

※

Though our lives were in disruption, Papa insists that I still study and makes me read the Torah with him every day. I don't mind because it is our special time where I could have his attention all to myself. Sometimes, Tadek would join us in these lessons. My father loves to tell biblical stories, spinning them into theatrical epics that keep us both spellbound. His interpretation is so visual that we ride with King Sennacherib against the walled cities of Judah and hear the prophet Isaiah thunder that G-d has sent an angel of death, "Which cut off all the mighty men of valor!"

My favorite sagas come from the Book of Daniel. Papa drills us in the Prophet's writings as lessons in trust and faith for the Jewish captives in Babylon. I plague him to repeat the tales of the lions in the den. Why didn't they bite the saint? And, of course, the mystery of the fourth figure that stood with Ananias, Azariah, and Mishael in the furnace. We boys hoot in glee at King Belshazzar being humbled by the disembodied hand that wrote on the wall. (This episode is always a great hit with us since Tadek and I have recently taken up the study of invisibility.)

News of the war filters down to us from passing town folk and signs posted in Borek Falecki requiring Jews to register here, there and everywhere and to observe hundreds of different rules. The best thing to do, Papa advises, was to keep your head low and to remain unseen, an idea that appealed to me immensely.

Being invisible becomes our all-important mission. Tadek and I are on the hunt for a magic formula that will render us present but completely undetectable to the rest of the world. With such a gift, one would be able to make free without parents or other adults yelling at you for your badness.

Not only that, it would be a good ruse with the Germans—a boy invisible could easily glide up behind some Kraut, kick him sharply in the arse and shake with silent hilarity as the surprised victim whirled about and cursed the empty air. Tadek and I speculate on what other soaring and daring wickedness could be the lot of unseen boys. Once we have perfected this art, we'll get our fathers to sell our secret to the Jewish underground and the allies, causing peace to break out and the two of us to become the youngest war heroes in Polish history.

Together we spend many hours staring into Mrs. Horowitz's full-length mirror, willing each other to become visually undetectable.

"This is what you do," I order. "You close your eyes and think very hard that you are disappearing from the feet up. You have to wish and wish until nothing of you can be seen—not even your ears! OK, think! Think that you're disappearing!"

Tadek screws up his features until his face looks like an imploded prune. I keep my eyes shut tight and will my hidden self up to the ceiling—I am about to become a secret vaporous force! It is a contest of who will open his eyes first. Ma Horowitz's mirror never lies—we cry out in dismal failure on discovering we are still both obvious in the glass. Only once does it work when Manek and my mother have us both on the hook for about fifteen minutes in the kitchen.

My brother, staring into the middle distance over my head, practically walks right over me, saying, "You know, Mama, I think Tadek and Romek finally stumbled on the secret of complete invisibility."

"How miraculous!" exclaims my mother as we boys press ourselves back against the kitchen wall and stare right at her! Her eye line didn't waver one centimeter, she looks right through us, keeping a straight-faced gaze on Manek and says, "We must write to the scientists at the Jagiellonian University about this—they will want to know!"

Manek slams open a cupboard door, pinning part of the not-disappeared me against the wall. "You're absolutely right, Mama," he agrees in serious tones, "Maybe Romek learned this technique from the Belzer Rebbe?"

"Well," Mama declares, "they say such mysterious events do happen in this part of the country. Where could those boys be? Maybe they are watching us right now."

She brushes right by Tadek, who has to stuff his sleeve into his mouth to stop from cracking up. I know Mama would never lie about such a thing. She goes over to the bread safe, brings out a length of half-eaten cherry strudel and says to my brother, "We better finish this before those two decide to become visible again—hand me the knife."

They sit down at the table together and my mother starts slicing into the strudel, red juices running everywhere. It has the desired effect; both Tadek and I explode into hysterical giggles but Manek and Mama keep up the act.

"Did you hear that?" asks my mother, shoveling the delicacy on to two plates, "that strange laughter?"

"Nah, it's nothing," says Manek, "just air trapped in the stove. Eat already."

✻

The house is shared equally between our two families and despite the cramped quarters, there is an easy communal spirit that touches everyone. The adults keep the place well organized and are mindful of individual needs for privacy and quiet.

Meals are taken together with all of us around the kitchen table and are usually noisy extended dining fests. My parents had brought out a considerable amount of money and supplies from Krakow and we are able to pool our food resources with the Horowitzs. We have coal and wood for the stove, a well-stocked larder; and considering the hazards of the time, we live with some degree of pleasantness.

Every three weeks or so, my father and Manek make an afternoon trip into Borek Falecki to buy whatever was necessary from the farmers' market and to glean news of German troop movements in the area. Both of them speak the Polish of the educated classes, and always present themselves well. However, it is their scheme to have no extended conversations with anyone, no eye contact; their business has to be done almost wordlessly. They court menace from many quarters by not wearing the star armband because my father's logic rules that, "A Jew in secret is a Jew saved. Who needs to carry the Devil on one's arm?"

To sport the band in the marketplace is to invite verbal abuse and exorbitant prices. To wear it on the main avenue means dodging the approach of any German military that might easily ask for identity papers and subject the pair of them to arbitrary arrest, to not wear it at all and be discovered guarantees absolute disaster.

It's in one such situation that made my father and brother short-term Christians. They were headed away from the village with their purchases when my brother sighted a unit of drunken soldiers spilling out of a tavern. A dozen military jeeps were also parked further ahead and several troop trucks were speeding into town from the opposite direction.

"It must be a platoon change over," said Manek. "There's way too many of them for my comfort."

Both men were standing outside the Church of St. Stanislaus the Martyr and its incensed interior never looked so inviting. "We'll go in with respect," said my father, removing his hat and urging my brother up the steps.

They sat, hidden in the pews for the next two hours, listening for the German militia outside. It was the afternoon confessional, and while the church was mostly empty, the occasional parishioner heading for the sinner's box caused Papa and Manek to bend their heads and fervently pray the Shema Israel. It was in this pious mode that Father Caspian Wilenska came upon them, eyeing them immediately as strangers to the area, (not suspecting that they might be Jews). The priest's head-to-toe admiring glance of my father's finely cut suit had Papa mentally rewriting a new history for he and my brother. (I would come to realize that the war was accelerating my usually scrupulously honest parent into a first class liar.) Manek subtly recoiled to hear his father smoothly introduce himself as Wadislaw Komarovski, a realtor from Warsaw.

"And this is my son, Martin. We're interested in evaluating properties in the area, those not under confiscation by the Reich, of course."

"How pleasant to meet successful men of commerce in these difficult times," boomed the priest, sizing up the two of them for a potential donation. He advised that they wouldn't have much luck higher up the valley, since the better summer homes located there, once owned by wealthy Jews, had been appropriated to billet the Wehrmacht units. My father swayed a little in his pretense when he asked what had happened to the former householders.

"As you know, they were declared enemies of the state well before the invasion," answered the priest, with puffed-up dispassion. "We hear they were removed to an armaments factory near Oswiecim (Auschwitz)—a temporary measure, of course. I understand that they are well cared for there. No doubt they will be freed when the peace is made evident."

"No doubt," said my father, his fingers flexing restraint along the rim of his hat. Manek calmed his own nerves and entered into the game quickly. He was a superb second player and even surprised Papa by his intimate knowledge of the Borek region and his ability to stay in character.

"We like to think, Father," he said to Wilenska, "that our investment efforts are above reproach. We deal with only with a limited number of gilt-edged clients who have moved their substantial Catholic funds to Geneva and Buenos Aires. Persons of quality seeking to preserve their resources for the day of armistice"

"Quite so," agreed the priest. "Such upstanding people are the lifeblood of a poor parish like mine."

The construct started to fray some when Father Caspian smiled broadly and said he'd hoped they might attend his mass during their stay. My father, with a straight face, explained his religious inclinations were so diminished it would be like King Boleslaw hacking St. Stanislaus to pieces all over again to have such a lapsed soul at the altar rail. Manek patted his father's shoulder and humbly declared that his parent's ruined faith had brought him too well below the waterline of grace. The priest sighed and shook his head sadly at the pair of them.

"Gentlemen, no one is outside the generous mercy of Christ." he opined. "The lost are particularly beloved of his flock."

He urged them that all could be righted if they would enter the confessional and square matters with the Almighty. By now, my father is in a quiet panic, not wishing to feed the priest's interest in them any further and Manek is giving him urgent eye signals because the stamp of military boots is coming up the church steps. Both men turn their faces away as an eager youthful soldier burst into the church with his Polish betrothed staggering on his arm—to be their savior from heresy.

The young woman, exhausted and panting from the huge bulge under her dress, sat down heavily across a pew, avoiding the instant condemning stare of the priest. The soldier whipped off his cap, shyly excused himself to all present for the interruption, and asked in bad Polish when could he and his pregnant lady be married, because he was about to be recalled to his unit in Lublin? Relieved that Father Caspian had more nefarious sinners to absolve, Papa and Manek made a quick exit unnoticed.

They usually made their return through the back streets, and then followed a route through the concealing forest that ran parallel to the highway. To walk on the open road in the middle of the day was also high risk, and many times my father and brother had to hide in deep waterlogged ditches as armored divisions thundered along within a few meters of them.

My mother waits anxiously for their return, frequently walking out to the back of the house. Tadek and I wait with her, hoping to see Manek and the determined figure of Papa come striding down the river path. In the long stretch of time before they appeared, Luisia Horowitz, sensing my mother's apprehensions, creates all kinds of affectionate distractions.

"Mala, dear, did I ever tell you about the time I danced at Wawel Castle?" or "Mala, I have some lace left over from my wedding gown, come, why don't we sew it on a blouse for Hanka—that way she'll have something pretty to wear when we all return to the city."

※

We have no real toys in the country house (except the lead soldiers I had gotten from Moniek) but Tadek and I invent all kinds of things to do and devise playthings out of old tin cans. In the front field, we play soccer with a ball constructed by wrapping rags around a can that would usually disintegrate halfway through the game. Another favorite pursuit is called *machajka*. This involves taking a length of wire, usually two or three meters long, threading it through holes we make in yet another can, stuffing it with paper and wood chips and setting the contents alight.

The fiery item is then whirled around our heads by the wire, sending a broad plume of sparks high into the air. The visual effect at dusk is stunning —the burning embers causing a Catherine-wheel arc to blaze against the dimming sky. It's a terrific game until it causes our fathers to come tearing out of the house yelling such inane questions as, "What kind of a schmendrick lights up the night in the middle of a war!"

"Idiochi! Nudniks!" Mr. Horowitz screeches, standing in the damp field in his suspenders and undershirt, gesticulating to the Tatra hills like an opera singer. "Do you want every German in Galicia to think the Akiva underground is holding a barbecue here? You want to send them an invitation, huh?"

They are right, and we stand completely defeated and frozen by this paternal rage. In the next instance, the two fathers start to argue as to which of us boys is the more demented and order us both to bed at once.

The spring eventually arrives and the fire games give way to long sun-filled days that Manek often spends with us, teaching me to swim and Tadek (who was already like a fish in the water) to improve his crawl stroke. My father and the other adults have tried to establish some kind of indoor curriculum for both of us, but studying was far from our minds. We muddle through some math and history in the mornings, but our impulse is for the river whose soft burble tantalizes us through the open windows.

My mother declares that Tadek and I will grow up to be as ignorant as wood, and that the war is a sorry excuse for our lack of dedication to learning. I am far too vain to deliberately slack off the religious studies (my standard road to impressing my father), but Mama's comment bewilders me. A foreign invader who kicks people out of their apartments and closes their schools seems to me like a very good reason to postpone one's education, until the future moves us in a more sensible direction.

Besides, the sunny weather is a magnet. Tadek and I have become aquatic champions, fin-crested warriors whose new habitat is the swirling water we lived in every afternoon. In our river paradise, we lay prostrate on sandy ridges in the shallows of the Wilga; our heads lodged against rocks, letting the cooling stream rush over us, bringing with it, a cascade of young frogs that breed among the greening willow roots. We take old soup cans and corral several of these yellow stripers to hear them ribbit frantically against the aluminum. If you stack the cans up on each other, it's only a few minutes before the bigger amphibians in the first can make spectacular explosive jumps, freeing themselves and their cousins trapped above them.

"If you didn't let them escape," says Tadek, "we could take them home and have an aquarium."

"It'd be like making them live in a prison."

"So what? They're frogs," he argues.

"So, I'm not arresting them," I counter. "They like it best here, in the river."

Further downstream, the watercourse widens out into a small trout pond. Its surface bubbles from the tumbling current but its depths are a transparent jade-colored world of streaming reeds, aqueous ferns, and a darting parade of sunfish, grayling and devious huchen (Danube salmon). I learn how to dive and stroke my way through this serene trench for minutes at a time. I like the soft nudge of the current at my shoulders, to look up through the river's face and watch the way it dilutes the sunlight, making the sky a dirty blue.

Borek Falecki

Tadek and I swim closely along the river's edge here because the water drops from three meters deep at the bank to a sudden plunge of over fifteen meters at its center. I can see this dark core yawning open and it makes me apprehensive. I have a fear that something sinister might dwell in its depths. Tadek bravely strokes across its lateral distance and back but I am not a confident enough swimmer yet to venture after him. If I want to join him on the other bank, I have to backtrack on foot and cross by the rocks upstream.

We collect rotting logs and ride them as wormy mounts along the miniature rapids from our bathing shallows to the deeper basin that I now call the "moon's pool," because when I sink beneath the wavelets, the light at the edge of the subterranean pit has an eerie evening cast to it. In these days of the sun-warmed river, of floating lazily on our backs above the reed beds, the war and the regime in Krakow seem very far away.

On the far bank of the pool is a compact grove of spruce and beech trees and as I float past it like an unhurried otter, my eye catches Turk's cap lilies, snowdrops, and purple slipper orchids. Here is the place where Tadek and I had surprised a family of roe deer drinking from a feeder stream that led into a duck swamp. The animals snorted at us and thrashed among the algae, leaping frantically over each other to get away in their hoofed terror.

We try our hand at fishing in the crudest ways, building a dam of branches at the point where the Wilga narrows just before the moon pool. We have no real nets to speak of, but Tadek's sister, Salka, sews us an item that resembles a long windsock from the startling red netting overskirt of a chiffon party dress long discarded. We set this makeshift trap within our twig weir but catch nothing but mud. After some re-jiggering, we haul up mineral pebbles washed to a glassy brightness and even some amber matrix. Tadek and I are arguing over these spoils when the chiffon windsock begins a slow convulsion in the water that grows to a violent churning. A cloud of cast-up sand and debris spreads around our bare ankles.

"Don't move," I whisper. "We've got something."

"Maybe it's a big carp?" says Tadek. "Quick, grab that end of the bag, by your feet!"

I am suddenly immobilized because the swirling muddy haze below us is clearing and I am seized by a paralyzing fear at what I see through the red netting. The face of a demon grins back at me, an elongated head blunt as a cannon's shell, malevolent white eyes and a long slash of a jaw opening and closing, lined with band saw teeth that tore at the fabric.

"It's a killer python!" I scream. "Get out of the water!"

I yank at Tadek by the waistband of his swimming trunks and he falls backwards heavily, kicking the chiffon bag high into the air. A muscular silver thing about a meter and a half in length goes twitching across our vision, a perfect shining arc set against the trees. It whips its tail and soars, snout down, back into the river, to escape us in a sideways scurry into the dark pit of the moon pool. There it circles around to stare at us, ghostly and sinister in the semi-darkness, lashing back and forth, as if waiting for our next move.

I am already hurtling up the bank, yelling again for Tadek to follow and get on dry land immediately because I can see the huge snake turning and turning in the water but he just sits there in the mud looking dazed. "Schmuck!" he shouts after me. "This python our mamas could have cooked for supper!"

❋

"Read this to me, right here," orders my sister and points to an open chapter of my book titled *Eels of European Waters*. I stare at the words and stutter over the page. Doing any kind of schoolwork with Hanka is always a humongous tyranny.

"The Ang...Anguil...lidae is a family of fishes that contains many freshwater eels," I began. "There are sixteen to twenty species in this gee...genus. They are cata...cata...drom?"

"Catadromus!" barks Hanka. "That means they live in freshwater and return to the sea to spawn. And they do not eat people!"

I am in disgrace and trying to weather it.

The reason I am being tortured by my bookish, domineering sister is that I left my friend to his fate by the moon pool and raced back to the house with every noble intention of fetching help, a grown-up to contend with the great serpent. I came hollering up the path, propelled by fear that Tadek was under attack, if not already having the life squeezed out of him by the deadly coils of the silver 'python', a statement that causes his mother to shriek in fright for the men. My mother grips me hard by the shoulders and insists I speak slowly while Manek and Papa are already sprinting down to the riverbank with Salka Horowitz close behind them.

Is Tadek under the water? Is he drowned? Mama paces her questions calmly. No. *Is he bleeding?* No, Mama. *A leg broken, did someone hurt him? The soldiers, is it the soldiers?* No, Mama. Through her hair, I see a sodden apparition slopping their way into the kitchen. A sludge-caked boy covered in dead leaves and wet ferns with leeches hanging from his chest like medals, a boy who has eluded his would-be rescuers. His bare feet come squelching across the tiles. Luisia Horowitz shouts a joyous welcome through her tears and makes a muddy impression of her son against her white apron.

Tadek returns triumphant but is utterly contemptuous of me, calling me a miserable piss pot afraid of his own shadow. It takes me several days and all kinds of trades of my best tin soldiers to win back his friendship. I have to apologize to his mother for shredding her nerves to near cardiac arrest, and, on severe orders from my father, I am condemned to learn, in mind-numbing detail, the biological distinctions between an eel and a python!

"You see? What trouble comes," lectures my mother sternly, "from numbskulls who will not mind their books? Dear G-d, save me from raising a mental defective!"

Manek arrived back at the house one evening with the radio he retrieved from our former apartment building, long hidden in a box behind the cistern of the sub-cellar. He and Yehuda Lipnicki smuggled the item up river to Borek in a canoe illegally acquired from the Krakow Rowing Club, the radio buried beneath sacks of stolen roots crops Yehuda intended to trade for shoes his children needed. My brother had made the Cantor promise there would be no singing on their short voyage. He put Manek ashore where the Wilga tributary left the Vistula upstream from the city. My brother struggled through the forest paths in the gathering dark, carrying the radio in a sack across his shoulders.

The dome-shaped contraption with its silk mesh speaker and inlaid wood panels still works very well but there is much frantic whispering among the parents about where to hide it a second time, since the forbidden item symbolizes instant arrest and execution. Our fathers construct a false section under the roof of the pantry and sank the radio down between the supporting wall and the sloping eave. The radio itself is listened to sparingly and always with an elaborate security ritual. Every door must be locked and blankets put up at the windows prior to the item being carried with much reverence to the kitchen table where we wait for it to be turned on. The Horowitz girls, (who'd studied the flute and French horn before they were expelled by decree from the Krakow Academy), sit alert with their sheet music, ready to rouse their instruments to cover any suspect voices leaking from the airwaves to the outer world, should we be raided.

Although I don't always understand what is being said through the static squall that blows out of the radio, Tadek and I are thrilled at the idea of doing something so illicit. Besides, we are fascinated by the effect that the news of the war has on our fathers. The BBC broadcasts in Polish from London send Papa and Israel Horowitz into heated fervors of backslapping nationalism when the latest reports have the Germans scurrying from some smarting defeat, followed by their storms of desperation at bulletins that the allied troops were taking a beating from the Huns.

On the morning King Leopold III of Belgium surrendered, both fathers became morose and had to soothe their distress with several glasses of schnapps. A few days later, they whooped with pride at reports of the RAF's daring in the evacuation of Dunkerque. It cheers all of us to know that might is not always in Hitler's favor and that the wider world out there is kicking back.

My father exalts Winston Churchill highly among his heroes. One night he pulls me onto his knee and urged me passionately to, "Listen to this famous man, Romek. He's a great warrior. Listen and remember. This is what it's like to live fearlessly!"

I bend my ear to the radio's worn speaker and hear the gravelly declarations of the bulldog from Westminster; the timbre of English vowels sound so alien to me at the time, like a cascade of marbles rolling across the floor.

"What's he saying, Papa?"

My father, all keyed up and full of inspiration, translates haltingly in Polish.

"He's saying that…Hitler knows that he will have to break us in this island or lose the war. If we can stand up to him, all Europe may be free and the life of the world may move forward into broad, sunlit uplands."

"What use are all these fancy speeches, Leon?" interrupts Israel Horowitz. "Churchill should persuade the Allies to get here quick and dig the Jews out of this mess."

I ask if we can go to this place called the "sunlit uplands" now please, but get no sensible answer, just my head patted in tolerance. My father's next tier of faith, beyond G-d, the Rabbis and Winston, goes directly to Roosevelt and all things American. For him, the Yanks promise to be robust hosts of deliverance against the regime that is literally draining the life out of us.

"Don't worry so much," Papa says, "we'll live to see the end of that lousy little Austrian yet. Roosevelt and his marines will stitch him up for good."

However, no one that summer comes to sew Hitler up in a sack like an unwanted cat to be drowned. Tadek and I saunter into the living room one afternoon and check with our mothers as to what had issued from the radio earlier that has driven my father's head down on his arms and is compelling Israel to pound the kitchen table in a rage at the collapse of something called the Maginot line and France being cut into two zones.

"You boys don't go in there just yet," orders Mama.

"Why not?" I ask.

"The Germans have marched into Paris," explains Luisia Horowitz.

The next week isn't any better. Salka carries cognac in to the fathers. "What's happened now?" asks Tadek who meets her in the hallway.

"The Germans have invaded the Channel Islands," answers his sister. "They're close enough to spit on England."

Papa argues that the English are a stubborn people and will fight at the ocean's edge to the last man rather than see the swastika fly over some palace called 'Buckingham'.

"Enough already!" explodes my mother who tries to put an instant moratorium on any more radio listening. "Why do we need these endless *tsores* (troubles)? So it's bad, but do we have to eat our own livers at every disaster?"

I blame the eel for all this broadcast misery.

Borek Falecki

The wriggling peril still swims through my mind, a glistening repulsive menace that frequently enters my dreams. It would rise up out of the river, startling my sleep, its mucus slather winding across my pillow to hover and fix me with its sallow death's eyes. I fear it is a harbinger of many strange events still to come.

✼

The high summer in Borek sweeps the valley like a furnace. The dusk comes down later and later and the shared attic bedroom, which faced south, catches most of the day's heat, making it a sauna to sleep in. On one such night, I awake from an eel dream, disturbed by the clattering of a branch tattooing against a shutter. I get up and lean out of the window to reach for the shutter's latch and see below me along the driveway the red glow of someone's cigarette. The red light moves and I pull back to hide behind the curtains but still have a view of the front field. I can see the figure of a man walking briskly up the drive. He stops a few meters from the front door, turns to the right and waits. A few minutes later, another figure of slighter build walks out of the northern side of the pines, as if they have come around the back of the house. The two silhouettes meet on the lawn but say not a word. I track them by the cigarette's glow as they head down the drive, arm-in-arm, and into the forest.

I swallow my panic and wait in uncertainty. I catch sight of myself in the dresser mirror, a frightened boy in the dark, wound up in the drapes, not daring to move. Also in the mirror, I see…Manek's bed is empty.

✼

We still go to the river to cool off and to play at fishing but avoid the moon pool totally. Ever since the python fiasco, Tadek and I are not allowed to frolic alone in the water without having a third person present, not a good situation because it means having a strict sister or two, either Hanka or the Horowitz girls, along with us. Salka and Gizia come down to the bank as if prepared for a beach resort on the Black Sea, toting baskets with parasols, towels, flasks of lemon tea, rugs, wide-brimmed straw hats and lotions that smell like violets but which attract clouds of gnats. The sisters order us to remain in plain sight. We pretend to obey and wait until they are settled down to tan their basted limbs, when we can swim away to a girl-proof spot under the willows.

Here, cradled by the cooling waters, we sink into my favorite game; the otter drift, floating peacefully on our backs, only our faces visible to the clear sky.

It's in this repose that we are almost stoned to death one hot July afternoon.

There is a large splash beside my face and another, then the swift shadow of a missile that whizzes close above my gaze. I turn to see several pairs of male legs standing on the opposite bank, and the grinning faces of three boys, peering through the reeds. The amusement in their eyes is not innocent; they are here to hurt. The next rock they hurl smashes painfully into my right ear. Tadek drags me up and yells something at them but we're forced to run and dodge a rain of pebbles. Our attackers are shouting, "Jews! The Jews are dirtying the river! Get out of here, filthy Jews, this is our place!"

More sickening is the terrible screams we hear coming from Gizia Horowitz. We charge back up the stream but the war-like boys are crossing the water after us, stones glancing off our shoulders. Up ahead, I see a tall male of about sixteen tearing at Gizia's bathing suit. The girl is sobbing and fighting back. Salka is kneeling near a tree, moaning and holding her bruised forehead. I am very scared and the only action I can make is to shout, "No! No! No!"

Then someone is coming, a heavy-hipped stranger blasting through the trees, a wind-weathered face belonging to a handsome, well-built woman wearing a black apron over men's pants and carrying a carriage whip. In one easy motion, she brings it down across the back of the boy attacking Gizia. He screeches in pain and falls; the blow is so hard, it tears his shirt in two. I remember clearly to this day that the crack of the leather framed the entire scene.

"Get off this property!" orders the woman roughly to our pursuers, lashing at our other assailants mercilessly, making them dance and snatch at their stinging limbs. They take off for their lives down the river path. Tadek helps Salka to her feet and covers her with a towel. Nevertheless, Gizia's assailant is now our captive, a lumpy Polish kid with bad acne. He moans and collapses to his knees, blood seeping through the cheap cotton of his torn shirt. The fierce woman kicks him hard and loops the whip around his throat. "Apologize or I will hang your skin on my barn," she threatens calmly.

The terrified boy is hauled to his feet by the neck. For a moment there's just the river's murmur and all the Horowitz kids standing together clinging to each other, staring at the tableau before us. I dare not move or say anything, not wanting to disturb the web of potency and command the woman seems to spin out of herself. Inside the collar of her blouse resting against her sun-browned throat, I see a thin gold cross on a chain. Even though the stranger was our defender, she seems so unstoppable; she now puts raw fear in me as much as our attackers just have.

"Apologize!" she orders the boy again and delivers a brutal slap to his head, which causes him to weep louder.

Gizia and Salka have recovered enough to pull on their cotton robes. Salka is calling the woman "Pani Tomaszow" and gently asking her to please end the standoff and free the teenage atrocity. The woman's response tightens the whip around the boy's neck. She pushes him forward. He coughs out an abject plea for forgiveness from the girls, from us all, and is hurled into the stream for his effort. He flees, thrashing across the flow without looking back.

The woman stares after him, standing at the river's edge, as if in possession of that too. The slant of afternoon light makes diamonds in the water and from the reeds. I hear the raucous commentary of black grouse, but fear had robbed us of the day. We sullenly gather our belongings and prepare to go up to the house. Gizia speaks words of gratitude to Pani Tomaszow who receives them with a regal nod of the head. The woman suggests we say nothing of the stoning incident to avoid upsetting the parents, assuring us that our torturers will not return. She then turns her gaze on me. "You, boy?" she asks, "You are Roman Ferber?"

I nodded mutely, eyeing the horsewhip now tucked neatly into the side of her belt. She sizes me up for the shrimp I am and pulls a sealed envelope from her skirt pocket. "You will please give this to your brother. You will not lose it, damage it or open it, is that understood?"

Salka says she will guarantee my delivery. My tongue is so much wool in my mouth as I hesitantly take the letter. I see Manek's name written in the most beautiful elegant script incongruous to the work-calloused hand offering it to me.

I look up into Pani Tomaszow's broad face, she's not smiling but something like gentleness making a slow approach seems to be rising in her large brown eyes.

6

Leaving Borek Falecki

SO MOSES COULD HAVE SOME TIME IN NATURE, my father temporarily retires the horse to the farm of our secret deliverer, Immaculata. Papa also arranges for Tadek and me to go visit him. During our first outing to her property, the woman declares that she does not always approve of young boys because of their inclination towards tomfoolery. She restricts our visits to once a week and orders us not to trample her crops, step on day-old hatchlings or chase the piglets nursing at their sow in the swampy byre. (I was never allowed to have a pet at our apartment. The chickens on the terrace were a malicious bunch of ankle peckers and had always refused my affections.) To roam the Tomaszow farm at will and wander among the marvelous array of creatures that dwelt there is an extra bonus on my freedom summer.

Tadek and I are meekly submissive in Immaculata's presence. She rarely uses our first names, but calls us "Boy Horowitz" and "Boy Ferber". While she rarely lets down her guard, she does take a detached interest in us. "You two might as well make yourselves useful. Nothing flourishes alone here. Crops and animals need constant care."

Under her exacting tutelage, we learn to milk cows, feed orphaned lambs, gather eggs without breaking them and herd her semi-feral goats from the meadow to the dairy without being gored. This last task becomes a wild onerous trial, one that we must manage alone. I think Immaculata knows that between us two boys and these braying maniacs, the hoofed team certainly has the advantage. Tadek and I facing down a dozen crabby goats led by a bad-tempered buck with razor-sharp horns and a murderous nature is a contest to which we could have sold tickets.

To get them to go anywhere, one of us has to be the bait. Tadek slowly opens the gate of their corral while I got the demon buck to start charging me to the fence. Where he runs, the other goats follow, braying hysterically. Then, I speed through the gap, up a slope and into the dairy, hoof beats uncomfortably close behind me. Once all the animals are inside, Tadek slams the door shut and the herd would immediately head for their feeding trough, while I stood on a hay bale, well out of skewering range.

Both Hanka and Mama think Immaculata a haughty, stern-faced Catholic with the nature of a disgruntled general. Her character confounds just about everyone in our two families but her steely disciplines have worked well for the mixed animal and crops outfit she runs with tireless efficiency, and the help of her three monstrously huge daughters, Adelajda, Tesia and Mirelia. The acreage of their land is largely reclaimed terraces from layers of collapsed hillsides. As Immaculata had told my father, she and her Amazon girls had won much of it for growing by combing the skin of the earth with

Leaving Borek Falecki

rakes, leveling the terraces flat and patiently turning up stones for weeks on end, until they were finally rewarded by a broad spread of fecund topsoil.

I hear Mama chatting with Luisia Horowitz that these women, somewhere in their thirties, must have a hard time finding husbands with so many young men away at the front. However, Luisia says that after their father had abandoned the family to go work in the Gdansk shipyards, Immaculata had bound her daughters to her with iron admonitions that they were never to marry. Spouses would rob them of the land and divide the farm into unprofitable allotments. For their part, the three muscular sisters were less grown women around their mother and more like skittish convent girls.

All four females seem to be comfortable in the presence of my father with his elegant manners, who walks up to their paddocks to buy their excellent produce with the hazardous currencies of Swiss francs and American dollars. However, Immaculata never queries the foreign money and is unperturbed that a nest of Jews lives nearby. My father always sweetens her asking rate for meat and vegetables and she is unfailingly generous in the weight of the goods she supplies to him. Papa argues when my mother complains of the prices he paid, "Mala, she's an honest woman. Besides, I'm buying more than sustenance. As long as we are a source of steady income for her, we are safe. Why would she kill the golden goose, even if it is kosher?"

✤

A bizarre scene has cut across my life, which I foolishly believe is the influence of the satanic eel from the moon pool. On a stifling August night, I had a dream of staggering fearfully through black trees, in which something threatening is waiting to erupt, a distant roar partially suppressed. Branches drip mucus on my face. I flail my arms and brush horribly against the water serpent that grins down at me in disdain.

In my struggle to escape, I come to fearful awakening in the calm of our room. The wall clock reads "3:00" and Manek's bed is empty again, but I hear him padding around the downstairs hallway. Tadek is lying as if slain, his mouth wide open, honking sonorously in a noisy sleep. I quickly pull on my pants and shirt but leave my shoes behind. I creep out to the landing to follow my brother with every intention of investigating his secret forays. The eel has willed it so! I wait until he has slipped the latch on the front door and exited. I'm down the stairs in seconds and out into the night swollen with summer heat. I pull the door gently shut and feel the bolt click into place.

I hear a light tread cross the parched grass and spy my brother entering the forest. Never in all my short life have I been outside at such a late hour and it takes me a moment for my eyes to adjust to the dark. The sky is star-pinned and their light barely supplemented by a waning moon. I can make out a shallow gap in the trees where Manek has walked and I head for it. I am not exactly a great stalker and step badly to fall several times over rocks. Sharp stones and twigs stab at my bare soles, spruce branches rake my hair and my bravado is long gone because of the assailing trees that mirror my dream and the immense loneliness of the night. The wildness of the place is alive with nocturnal bustling. An animal scurries away from me and I hear the mournful shriek of some bird spiraling away through the pines in fear. Maybe the saw-toothed eel is here too.

A fervent whispering emanates from the spruces, two dark silhouettes are seated together, their backs to me; a stab of flame from a cigarette lighter outlines the face of my brother who has his arm around the shoulder of… Immaculata Tomaszow! On her lap is a clutch of papers and she is looking earnestly into his eyes. Manek is reciting something from a list; his tone is pleasant but urgent.

The two of them clasp hands in some kind of agreement. Manek smiles approvingly and kisses the woman's forehead! I stoop down in the bracken, utterly mystified. It seems to me that this is what men and women do when they're what Hanka calls "stuck on each other." Meet in secret in dark woods and stare goofily into each other's faces. My G-d! My seventeen-year old brother is mad for a woman older than our mother! What if he marries her, I thought. We'll get the farm, the crops, all the animals and to stay here forever—not so bad. Oh, but we'll inherit three huge stepsisters, Immaculata's drill sergeant ways, and the nasty buck with the bread-knife horns. My parents will faint dead away and never recover because Manek has gotten himself a Christian wife and there'll be endless ructions if Mama ever tries to get her to convert.

I steal away from them as quietly as I can. Once on an open path where I can mark the roof beam of the house, I run like an Olympian athlete for the front door. I want to be back in my bed, to hide away and not have to look at my brother, to shelter his secret that I know will weigh me down forever. It's not a night for sleeping.

✻

The Tomaszow women own two fine dusky Percherons named Dobry and Dolek that, even in his restored health and handsomeness, put poor Moses to shame. These proud alert creatures, sheer mountains of horseflesh, dazzle us with their rugged banks of muscle. When the hefty sisters walk the beasts into the plough harness, it is as if the mighty equines and the women are scaled by nature to complement each other.

We sneak up to the farm late one afternoon (not on one of the permitted visiting days), intent on fussing with the Percherons and have brought them a bag of apples. Dolek is out in the fields with the women but Dobry is in his stall, a huge mass of standing horse sleep. He comes awake with a soft whinny, looking down on us with his luminous fringed eyes. Tadek and I stand well below his titan's frame and the level of his stall's gate. We are so awed by the animal in these moments we cannot speak. We love to watch Dobry's jaws mash up several apples at a time. I am feeding him the fruit at a rapid rate when it comes to me by instinct in that hour that we were not

Leaving Borek Falecki

alone. Tadek looks up at me, his eyes silently telling me the same thing. He signals for us to be silent and to hunker down in the straw.

From the other end of the cavernous barn, from up in the hayloft came rising whispers, a male sibilance asking, "Is it safe?"

A girl's soft voice answers, "Yes, Papa, we must go now."

Through the stall's slats, I see a dark-haired well-dressed man of about thirty descend an unsteady ladder followed by a gray-haired elder, the image of the younger man. The old father then carefully helps a woman down with a tiny infant in her arms. Two more women, who look like kin to her, come next, then a young girl, and lastly a boy our age. The younger man pulls back the straw below the ladder to reveal several suitcases. Outside in the yard, we hear the throttle of the Tomaszow's cattle truck and the shunt of brakes. Tadek and I watch in utter astonishment as the parade of loft people quickly cluster into the shadows of an empty stall.

The double barn doors swing open and Adelajda enters, wearing her harvesting overalls. She gives a low whistle. Tesia backs the straw-filled vehicle into the barn's dusty interior. Adelajda silently beckons to the eight travelers. No words are spoken as she helps them and their luggage up into the truck. Tossing in bales of hay after them, she then drops the pins into the tailgate, rejoins her sister in the cab and they drive away.

I whisper to Tadek, "Who are those people—are they Tomaszow relatives?"

"Can't be, they're normal size," he hisses back.

He stands up too quickly to see further and smacks his head on Dobry's hard shoulder. The big horse is startled; it whirls on his haunches and his giant backside slams Tadek clean out of the stall! I leap after him to avoid being stepped on. It's not a good moment because coming up the yard we hear the tread of Immaculata and Mirelia. Immaculata is winding a lead rein around a metal bit in her hands and is actually laughing at some joke with her youngest daughter, a satisfied light in her eyes. They mercifully pass by the open barn doors, after which Tadek and I debate how to leave without being discovered. We hide out with Dobry for hours, until the day begins to wane—another dumb move. Now we're in the time zone of parental fury unless we can get home before dark.

Tadek finds a low window behind the hay bales, opens it and we're through it like ghosts, keeping to the shelter of the trees until the deepening silhouette of the Horowitz house comes into view. We enter by the kitchen door as nonchalantly if we'd never been gone. Salka, Gizia and Hanka are at the stove, involved in some female cabal about clothes and makeup. They ignore us except to give strict orders that we are not to disturb my Papa and Manek.

※

Many months from that day, Manek will confess to me about that evening when he and my father were locked in the cellar with three others. A certain amount of money was on the table, payment for new identity cards. I recalled the murmur of voices through the floorboards, and pieced together for myself the secrets of those who came and went from the house at night. One of them I now know intimately. My brother is brokering, not true romance with Immaculata Tomaszow, but freedom for Jewish families whose professional standing makes their survival imperative, those necessary to rebuild the world anew in their despairing communities. Men and women bound for Palestine or England, for whom there are outstanding warrants for their immediate hanging: clerics, scholars, teachers, journalists, philosophers and doctors; all talents in the first line of targeted destruction.

My mother will complain tomorrow how that tyrannical Catholic matriarch is bleeding us dry! However, Papa will shush her, saying look how Romek has grown brown and sturdy from his time on her farm, how the good food from the Tomaszow's fields has broadened our boy's frame and caused Manek and Hanka to glow with robust health.

He will never tell Mama of the hidden chambers above the hayloft. Strict silence is understood for the security arrangements; not just to protect us but also the unseen travelers and the Tomaszow women from being dragged away to be shot in St. Magda's square in Borek. My father kept his subversions well. He had a deep respect for the farmwoman and her rough strengths. I will learn from his conversations with Manek that Immaculata buried the money we paid her in an old cistern in her farthest field. She also kept several guns around her house, claiming she would rather shoot her daughters than have them suffer arrest and interrogations. Eavesdropping from my place of invisibility—a disused water pipe in the pantry above the Horowitz's cellar, I discover how she lies easily to Father Wilenska at confession on her feigned obedience to the new German legalities. How much of her farm profits not only bought liberty for the hunted but sustained the handsome red-haired Jew she had once married, who drinks it away under the guise of a Christian boozer in the waterfront bars of Gdansk.

Immaculata always reads his letters, his love still strong for her and plainly stated on the cheap notepaper. Her replies are in cash only. She knows he will never return and has long come to the understanding that their impossible passion, however unquenchable, is a pockmarked, messy arrangement; full of barbed uncertainty but deep in her flinty soul she has no problems recognizing the splendor beneath the dross.

❀

A white knee-high fog hovers over the meadow behind the house, dampening the lazy harvesting efforts of Tadek and me and causes the illusion that low-lying shrubs are floating above their roots. The March air is spiced with the cadaverous rot of leaf mold and sodden earth. Clouds, fat with more rain, drift across a sullen sky. My mother yells from the house as to how much 'borowiki' have Tadek and me have picked by now, and is it possible that she might get them into the breakfast pan in this lifetime? My friend shoots me a guilty look. At our feet lay two pathetic mounds of boletus mushrooms. Both of us have been traipsing about the field since early light collecting the ochre fungus that seems to have surged up through the fog drippings overnight. My hands are stained with mushroom spores and I smell like an old attic.

We fruitlessly pursue, for an endless time, the startled dash of a young fox we'd disturbed in the bracken. I heard him bark as he dragged a rabbit doe screaming and growling down the river's slope and caught a glimpse of his sharp black ears, his fiery pelt with its winter luster, a swift little murderer weaving through the mist, leaving a bloody trail of his struggling kill.

Beyond us, on the damp bank the death fuss had quieted into watered silence. I remember pushing away the nagging presentment that the hunt we'd witnessed was an omen, more than just nature turning the wheel of consuming instincts.

Behind the house, the river stream narrowed and clattered through a deep clay cut. Tadek and I charge our way into a dripping swale of blackberry canes, where stunted spruce firs and miniature alders drove their roots between frost-shattered rocks in a determined grip to grow at any angle to the stream. On the opposite bank lay the half-eaten rabbit, blood and intestines rouging the withered reeds. Grass is flattened and the mud churned with the violent stamping of two sets of claw prints. A red plug of fox fur sways from a knurled bough projecting above the water. Tadek glances at the slaughter and turns away immediately. I silently give the rabbit her due—wrestled her hunter to exhaustion, and took a piece of him with her.

Up ahead, pale clusters of mushrooms sprout abundantly in the runnels of tree roots. We splash along the stream's lip and squat to pluck our own quarry at great speed because we hear my mother maneuvering over the field with shouts of hazardous impatience.

"Hurry, Romek, fill the sack," urges Tadek, "Pick! Pick!"

"I'm picking! I'm picking!"

I pull and dig, grabbing at just about anything fungus–like. My friend is more diligent, hauling the boletus out in entire colonies. The bag is full by the time my mother's face appears through the trees.

"You boys down there?" she calls. I look up and see her on the ridge above, hair pinned up elegantly and lipstick bright, glamorously casual with a canvas apron wrapped twice over her good dress and old rain galoshes flapping around her slender ankles. To my relief, her face wears what I call her movie close-up smile.

"We have a lot, Mama," I exclaim proudly.

Tadek and I clamber up the bank and open the sack to show her.

"My brave little foresters," she croons. "There's enough there for breakfast and for soup tonight."

I make a face. "I don't want to eat these gritty things all day. Can't we have something else for dinner?"

"No, Romek, most of the food is already packed up," she answers me gaily and starts up the field with a quick squelching step. She waves for us to follow her without turning around.

"Packed up, why?" I call after her.

My mother stops and flexes her shoulders (a gesture that meant nothing but trouble) and says in a steady voice, "We're going back. Back to Krakow... where you'll see all your friends again."

My stomach knots up and I fight the urge to cry. Tears surge from Tadek's eyes, mostly for shame—he had overheard our fathers whispering about our leaving the night before but has said nothing at all to me.

"But we don't want to go back!" I moan at the shimmering wet trees, at the implacable iron-stained sky, "We like it here!"

In the distance, a dull chasm of cloud opens beyond the tree line and a vein of lightening silently enters it. A low wind brings huge spatters of rain that soaks us all in no time. My mother turns and pulls us into the fabric of her damp apron, her fragrance overriding the earthy stench of boletus.

"My poor cubs," she says and kisses Tadek's hair. He hides his face in her hip and weeps softly. She raises my eyes to hers.

"We have no choice, Romek. It's an order. We have to leave...tomorrow. Papa will tell you more. The good news is that we have a new apartment and we're all going to live there. Both the families will be together, just like now, how about that, huh?"

We both stare up at her in mute misery. Strands of dark hair fall across her cheek. She fiddles awkwardly with a hairpin and her flecked brown eyes dart between Tadek and me. In her gaze, I can sense her honing what to say next to make the situation better.

"I've been keeping a jar of serwulatki (hot dog wieners) for a special occasion," she says, smiling radiantly. "I'll open them and Luisia has a few cabbages in the cellar. We'll make bigos (cabbage stew) and roll out some mushroom pirogi (dumplings). We still have some sugar and Hanka will bake a chestnut cake for desert. You two dry your tears. Come on, we'll dine like kings."

The idea of eating well puts some salve on our wounds, as she knows it would. We both cling to her as she marches us up to the house through the pelting rain.

Leaving Borek Falecki

The last night in our country refuge, we make a merry feast that, to me, stinks of towering falsehoods. Manek and Hanka talk excitedly of how maybe, back in the city, they can continue their studies in some fashion and both sets of parents jaw on about seeing old friends and familiar faces. Tadek is swept into the forced jocular atmosphere but I morosely watch them whip up their fake delight, and keep silent for once.

I go to bed with a leaden sense of foreboding. In the cot across the room, Tadek mutters in his sleep and snores like an old dog. Our mothers, the Horowitz girls and Hanka have already retired but the men remain downstairs, drinking the last of the schnapps and speaking in low voices.

I strain to hear their conversation and my brother's clear tones drift up to me. He's reading yet another edict aloud to the two fathers.

"Jews may not travel by train between cities in Poland, they may not buy books, and in particular, they may not buy German books, Jewish peddlers and merchants are prohibited from purchasing or selling goods in neighboring villages, they may not enter the central post office, or send mail abroad. They are forbidden from owning phones, radios, and they may not run bakeries or own coaches or deal in textiles and leather."

"Who will sew a coat or make the shoes?" Mr. Horowitz laments. "Are we to look like beggars before our wives with our *tuchas* (backside) hanging from the pants?

"Izzy, you worry too much," my father assures him. "The day you bare the treasures God gave you, I'll take a needle to your suit myself."

Listening to them, I spend hours staring into the thick darkness, fantasizing whether I should run away or not. I consider the distance it would take me to walk to Russia, how lonely I would be…and what if? What if I never saw my family again? I even rehearse how that would feel, a cutting grief, like the rabbit having her innards torn away even as the life still lingered in her. I weep quietly into the pillow at the very idea.

The next morning, we are all reversed. There was a somber atmosphere in the house. Everyone wears a martyr's face as we busy ourselves for the departure. Even my father is remote and silent. I go about smiling and whistling, packing things up and offering to help with loading the cart.

"Must be the mushrooms," remarks my sister. "The ones that make you hallucinate. Romek is suffering from too much niceness."

"Savor it while you can, Hanka" argues Manek, "the effects could be short-lived."

He pulls lightly on my ear and says affectionately, "What have you been up to, you little pirate, that you're sugaring your way around everyone?"

"Nothing bad," I answer. My brother smells of mint soap and balsam hair oil.

"Where we're going," I ask him, "It won't be so great, will it?"

"We'll make it great, Romek, I promise you."

His eyes lighten as he smiles into mine and I see a subtle but utter fearlessness there. My brother has an unending supply of audacity. Maybe his bravery will be contagious, hopefully, courage I would grow into.

"Come with me," he says, laughing. "We're going to get old Moses and I'll let you put him in the harness."

"Manek, where's our new apartment?" I ask him. We start out the kitchen door and down the lawn's path together.

"It's on Krakusa Street. The Germans have arranged a ghetto across the river," he answers, walking at his usual focused pace, a fleeting lope that ate up distances.

"What's a ghetto?" I blurt as I hurried after him.

"A place apart, such as they have for Native American people in the USA."

I have a fleeting vision of our new address rising out of the Great Plains, of lantern-jawed heroes in tall hats, dusty towns and clapboard streets, images banked from the few scratchy black-and-white westerns I used to watch with Moniek Hocherman at the Wanda cinema. "Will there be buffalos?"

"No buffalos. It's Podgorze, not Kansas."

I ask if we could say goodbye to Immaculata, the big daughters and their animals but Manek says that it is best to leave without any ceremony. As we walk away from their fields with Moses, my last sight of the Tomaszow farm is the dark silhouette of their barn and its pointed gable that has been, according to Papa, the freedom station for over sixty-three Jews and twenty-eight members of the Polish underground.

✧

Long after we are gone from Borek Falecki, Immaculata will totally disappear from the world, as will her daughters. Father Caspian Wilenska will betray her for harboring Jews and resistance fighters. The priest will argue with the local Reich commander that her hard-working farm should be turned over to the Catholic Church. Of course, he will lose on the deal but not as badly as the Tomaszow women, who will all perish in Treblinka. Immaculata will refuse the walk to the gas. Defiant to the end, she will fight like a tigress and give her jailers holy hell, even though they will beat her bloody and break her fine jawbones. She will force the soldiers to shoot her against the wall, having regally earned a warrior's death.

In the not-so-distant future, I came upon my father one afternoon, with his eyes moist and caped in his tallit, praying over a dog-eared photograph of the woman and her daughters, all young and ripe in a more peaceful summer of 1930. There is the man in the photo, Adam Tomaszow, wearing a full beard and coiled payess. His glance toward his Christian wife bears a delicate tenderness. Her hand is linked in his and in her face too shines an unshakeable devotion. Whatever harsh forces of priestly or rabbinical disapproval over their rebellious marriage had forever separated them; it seemed to me looking back at that time, if she could not be with Adam, she would be for the sustenance of his kind.

However, my wailing complaint rose loud and clear—why didn't she help us too, Papa? Get us out to the Adriatic Coast and to Palestine. I could have grown up in Jerusalem and been a true child of the Book. We had money saved and Mama's hidden diamonds? We could have paid to get away. Didn't Pani Tomaszow like us enough to send us to safety in the truck with the others?

"Don't get so heated, little Romek," said my father, whose words first calmed me and then astonished me. "It wasn't as if she never offered us a way to leave. I politely refused her help many times and with good reason. We *are* true citizens of Poland. I will not have my family driven out of our country and see our ancestry uprooted. You will understand why once you're older. No man's power is forever, Hitler will learn that soon enough and we'll be restored to the life we once knew, I promise you."

He ruffled my hair, his smile comforting but I heard the lie resonate deep within him. Given the fact that we could have been long gone over the Mediterranean's horizon to permanent safety and, to know that he had declined our deliverance, was the first time in my life that my father had ever disappointed me.

❦

Otto von Watcher, the Austrian Governor of the Krakow district, had issued the decree on March 3. Copies of the notice are plastered all over the town's market square in Borek. Manek has done the dangerous thing of ripping one from the wall of the St. Stanislaus Church and hiding it down his pants. He and my father have waited until they are deep into the woods on the town's outskirts to read it.

"The Regulation for Restrictions on Residence…a Jewish residential area…in the city of Krakow…any Jews remaining in the Kazimierz, or those billeted in outer environs…must take up domicile by March 20th, 1941. The Jewish quarter to be located in the district of Podgorze…under guard at all times… The main gate will be located on Limanowskiego Street and the Rynek Podgorski. Gate Two at Wieliczka Street and Limanowskiego will be reserved for military vehicles only. Gate Three will be situated on Lwowska Street, Gate Four at Kucik Street and the Plac Zgody. Any person contravening this Decree, or the Regulations for its execution, will be punished in accordance with…etc."

News from the city reports that the Ghetto is comprised of twenty hectares made up of fifteen streets, three hundred and twenty houses with just over three thousand rooms. Most of the buildings are just two floors high, ancient and dilapidated. Before the war, Podgorze had just a few thousand inhabitants but in March of 1941, the relocation of Jewish families boosted the population by an additional fifteen thousand souls. Dr. Fritz Sipher, the editor of a Jewish paper, has an admiration for my brother, possibly because of Manek's activities with the Akiva resistance group. As soon as the relocation decree is announced, Dr. Sipher requisitions us an apartment on the corner of Krakusa Street and Wita Stowsza.

Our families are allowed two suitcases each, nothing more. We once again put on the overcoats with money and jewelry sewn into the sleeves and thickened hems. I have a silver chain patched into my jacket with the name of Moses (the prophet, not the horse) inscribed on it. (My father insisted I give up it to him for safekeeping. I still have that chain to this day.)

When the men load up the cart, a light feathering of snow idles down around their shoulders. A ravenous chill sets in as the morning comes on and looses a tempest that howls and spins into a whirlwind of ice. It stings my cheeks and melts along my eyelids. My mother orders us kids quickly up into the cart. Luisia gets up by her two daughters, then Tadek and me. My father covers Moses with the rain canvas and we make tents of shawls and blankets against the lashing flurries.

Hanka on the buckboard takes the reins while the men decide to walk beside the wheels to guide the horse through the oncoming blizzard. A screen of slanted snow obscures our last view of the Horowitz house and the entire landscape. Soon we are enveloped in an endless white. The dark suggestion of birch trees, a roof, and a hill here and there barely lessens my rising fear of being suspended in a deadening blank emptiness, no comfort of fence rails or solid boundaries anywhere.

I recall my inner state in those hours; yearning badly for all we had left behind. Now, in retrospect, I consider who willingly walks back into the waiting jaws of an enemy? I was just a boy with none of the well-forged disobedience that liberty needs, and, although the inclination was strong, I had no courage at all in that year of my life to be a runaway. Love had me tightly harnessed to my family.

In the blurred distance, I see a vast moving shadow on the horizon, a long bleak file of travelers churning through freezing wheel ruts walking and leaning into their route to defy the weather that punished their forward stride. We halt at a crossroads where a roadside Christian shrine rises to mark a parish boundary. A statue of the Virgin with the baby Jesus in her arms stares out at me from behind a pane of glass and a garish froth of silk flowers. An immense train of people flow around the cart on either side of us now, dragging small miseries of children and sacks of possessions. Manek gets up beside Hanka and carefully takes the reins.

We inch forward through a sea of dark shoulders laden with baggage of all types. Many gaze up at us with a sour resentment, as if we've stolen the privilege of riding the creaking cart. Men, faces dark under their caps, suitcases tied to their backs, stagger ever forward. The women speak in despairing murmurs, urging along white-haired elderly relatives, so strong is the pained bewilderment in the gaze of these old ones, it seems to me

Leaving Borek Falecki

they have stepped off the world into some alien place at the far end of nothing.

As we near the city, I see the black arches of the Podgorze Bridge rise above the congested roads, the gray tremulous flow of the river. A tremendous cacophony heaves up into the pallid sky, the roar of exiles with swaying towers of furniture on flimsy carts, going and coming, struggling to pass each other on the narrow bridge road. We will not cross it into Krakow proper, as I now ached to do, back to the welcoming route to the familiar apartment on Waska Street.

Manek pulls our cart up short on the edge of the Rynek Podgorze (Podgorze Square) where thousands of Jewish families are swarming around the slow wheels of German military trucks that cruise through the crowd barking orders operatically from megaphones. Clerks with small card tables are assembled at makeshift desks where they set down their lists, rubber stamps, inkpads; they fuss with their pens and inkwells, rub the winter mist from their eyeglasses on their jacket sleeves, and look skeptically at the spread of humanity before them. My father remarks that they remind him of bookies opening the shop before a race. My mother shushes him so she can translate the mess of German orders being shouted over the square.

"Everyone should walk from this point," orders Mr. Horowitz. "We'll have to wait for our entry papers to be examined. Manek, you know what you have to do?"

"Indeed," he jumps down from the cart and lifts us down after him. "Romek, Tadek, say goodbye to Moses."

Manek unhitches my equine friend from the shafts and ties on the lead rein. I lean up into the horse's warm mane and hold on tight. Moses is half-sunken into the waking sleep that his kind can achieve with one hoof bent into the cobbles.

"Manek, you're not taking him…to the slaughterhouse, are you?" asks Tadek.

Please, no, let it not be so, I whisper to whatever angels guard horses in their old age. Manek peels me gently off the animal's neck and says, "You guys will see him again someday, I promise. He's going to the lumber mill, where he'll tow railroad ties twenty yards from the saw barn to the pile. He'll have a warm stall and be well fed. Poldek Kreuski raised him from a foal, said he'd always buy back old Moses. That nag's better than a wife to him, eats less and doesn't argue."

Manek walks the horse to where I see a young but prematurely bald man with a carpenter's apron under his jacket come forward with a travel pass in one hand and a halter in the other. Moses nickers with pleasure at the sight of Poldek who reacts with equal joy. He and my brother pull the horse into a side street as an envelope is exchanged between them. My unhappiness is complete when I see Poldek strolling away with my beloved mount.

My parents come over and we all find a place to sit along the curbside. The Horowitz family joins us and Luisia offers us some of her homemade cheese and pickles. The megaphones bellow a cluster of names, "The following families of Abusch, Josef, Altmann, Eliasz," and "Bejski, Mosek, Bernstein, Mendel, Bolazcy, Szmul, report to table three immediately!"

By the time the recitations got to "Davidowitsch, Wigdor," I begin to drift into a light slumber, settled across my mother's lap. Who knows how many hours before the lists under F are announced and we would rise to stand at the tables with meek respect for the spinsterish clerks, who stamp, sign and wave people with absurd grandiosity through the barbed wire gates of the Ghetto. But Manek is jostling me awake as our name is called and I find myself carried over my father's shoulder when it comes our turn to enter into our confinement.

PART II: 1941 ~ 1943

7

The Krakow Ghetto

THE FOYER OF OUR ASSIGNED APARTMENT has a worn oak floor, aromatic with age and linseed oil. It ends at a small, dilapidated kitchen where the floorboards meet uneven gray tiles. There stands a very basic stove, three spavined shelves above it and beside it an ancient sink veined with cracks in its discolored glaze. A pump handle sits precariously attached to the pipes that once supported faucets and the toilet is down the hall to be used by nine families.

The Reich had decreed that there should be four ghetto dwellers to one window. Our new residence was a corner apartment with a decent number of windows that exceeded the four-to-one ratio. When I asked where my bedroom was, my father opened glass-paned doors, each leading to two large empty rooms, one for each family.

"You won't be alone, Romek," he says jovially. "We'll be like gypsies; this room will be our caravan, with the Horowitz clan camped next door."

"What do we sleep on, Papa, the bare boards?" asks Hanka.

My uncle Solomon Ferber, dressed in the uniform of an OD (the Ordungdienst, Jewish Police) who had escorted us to this address, is casually buffing his nails by the stove. Of all my father's brothers, Solomon was stamped with amazing good looks, which allowed him a delicate vanity. He had a welt of curly black hair, a sultry luminous gaze, a patrician nose and a full mouth. A man possessed of exquisite manners, he was renowned for winning hearts and minds of both genders. He also had a droll and snappy sense of humor.

"Don't worry, sweet Hanka. There are mattresses and blankets in my cellar. I've been saving them for you," he says, grinning through white teeth, even as a picket fence. He strokes Hanka's hair affectionately, as if seeking a mirror to his remarkable self in her own dusky prettiness.

From my talents as an eavesdropper, I hear Mama say that Solomon's striking visage could be publicly disturbing, that he was the envy of many husbands and black-garbed orthodox men who distrusted his delight in his own beauty as something G-d would begrudge. Prior to marrying my Aunt Halina, this uncle had broken the hearts of several shop girls, the sisters of friends, virginal amazons of the academic stripe, who put knowledge above passion, and had side-stepped the lusts of men who my mother labeled as being "Of the Greek persuasion." (At eight years old, I really thought they were from Greece.)

Mama interrupts Solomon's preening by asking the men folk if they don't want the kids to sleep standing up, to please go with him at once to collect the bedding.

The Krakow Ghetto

After they leave, I wander from window to window, for a limited view of the upsets happening on the sidewalks. The Ghetto is filling up. All along Krakusa Street, families are swarming to their allocated burrows, shepherded by a fleet of ODs on bicycles shouting out addresses. Now and then, they will brake and salute as a German staff car roars by carrying a passel of officers.

From the room that will house our family, I can see the Ghetto wall and a thin strand of the Vistula glistening far away. The shining ribbon of water arouses a yearning for escape. I close my eyes and I'm riding the fast current thousands of kilometers to the Baltic Sea where I would most likely drown from loneliness. My mother came in, black market chocolate bars in hand, to interrupt my reverie.

"We'll open the powdered milk and have some hot chocolate when the others get back," she says brightly. "Maybe I'll save half of it for a special occasion."

But there can be no special occasions, not ever, in this place.

I shall remember forever the shape of the Ghetto walls, curved in the style of *matsevot* (Jewish tombstones), and the high wired fence that surrounded us. The wife of Krakow's Austrian Governor, (Baron Otto von Wächter), had gaily described these barriers as "elegant in the Hebrew taste." Every night at seven, the guards would lock the gates promptly, the curfew hour when only the foolish, the desperate or the Jewish underground would risk exposure in the deadened silence of the streets. All windows and doors overlooking the "Aryan" side of Podgorze were bricked up lest our presence offend Christian eyes. We are condemned to be shut away for the next two-and-a-half years in some fifty acres of streets that Hanka deemed the "Jew Zoo."

✻

A heavy snowfall seals the windows of our apartment, watering the daylight to a pasty gloom and buffering the Ghetto in a stone quiet. Tadek and I, jacketless but with wool gloves on and paint scrapers in our hands, are the snow-scouring team, a task that has be done twice a day to stop the window sashes from freezing.

"OK, Romek, it's thickened up again," Tadek calls out, "time to clear."

I throw up the windows in the Horowitz's room and the snow blusters over us in little drifts. We scrape away at the panes, guffawing like heathens and spearing each other with broken icicles. My mother, Luisia Horowitz and her girls are playing their umpteenth game of cards at the kitchen table. Mama issues a stern order that we are not to wet the floor or dump snow on innocent pedestrians.

Earlier that morning, we'd already doused two girls who squealed nicely at the icy cascade on their shawls, and a furtive rail of a man, hair like matted snakes, dressed in a woman's tattered velvet opera coat and walking a

German shepherd dog on a length of string. Tadek had fired off a snowball at the dog that had caused the man to drag his charge to the gutter, where both he and the young animal barked up at us.

"Crazy little bastards, your parents should wallop you senseless!" The matted head jiggled with rage. The man's skin was the color of chalk and pitted with open sores.

"Where'd you get the dog?" Tadek called down. The shepherd was a handsome, full-muscled creature, his golden eyes shone with eager adoration as the man brushed the snow carefully from his pelt.

"He was my father's," said the sick-skinned man.

"Liar!" I teased, seeing the iron cross swinging from the expensive leather collar. The man tracked my gaze, fumbled the collar open and quickly stuffed it in his pocket. He seemed suddenly very perplexed and said something of tender urgency to the beast. He stroked its brindled ears and turned his diseased face up to us again.

"I have five kids. The bread ration is not enough…not enough," his voice trailing away. He and the dog stared at each other in mute questioning. The man pulled the green velvet coat closer around him and shuffled off in the direction of Targowa Street, the animal high stepping amiably by his side through the snow.

I like the window-cleaning task, I like scanning the icy streets to see what dramas would occur and, if we scrape snow late in the day, it gives me a chance to greet my father, or Hanka and Manek, as they came crunching down the sidewalk from their compulsory labor assignments. Staring out from windows is still high on the list of the verboten and likely to elicit a leather-handed beating or worse from the ODs, the Polish police, or the German patrols. Despite these ferocities, eyes go hungering everywhere.

Six is the wanting hour when other faces are also pressed to glass panes; numerous bobbing shadows over lamplights or burning candles, darting glances that gave a ghostly ripple to lace curtains and disturbed window shades up and down the street. Many would even risk loitering in the gloom of their doorways, ready to dart back at the first sight of danger. A crucifying terror lay at the core of this daily waiting. Shouts of greeting clamor the air, as families swarm around their returning loved one crossing the threshold. If the scenario were otherwise, from over the rooftops we would hear the sobbing screams and laments: a father randomly arrested at the Gates, a child picked up, another shot out of hand at the freakish displeasure of a guard. Each day more of us fell away from existence.

In the mornings before the men and Hanka would leave to march out with the work detail, my father would gather everyone in the kitchen to recite the Modeh Ani.

"We thank you, G-d, for our waking up and being alive."

The Krakow Ghetto

I am not pious in this. Gratitude for opening our eyes on yet another day in the Jew Zoo seems utterly stupid. Papa, as always, senses my bitter little festering and whispers to me, "No matter what happens, you are to study hard, behave well, and protect your mother. Do you understand me?"

I nod, hiding a tear or two; any disapproval from him is a biting wound.

My father had been assigned to a papermaking factory across the river, Israel Horowitz to a factory line assembling things I have never heard of. Hanka swabs floors at the Krakow airstrip, and my brother now catalogues books for an educational institution that would never have admitted him as a student.

Both in and out of the ghetto, invisibility counts for much. Of all my family, Hanka, who easily kindles males with her rustling silk voice and her zaftig physique, is the most vulnerable, the one who risks the predatory gaze of the Luftwaffe pilots who roar their Heinkel fleets daily into Krakow. Since many soldiers secretly disobey the racination laws, Luisia and my mother announce it would be prudent to downgrade my sister's charms.

"How will you do that?" I ask.

Each morning, something like a misshapen quilt walking upright in crude work boots would emerge from our apartment house on Krakusa Street. Sacking packed under my sister's filthy raincoat to conceal the swell of her hips, ebony hair buried beneath a greasy kerchief. Lay the flour paste on evenly, Luisia had advised, don't forget her hairline and the neck, just a light dusting of soot and cigarette ash on the cheeks. Rotting onions wrapped in ammonia-soaked rags in the pockets for the right odor. Not even a blind man would touch her! Our father had gasped to see his pretty girl child reduced to such a grubby monstrosity.

At the ghetto checkpoint stands a young OD, still reasonable in nature. He compares Hanka to the alluring, fine-boned face that stares out at him from the photograph of her Kennkarte (her worker's ID card) and assumes that he has before him a punished, drained creature from the Montelupich prison. She stands among other women looking equally slummy and ruined. Her stench makes him gag. The youth, with his hand over his nose, kindly recommends to her the public Mikvah on Josefinska Street, where the hot water would cleanse away any measure of degradation. Hanka nods submissively but does not raise her eyes.

At the airfield, the onion-scented fright is down on her knees, scrubbing the women's toilets, glad to be out of human view. Sora Finkelstein, hair dyed Jean Harlow blond, who poured beer for the pilots and sold them cigarettes, stands at the mirror, daubing her mouth with black market lipstick. Hanka, in the farthest stall, hears the restroom door burst open, a man's sudden footfall, the gold lipstick tube drops in shock, rolls her way. She hears the pilot's coaxing tones in bad Polish, Sora's protest and the thread of fear that spikes it. A turn of the lock, the barmaid pleads, the man grows angry, "Two minutes, that's all," he demands. He starts a sibilant rant about good German boys and the demonic Jewish whores that tempt them, ever since Sheba, Jezebel and Herod's daughter.

There is little struggle. Hanka listens to the first slap and the slam of the other woman against the tiles. From a gap where the hinge met the toilet's door, my sister sights the man's boot kick the cheap black woolen skirt underneath the sink. She climbs onto the lavatory bowl and clings to the pipes, her breathing noiseless, praying hard not to be discovered. Sora silently endures, but for the sooty young hag in stall number eight, there would be one fist in the face for being dirt ugly, and another for witnessing the stain of the Jewess on Aryan flesh.

❋

Tadek and I are required to clear more snow, this time on the streets with our fathers. What a prize! It wins me the chance to be in the open air with Papa for a whole day. The jeep with the bullhorn trolls the Ghetto streets ordering all men and boys to report to the Plac Zgody. We will be marched across the river with shovels issued by the Labor Office for snow removal work.

"Surely not the boys too, they're not regulation age," my mother protests.

Manek's arm is already in his overcoat, "Von Wächter's got some generals visiting from Berlin, and he needs to show he has the city in hand."

"Let's go, Papa, please," I pester, fearing the opportunity to be outside for just a few hours will suddenly evaporate.

Over a hundred men and boys assemble to clear the driveway at Wawel Castle among trees shrouded with snow and sunken gardens lined with topiaries, a zoo of white, iced animal forms, frosted privet cones, box hedges and miniature poplars all frozen rigid. Manek is sent further down the hill with another team to haul out dead shrubs.

From the stone ramparts of Kasimir's tower a red and white flag emblazoned with the Swastika wafts above the city. The sky is razor blue, the air sweet with cold. My father inhales it with the same satisfaction I'd seen in him when sipping a fine champagne. In his face shines a small blaze of happiness that he hopes will spark me too.

"This is not so bad, Romek," he declares enthusiastically, propelling a huge heap of snow from his shovel. "The exercise will make you strong."

On my shovel is a tenth of his amount. Rather than hurl it at the growing mound, I aim it at Tadek who squeals in protest, "Snowball fight, now!"

Tadek charges me in the belly and two of us go crashing into the snow pile, yelling and snorting ice crystals from our mouths. Four other boys join us in a raucous skirmish; globes of snow fly in all directions.

"You think this little war within a war is such a brilliant idea?" asks Issac Horowitz, but winks at my father while he shovels alongside him.

The Krakow Ghetto

"Let them play, Izzy," says Papa, "G-d knows, it's seldom they have the chance."

Despite the pleasant weather and camaraderie, the adults are anxious about being a hair's breadth from the seat of the Reich's governor, his Wehrmacht, and the SS platoons housed in the former palatial barracks of King Zygmunt the Great. My Uncle Arnold is one of the ODs assigned to supervise our section. Out of sight of the German guards, he's generous with candy for the kids and cigarettes for the men. Arnie is discreet about having his own brother and Tadek's father in the detail, but he regales us with the story of the Dragon's cave that burrows into Wawel Hill on the riverside of the castle's heights.

"You know it was Prince Krak," explains my uncle, "who had to rid the people of the dragon that was devouring their cattle and every virgin in town. The dark cavern over there on the western side is where the Krakus used to wait for the fishermen to bring their daughters to be eaten alive."

"I don't think the monster ever left," mutters Issac. "I see its chariot coming this way."

We have excavated the drive almost to the gates when Arnie shouts, "Caps off. Attention!"

Men and boys part on either side of the snow banks to stand and salute the Nazi staff car that lumbers up the cleared path, a huge shiny black Daimler. In the back seat sits a well-dressed woman wrapped in a fox fur coat, her yellow hair braided elegantly around huge emerald earrings. Arnold says she is the resident harpist who discreetly played Baroque pieces in Wawel's tapestry-lined stateroom while German generals sipped their aperitifs.

By mid-afternoon, Issac and Tadek are sent off with a party of about twenty-five workers to clear the paths around the Planty Gardens. Manek, Papa and I find ourselves shoveling the sidewalks of Florianska Street, an upscale main thoroughfare we had not walked in two years.

"Look, Papa, there's the Eugeniusz bakery," I cry, pointing at the window of the luxury patisserie filled from end-to-end with a monstrous sugar-tiered wedding cake corralled by glistening fruit pies. "Can we buy some kugel for Mama?"

"No, Romek, I'm afraid that's not possible," says my father with a face of stone.

My brother tries to explain that the cake parlor now has a sign that reads "No Jews."

I start laughing at the very idea until I see despair creeping up my father's face like a flame at the edge of a newspaper. "Dig, Romek," he commands.

All up and down the gutter, our ghetto team shovels snow into the drains. We are one long line of David's blue star. Three women stop and stare at us, shake their heads in pity and then turn to cluck sympathy at each other. A priest passes by the line of Star brushers, makes an elaborate sign of the cross in the air and darts quickly to the other side of the street. I can't tell whether he's blessing us or invoking protection. Two young men dressed in fine wool coats approach. "Well, what do we have here?" they carp in disdain, "Zyds actually working and for no money."

"Don't look at them, Romeczku," whispers my brother.

One of them, an oily-haired capon kicks hard at my father's shovel. The snow flies everywhere and Papa teeters back onto the pavement to win his balance. He ignores the insult and goes on working.

"You, Zyd!" said the capon's partner, also a well-coiffed boy with the fur collar on his expensive coat turned up against the wind. "Don't you know the sidewalks are for your betters?"

He prods my father in the chest. Papa suddenly grabs the gloved fingers and holds on…and on. I drop my shovel, shocked and rigid with fear. Manek stills my quivering shoulders with one touch. The Fur Collar looks flummoxed and tries to pull his hand away but Papa grips it tighter, not taking his eyes from the young man's face. The youth is highly uncomfortable to be so snared with Jew breath misting over him.

"I see no betters here," said Papa quietly. "I see ill manners and a lack of good conduct."

The dozen other men on the snow detail drift closer to watch.

"One shout from me," grates the capon, "and your filthy Jewish hide will be blown all over the street."

The Fur Collar still attached to my father's hand tells his friend to back off. However, the fool snatches up my shovel and starts swinging it. I wrench myself from Manek's grip to leap between Papa and the gloved offender, crying to the sky, "No! Please, no! That's my father!"

Papa, with his free hand, quickly pushes me behind him, where I sob into the tails of his coat. "Manek, please call the OD," he orders in a cool voice, "and we'll settle this nonsense. It seems these gentlemen have a complaint."

An odd circle assembled around us. Ghetto men on the inside, ordinary Poles ringing them, followed by more snow-driving Jews on the outer edge sealing the crowd. Manek looked desperate. "Let it go, Papa, please."

My father gives a tug and releases the prodder; the glove catches in his hand. The youth steps back, takes the shovel from his friend and gives it to Manek.

"May…I have my glove…Sir?" he asks Papa with polite contempt.

My father gives a gracious nod. "Of course," and hands it back to him.

From down the block comes a terrific shout from Uncle Arnie, who warns us to get back on the job immediately because the duty patrol's jeep is turning out of Wawel's gates, carrying Sergeant Fritz Goertner, known as Fritz the

The Krakow Ghetto

Flogger for his love of the steel-tipped whip. The two young Gentiles quickly merge into the dispersing crowd. My father turns and dabs at my tears with his coat sleeve. "Romek, you can stop crying now; we have work to do."

※

Tadek and I play football with girls. The opposing team is Bella and Sara Abramowicz, both taller and two and three years older than we are. They live on the floor below us, crowded together with four other siblings and another family with two infants.

It's a fine dry day in late April and our field is the southern end of Krakusa Street. (In the first months of the Ghetto, we were able to play outside for a brief period each day, not always a safe activity but not yet a forbidden one.)

On this afternoon, the four of us had crossed the main tramline that ran down Limanowskiego Street. We kick the ball until the number three trolley carrying Polish workers to the Aryan sections of Podgorze rumbles between Gates I and II. Although the trams are never allowed to stop inside the Ghetto, food and other essentials are often thrown from the speeding vehicles. (My brother, in one of his many secret deals, had arranged a food drop for us on this particular afternoon.)

Sara and Tadek are stationed on one side of the metal rails with Bella and me on the other because we have no idea of what face to look for, or on which side of the tram they would be riding. The rails vibrate through the decaying soles of my shoes; the shuddering meets the excitement I feel at being assigned such a grown up task by Manek. A horn bellows and the green hub of the tram appears in the distance. I see a row of faces leaning out, taking fresh air at the windows.

"OK, Bella, about now," I say nervously.

Bella steps out into the middle of the tracks and bends in a pretence of tying her shoe. The bright red sweater she wears and the cascade of yellow hair makes her a colorful signal. The driver sights her and the tram slows down, as it grows closer.

"OK, you can move now," I call to the girl.

"No, not yet," says Bella, eyeing the gap between her and the oncoming wheels.

There was nothing for me to do except run alongside the tram before it reached her. I scan the faces at the windows. The men are friendly and wave, but no one proffers a package. At the end of the row, I see a lovely woman with her dark hair in fashionable rolls beneath an elegant broad-brimmed hat. She smiles and raises a white-gloved hand to me.

"Happy birthday, little Romek," she calls out the sweet lie.

In an instant, she lowers a large canvas sack through the tram's window into my arms. The men inside applaud and also shout birthday greetings. The woman blows me a kiss and quickly retreats inside the car. I watch the curved silhouette of her hat as she takes a seat. The tram glides by like a big emerald boat and I'm staring across the tracks at the huge grins of Tadek and the two girls.

"Let's take a quick look," says Bella eagerly.

I loosen the ties of the sack. Inside are numerous cans of fruit, corned beef, flour, sugar, tea, coffee, powdered milk, dried eggs and soap—a miraculous abundance to be shared among three families.

"Wonderful! We'll help you carry it all home," offers Sara.

Back in our kitchen, the two mothers divvy up the food for distribution, but not before Mama opened a can of peaches just for the four of us.

"All my brave angels," she clucks. "You deserve a treat."

We are lions at a kill, eating and grunting with delight, the sweet juice dripping down our chins. Bella has a contest with me to see who can allow a peach slice to rest on their tongue the longest. We both sit with our heads back, open mouths exposed so Tadek and Sara can judge accurately. Three minutes go by in exquisite torture, the perfume of the fruit is so delicate and wonderful I want to weep but I cannot stand the temptation, I take a large gulp and let Bella win. Tadek calls me a "damp pants" for not being the peach-tongue champion and demands that we challenge the girls to a return football match.

The next afternoon the goal posts are once again chalked on the cement of Krakusa Street, the farthest one toward the entrance of the Roza Rockowa Jewish Orphanage where some of the kids press their faces to the window to watch us with envy and interest. Posturing like Olympians, we go dashing onto our "field" to face Bella and Sara.

The Abramowicz sisters are talented ballet school dropouts long since their parents surrendered their bank accounts under German decree. Despite their stick-thin limbs, their dance training still lives in their feet; they are demons on springs at the running kick. They leap, swerve and pirouette away from our blocking with lightening ease. An hour goes by and Tadek and I are losing miserably.

"We're six goals to one!" chimes Sara proudly.

"We'll let you have a free penalty kick, OK?" says Bella.

"Don't do us any favors," mutters Tadek.

Bella takes the ball (no more than our usual tin can tied up in rags) and places it on the forward line by my feet. I step back and charge, my aim spectacular. The ball soars almost the length of the block. We chase after it, even as it rides the air. Bella leaps for it and collides with Tadek, both of them grip the prize, knock heads and fall but our side claims the goal.

Bella has suffered a scraped knee and I gallantly sponge at her wound with my shirtsleeve. Through the strands of her golden hair, I see the orphanage kids at the windows begin to gesture wildly and make odd faces at us, as if they were mouthing an "O" sound.

"Ignore them," Bella orders. "Some of them are not right in the head. Who's got the ball?"

"I do, OK," says Tadek, staggering up, "That puts me and Romek two to six."

"How long do you guys want to play?" Sara asks.

"Until we beat you," I reply, my hand lingering on Bella's knee. I see over her shoulder that the orphans are now being pulled away from the window by their nurses and a small gray-bearded man, Dr. Kunznetski, the resident physician for the orphanage. The adults are waving us away too and also making urgent "O" sounds that I finally understand as "Go…Go now!"

I stand up quickly, an electric jolt of danger through my shoulders.

Shlome, an older Abramowicz brother, is racing down Krakusa Street with four other boys. In the far distance behind them rolls a military truck with soldiers and several kids standing in the back.

"Run!" Shlome screeches, "It's a pick-up sweep!"

Bella leaps up and grabs Sara's hand. The nine of us tear toward Rekowka Street to to collide with the orphanage doctor, who now races in tandem with us.

"Where are you going?" shouts Dr. Kunznetski.

"The Zucker Synagogue, to hide!" I holler.

"Don't, they'll outdistance you. Come with me!"

He grabs me by the elbow. Together we turn swiftly and create this gravitational pull with the whole pack of us kids pounding toward the orphanage gates. Within seconds, we're behind closed doors. A large amiable looking nurse appears in the lobby. She hugs Sara, who is crying with fright.

"Nurse Fryowka," orders Dr. Kunznetski, "take these children and put them in the spare beds in the isolation wing, quickly now! They must not be seen."

"But we're not sick," says Tadek.

"For an hour you can be quarantined with possible typhus," advises the doctor.

"Better put the flag out," says the nurse as she marches us into hiding.

Dr. Kunznetski gallops up to his office on the top floor and lowers a flag with a double red cross painted on it out of the window—a warning of infection swarming among his charges. The quarantine ward has beds for twenty or more, we strip to our underwear and are beneath the blankets in seconds. The room smells of furniture polish and iodine. I hear the slam of the truck door, the clatter of boots on cobbles and orders shouted.

"Are they going to take us away?" whispers Sara, still tearful.

"Not if we get out of here first," Bella hisses back. "Everyone keep their shoes on."

She and Shlome have managed to pry open a window that leads immediately to the dining hall of the orphanage just a meter or so below the sill. They stand at the ready, blankets wrapped around their half-nakedness. I hear the good doctor pounding back down the stairs. Urgent whispers drift up from the hallway below, voices speaking in German and Polish, one with a crisp edge of authority. Tadek and I are bedded near the open door. I slip from the covers and crouch down to listen.

"Good day, Lieutenant Taubenschlag," the physician offers a greeting to the owner of what I can see through the stairwell is a pair of highly polished military boots. The Lieutenant's voice answers with exaggerated cordiality.

"And how is your *kinder* (children) population today, Herr Doctor? More or less?"

"The same...but we have five patients with scarlet fever and four suffering from mumps, a disease that can be unforgiving in men of your age. Ruins the sperm count."

"It never ceases to amaze me that our presence here always seems to bring on epidemics," comments the Lieutenant in an acid tone.

"As an educated man," replies the doctor firmly, "you can understand how the stress of our living conditions lowers the immune systems of the young. The children in the truck? Another clutch of subversives?"

"You cannot have them. Not even for the usual price," declares the soldier curtly.

"Where are you taking them?" Kunznetski asks and I hear the caution in his voice.

The Lieutenant doesn't answer the question. He demands that the doctor call his nurse with his usual medicine. I see Fryowka appear as if on cue and hand off a small box of glass vials plus new injection needles to Taubenschlag who actually sighs with pleasure at the sight.

Tadek joins me in the shadows of the upper landing. We see the doctor put a fatherly hand on the man's shoulder.

"It's my duty as a physician to advise you," Kunznetski declares. "That to increase your usage carries certain dangers, loss of consciousness and possible coma."

"I understand but it's my one haven in this sea of misery," the Lieutenant replies.

"Yes, I'm sure it makes your job easier," says Kunznetski boldly.

The Krakow Ghetto

"It's not just my job but my orders. We will leave you...for now, good day, Herr Doctor."

The child collector shakes the doctor's hand, swivels on his heel and marches out.

Nurse Fryowka and Kunznetski turn our way to come up the stairs. Tadek and I quickly dart back into bed.

"He will overdose, sooner or later." the nurse is saying.

"You can depend on it," the doctor answers. "And on that day, my dear Fryowka, we'll probably be faced with a more effective evil. Come, we have to filter out our renegades and send them home, their parents will be missing them."

❊

In the early months of the Ghetto's existence, life has a tenuous veil of normality. New stores, dairies, patisseries and even a small number of restaurants and cafeterias temporarily flourish. Shops are reasonably stocked and very crowded in the morning while supplies last. There is a post office that issues special stamps in Yiddish that trademark the community, although I doubt that any of the mail made it past the German censors. The Reich, fearing information leaks, soon shut the service down.

Nachim Hirschel, the owner of the failing Café Ramowka on St. Benedykta Street, struggles to create meals of astonishing invention. His only child, fourteen-year-old Aron, is often seen swaggering into their courtyard with dozens of dead pigeons swinging from a pole, destined for the café's menu. The Hirschel kitchen produces amazing soups that are fragrant variations of potato peels, beets and turnips, with light salty onion dumplings. Bread and cakes conjured out of chestnut or acorn flour and honey (and sometimes filled with sour cherries) issue forth from the café's oven.

I like Aron's sense of independence and boldness that rested lightly beneath his practical personality. Tadek and I tried to win his friendship by offering him a tattered 1941 calendar that had faded photos of semi-nude women I weaseled out of Uncle Solomon. This gift purchased the hope that Aron would take us to the rooftops where he would bring down birds with his slingshot. We thought ourselves decent enough expert shooters and, in my mind, it would be the manly thing to do for our mothers, who might duplicate the succulent braised pigeon stew Nachim boiled up.

"Come see me when your pants are long," is Aron's decision. "I hunt up there alone," he says, pointing to the guttering high above the Jewish Orphanage. Seeing our faces shriveled with disappointment, he hands each of us a pair of kills for the home pot.

Giving the feathered corpses to the maternal team is not our proudest moment. Luisia shrieks in horror and flees the kitchen. My mother swallows her shock and plucks the birds, whose naked skins revealed sores and embedded fleas. She saves and washes the feathers in vinegar for my Aunt Cyla's hat-making business, but commits the pitiful carcasses to the trash.

"Are you boys trying to kill everyone with the botulism?" she asks in disgust. "Who could dine on such dreck?"

"People eat pigeons in the restaurant all the time," I protest hotly.

"That's because Nachim soaks the meat with every kind of spice under heaven. I'm surprised he hasn't poisoned half the world by now," Mama rants.

Papa had often tried to coax my mother to eat at the Ramowka.

"Come on, Malia, we'll make a night of it—just the two of us," he would announce gaily, slipping his arms around her waist and kissing her cheek. "We'll take a bottle of the Hungarian Tokay I've been saving and have Nachim cook us up some of his best pirogi. It'll be like the old days."

Mama declared that she would rather set her face on fire than consume the toxic menu at the café, and who could enjoy a romantic dinner when it entailed tearing down half the ceiling of our quarters to get at the concealed wine and the stored liquor?

However, my brother and Hanka have what they the call the "Freedom Hour" (a brief time before curfew) at the Ramowka when they sit at the bar with their friends, sipping bootleg vodka that scalds the throat accompanied by Nachim's homemade goat cheese and pickles. The restaurateur's wife, Felijca, kept Anatolian goats in the cellar that grazed on food waste. The three black females dropped young regularly, kids that lived long enough to be suckled to firmness and then were slaughtered for the kitchen.

For another bribe (a bar of lavender soap begged from my mother), Aron Hirschel allows Tadek and me down the stone steps to see the newborn animals. The cellar extends far beneath the building and is composed of a series of large connecting chambers. One has a door that was mostly always locked.

The stench of ripening cheese, root vegetables and goat crap hits us in the face. Out of the shadows, the goat mothers clop forward, pressing their wet, sour muzzles into our hands. Their downy infants stagger behind on uncertain legs. In the gloom, I see the outline of the male goat chained up for the sin of his wild charges against visitors. I step back quickly, since I have a wary history with his species. He snorts defiance and knocks at the brick wall with his magnificent horns.

Aron lays one of the kids in my arms, a tiny female the color of gray gloves who suckles at my fingers hungrily. She has a clean, sweet odor, like sun-heated grass. I could have walked with her and her kind on any June day down to the river at Borek Falecki. The small she-goat coaxes a green summer to arise in that dark, reeking basement and my heart teeters to know that Aron's mother would soon come for her with the blade.

The Krakow Ghetto

Above her baby-mashing jaws I hear a conversation from somewhere far in the cellar's darkness. Dominating the chatter, I suddenly hear my brother's voice. Aron's hand is on my shoulder, "Let's go! We can't be found here," he exclaims.

"Why not? It's just Manek," I say.

"No questions, we have to leave now!"

Aron pushes us hurriedly through the mass of animals and up the cellar steps.

※

Tadek's father smuggled home a few ball bearings of various sizes from the assembly line he worked on so we can use them as marbles. The noise of rolled steel on the timbers of our living quarters sounds like a small freight train rumbling through the apartment, causing the parent quartet to banish us to play in the hallway. Manek finds us there one evening as we sent the metal orbs thundering down the cracked linoleum.

"You two have to absolutely stay away from the Ramowka and Aron for the next few weeks," he orders in tones that command there will be no argument here.

Uncle Solomon stops by to affirm the same edict with the parents. It seems that certain low ranking officers of the Gestapo have discovered the pleasures of pigeon stew and roasted goat. Nachim was ordered to open on Shabbas and (except for his family) keep the restaurant Jew-free for military personnel.

Preparing cuisine for the enemy became a nerve-shredding enterprise for the Hirschels over the next month. Aware that periodic thinning of the Ghetto's population mainly targeted children under sixteen, Aron's parents sent him to concealment on the rooftops whenever the soldiers dined in the restaurant. Walking with my father from the Jewish Aid office on Josefinska Street, we'd catch a fast glimpse of the boy stepping gingerly along the roof beams to some of his favorite hiding places between the chimneys.

"Don't ever call to him, Romek," Papa warns. "Eyes will follow your shout and he'll be discovered."

It is not the bellowed name of Aron that would eventually betray his family but a combination of over-spiced goat sausage and the whisper of collaborators. After eating the last wonderful meal the Ramowka would ever serve, the Germans arrested Nachim and Felijca for allegedly trying to poison the warriors of the Reich. Flogger Goertner was on the detail that took the Hirschels away. He and his soldiers went to the basement where they bludgeoned open the walls looking for weapons, valuables and any whiff of insurrection. Finding nothing in the broken bricks, they beat and shot the goats, throwing the broken animals, some still braying with life into the same truck that would take away their former owners. From the rooftops, Aron watched them drag his parents from their home.

His mother was screaming, *"Zostain pszy ptakah, Aron! Zostain tam na gorze!"* (Stay close to the birds, Aron! Stay up there!")

Goertner, short on patience with it all, knocked her to the pavement, gashing open her cheek. Her husband lifted her tenderly into the truck, where they stood upright and stilled in the blood of their dying goats.

High above Benedykta Street, the boy weeps at his mother's wounded face upturned to the chimneys, he sees the animals convulse from their wounds and roll their white eyes. He runs the length of the rooftops to watch the truck grow small along the avenue of Limanowskiego, the escort jeep riding behind it. Outside the Ghetto gates, Goertner wants the job finished quickly; he makes the couple stand back to back so he can shoot them through the head with one bullet. Their bodies are thrown into the Vistula where Christian anglers, rods and lines draped through the chilly spring waters, cross themselves as they see Nachim and Felijca float by. It does not occur to them that their catch will be washed in Jewish blood.

My father and Manek unfortunately become the recipients of the Hirschel finale. Aron hides alone at the café, determined to hold on to his parent's business because he believes they will be exonerated and return home soon. No one has the stomach yet to tell him he is orphaned. He waits for a week then another, no parents return, no one comes near the place. The boy consumed the last of the café's stores but would not risk pigeon hunting during the daylight hours. He is too old to be placed in the Kinderheim (the children's home) but too breakable to stay alone permanently.

Both the Horowitz's and my parents agree we should go get him and bring him to our apartment to live with us as an adopted son. However, there is a new identity to be forged, paperwork to be filled out and Uncle Samek, my father's brother-in-law, also an OD, says that he can filter the documents through the right hands. The process commences slowly.

Manek and Papa check on Aron frequently, bringing him food and finally let him know that his parents are deceased. The boy becomes withdrawn and broody. He beds down in the cellar where the lost screeching of the infant goats against his mother's knife tears into his sleep. He dreams he hears his father upstairs, firing the ovens to bake bread, and the jocular argument of Felijca warding off her husband's flirtations. Aron awakes in gloom, to the smell of brick dust and an immense silence such as he has never known. Several times a day he sits at the best table in the abandoned restaurant and stares endlessly at photos in the family album because his memory will no longer summon forth the image of his parents. The hours are blunted, the stillness a famine of voices. He begins to feel he might not exist.

Aron yells at my father and stubbornly refuses to be part of our family. He now believes that maybe Manek and the single meeting of the Akiva group in the cellar have caused this fantastic unraveling of his life. The nearest he gets to our apartment is clattering over the rooftops of our street in the midnight darkness to raid whatever nests he can find.

The Krakow Ghetto

A rage of wings, threshed open and beating, no merciful air currents to bear up the pigeons whose backs are broken from the sling. Five of them plummet, twirling like loosed seed cases in the autumn, never to be planted. They tumble and murmur in resignation, a silver dash of feathers all down the night, spiraling around the descending figure, hands and talons falling together, grabbing at the wind.

Papa found Aron lying in the courtyard; his head open on a cloud of dried blood, his eyes finally content, gazing skyward at the frayed plumes that still fluttered from the broken gutter pipe. Around the boy spread a corona of birds, wings outstretched, accompanying him on his last hunt. My father shouts in anger at Tadek and me not to stare so disrespectfully but to fetch Manek and ask him to bring a clean sheet—quickly!

In our absence, my father takes the boy's broken hand and prays the Kaddish.

Uncle Samek and a Rabbi from the Judenrat come running to wrap the body and take it away to the burial house. Manek and my father follow on; arguing in whispers to convince the Rabbi this could hardly be a matter of suicide. My brother's sorrow is like stones stopping up his breath, he feels gutted at the shape of despair in the shrouded form on the burial cart. "This boy, this boy..." he keeps saying to himself.

He dare not raise his eyes to the rooftops.

8

Taken

MY PARENTS AND THE HOROWITZS have the maddening adult habit of clamming up on any Ghetto news that might distress us kids. The result sets our curiosity ablaze and eavesdropping becomes my finest skill since my constantly failed experiments at invisibility. The things I hear are tales of the streets replete with more arrests, as the maw of the Beast opened wider.

A family shriveled by absurd and random selections. Two children under five taken, eight-year-old twin boys left behind, not being in the house at the time of the raid, their mother arrested with her newborn, and the father, a skilled engineer, reassigned to munitions production in Zamosc. Remaining is their twelve-year-old girl, Andzia, who, along with the twin lads, hid in the cooling ovens of a nearby bakery to emerge dehydrated and reeking of yeast.

I hear Uncle Arnold telling Papa that he revised Andzia's Zjezdzie Street residency on paper, recreating her as a twenty-eight-year-old widow named Magda with three kids. He lies about her age too so the real girl can stand in line at the rations depot and collect food for her now fictitious mother and the twins. Neighbors keep the secret well, watching over the little family, and offer no details to decorate the carnal figments conjured up by bored OD men.

My Uncle Arnie has a clerk named Yankel Gorowski, who processes all manner of disasters ordered on paper (arrest writs, labor indentures, selection lists, confiscations, etc.) in the offices of the Judischer Ordungdienst (the Jewish Police). Yankel, who Hanka deems as "unfortunate looking", lusts for the unseen Magda and has yearnings to throw aside the narrow cot in his mother's kitchen and drag his miniscule authority up Magda's stairs to tempt her with tasty black market luxuries.

"A lonely woman," opines the clerk, gazing out from a long doglike face cratered with acne scars. His shoulders, hooped to the left by scoliosis, give him the aspect of a warped fence. "Probably needs a little livening up."

"Hmm, you think?" questions Arnold, with thoughts crowding him on how to whittle Yankel's lust down to nil. "Females that secretive," he advises, "are quicksand. One false step and you're under the mud drowning."

"She's a Ghetto girl, can't be spoiled for choice," Yankel argues.

Women, married or no, confined in these streets, are like a deluge that rained fish. You could trawl the sidewalks any day and net so much flesh. Even the most pious females are easily pitched into raw debauchery if there was extra food promised, or an infant to be smuggled out to Jesus and the nuns of St. Agnieska's Convent.

Taken

Andzia is a doe-like beauty with chrome-colored eyes, and had no idea of the thrall her soft look provokes. A small schematic of her pretty mother, Yankel considers, on encountering the girl at the rations depot, a forerunner he easily resizes into a more mature vision of a ripe mouth, body lusciously blossomed, and a gaze from under half-closed lids that has the effect on a man of being slammed by a cyclone. Uncle Arnold realizes that no sucking sand would easily dissuade his bent nail of a clerk from the venal feast he dreams is Magda.

"Why don't I drive you by her place tonight?" offers my uncle kindly.

In an open jeep borrowed from the checkpoint detail, Arnold ferries Yankel across the Ghetto, watering his impatience with frequent stops for beer and vodka. He detains the clerk in the front seat, well provisioned with a bottle, while he visits our apartment and pulls Manek into a feverish discussion out on the landing. I try to listen through the half-open the door but was discovered and hauled away by my father.

"Yankel, let's approach Zjezdzie Street slowly," Arnold advises in parental tones. "We'll take a couple of turns around the block, see if Magda's home."

A candle-lit window on the second floor overlooking the street is frothed up with a dense lace curtain slowly succumbing to moths. Two silhouettes sit across a table, the form of a wine bottle and two glasses between them. The jeep pulls up and Arnold clumsily brushes against the horn. A female shadow, with breasts tilted high, is seen to lean over and kiss a male profile wearing the peaked cap of an SS officer. Yankel stares up at the tableau as if he'd been shot and and frozen by the bullet's impact. The scabrous whore! It's against the racination decree; the unknown Aryan defiler will be at the Russian front this time tomorrow. As for her, sign the bitch up for the deportation transports, the kids too, we'll fix the paperwork ourselves!

"I don't think so, Yankel," soothes Arnold as he drives away.

A risky business to witness such things, advises my uncle, could be head-on-a-plate time for a lowly Jewish clerk looking to unseat an overheated Ubermensch.

❂

Three nights later, Tadek and I are playing soldiers in the kitchen, wearing pots and pans as helmets with the chairs overturned and arranged in a makeshift fort. Our "spears" are soup ladles and large wooden spoons. Whoever gets the most hits on the helmet of the other wins the field and then the battle would begin again. Implements are ringing off my headgear with deadly regularity.

"Romek, you couldn't hit a wall if it fell on you!" snarls Tadek the victor.

"You noise mavens! Keep it down out there!" Mama's order cracks from our living quarters.

I look over in her direction, leaving my left flank undefended, a painful mistake. A heavy ladle comes spinning into view, a well-aimed direct strike. No prisoner confined in any medieval tower ever suffered the resonating clang as that which is drumming through the aluminum around my skull. My lip is split open badly and I can't hear anything but echoing steel. My barricade topples then I topple and fall against the small cupboard under the sink. I grab at the door to break my fall and out spill buckets, cleaning rags and a military cap with the badge of the SS *Hoheitsadler* (the eagle on the swastika symbol) set in its band. I pick up the hat with my bloody fingers. The sight of the item made Tadek gasp.

My mother sends Manek running in to see who had been slain by spoons. He lifts me up and out from the scattered chairs and takes the hat.

"Whose is this?" I stutter accusingly through a swollen mess of my mouth.

"It's borrowed," grins my brother. "I have to give it back to Uncle Arnold."

"Manek, you're not...you haven't," asks Tadek in a small voice, "become German?"

My brother can't stop laughing for quite a while, jiggling me in his arms while I scatter rosettes of blood over the tiles. The carousing draws Hanka into the kitchen. She takes one look at me and says, "What happened to you, Liver-lips?"

Manek sets me down on the kitchen table and my sister runs a basin of water to wash my wound. "Mama will faint if she sees you like this."

My brother places the SS cap on her head.

"Hanka, you look stupid in that," I say.

She winks at Manek but dabs at my lip with a stinging smear of carbolic soap.

✹

The oral sagas continue. The lip wound sets off a tooth infection, causing my lower jaw to balloon painfully. It is a raw, blustery Sunday afternoon when Manek asks me, "Open your mouth. Let me see those choppers. Wider."

My brother puts a finger in my gums and begins stuffing them with cotton wool soaked in menthol oil until my cheek is the size of a golf ball. The oil tastes venomous. My mouth tightens as if pulled by purse strings.

"Romek, I need the loan of you and your face for a couple of hours," says Manek.

He ties my jaw up with a lengthy wool scarf and hustles me into my overcoat.

"Go...go, going with you?" I whistle out a thin plume of words, wet and spitted.

Taken

Manek nods and pulls on my gloves. "It's a two-man job and you're the star, my reason to be on the street, if we're questioned."

I exhale an entire eucalyptus forest in an attempt to look as thrilled as I felt. My numb expression doesn't obey. No matter, I would have gone with my brother to the cold pits of the ocean or the waterless plains of the moon just to be with him.

We sally at a good clip up Josefinska Street, my hand comfortable and assured in Manek's broad palm. Frequently, he wheels around on his heels, taking a few steps without a break in his stride and then rights himself.

"Why are you walking backwards?" I ask.

"It's the Ghetto dance," says my brother with a straight face, "You can do it too, Romek, so you can see who's coming at you."

Right before we make the turn into Targowa Street Manek declares, "A man is walking toward us very fast."

A voice calls his name and we stop. My brother picks me up and whispers, "You are in great pain, remember."

We turn to face an OD named Azriel Feiner who lives in our Uncle Solomon's building. I moan and hide my face in Manek's shoulder.

"Hey, Manek, what's the hurry?" asks Feiner. Through my wool muffler, I see a flush-faced older man with fatted eyelids resting on sloping cheeks and a heavily drooping mouth that appear to be migrating down his chin.

"My kid brother, high temperature," explains Manek.

"Could be the typhus, you'll have to report it," says Feiner in official mode.

"Don't think so, there's no rash and my mother keeps him lice free. More likely an infected tooth," replies my brother, slowly backing us away from the man's suspicious glance.

"There's a good German doctor in the barracks, Surgeon Koenig, who has a fully equipped clinic," offers Feiner. "He'll make an exception to treat the kid."

"Ah, the collector of Jewish body parts?" demands Manek.

I lay over my brother's shoulder like a comatose fluke but inwardly quake at the idea of this Koenig and his bottled specimens. Feiner manages to laugh. "Old women's gossip," he says. "You're too young to be that cynical."

"We have to be on our way. Good day."

He raises his cap to the OD and we hurry on.

"Tell me when you can no longer see him," whispers Manek. "You're killing my back, you little ox."

I jump from his arms to the sidewalk. "You don't like that man, Feiner?"

"No." says my brother. "He's a finagler and gonef. Not to be trusted."

I run beside my brother, asking if we can work the ruse again. I believe I performed the sick waif very well. "Maybe this time I can be dying," I suggest.

"You'd never get the part, too much competition," says Manek.

All the distance to the Plac Zgody, Manek teaches me road rules for moving through the Ghetto in daylight hours. Don't be engrossed in conversation because you'll never hear the military truck closing in, see each basement and open door as a shelter, if you hear shouts and gunfire ahead, stride away in the opposite direction, never raise your eyes to any German soldier, and get out of their sight as quickly as possible.

✽

We hurry on to the Apteka Pod Orlem (the Eagle Pharmacy) and into the righteous presence of its owner, Tadeusz Pankiewicz, a neatly dressed man with a bow tie set between the winged collars of his white coat. He has solemn eyes, thick brows and a precise dark hairline enclosing even features. He is known, so Manek says, for always maintaining an aura of calmness, no matter what disasters were erupting outside his front door.

When we approach him, he is lining up apothecary jars in some chemical order along a shelf. Nearby, two women in white dresses are weighing powders on a brass scale and debating the addition of a third element to punch up the efficacy of a medication they're preparing. Manek greets them all, and the pharmacist, smiling broadly, turns to us.

"Why is this boy's face tied up like a ham?" he asks my brother. "Tooth abscess?"

"Neuralgia, some infection," answers Manek, the exchange a prearranged code.

"We have a solution for that. I understand you have other needs, Pan (Mr.) Ferber?"

My brother hands Dr. Pankiewicz a list that he reads over carefully while ushering Manek into his lab beyond the main shop. My brother looks back at me sternly and orders, "Wait here. And *do not* touch anything, OK?"

Looking ridiculous with my face in the wool sling, I wander among the smooth wooden counters cluttered with rows of exotic glass vials, blue and white china medicine pots labeled with unpronounceable Latin names. The shelves are crowded with boxes of dried herbs and twisted roots that resemble miniature desiccated men, glass cases with several rock crystals I believe to be diamonds, bandages and limb splints, steel bone saws yet to be bloodied, quinine potions, camphor liniments, crutches for the short, tall and in between, and evil-smelling poultices of mustard and garlic.

I am struck by how various aromas take dominance in different areas of the pharmacy. Upon entering, one is swamped by winds of sulfur and iodine, followed by a heady tang of cloves, ginger and arnica. A cloud of aloes, turmeric and methyl alcohol float around the scales where the two women are scooping pills into small envelopes. A false leg tinted an alarming pink with leather straps lounges in one corner, above it on the shelf, rests a fine violin. It occurs to me that maybe Dr. Pankiewicz plays it to console himself from doling out medicines to sick people.

I drift over to gawk at the artificial limb and catch a faint odor of bitter almonds. To my right is a glass case bearing the skull and crossbones symbol. I consider that the gleaming salts of cyanide must be a medicine for pirates. One of the nice women, whose name was Pani (Mrs.) Aurelia, comes over to me.

"Hello, Romek, Dr. Pankiewicz thinks it would be fine to remove the dressing from your mouth. Will you let me do that for you?"

Pani Aurelia wears her hair curled in golden rolls around a broad face, her gaze is serene and her voice full of quiet concern. She sits me down in a chair and takes the oily cotton from my gums with a pair of calipers. Next, she shines a light down my gullet, pressing my mouth north and south with a silver spatula. "Your lip is a little swollen but it's not looking so bad," she says. "The toothache must have gone away. I have some pear juice we keep especially for good children who have taken their medicine."

I am given a small glass of the delicious ration, a rarity I hadn't tasted in a long time. I sip it slowly while gazing at a large chart of a man dressed only in his musculature with all his inner organs colored and labeled—an image I thought would be a good reference map for the knife-handy Dr. Koenig. Below the skinless man, a single artificial blue eye stares out from its presentation case. The lettering offers an improved appearance with a Koslowski ophthalmic prosthesis custom fitted by the Modified Impression Method. All eye colors matched.

The pharmacist had left the doorway of the back room ajar. From where I sit, I can see a microscope resting on a bench, piles of books and more jars of pills and powders. On a table nearby, a dozen Torah scrolls are stacked, partially uncovered from their velvet sleeves. The sight of them mystifies me because I'd heard my parents say Dr. Pankiewicz was the only Catholic allowed to remain on his own premises in the Ghetto, quietly spooling out delaying tactics until the Germans stopped offering him a confiscated Jewish pharmacy in the city center.

Finally, Dr. Pankiewicz comes striding back down the shop with my brother, who is carrying two bulging linen pouches.

"Ah, so, Romek here is your little pack horse?" he asks kindly.

"Small but giant in spirit, eh, sprout?" my brother comments.

Manek kneels before me and carefully pins one of the pouches into the center of my wool scarf, turned up my coat collar and tied up my head babushka style. In profile, I look like a hunchbacked dwarf. The weight of the bag rests along my neck and I can hear the slurp of liquids whenever I take a step.

"What sickness do I have now?" I ask my brother.

"A severe attack of being fresh," says Manek, hiding the other pouch down the back of his pants, "which will be cured by the time we reach home."

"Go slowly, both of you," advises the pharmacist. "You don't want the morphine vials to leak."

"Might not be a bad thing," says Manek, grinning. "Could make my arse very happy or shut Romek up for a few days."

⁕

Like many who have grateful memories of the Eagle Pharmacy from those Ghetto years, I recall that Tadeusz Pankiewicz was an exceptional rebel. My father would say that the innate wisdom of his science nourished his unshakeable sense of justice. When Dr. Pankiewicz looked into his microscope, he roamed ecstatically among the subtlest wonders of creation. "It's there, Leon, that I find another Eden," he once told my father, "a rare world of sublime order and grace. You must see for yourself."

He would urge Papa's eyes to the microscope's lens and point out with boyish delight the geometric schemes of tiny javelin-shaped crystals called raphides, the beautiful prismatic sugars of plants carved into lacy tetrahedrons, as delicate as snowflakes, and spectacular bio-crystals known as druses. "Look carefully, my friend," Dr. Pankiewicz would say, "the druses appear like microscopic carnations, but their minute rigid petals are sharp enough to lacerate the tough shells of invading insects; evolution's armor custom-made for the defense of flowers. This slide here shows plant crystals that are faceted precisely to capture sunlight for the bloom's development. The world was made in wisdom, no?"

Papa would counter with why so intricate a sensibility deep in the cells of lilies does not translate up to peace among our own kind? The pharmacist did not answer him immediately but fussed among the petri dishes that contained his bacteria farm. "These organisms are relentless entrepreneurs," he said, "they reproduce by the thousands every twenty minutes. I have no answers, Leon, for the madness that surrounds us in this time. As for the lily, most flowers are models of biochemical harmony. Such natural sophistication is beyond brute force."

My father would shake his head and complain to Mama that maybe this good man suffered from some kind of angelic madness, infected by his zeal for the speedy conjugations of viruses. However, I would also hear Papa say that the deeds of heaven perfected in the Apteka Pod Orlem would fill several volumes. The pharmacy stayed open twenty-four hours with Dr. Pankiewicz often sleeping in his lab close to the exotic beings of his infinitesimal universe. He and his staff became a daring conduit between Ghetto residents and the rest of the city, relaying valuables, cash, food, and messages back and forth. Medications were never refused to those in need, and hair dye flowed liberally for whoever had to look younger to avoid the deportations. There was also free Luminal to induce a heavy indigo sleep in the smuggled infant. The young one might awaken bewildered to find themselves in the arms of a new Christian mother, but far beyond the reach of the devourer.

The pharmacy often swarmed with escapees of all stripes while its proprietor keenly observed the balloon-shaped staphylococcus that pulsated under his microscope, busy making itself hundreds of relatives by the minute. Life will not be denied, he marveled.

My father came home with the news that he ran across the carpenter Dr. Pankiewicz hired to build a hidden closet, this time to conceal Torah scrolls and other religious objects entrusted to him. Their refuge was enfaced with shelves on which neutralized specimens of tuberculin bacterium sat as sentinels.

The Eagle Pharmacy was also a sulfur-infused salon for lawyers, writers and journalists joined by botanists, biophysicists, zoologists and eager physicians who hunted new theories along the trenches of infectious diseases. Many of them were Jewish academics who could no longer teach, research, or publish findings, but who debated their luminous theories with impassioned zest, lest their knowledge languish and fade into the darkness.

Manek ferreted out the full story on Colonel Irmfried Koenig who graduated medical school with a specialty in deep-tissue surgery, Heidelberg, class of 1927. There was no territory of the flesh that this physician had not entered into with his scalpel.

Arterial systems were like summer highways to him, the chambers of the heart and their orchestration of the blood a composition he thought finer than the living woman stretched against him in the night. Whether the body under his blade was animated by breath or not, it was the structural mysteries he sought, often by opening the still warm innards of the recently executed. He requested the firing squads to be sure to divert a healthy young corpse or two his way and he was particularly fascinated by the anatomy of deceased women in the late stages of pregnancy. In any other life, he would have been an excellent clockmaker.

Koenig erroneously regarded the pharmacist as a kindred soul. The two would often discuss new methods of controlling sepsis, Pankiewicz offering data on clinical outcomes in his quiet steady way. He'd already heard of the morning's roundup ordered by Dr. Jost Walbaum, who had demanded a certain number of young Ghetto women be delivered to him to be examined for "anthropological research." Koenig waxed on about antibacterial proteins while the pharmacist listened respectfully, leaning against the lab bench where the lower cupboards hid nineteen-year-old Riva Gluck, who had earlier slipped away from the roundup.

I begged Manek to take me again to see the curiosities at the Eagle Pharmacy. Not believing that there were creatures in existence so tiny they could fit a hundredfold on the head of a pin, I also plagued Papa to ask Dr. Pankiewicz to let me look down his microscope.

"When things are a little calmer, Romek, we'll go back," said Manek.

"But I want to see the small animals now!" I whined.

"Take the time to learn about them and I'll make that possible," Papa promised.

Tadek and I have not left the apartment in two weeks, not even to play in the hall and the streets were now strictly forbidden, infested with regular patrols looking for prey, especially for younger kids who had no labor value. There is an ominous discussion among the adults of a home education scheme being instigated for Tadek, his sisters and me. This conspiracy involves the Abramowicz parents from downstairs who have offered up Bella, Sara, and brothers, Shlome and Lazer as our soon-to-be classmates.

"It can't happen. We have no books or pencils, nothing that makes a school," I remark smugly, confident that this outrageous idea will soon wither from lack of resources. However, the parents are set like cement against any refusals.

"One *am-haaretz* (ignoramus) of a boy is bad enough," Mama declares tartly. "But a whole troop of ignorant children is not to be tolerated."

"But, Pani Ferber, we have no Belfers," says Tadek.

"We do have Lydia and Ester Rosenfeld," commands his mother.

The sisters Rosenfeld are former schoolteachers and the granddaughters of a famous Rabbi, Chaim Rosenfeld, whose pious ancestor, Rebbe Meir Rosenfeld, once hosted a great Hasidic Court in Lublin in 1730.

His descendants, Lydia and Ester Rosenfeld, who had lived and taught in the village of Lagiewniki, are two of the thousands of country Jews funneled into the Krakow Ghetto from surrounding communities during the war. They are billeted across the street from us, with three other middle-aged women and two couples in their seventies and eighties in a damp basement. My father never liked this warehousing of elders and thought that Lydia and Ester would appreciate a respite among young ones.

"I have many years experience teaching English, Latin, history and French," explains Ester to my mother at an invitation for tea. "I also give musical instruction, and if no instrument is in the home then I resort to the human voice."

Ester Rosenfeld is a lean, long-necked woman with a still-dark braid coiled around her austere head. Her eyes are a washed-out blue, her aspect handsome but reserved and virginal. However, her hands are still supple from many years of playing the piano. Her younger sister, Lydia, has eyes of a more definite sapphire, her body solid, with muscular hips and broad shoulders. She carries herself with an athlete's strength, has a blunt direct speech and wears her graying hair in a heavy tumble around her shoulders. Whereas Ester has an ethereal manner, Lydia charges at life with a determined energy.

My mother speculates as to whether their parents ever secretly yearned for one composite daughter sharing both their enhancements. Unlike the literary and romantic-natured Ester, Lydia is very much a creature of the physical world, a multi-talented biologist who has studied astronomy and several other sciences. She shocks my father by declaring herself an agnostic, believing only in the tangible and messy forces of nature. The combined intellectual talents of the two women form a deep well of learning and they are enthusiastically hired by all the parents concerned.

Since both women work a shift system in the afternoon labor detail, Papa arranges that they should cross the street for several hours each morning to the small schoolroom that will be our kitchen table. Although the sisters protest at being offered any payment, our tuition fees will be made up of small donations of rations and even a little money, if it can be found.

"Pan Ferber," Lydia declares gratefully to my father, "we haven't been allowed to teach in such a long time, it will be a joy to have pupils again."

While my parents hide all manner of canned and bottled goods in the crawl space above our ceiling, the Rosenfeld sisters shelter a small but precious reservoir of books under their basement floorboards, which they generously share with us. A manageable curriculum is established for four hours a day, two devoted to math and science, the other two to history and literature. What I thought was going to be a school with the severity of the Belfer's classroom, where G-d and the instructor sit at a high desk, ready to impale you for the smallest transgression, was, in the hands of these two women, transformed into a daily wonder.

The minute my father and the rest of the household leave for their work assignments, Mama and I wash the kitchen table and line up the chairs on either side of it, with a more comfortable one set out for the tutor and a small side table where she can place her texts. Salka and Gizia Horowitz, as the oldest pupils, are appointed as class monitors to help the younger ones with their studies and pull the reins on any slacker.

We have no slates or a blackboard but Manek, the miracle maker who could procure just about any item, supplies us with pencils, boxes of crayons, and rolls of blank newsprint sheets that we fold into four parts to serve as notebooks and drawing pads. I am first to take my place in the "class" and I save the seat next to me for sweet Bella, who secretly enjoys my adoration. I feel an odd exhilaration about our little enclave, of being lifted up into something brighter and more hopeful. Tadek and the other kids arrive and take their places around me. My mother and Luisia Horowitz always stand by the front door to greet our teacher graciously before they retire to the other room.

This morning Pani Ester enters first and with some ceremony. She takes off her coat and produces from her pocket a small French flag. Today is our first history session. She sits down and from her canvas bag brings out a Polish edition for children of *A Tale of Two Cities* by Charles Dickens that she will use this week to illustrate one of the most volatile revolutions ever, and to show us how a nation under duress does or does not construct civil rule. From this one tome, we will be taught history, drawing, and some basic French and English phrases.

Ester begins an excerpt from the story, telling it while barely consulting the pages and reciting with such drama and color that our kitchen fades away to the boulevards of Paris, the towers of the Bastille, and there's Tadek and myself, marching with the revolutionaires to burn down its tyrannical gates. Ester holds up a map of France in relation to Poland, then illustrations of: a woman dressed as Liberty leading the people; the dreadful guillotine; and a man swinging the loosened head of King Louis that Tadek and I found wonderfully gory and comical but which horrifies the girls.

(Many years later, I realized what Ester really taught us that morning was not just about the temporary nature of power, but the rise of a new terror: institutionalized violence, the willful elimination of those deemed undesirable by the state. The lesson remains with me to this day.)

Ester makes each of us read a short passage from the Dickens book in Polish, then, just for our ears, she reads it again slowly in English, a language I thought at the time would be utterly impossible to learn. Next, we have a wonderful drawing session, coloring soldiers, cannons, street battles, and unfortunate aristocrats.

"Did you ever go there, Pani Ester?" Tadek asks, "to the Paris place?"

She's guiding my hand, helping me draw a horse from a photograph and I smell the mint tea on her breath as she answers slowly. "No, but I knew a man from Passy, he was a talented organist and played the masses of Bach and Handel at all the concert halls and churches in Warsaw and Krakow. I was very young then and my parents thought I was not ready to travel so far from home."

Her pencil shakes a little as we sketch out the animal's mane together. I remember the full tale from shreds of my mother's gossip. The Frenchman from Passy and Ester had been bound by music and a brief but volcanic passion. Her parents were obliged to each other, dried in some narrow chute of duty that sealed their marital days. They had no map to the heated rapture of Ester's new terrain, no practical counterforce for such incendiary love. Their Rabbi spoke to her with severity, of obedience, of righteous arrangements, and upholding a daughter's place. The lover's marriage offer was refused by Ester's parents but she had said "Yes" and vowed to the French musician to wait for him until she was of an age of independence.

Taken

The organ maestro left Poland in 1916 to seek obliterating solace in the blood-leached fields of Verdun. Ester, emptied out from longing and the formal telegram announcing his death, sold her piano and gave away her bridal linens to the Community Hospital. She refused all further suitors and lived as if caped in a stone silence that unnerved her father, provoking a rabid and perpetual desolation he would never comprehend.

When Lydia Rosenfeld comes marching up our stairs, she scans the expectant faces around her and announces boldly, "Today I plan to travel with you to the moon!"

She takes out a tennis ball from her bag of books and bounces it aggressively off the floorboards, then hauls up a chair, angles it, and makes us repeat the same action all the while sliding the chair away to the window. "A ball thrown upwards from a speeding ship falls vertically on the deck because gravity prevents it from moving along in the same direction as the vessel," she explains.

I find the class a little heavy going, especially the geometry session.

Salka Horowitz lets me copy answers from her notes but then my mind drifts away from obtuse triangles to the amazing tints in Bella's hair. Lydia's eyes miss nothing and she launches into a free roaming lecture of why the tresses of my adored friend are yellow, low in pigment, susceptible to reflection, while my dark locks are frizzed storehouses of melanin. Amazingly, she encourages us to pull hairs from each other's heads to compare color. We squeal and giggle in a mayhem that our teacher seems to enjoy, and we hold the strands under Lydia's powerful magnifying glass. She steers the lesson from the construction of follicles to the nations of the equator and the capacity of the human hide to turn brown and black.

Next, Lydia brings forth a splendid map of the heavens and spreads it out on the kitchen table. At first I see nothing but white spots, arrows and trajectories on a dark blue ground but soon we are cruising through legions of icy comets, celestial debris, and the moons of Jupiter.

"The are two types of planets," Lydia explains, "many are small, rocky places with cores of iron and other solid elements while the larger orbs are immense domains of fire and gas where it is believed that no life has yet gained a foothold."

I ask her how old are they and how big is the void in which they spin.

"These are worlds without end and ancient enough, Romek," she says, "it's impossible to count their numbers, they stretch on forever, and the heavens they traverse have no known boundaries."

I ponder the idea of endless space as we cut out planetary circles from cardboard, color them, thread string through the edges and sling them from the coat stand to recreate the universe in our kitchen. Gizia and Sara draw and shade outer coronas to be glued on to my Mars and Saturn. Tadek and Bella construct a series of comets with fire-charged plumes. Soon Lydia has all the heavenly bodies looped over the hat hooks and lined up in proper conjunction to the sun. Solar distance is measured in so many millimeters of string to every million light years, with the earth and moon swinging their way to the front door.

She crams fact after fact into our well-pigmented heads; how, by using simple geometry, Galileo calculated the height of the mountains of the moon from the shadows they cast; that the last Jewish astronomer in Spain to have a lunar crater named after him was Abraham Zacuto, and how the chemicals of exploding stars lives deep in our bones. The morning goes too fast and at noon I help Lydia gather up the map, the paper galaxy and her books.

"Romek, why the long face?" she asks me.

"I don't want it to be over," I say glumly.

"It doesn't have to be. Here, you have good reading ability, you can prepare for the next class."

Lydia hands me a child's primer on astronomy. "Too bad I don't have my old telescope any more, it was a marvelous instrument," she laments. "You'd be able to see close up how certain planets have hills and valleys, landscapes as a magnificent as any of those on earth."

In the middle of the night, I thrash around in my layer of quilts and angle myself near the wall so I can view the star-packed sky through the window of our room. A white bone of a moon bowls its way through ribbed clouds, edging them with a delicate rosy hue, turning them opaque at intervals. The intermittent light drifts across our single room, ghosting over my mother's sleeping face, she rests easily against my father's shoulder, a man who slumbers so deeply, his breath is barely audible.

My parents share a bed while the rest of us are camped on the floor. I'm settled on one side of Manek with Hanka on his right. Secretly awake, I hear the two of them whispering. Their voices rustle and drift, as the nocturnal hiss of some reptile.

"Are you sure? How many were there?" Hanka asks.

Manek recites, "At least fifty from the list that Uncle Arnie had to sign up. Jonas Esinski arrested for failing to report for the work detail. Yehoshua, that's Josefa Aharonson's boy, food theft, Magda Brumer for selling herself while classified as tubercular. She's scheduled for the Lvov transport, if her lungs don't bleed out beforehand, and Max. You remember Max Gorfein? Picked up for striking a supply officer...sentenced for execution!"

"Shush," orders my sister in her normal voice, nudging Manek. "Romek's lying there like a crab in sand—pretending to be asleep, the little faker!"

Taken

I clamp my eyes shut tight but she leans across my brother and snaps my earlobe into suffering between her thumb and forefinger. I moan in pain and manage to utter "But I didn't hear anything!"

"Let him be, Hanka, or he'll wake up the entire world," pleads my brother.

Hanka releases my throbbing ear and rolls over, her back to both of us. Soon we hear her snoring softly. Manek rearranges my covers and stretches his arm protectively across me. For a moment, lunar light surges full into the room, overflowing the scant furniture and the crammed-in bodies of my family.

"What did you learn in the kitchen Cheder today?" Manek asks softly. He knows I like this quiet time just between the two of us.

"The names of stars and that the moon is about three hundred and twenty three thousand kilometers away." I whisper proudly.

He points through the window to the spangled sky.

"What stars can you name for me?"

I raise my head to see through the window better. "Look, right there, those seven are called the Little Bear and the first one on the bear's tail is the brightest star of all. Its name is Pol...Pola, Polaris."

"Very good, Romek!"

"And you know what, Manek? Pani Lydia says the sky never ends, not ever," I declare. "Do you think that's true?"

"Shush, not so loud," urges my brother. "Pani Lydia is right, if you were to ride all along the edge of space you would never reach..."

Manek stops talking abruptly and places a hand over my mouth. We both freeze. Down in the street a scream of brakes, the groan of a heavy vehicle as the tires mount the sidewalk, men's voices, and the staccato of orders shouted. My brother stands up in one smooth leap. He pulls on his pants and waits, not moving. We hear voices slurring loud commands, bottle glass shattering on the pavement, a rallying cry of soldiers agreeing on something, an engine sputters, the sound of wheels reversed and the danger roars away.

Neither of us speaks for several nervous minutes.

"Will they come back?" I eventually whisper to my brother.

"Don't worry, go to sleep," assures Manek. He lies down and coils around me, holding me tight in the quilts. I sense his eyes are open and watching the dark for a long time. Eventually, I feel his body grow slack, loosening away from the menace that might have come bellowing up the stairs.

I remain absorbed in my Polaris star, perfectly settled in one pane of the window. It comforts me to think how bright it rides high above this second hand apartment of ours, shimmering beyond the ghetto and these exiled sleepers in their confines, above the barbed wire fences and the watchtowers, and the trucks that are parked ready for the morning's deportees.

My radiant star wheels free of the checkpoints and the armed guards, untouchable and undiminished—I am grateful for the space it plays in, out there, where there are no walls and endlessness is a country unto itself.

9

Bitter Hours

WE HAVE PLANS TO VISIT BORIS PINSKI, the seven-fingered black marketer, seller of stolen identity papers and passports, arms dealer, blackmailer, saboteur, pimp (for either gender), forger, sometimes assassin and an odd defender of the old and weak.

Mama and I cross the Ghetto's main thoroughfare and crunch our way over old snow to Czarnieckiego Street. The day is dry and sunny but the cold has a piercing bite that shrivels me in my deliberate disguise of rags. Our reflection in the empty shop windows mirrors a beggarly mother and son, dirty shadow people. We blend in with several other women and kids just as tatter-dressed, rakers of food trash, mendicants looking to sell buttons, nails, scrap metal, discarded shoes, old clothes or whatever was at hand for a measure of sustenance.

Secretly, I am a strolling bank vault. Earlier that morning Gizia Horowitz and my mother had bandaged to my bare stomach her six-strand pearl-and-diamond necklace with a medallion filled with rubies. A diamond-and-platinum bracelet is taped to my back. If I bend forward even a centimeter, the clasp of the necklace stabbed painfully into my navel. However, it is a morning when I would willingly go to the rack because my mother has enlisted me in one of her food and money-finding missions and I am puffed up with the importance of it all.

One of Pinski's bartering parlors was an abandoned house in the shadow of the Hospital for Infectious Diseases on Rekawka Street and access to him was a highly coded affair.

We arrive at the hospital to be greeted by Pinski's gatekeeper, Nurse Gurewicz, a woman shaped like a huge boulder from a significant rock fall. I recall her substantial expanse in a white uniform and her winged cap filling the entire admitting office.

"Is this the boy?" she rasps, surveying me through small olive eyes hidden deep under a mannish brow. Her voice has a high-pitched wheeze, as if the words have a tough battle rising up through the frontlines of her flesh.

"Yes, Nurse," answers Mama carefully, "he has ringworm and nothing seems to heal it."

Nurse Gurewicz grips my head with one hand and the daylight disappears. "Where is the rash?"

"Around his mid-section," my mother says, uttering the magic phrase. Gurewicz smiles, her several chins quivering as her eyes sink into dark slits. "Come with me," she orders.

We follow the white mass of the woman into the hospital's basement along chilly corridors painted an institutional green and biliously illuminated to halt at what I thought was a supply closet. Gurewicz unlocks it and swung open the door on a hidden staircase. She gestures for Mama and me to ascend it. Her keys rattle the lock fast behind us, but we sight the daylight of a room ahead.

The staircase terminates into a huge parlor furnished with towers of cardboard boxes. At one end, a squat looking man is writing at a broad oak desk. He turns and I see thick lips, buffalo jowls, and a head totally shaven rising out of an expensively tailored suit. He gets up to greet my mother, opening his arms in a grand gesture.

"Pani Ferber, what a pleasure! And this is your beautiful child!"

He kisses Mama's cheeks lightly and urges her to sit down. I gaze in fascination at the three fingers of his right hand that terminated at the knuckles, and whose stubs are crowned with heavy gold signet rings.

"As you know, times are difficult," begins my mother delicately, handing him a list from her pocket.

"I shall do my best to ease them a little," replies Pinski, striding briskly over to me. He lifts me up and stands me on the desk. His shorn head reeked of lime cologne and his stone-colored eyes fix on mine with a gaze that brought me fear. The stubs of his fingers probe at the fortune under my shirt.

"I hear you are a most valuable boy and such a good son," he says kindly.

He pulls off my sweater and was about to open my pants when I pull away from him. "No! Please let Mama do it," I demand.

"Of course, dear heart," he soothes. "I certainly lack a mother's gentle touch."

Not gentle at all is the removal of the sticking plaster that took off a layer of skin. My mother trims away at the tape and bandages with nail scissors and I weep silently through gritted teeth. While I suffer, Pinski walks around the room with Mama's list, concentrated and efficient as a grocer, gathering up various food and clothing items and dropping them into large cartons.

"It will be risky and physically impossible for you and the boy to carry so much," he boomed. "I will have the whole shipment driven to your home by my man, Fredek Lempl. He has a permit to travel in and out of the Ghetto. He'll make sure you're not compromised; you don't even have to set eyes on him."

Finally, my belly was free from its riches. Mama puts my clothes back on while Pinski gazes in reverence at the shining necklace.

"How magnificent!" he gushes, holding the pearls up to the sunlit window where the rubies cast scarlet glints over his plump cheeks. "And your courageous little emissary here, what promise he shows!"

Bitter Hours

The man turns to me with genuine delight, grinning through perfect and gleaming teeth. He caresses my face tenderly and appears concerned at my tear-stained upset, his crippled hands as soft as a woman's, but I find their touch insinuating and unpleasant. They hint at the strange tides that surged in his nature that swung between combustions of murderous violence and random generosity.

I'd heard Manek tell that Pinski had once strangled a Sinti (gypsy) man who had cheated him and in the same day prayed for forgiveness at a memorial mass for the only woman who ever possessed him, his mother. A civilian Gestapo member named Hans Keppler also met his end on Pinski's orders for beating an elderly Jew in the street. (The black marketer made sure that whatever resources the deceased owned were secretly assigned to the injured patriarch.)

"You did very well for your family, dear Romek, and you must be rewarded. What is it that would please you, eh?" Pinski says, happily rubbing his remaining fingers together as if the genie of the lamp would appear between his one-and-a-half hands. "Tell me, my fine boy, what do you dream of owning?"

Mama protests that the supplies and the cash she negotiates are enough, but he's insistent.

"Please, Sir, I'd like a telescope," I ask hesitantly. "That will let me look at the stars, at their hills and valleys."

From the stark bewilderment in the room, one might think I'd requested that he drain the oceans. My mother looked stunned and Pinski's eyes widened in fascination. His gaze bores into mine as if looking for some hint of failed sanity. Finally, he nods and smiles broadly.

"You are a very remarkable boy," he says. "Give me a few days and you shall have a telescope so splendid it will make Copernicus spin in his grave."

"We should be going, Pan Pinski," my mother responds, "You have been more than kind."

"Keep this safe," he cautions and hands Mama a bulky roll of zloty bills. She quickly stuffs money inside her blouse. Pinski inclines a bow and says, "Everything you requested shall be at your home by the time you reach it. G-d speed and don't forget me when your needs become so pressing."

He smiles, teeth and eyes a feral glitter, and escorts us out of the empty house through the front door.

❂

In the street, I hurry quickly behind my mother's edgy stride.

"If we see the soldiers approaching, you are to run and hide, is that understood?" she orders.

"What will you do, Mama?"

"Help my interrogators count the money."

"But Ghetto people aren't supposed to have money," I pushed.

"Don't split hairs with your mother. I'll say I was on my way to turn it in."

We reach the corner of Benedykta Street when Mama halted our steps and listened intently. The street is utterly deserted, its stones sullen and hushed. I turn around. There are no sidewalk paupers to be seen, not a living soul. The road behind us is a long cement void, save for the electric buzz of the tram tracks. A very old woman in a greasy black apron exits an apartment house to empty a slop bucket into the frozen gutter. She stares up at us in surprise and pity. She too raises her head to listen. In all my short life, I had never heard a quiet so dense, not even a bird cry, but these two women, strangers to each other, seem to catch the slither of a certain malevolence rising in the potent stillness.

The old woman beckons urgently to Mama, quickly pushes us through the doorway of her courtyard and locks us in. We are concealed behind doors as antique as our crone rescuer, with many gaps spavined open in their decaying carved panels that offered a fair view of the street. We glue our eyes to the holes.

Far away comes a distant tapping, like a thousand small hammers on paving stones, followed by the rumble of wheels. All three of us draw back from the far sight of the heavily armored German vehicles moving down the avenue. Next, a huge sea of elderly people—their faces set in apathy, marching listlessly inside an escort of armed foot soldiers. What I remember vividly is each person in the crowd carried a loaf of golden-crusted bread, as if they were making a pilgrimage to some temple of Panis.

The old woman crosses herself, pats my head and says, "Don't worry, little one, here you are safe."

"Why are they taking these people away? Where are they going?" Mama asks fearfully. The crone, whose name was Pani Dembitzer, regards my mother's distress, and places a shriveled hand on her arm. "The Ghetto is overcrowded," she explains, her voice like snapping twigs. "An order was announced to reduce the population by a thousand or more, the old and unemployed were kept overnight at OD headquarters, and now they're headed for the railway station at Plaszow."

"Where will they be sent?"

"Some say to work in the Ukraine or to the settlements around Kielce," answers the ancient face. "It could be worse. No harm will come to them."

My mother takes up a position at a door chink again and stares out. I see something like a current shudder down her spine. In the next moment, she's pounding on the worm-eaten panels with her fists and yelling, "No! No!"

Her voice rings off the vaulted courtyard. She hurls herself against the doors and tugs violently at the corroded bolts. I try to help her because she seems

Bitter Hours

so panicked to get out. Pani Dembitzer hauls me back and gives out a loud hiss. "Be quiet! You put us all in danger!" She turns and asks me in anger, "Boy, what's wrong with this woman? Is she from the insane asylum?"

Outside, we hear a military voice call a temporary halt and through a keyhole at my height, I see a well-tailored general standing up and shouting orders to someone beyond my sight. The host of captives stand like frozen ghosts. A ferocious terror comes alive in me, raking my insides. My mother sobs and seems out of control. She slides down the doors to the dirty tiles—her forehead scratched and bleeding. I sit down beside her. The old woman is stroking her hair, "Is there someone out there that belongs to you?"

"My parents!" Mama hoarsely grieves through her tears.

"What! Mama, where are they?" I demand. I look again.

There, in between the shoulders of the armed escort, are the familiar profiles of Dziadius (Grandfather) Shya and my Babcia (Grandmother), Meresa Chilowicz, staring straight ahead, my grandfather holding his wife's hand tightly.

"Let's go get them," I beg. "We can give the soldiers the money."

My mother looks utterly fractured and hangs on to me, "No, Romek, it would make no difference," she says.

Outside the doors we hear more shouts and the clatter of the human tread resumes. The old woman stares hesitantly at the two of us.

"Why didn't the uncles tell us?" I ask and cling to her as I see the tears coursing down her cheeks. She whispers, "They may have thought it unnecessary. We're supposed to be protected from certain things."

"We have to do something," I say, ready to do anything so that she doesn't hurt so much. The old woman reaches into her concierge's vestibule, brings out a chair, raises up my mother and makes her sit. "You can wait here with the boy, until they're gone," she says.

I watch through the holes in the moldering doors as my grandparents disappear around the corner with all the marchers. We stay hidden until the street outside the courtyard of Concierge Dembitzer is finally empty so we can leave in safety. My mother races us home so fast I skid on the sides of my boots and plough a boy-trail through the snow from her dragging me.

Turning into our apartment house, we run into my uncles Solomon and Arnold, and Manek and my father all gathered in the lobby. In their faces, we read the impact of the what-to-do discussion they'd been having. At the sight of the men, Mama starts to weep again. Papa hugs us and assures her, "We'll get them back, Mala. Don't worry."

I stand in the midst of them, tall trees of regret and heated emotion, making a rapid-fire hash of the conversation above my head. How could this happen? Who knew? You should have warned us! What if they send them to the Russian side, how will we ever find them? My Uncle Solomon says that

Kielce is full of Zionists, Tzaddiks and good Rabbis but it's rumored that over twenty-five thousand Jews are crammed into the Ghetto there—you think they need houseguests? It's not a problem; we know ODs there who can help us, who can maybe arrange travel permits for Shya and Meresa.

Manek instructs my mother, "Mama, can you give me about six hundred zlotys? Gershon Nowak has arranged a car and a travel permit. If we start driving in the next hour, we'll arrive about the same time as the train."

"How will you get in and out of the Ghetto?" I ask my brother.

"There'll be no problem if I'm with you," says Uncle Arnold. "I know the captain in charge of the transport."

My mother sits down on the landing, one exhausted sack of fear. Behind her stand the boxes from Pinski's emporium that I can smell contain fruit and fresh coffee among the provisions. However, the idea of eating well tonight is diluted by our latest emergency. Mama hands Manek the money he'll need for bribes. Papa beckons to me and we help her upstairs into the apartment.

※

A colony of immense cockroaches nested in the cupboard under the sink in our kitchen. My mother had previously poured boiling water into their realm in the hopes of killing them off, only to drive the swarm below into the Abramowicz's apartment. Tadek and I captured two of the largest of their clan, handsome (we thought) shiny-backed creatures at least forty millimeters long with splendid antennae. We kept them in matchboxes as pets. For two nine-year-olds who could only venture into the streets under very restricted circumstances, the discovery of this wildlife was as entertaining as any zoo visit.

We named our new pets "Royal" and "Giant" and liked to race them on the hallway linoleum (not always a successful game since the insects had their own stubborn routes built into their chitinous skulls and frequently made off to hidden freeways among the wiring and the water pipes).

"You boys keep that disgusting vermin out of the home or else!" Mama would warn us, sprinkling a line of salt along the doorsill to our living quarters to prevent these racing champions from bedding down with us. I feed my little winner, Royal, stale breadcrumbs and the dregs of leftover tea, although he seems to prefer the open jar of horse glue in my father's toolbox.

"He likes the protein," advises Lydia Rosenfeld, who delights in our sudden interest in insects and peppers us with all kind of scientific facts. "Romek, your racer is a cold-blooded species, cheap to feed. A single meal is enough to last him a whole month."

At night, Tadek and I cover Royal and Giant's boxes with a heavy book and place them under the sink. However, more than once they manage to burrow their way through a cardboard seam and escape, as if to be returning heroes to their kind. Recapture meant Tadek and I waiting in the

Bitter Hours

dark for the very faint patter of the insects as they emerged to rule the kitchen tiles. Throwing on the light would send them into a darting frenzy, and since their clan all look alike, we had our pick of big racers who would receive the same names no matter what.

Like Royal and Giant, we learn to scatter too.

❦

I travel in the warm flux of an amazing sleep that sways me between a spectral dream and the thin haze that hovers just beneath wakening. I no longer feel the blankets or the hard floor beneath me. There's a chorus of whispers above my floating trance. My mother is scrambling about restlessly, urging someone to put my shoes on and make sure that I'm wrapped warmly in a quilt.

My sister is protesting, "I can't carry him. He's a dead weight!"

Then I hear my brother demand, "Give him to me!"

I moan in sleepy agreement. I'm handed off into Manek's arms and wind myself into the cradle of him. My father's voice flares up in my consciousness, commanding to make sure that I remain invisible (and I think that maybe my experiment to be unseen is finally working). In my semi-dream, I speculate, without any sadness or hurt, if I'm to be given away. Salka and Gizia meander across my vision, they too are both struggling to carry a rolled-up rug. They stare at me watchfully and stagger out of view with their heavy burden. Tadek is nowhere to be seen. The apartment is reduced to faint shadows.

I'm in Manek's arms and we glide down a rush of cold air, along a pathway of intermittent lights and dense pools of night. Close behind us, I barely discern the steps of others following us. We move like a school of fish, darting together beneath the tall silhouettes of chimneys, the lead scales of rooftops, through a pursuing urgency across courtyards until a strong undertow of sleep plunges me into the deep end of silence.

Still tightly quilted, I open my eyes hours later to a lace sheet on either side of me filtering weak sunlight. Just above my face is a metal arrangement of diamond shapes. Footsteps beat along floorboards and I see a pair of high-heeled shoes come drumming by, propelled along on narrow ankles, a drift of perfume from the edge of a hem. My forehead slams against iron mesh and I come fully awake. A woman's pretty face suddenly apparitions at my floor level, whispering to me, "Shush! Don't make a noise. You have to stay very quiet, not so long now."

I'm under a bed, right up against the box spring, in the home of my Aunt Cyla, the hat maker, my father's only sister and wife of another uncle, the OD, Samek Wiener.

"Where's Mama?" I whisper back. "Where is everyone?"

"They're fine," mouths my aunt. "You'll see them in a little while."

A girl's voice calls to her, "Pani Wiener, is the green velvet toque ready? Pani Schoenholtz is here to pick it up."

Aunt Cyla winks at me and blows me a kiss. Her patent leather pumps retreat into the kitchen that is also her hat-sewing operation. I view another player at shoe level, her young assistant, Ewa Urbanowicz, ankles thick as logs, lisle stockings rising to a heavy-hipped but shapely figure in a beige cretonne dress. The clack of the sewing machine starts up, driven by Ewa's powerful hams. Across the room, I sight the cradle of Cyla's infant son, my cousin, eight-month old Lonius. Shifting my position, I can see Cyla escorting a woman named Frida Schoenholtz to a gold-framed mirror where she sets the green toque carefully on a crest of peroxide hair.

Aunt Cyla darts around her client, full of amiable flattery, patting curls in place under the hat's brim, raising a feather here, arranging the net veiling just so. The heavy-bosomed woman beneath the hat is from across the river, the wife of a wealthy German attorney. Both are Nazi party members of high rank, the husband representing his nation's industrial interests in Poland. Frau Schoenholtz makes a special trip into the Ghetto because she knows Cyla's creations can be purchased cheaply and still retained their renowned pre-war chic. The woman's chauffeur, a thick-necked Polish boy named Jaroslaw (who was allowed a pistol on his belt for his employer's protection) hovers by Ewa's sewing machine, his inane flirting drowned out by the treadle's clicking song. The seamstress, well versed in the punishments for romancing with Aryans, ignores him.

I stay underneath the bed for the next four hours, waiting, listening, and daydreaming. I'm parched, hungry and am dying to pee. Eventually, I hear Ewa bid my aunt goodbye and the door lock behind her. In the next instant Cyla drags me out of hiding by my nightshirt and shoves a chamber pot under my butt. "Don't worry, I won't look!" she exclaims and hurries off to move Lonius's cradle into the bedroom. Cyla returns and calls me into the kitchen to eat pea soup followed by her superior banana and raisin pudding. I down many helpings of everything until my stomach hurt while my aunt entertains me by modeling her hats.

"Look at this one, Romek," Cyla commands, whirling around with what appears to be a nest of stray pheasants on her brow. She makes a clucking noise and cracks me up by doing a chicken strut across her kitchen. She rams on my head a red felt cloche with the wings of blue-black crows taking flight from its crown, hands me a silver mirror and announces, "Don't you look swell?"

I see a pale skinny boy in an old patched nightshirt, a green scab of soup on his upper lip, half moon shadows of stolen sleep under each eye, and dead birds rising out of his greasy hair.

"Not overawed, huh?" Cyla asks over my shoulder. "I know what you need!"

A tailor's body model stands by her sewing table. I hear a loud click and am astonished as she carefully lifts off the upper section and lays it on the floor.

Bitter Hours

Deep in the belly cavity sits a small but illegal radio—now I am impressed! Cyla fiddles with controls, a crackle and sputter of indecipherable voices, and then the Tommy Dorsey orchestra, courtesy of the BBC Home Service, blasts into the kitchen.

"Give me your hand," shrills my aunt above the louche saxophones riffs.

She sweeps me into the living room. Head feathers at the dither, the two of us leap and rumba like some wild tribal horde. For the next hour, she merrily dips me, swings me, whoops and waltzes me until we make the dust rise from the carpets. The red cloche flies off when I make a clumsy glide away from her and I fall down, chortling so hard that the soup threatens to return up my gullet.

Cyla laughs too, hauling me to my feet and we stomp away to Irving Berlin's *This is the Army, Mister Jones!* "Shake your hips like this, Romeczku, the way they do in the American movies," she urges, swiveling her slender frame on one foot.

We drink lemonade from wine glasses and she teaches me the Yiddish words to *We're Gonna Hang Out the Washing on the Siegfried Line.* (I would later learn this song stuck in the craw of the German High Command for poking fun at their defenses.) We eventually collapse exhausted on her sofa and listen to Big Ben far away above the Thames chime five-o-clock. I loll content against my glamorous aunt, always a wacky but elegant woman, a lightning wit and a natural comedienne who should have been on the stage. The happy waning afternoon eventually leads to the question, "Auntie Cyla? Why am I here?"

She smiles beautifully and says, "You're here because I miss my sweet Romek and I stole you like a treasure in the night."

She hugs me and kisses my cheeks noisily. I know she's lying but I love her and the wonderful fib just the same. I feel a warm sadness when my mother shows up with my clothes, a look of relief on her face. In that moment, I didn't mind this game of going to sleep on the floor of our apartment and magically waking up in some other place. Maybe it's all part of the invisibility business?

❀

I soon learn the real reason for my night travels: Lieutenant Taubenschlag, hunter of children. My homecoming is a celebrated feast where Tadek and I are given a hero's welcome. Papa had opened the cache of food luxuries suspended above our fake ceiling and brought down several precious jars of chicken stew, dried peaches and a small bottle of sherry for the grown-ups. Luisia Horowitz had baked a honey kugel and frothed up an icing glaze from a careful issue of sugar and molasses. My father insists that his lap be my chair at dinner. His eyes are moist; he keeps stroking my hair and saying, "Beautiful boy. Just look at him, Mala, he's growing up so strong and sturdy."

Hanka squeezes me too and distributes to Tadek and myself the candy bars she'd traded for shampoo at the airport. Manek gives us a small wooden horse carved from one piece of wood that we were to share like brothers. The evening is double crowned by the news from Uncle Arnold that he and Manek had managed to buy back my grandparents, unscathed, from the Kielce transport of the bread carriers.

Here we all are, returning from different compass points: Tadek and Shlome Abramowicz and nine others from a crawl space under the roof of the Madritsch Confectionary factory, Bella and Sara Abramowicz from behind the shelving of the bacteria collection in the Pankiewicz pharmacy. Gizia was dressed in high heels with full woman make-up and was serving behind the pharmacy counter when the roundup began. Her effective shield was a silver cross on a chain loaned to her by Pani Aurelia. The patrol passed her by. All over our community, kids had been tucked into impossible spaces; lowered into disused chimneys, sub-cellars, drains, bakery ovens, water pipes, and even stuffed beneath the cold-water tank of the public bathhouse on Josefinska Street.

I learn that from the fifteen hundred souls that had been removed from the Ghetto the previous night, Lieutenant Taubenschlag, like the *Rattenfänger* (rat-catcher) of Hamlin, had netted himself over three hundred children. The sharp lament of their parents rose up like mournful smoke over the Ghetto streets.

※

The selections make it even more vital that Tadek and I press on with our plans to become invisible. I plague Lydia Rosenfeld about this highly scientific problem. She surveys me cryptically and I sense a kind of despairing patience billowing out from her. "It can't be done," she declares with authority. "Small boys, like all mammals, are made up of solid matter. They exist to be seen. Few things are visually undetectable in nature: certain gases, electricity, the forces of wind, and the thoughts of a liar. Get smart; try camouflage."

Tadek and I refuse to be discouraged and attempt the "We think we are, therefore we'll become so," routine. We decide to test the camouflage experiment on Bella's mother, Pani Teofila Abramowicz, concealing ourselves in the gloom under the stairs while she ferried a mass of laundry back and forth from the courtyard. The woman passes within inches of us. Her gaze is tensed on flapping sheets and a sky burdened with oncoming rain. "It's working," Tadek whispers to me, "we look like wood grain."

It appears that total stillness has a lot to do with it. On her third trip back from the clothesline, her basket full of garments, Teofila catches only the glitter of our eyes and lets out a heart-stopping scream that makes me dizzy with panic. Her two strapping sons, Shlome and Lazer, fly out of their apartment swinging splintered chair legs as clubs. Their mother leaps back and her terror causes to her to heave the laundry basket almost to the second floor landing. The hallway is suddenly awash in Abramowicz shirts, socks, and underwear, all drifting down in a tumult of wild protests and shouts.

"Oh, G-d, it was a filthy pervert," Teofila shrieks, "waiting to strike me down…there in the dark!" She points operatically to our former hiding place. Tadek and I had darted into the storm of clothing, pretending we'd just arrived to be helpful, and are now wading out of the sheets, ending our cover as bed linens.

✷

My father had warned us all that the OD, Azriel Feiner suffered a jealousy in the blood, the querulous craven type that walks with a man daily. If good fortune took up residence with one man, it was because the lucky bugger had seduced it away from him. Azriel's dissatisfactions honed a sharp blade in his nature and made him extremely dangerous in the climate of the Ghetto. Here, where luck was fleeting at any hour, he could easily enact refined punishments against the blameless for all past disappointments, real and imagined. His position as an OD was tailor-made for squaring his accounts of joys subverted; payments settled by random arrests and torn-up residency permits or ration cards.

The source of Azriel's bile seemed to be his historic failures with women. My mother declared that he was not a handsome man by any stretch but could have been a passable short-term contender for a certain type of female. Much to his own astonishment, Azriel managed to marry a wisp of a widow, a Catholic woman named Drevna Malinowski who willingly entered the Ghetto (unconverted) to live with him. His wife's dog-like affection diluted his venom somewhat.

They live at the same address as my handsome Uncle Solomon and his family, who often encounter Pani Drevna taking her discreet steps down the stairs, hugging the wall as if she would fade into the wainscoting. Solomon, with his stunning looks and impeccable grace, always raises his hat to her and offers to carry her packages up to the Feiner apartment. My uncle would tease Tadek and me on how Drevna must also be working on the alchemy of invisibility. She passes by frequently unseen but is definitely sensed by her dank after-presence.

Azriel and Solomon cross paths at the office of the Judenrat where Azriel would be unnerved at the reflection in the window of the two of them bent over documents of potential removals. Solomon's fine-boned regal looks are multiplied on the numerous tiny windowpanes. His dark hair shines with bluish tints and a rich confident tone in his voice causes people to look up whenever he enters a room. Standing beside Solomon, Azriel must see in the glass a misshapen ape-like creature, a sloping head covered with anemic strands of hair, a colorless gargoyle forged in envy.

I am there when the worst happens, and while my cape of invisibility worked for me, to my endless sorrow, it does not shield Uncle Solomon. I had been sent to sleep at his home because we'd heard that another night action threatened to sweep up more kids. Solomon, my Aunt Halina and their daughter, my teenage cousin Sonia, are billeted in a place similar to ours—a very basic two-room apartment with a foyer, but because of my uncle's position in the Jewish Police, they live there exclusively.

We are seated at dinner, enjoying small careful portions of smoked sable that had secretly been routed through Rabbi Geller of the Zucker Synagogue. At times like this, enclosed in some pleasant evening with family, the presence of the strife beyond these walls recedes, leaving a short-lived gift of the moment. Sonia hands her father another slice of bread when an explosive pounding hits the front door. My aunt quickly drags me by the elbow into the bedroom, pushing me between the wall and the closet, hanging several dresses on the outside door to conceal me.

A cacophony of voices; I hear the front door splinter open followed by shouts and threats, Halina's gentle pleading, and Solomon saying "I'm innocent of any crime. I am a respected member of the Ordungdienst!"

There is a five-second silence then an order in German from a new voice. Halina had no time to slam the bedroom door fully, and I can see through the slit another OD man and the Gestapo investigator dressed in a well-made suit and a soft leather coat. He's holding the arrest order in his hand that accuses my uncle of sabotage. He demands that Solomon get his jacket and leave with them immediately. Aunt Halina, trying to keep the tremble out her voice, asks "Please, Sir, where's the proof of this charge?"

Solomon is calm and steady. To his wife he requires gently that she must avoid a scene, these authorities can't stand the tidal hysterics of women, the pitch of their heart-destroyed cries sets off a storm in their heads that transmits to the un-holstered pistol. Sonia holds on to her mother, her eyes drinking in her father hungrily, as if to shelter him in her gaze. Solomon kisses his wife and daughter, whispering that they should speak to Uncle Arnold and my father. The waiting Gestapo men shift their feet impatiently. My uncle puts on his jacket and walks out with them, looking forever fabulous as he goes down to oblivion.

I wait with my aunt and cousin all night. No one slept much. Halina keeps to herself in a chair by the window, silently looking out. Sonia and I sit in blankets on the kitchen tiles where she eventually cries herself into a parched sleep. I put my arms around my slumbering cousin, wanting so much to rewind events all the way back to the sweet hour of suppertime.

At growing daylight, when it is safe, my mother, Manek, and Uncle Arnold come to the apartment to bring comfort, food and some plan of action. I am banished to the bedroom to wait, and strain to hear the fervent hum of their conversation. My father had been told of his brother's arrest prior to him leaving on the work detail, and of the report that Solomon is on his way to one of the concentration lagers. He had spent the day street sweeping, driving his broom with the unending fuel of his grief.

Bitter Hours

I'm sent back to our apartment to be with Tadek, where the adults aren't telling me anything. My father comes home, his eyes bloated and red. He refuses to eat, goes into our room and closes the door. My mother keeps asking me tenderly if I am all right and drafts me into peeling potatoes. Manek and Hanka drench me with such an overflow of affection, I begin to think that the arrest has left some secret sign on me.

Azriel Feiner sits at his dinner table, across from his specter of a wife who smiles with her blanched love for him. She pours him a tall glass of vodka and leans back, gratitude in her eyes that this man has claimed her when no other would. Now she can haunt the world with her small meager soul, her private masses, her stringent devotion to the Virgin who aids her in avoiding the marriage bed, and still be anchored by her ugly Jewish spouse.

Azriel's inner existence is so pocked with his own distortions that it competes with the dense web of menace and despair that shrouds the Ghetto. Drevna will pray for him to be delivered from what she thinks is a racial trait of gloom, that she will eventually convert him and be rewarded in the hereafter by the Queen of Heaven for adding to the ranks of her nailed son.

Azriel drinks the harsh vodka, letting it numb his liar's throat. He is very careful these nights not to seat himself opposite the window, where the gargoyle of his treachery can grin back at him. He will never be beautiful.

One sunny afternoon, Tadek pulls me aside and whispers, "Romek, come and see, there are strange 'turtlebacks' on the wall."

He drags me to the window. All along the far ramparts enclosing our section of the Ghetto are what appear to be an unending row of green metal domes, they look like inverted washbasins, some bobbing and switching places along the bricks. We hear the shout of an order and a long line of steel helmets ascend into view with several hundred rifles pointed into the streets. I see men's faces set in shadow beneath their headgear, scanning the scene and adjusting their gun sights.

"Get down," I cry and pull Tadek to the floor.

We crawl on our bellies into the kitchen where the mothers and the Horowitz girls are sewing. "What are you boys up to?" Luisia queries, "that you should be sweeping the floor with yourselves?"

"Soldiers on the wall!"

My mother goes to the window, looks out and jerks back. "Gizia," she says calmly, "Please get the kids upstairs."

"What's going on, Mama?" asks Tadek.

His mother orders that we are not waiting to find out. Gizia takes me by the hand and Salka grabs her brother. Up the stairs we run and into the darkness—to a deep eave in the slope of the roof where my father and Issac Horowitz had loosened three panels and nailed them into one disguised door on runners that could be bolted against any outer force from the hiding side. Salka slides the door back and the two girls hustle us into a wide but low attic space that ran the length of the building, with plenty of room for us kids to hide.

From the moment we are inside, the one major rule is "no talking." We hunker down on coarse blankets, keeping as still as stones and began the customary hours of waiting. I can hear my heart beating loud against the attic floor that reeked of old dust and mouse droppings. The recitation in my head shunts back and forth: please don't let me return to our apartment to find that I've been orphaned.

The faint crack of gunfire echoes over the roof slates coming from Gate One to be answered by retorts from Gate Four on Kocik Street. "They must be all around us," whispers Tadek.

Salka clutches at her sister and the two girls cover their heads with their arms. My mind has narrowed down to one huge knot of unease. I imagine my father, Manek and Hanka, waiting at the checkpoint to re-enter the Ghetto, the delay a numbing ferocity as they watch families spill into the streets from the bellowed order of the duty sergeant with the bullhorn. I send silent words to Papa wherever he is in the moment. We are here. We are safe. Please let the badness sidestep us.

I hear dogs at some distance baying pitifully and I recall Papa reading from the Book of Enoch that Samael is the *Mal'akh ha-Mavet*, the Angel of Death, who is full of eyes, a foul magician of Talmudic literature who soiled the sky with his droppings that became the dark spots of the moon. Samael, the Prince of demons, of whom it is written causes the dogs to howl when he enters the city to harvest the lives of men.

"You can't see us, you'll not take us, not us," I whisper softly into the blanket.

I hear my mother's voice drift up from the landing below answered by the deeper tones of Uncle Arnold saying, "Keep the kids out of sight until it's over..."

"What's all the fuss?" Mama asks him. "Our permits are in order."

"It's a sifting operation, Mala," Arnold assures her. "Kunde ordered it. I'll make sure that you, Leon, and the others are not bothered. Let's see what they do next."

I would learn later what *they* did next on the orders of SS-Hauptsturmführer Wilhelm Kunde was to move the ODs and Polish police led by Symche Spira, through the Ghetto like an infection, like an organized quail shoot. They flushed out the unemployed, the pregnant women, very small children, disabled men, healthy men for whom no work had been assigned, the elderly, the sick, and anyone who did not have the saving grace of proper documentation.

The Plac Zgody is thronged with these captives and their meager baggage. Over four thousand of them sit in the blazing June sun for several hours while German clerks move among them checking off names with mechanical efficiency and collecting valuables and money before they were escorted to the Plaszow railroad station.

My father heard from a neighbor who'd jumped from the train just before it reached Belzec and hid in a swamp, how they were marched alongside the Bug River. Escorted over its fertile banks and sandy scarps, by thickets of peat bogs and the ascending towers of anthills busy with community, through old forests acres studded with yellow foxgloves, Siberian Iris, and spotted orchids. Their slouching feet disturbed the blended songs of corncrakes, ringed plovers, black terns and bank swallows. Their route was fringed with ancient oaks and sweet chestnut bowers while the sun loosened sharp aromas from lime trees, blue pines and flowering ash above them.

Many of these scented branches had been cut down and neatly woven into the barbed wire fence, creating a dense leafy arbor that totally concealed a narrow enclosed trail. The guards called this lush green path "the tube", which led to a disguised terminus, reaching deep into the gaseous domain of Samael, in the Kingdom of the *Mal'akh ha-Mavet.*

10

Betrayals

MY VIBRANT AUNT CYLA was the only daughter among eight sons of my father's family. Blessed with entrepreneurial talents, she had successfully run her own dressmaking and millinery shop with a staff of seamstresses, but after 1939, her business was among the many Jewish enterprises the Reich closed down in Krakow. In the Ghetto, she managed a modest flow of work as a tailor for uniforms, remaking dresses from rags, and taking hat commissions from wealthy German wives. Of all my aunt's former employees, Ewa Urbanowicz had stayed loyal and, in return, Cyla kept her on the job that ensured the girl's survival.

The girl treated my aunt as a peer, unloading on the older woman the most lurid teenage confessions that could endanger them both. Cyla thought it wise not to inform her OD husband, Samek, of these secrets but in the event that Ewa fell into the snare of any collaborator, my aunt wanted someone else to know: her private ear was my mother. The seamstress's story eventually filtered down to us all as a high-risk romantic fable.

According to Aunt Cyla, Ewa celebrated her nineteenth birthday by sneaking out of the Ghetto hidden under the back seat of the Schoenholz's Mercedes *Tourenwagen*. The Polish chauffeur, Jaroslaw Graczewski, easily came and went through the Gate One checkpoint with a pass on the Reich's letterhead signed by his German employer.

Jaroslaw, a dull loaf of a man, unmarried and closing on twenty-eight, was the only son of parents who were caustic over conceiving him in middle age and regarded him as an unwanted pestilence and a drain on their finances. The Graczewskis were custodians at the Radovski Catholic Reformatory on the Aryan side of the city. Their credentials for the job were outstanding; they had practiced the bunched fist on Jaroslaw frequently, and had a full repertoire of capricious punishments for very young inmates. Their slap-and-strap disciplines herded many an adolescent along the razor's edge of brute criminality.

Jaroslaw managed to survive his rough upbringing and actually rose to favor in the eyes of his venomous parents when, at the age of fifteen, he began to bring home a salary and choice cuts of beef from his shift at the slaughterhouse on Zalieskego Street. His job was to pummel terrified cows down a chute where their necks would be locked in a steel collar, readied for the stunning hammer and the knife. Already inhaling the ferrous stench of their killed predecessors, the animals would roll their eyes piteously and moan against the vice that held them.

On slow days, his manager, Nestor Duchovny, had him sweep the blood-swamped floors and shovel the wreckage of bones and sawn off hoofs into the rendering vats. However, the boy soon grew tired of cow-terror and the

Betrayals

constant rotation of pastoral life into hanging meat. Nestor promoted him to be a relief driver and ride the insulated trucks that distributed the carved-up produce to butcher shops all over Krakow. The work brought him surprising connections within the Reich, due to the regular deliveries of saddles of beef and spring lamb to a fine townhouse of a munitions importer on the Maly Rynek.

The Graczewski parents, no longer satisfied with free steaks, pinned even higher hopes on their lumpish son when Jaroslaw was hired to the enviable and well-paid position of valet and chauffeur for Advocate Dieter Schoenholz. Against all the ironbound conventions of the day, Jaroslaw was reasonably well liked by his German employers.

Advocate Schoenholz appreciated the lad's easy company. He was so much more compliant that his own warrior son, Albrecht (a young victor general in the invasion of France). The Advocate's wife, Frida, a shrill obsessive woman, doted on Jaroslaw and was abnormally fixated on his eating habits. Although he would never be allowed near their dinner table, Frida ordered her cook to set aside generous portions of their menu for the chauffeur. After her husband retired to his study to deport more workers to the Krupps factory in Germany, his wife would glide below stairs to feed her pet Pole.

"Dear boy, I don't how you live," she'd croon to Jaroslaw between ladles of creamed spinach and roast duck. "This country is so primitive. We have to barter every morsel from farmers who would cheat their own mothers. And there's not a decent couturier to be found anywhere in Krakow, one is forced to do business with the Jews across the river."

Jaroslaw stuffed his mouth in hurried nervous spoonfuls. By eating, he only had to make the slightest of replies to her. "I'm glad, Pani Schoenholz, that you were able to find a good hat maker in Podgorze," he said unctuously.

He had a peasant's suspicion of being favored by his betters and, given the fact that Poles were only a marginal step above Jews in the Nazis' distortions of race, he feared the Schoenholz's kindness might be the crocodile beneath dark waters. One false move and the tearing jaws would rise up and open. Pani Frida poured him another glass of Riesling and pushed the crystal goblet his way.

"Drink!" she fusses. "Dieter, bless him, has this wine brought in from Austria."

From a confiscated cellar where the owners were shot against their own fermenting barrels, as Jaroslaw well knew.

He ploughed through dessert while the woman voraciously watched his every mouthful, occasionally dabbing raspberry pulp off his chin. He managed a cream-filled smile and a childhood tale came to him of helpless children lost in a forest who are fattened up by a witch for her cannibal pleasures. Frida's food fetishes were insufferable, time to fib his way out of the kitchen to the garage where he could rest his ruined digestion and

Journey of Ashes

polish the fixtures of the Mercedes. He wiped his mouth and made some courteous noise about having to check the vehicle's oil level. "Thank you so much for the splendid feast, Pani Schoenholz."

She nodded in satisfaction and rose too, to ascend to her private sitting room at the back of the house. Jaroslaw took heavy, pained steps to the garage, a walking gastric disaster, his belt cut into his tightened gut and the sugared dessert made his nerves twang. He slumped down on the running board of the car and decided that silent revenge against Frida's force-feeding was in order. There was no riper payback than driving across the Pilsudskiego Bridge with the Jewish maiden of his fantasies concealed beneath the beige suede upholstery. He glanced at himself in the car's mirror and grinned as he imagined the horrors to be endured by Pani Frida if she ever knew of such contaminations.

❀

Food and the machinations of getting it were among the most ludicrous, if desperate episodes of Ghetto living. We gratefully take the pocked rations distributed by the Judenrat but always have to find a way to supplement the basics from our secret pantry in the ceiling. The mothers combine the food allowance of each family, using potatoes and onions that came our way to enhance the one ration issue that never ran out: beet soup. Otherwise, it tasted like grit-filled mud and human sweat.

My Uncle Samek calls on us to escort my mother to collect our weekly rations allowance. He grins at me, cups my chin with his hand and comments, "Mala, this boy is as pasty as week-old dough. You should air him out; he looks like a dried-up fly."

My mother, busy collecting the large sacks we would need to carry the provisions, glances in my direction, "So Romek doesn't have a Riviera tan. He's always been a fair-skinned mite."

"Let's take him with us. There'll be no trouble—I'll be there to see to your requisition," assured my uncle.

A long column of people snake out of the door of the Judenrat's office, waiting for the officious stamps on their rations book that will take them to another line for their meager allowance of groceries. Uncle Samek sweeps us to the head of the queue, provoking ugly mutters from the crowd. Who's that woman with the boy? Why do they get to go first? Must be servants for some general? You shouldn't be so harsh. Workers assigned those jobs tread on thin ice every hour. One dropped plate and they'll be bleeding for a week.

I well understand but have never forgotten the hissed accusation of one woman, "Collaborators! Just look at them, privileged enough to sup the blood of their own! No sense of decency."

"Don't listen to them, Romek," my mother orders softly as if she's speaking from some great distance. The resentment wafting our way is too much.

Betrayals

Uncle Samek returns us to the streets via the back entrance and we make our way to the rations station.

On route, Samek regales us with the tales of the rations manager—the legendary Zigo Kousevetski and how he had come to lose his right eye in resisting relocation from his home in the Kazimierz. On multiple occasions, the Polish police arrived at his furniture warehouse to evict him to the Ghetto. The first time he bought them off.

"A little while longer, so I can fix up my business in good order for you," he wheedled. "You wouldn't want me to deliver you a shambles?"

The next time Zigo got them drenched drunk and handed them his plump eighteen-year-old daughter, Golda, for their pleasure. They left with monumental headaches and fond memories. The attempted removals stacked up expensively and he borrowed cash from Boris Pinski to pay off his evictors. Pinski loaned it without interest for the fascination of seeing how long the siege would last. Zigo was convinced that enough delay would wear the authorities down until they would eventually let him alone.

"One Jew less in Podgorze makes room for another," he argued to the officers he'd addled with slivovitz. "If I stay, I make you good money, what's not to like?"

The SS Oberscharfuhrer, Axel Hoenigmann, an expert in confiscations, found much not to like. "Get him out or shoot him!" he ordered. "We need the warehouse. He has one hour or he can start sawing his own coffin!"

The Polish constable returned with two Ukrainian guards known as "the Blacks" because of their uniforms, who put easy cash and luscious Golda way below the chance to bleed the unruly Zigo. He foolishly battled them relentlessly down the length of his cabinetmaker's shop, striking back with hammers, chisels and block planes. The guards refused to murder him because the chase over the workbenches was too comic a sport for them. It all ended when the men pounded Zigo with a small inlaid table he'd been meaning to finish. His eye was driven from his head to stare back at him from the blood-soaked sawdust. Nostalgic for favors previously rendered, the Polish constable allowed him a doctor's visit to treat the empty socket prior to shipping Zigo across the river.

✦

At the rations depot, the former carpenter stands behind a bench made from an old door, a subdued Cyclops but with one eye keen for shortening the scales when he weighs out our basic issue: potatoes thriving with blight, musty flour, stale turnips diverted from cattle feed bins, and ground chicory rampant with weevils. Mama and I have no privileges of being first-served on this line. The shoppers are mainly women, and a few men, dirty, unshaven and listless, for whom no work had been assigned. They stay silent, fearful that any conversation will betray their perilous state of unemployment: always a solid guarantee of deportation. I'm already bored and complain loudly that my feet hurt. "Nonsense, Romek, be grateful for the shoes you stand in," my mother whispers tartly. "At least they're not letting in the daylight."

I pull at a loose button on my coat and feel around on the sewn yellow star where Mama had hidden a coin beneath it for good luck. The hard press of metal was still there. She pulls me close to her, her mood switched to mollifying me. "Be patient. We'll be next," she said.

We step up to the counter and I watch Zigo. His head darts ineptly from one customer to another, like a pigeon feeding at spilled grain. His helper, a moody disheveled girl called Nadia, fulfills the chits with surly resentment, as if the world were ransacking her own pantry. Next to us stands a young mother with four children, stepped in age. I see their faces as they turn to leave with their supplies, full of uncertainty and bitter gratitude; dark pits of need beneath their eyes, their ethereal skin stretched tight by hunger. They emanate the stalking breath of future illness and worse.

Mama forbids me to stare at Zigo, but it's hard because when he turns to the right and bends to collect our rations, we have to shunt a little ways down the counter so he can see who is next for cheating. My mother packs up all our requisites. From the basin of the scale, she empties the two kilos of potatoes into one of the sacks and peers skeptically at the cluster of dusty tubers.

"Something wrong, Pani Ferber?" asks Zigo pleasantly.

Mama had a plan in hand that would usually score against the mounting odds of food shortages. She'd ask Zigo are there any carrots available today? The former carpenter would answer that if he had them by the bushel, he would willingly offer them for the sake of the puny boy at her side. Mama would then hold up a potato for his inspection and slip him a ten zloty bill beneath it—a deposit for later when Hanka, another victuals diplomat, would take up the field. Zigo smiled approvingly, his one remaining eye sparkling goodwill at her.

Because of their jobs outside the Ghetto, Hanka and Manek were artists of the quick barter and regularly tracked down fresh eggs, rare fruit, chocolate, and occasionally meat from underground connections across the river. The tuber transaction was complete when Hanka would meet Zigo on a quiet corner at the interior wire fence and he would hand her a gem—a sack of exquisite carrots and fresh apples in exchange for his final payment. Even these became currency. We would conserve some and buy other goods with the remainder.

❦

My father is perched on a ladder with half his body well up into the hidden food space above our kitchen ceiling. Israel Horowitz stands below him, writing up an inventory recited by Papa.

Tadek and I were at the table making crayon drawings, the result of Pani Ester reading to us from a child's edition of *Macbeth* the day before. We had relished the gruesome witches' brew and I'd begged our teacher to let me read it aloud, *"Maw and gulf of the ravened salt sea shark, root of something digged in the dark…"* I recited badly and stopped at the freakish line…*"Liver of blaspheming Jew…"*

Now I had Macbeth's head on a stick, and several pages of badly drawn ghosts and the magical dagger that floated in the air (a scene I thought to repeat by suspending a knife over the tiles that barely missed Tadek's foot when it fell). However, our sketching in the kitchen was a chance to listen in to the two fathers rather than study.

"One dozen cans of peaches, five boxes of tea, the large size," dictates Papa. "Six cans of corned beef, Mala's preserved tomatoes, around five jars or so."

"How about the salt and coffee, Leon, and the powdered eggs?" asks Israel.

"If we're careful, we might have enough for three weeks or more."

Papa comes down off the ladder and pulls Tadek's father into the Horowitz's quarters, where they argue like two grocers going out of business. Slivers of their conversation reach us, its pitch hoisted by concern and anxiety.

"We'll make smaller meals," I hear my father say.

"Weigh everything out very carefully, so everyone goes on a diet," Israel agrees.

"Surely not the kids?" Papa queries. "You can't stop children from growing."

Papa suddenly glances our way and hurriedly closes the door to the room. I hear more frantic debate about how the rations are diminishing.

"What happens when there's nothing left?" asks Israel. "The food from the depot would poison a rhino. Look around you, Leon. One can always tell who's living off that dreck; their faces see the grave coming closer every day. If we stay here, there'll be no good end. The situation gets worse by the minute."

"Izzy, we'll manage somehow," says my father.

"Leon, you can't rely forever on men like Pinski and Kousevetski, and we shouldn't let Manek and Hanka keep taking chances—luck is a fickle thing, and they're certainly draining their well of it. There'll come a day when the food connection is an informer, when the meeting in the alley has them facing down their executioner!"

"I've spoken with my older children about it," says Papa. "I don't like it either and have tried to forbid them from being so reckless, but in their situation subversion becomes a fire in the blood; it makes young people feel they're living for something. So they're fighting and conniving instead of studying and falling in love."

Tadek and I creep from the kitchen table and put our ears to the door. Forget about the witches on the heath, we're waiting for the utterances of the fathers to chart our destinies to new frontiers. Israel, as was his habit will have his hands hooked into his suspenders, waltzing his speculations up and down the bare floorboards. I hear the beat of his shoes ahead of his reasoning. "And, Leon, too many favors from your OD relatives aren't good either, it draws the wrong kind of attention."

My father counters, "Izzy, they give us an edge—for now. I don't believe the world will just leave us here. According to Cyla's radio, it's only a matter of time until Eisenhower and Churchill sweep these Krauts into hell. Look at how the Brits flattened Cologne in a few hours and the Americans are already in England. We'll live to see Eisenhower cross the Vistula. Think of it, Izzy, the streets will be a river of dollars, every lost business in the city will be riding home on U.S. war loans."

Tadek taps my shoulder and asks, "Romek? Is it true the Americans are coming to Krakow?"

"If Papa says so, it is so," I say.

"Well," whispers Tadek, "can he get the Yanks to bring us stuff?"

"What kind of stuff?"

"We'd like a big car with fenders like fish fins and silver teeth in the front. My dad will pay for it. We'll also need some of the brown soda pop, the one with the red letters that blonde girls in the magazines drink, their soldiers get it for free."

"Tadek? Shut-up. Your arse is falling out of your mouth."

"You shush, piss-face! They might hear us."

His father is arguing back. "Leon, you're killing us with your optimism. We should try and get away from here, get out, now!"

"And go where?" argues Papa. "You think we can all stroll through the Ghetto gates and tell the guards we'll be back after they lose the war? Should we walk the highways of Poland with so many kids? The roads are infested with more military than the country has fleas."

"Switzerland!" Israel suddenly blurts out. "The Italian Alps! Combine what money we have and buy our way there."

A taut silence ensues when I know my father will take a long intake of breath because he's weighing every word. Then he speaks again, his voice full of gentle coaxing. "Izzy, my good friend, the Alps are far away, and too much risk for all that distance. It would take a mountain of money for Pinski or the partisans to get us there, and no one is starving yet. Don't worry so much. Are we not resourceful? Are we not capable people? So we may have a problem, but we'll find a way to make it right."

Tadek stares over at me, his fingers bright orange from giving Macbeth flaming hair. "Romek, where's Switzerland?" he asks.

"I don't know, but Mama says they make a lot of chocolate there."

Betrayals

Jew-on-Jew abuse and exploitation was not unknown in the Ghetto. As my Papa said, the war divided the hearts of men into those who would generously share their last crust with another and those who would just as easily steal your final breath. It took considerable bouts of eavesdropping on the four parents and several weeks to piece together a heinous crime that I wished I'd never discovered. Initially, it would touch our family from a distance because of Aunt Cyla's seamstress, Ewa Urbanowicz.

My parents had once known the Weingartens, a cultured family, wealthy enough to buy their way out of Poland. They gave thousands of zlotys to Ewa's cousin, an OD named Feigel Birkner, who smuggled them away from the Ghetto hidden in the false bed of a truck. They emerged to ride in the fresh air once they were well clear of Krakow. The Weingarten mother, Beile, a loyal customer of Aunt Cyla's, had the family dress in their well-made summer outfits to bear the heat, as if they were just taking a leisurely trip into the countryside. She and her husband, Witek, along with their two teenagers (a daughter, Czesia and their son, Herschel), smiled and waved as the truck sped past local farmers working their smallholding plots, ringed by marigolds to deter hornworms that would devour their crops.

The warm summer air was honeyed with anticipation. No detail had been left to chance: doctored passports, forged transit visas, money and jewelry well hidden, nothing to betray them on their way to Gdansk and to the boat that would ferry them across the Baltic straits to neutral Sweden. The Weingartens had kissed their elderly parents goodbye on a Sunday morning, with the pretence that they were taking their children to the Jewish Community Hospital to be deloused.

Beile resolved that one made certain choices to win this blessed day. Besides, her ancient parents and in-laws were not likely to thrive long under the current conditions. It was time to preserve her nestlings for the future and go where their pre-war entitlements could be reassumed. As Swedish citizens, with a healthy bank account in Stockholm, they would enter the most illustrious of company. As the truck sped along narrow rural highways, she put on the hat that Aunt Cyla had made for her just the week before, a delicate lilac concoction with a stiffened scalloped brim.

Around late afternoon, not far off their route to Bydgoszcz, Feigel pulled the truck over to a deserted farmhouse, left to him by his brother, so he said. They could rest a while and have a late lunch. He had brought a picnic basket filled with delicacies that such a fine family would have dined on before the war. Wouldn't they like to come in? Everyone could sit at the dining table and enjoy the meal.

The Weingartens eagerly entered a ruin.

The roof had collapsed leaving the living room, devoid of furniture, strewn with debris and open to the skies. Weeds forcing their way up through the tiles gave evidence that the home had long been abandoned. In the sliver of time it took the family to realize that the promise of gourmet dining was also false, Feigel shot Witek Weingarten in the back of the head. Always wise to take the older males out first. Thirteen-year old Herschel, deafened and shocked by the blast, thought his father had only fainted and cried loudly for Witek to get up. "Papa! Are you ill? Papa? Please, get off the floor!"

Not fully understanding the sharp jaws they were in, he bent down to his dead parent, making it easier for his executioner to push the barrel into his glossy black hair. Feigel never liked his clients to suffer long. A swift shout from the gun and Herschel fell embracing his father. Beile came wailing and kneeling between husband and son, checking pulses back and forth, and wrapping the spouting wound in Herschel's head with her chiffon scarf. Pretty Czesia was screaming unceasingly a hollering that sent nesting birds racketing up out of the decaying thatch. Feigel was hesitant, too bad; the daughter was beginning to bloom nicely. He came close to calm her but she was a quivering pillar of unending noise. He put the gun against the bodice of her pink linen dress and fired.

Beile, now splintered into disbelief, staggered around the decrepit room, pointing wordlessly to each of her dead. She and Feigel made several turns together in a tight silence broken only by a light wind in the roof timbers. The betrayer was so fascinated by her iron quiet, by her lack of expression, giving no more words to outrage that he waited to fire again. Then she was on him, gripping his head with a tiger's strength, tearing at his face with her manicured fingernails. It seemed to him that they fought endlessly all over the desolate room, skidding in the blood of the slain. She knocked him down with powerful blow. Her warring grip on his throat was beginning to terrify him; there was no give in the bitch at all. Feigel fired the gun but his aim went wide, blowing a finial off the fireplace. His next shot finally stilled Beile, and she fell away from him to die upright on a wooden bench.

He pulled the bodies out to the well and sent them down it. He ripped the padded interior covers from their suitcases to find the money and their valuables. Their passports and the transit passes he'd purchased from Jaroslaw Graczewski, bearing the forged signature of Dieter Schoenholz, he burned in the fireplace along with his stained clothes. Naked and feeling lightheaded, the OD sluiced his bloody footprints away with several buckets of water from the outside pump, and washed himself down.

He reentered the house and took Witek Weingarten's second suit to wear along with a silk tie and an expensive handmade shirt. The dead man's shoes didn't fit him so he made do with his own damp boots. As he dressed, Feigel admired himself in one of the few windows in the cottage that remained whole. The suit settled well across his shoulders. In the cobwebbed reflection he suddenly detected a subtle disruption in the thickening quiet. There was no face but his in the windowpane, gilded by the fading day, yet they were not gone. It seemed the tiles and walls were coated with their latent presence. The wind was fingering through the thatch in a slow sigh. Feigel saw how tight his jaw had become, he was afraid of the gradually darkening sky, of the lonely walk to the truck in the driveway.

He gathered up the gold watches, the money and the hand-embroidered pouches that sheltered cabochon emeralds, rare brooches and necklaces plus several glittering unset diamonds. The elegant garments of the women he packed carefully to save them for his cousin, Ewa Urbanowicz, hoping he would one day persuade her to feed the voluptuous hunger she always induced in him.

He held up a cocktail dress of rich lilac chiffon ribbed with silver threads, the late evening sun provoking its brilliant iridescence, the straps and bodice insert embossed with black velvet appliqué. Feigel swung it around as if was full of woman and tucked his hands inside the velvet bodice cups. He caressed the lining and, out of the awesome sting of his desire, saw Ewa rise up, a naked Venus in a shell of swirling lilac. She would wear it well, along with the mauve hat Beile had dropped into the Rose of Sharon bush that still bloomed beside the decaying front door.

Fredek Lempl, a trusted runner for Boris Pinski, was a well-recognized face with the German guards at the Ghetto checkpoints. To ensure that his business was protected from intrusion, Pinski slyly made it known to the Ghetto's commander, Wilhelm Kunde, that no favor was too impossible for a fellow Christian, that there was no resource, gift or luxury that existed under heaven that was beyond the reach of the black marketer.

Pinski kept Lempl hopping; his sleek green Adler was seen driving all over the Ghetto, collecting favor money for extra food and delivering a range of quality goods offered to inmates who could still afford the short-term comfort of eating well – for now.

As for Pinski's military clients, Lempel taxied in crates of expensive champagne, excellent foie gras he passed off as the French variety (but prepared from the equally inflated livers of murdered geese by two grandmothers in Czestochowa), aromatic cigars, and vintage cognac riskily diverted from the Schoenholtz's cellar by the light-fingered Jaroslaw to Kunde's headquarters on the Plac Zgody.

The deliverer also had a provisions drop at the Zucker Synagogue and a loyal middleman in its keeper, Rabbi Efroim Geller. Services had long been banned and the temple ransacked of its menorahs, pews, and cantor's chairs. The *Aron HaKodesh*, (the Holy Ark) was empty of its rare Torah scrolls, now under the discreet protection of the Eagle Pharmacy, still wearing their golden shields and regal mantles. The synagogue was a bare stone tract but far from being depleted of spirit.

Rabbi Geller would sweep the marble floors every morning, happy to be alone, no longer distressed for the lost fixtures and the ritual textiles. He would gaze with pleasure at the soaring vaulted roof and the leaves of Eden hand carved in ash wood that sprouted along the screen of the women's gallery. Visits by Lempl prompted him to thank G-d for Pinski and conceal innumerable jars of pickled herring, bottled fruits and smoked lox wrapped in cedar bark, in a spacious recess beneath the altar of the Ark. Cash-paying customers would drift in a few at a time, make hasty reverence to their Maker and meet the Rabbi behind the Bimah. Whenever Hanka or Manek made mention they were going to the Zucker temple, Tadek and I knew that some fabulous treat was in the offing.

On one of his busy rounds, Fredek Lempl stopped at our building, so well dressed that the tenants thought him a plain-clothes Gestapo strongman looking to fry us on the brazier of interrogation. He pounded down our corridor and I heard him loudly demand if a Roman Ferber lived here? Thankfully, both my parents were home and Papa asked my mother to hide Tadek and me in the closet at once.

"We may have to open the door to him," I hear my father say calmly. "And hope that Arnold or Samek can fix the outcome. He must have made a mistake in the name, maybe it's me he wants?"

Tadek and I have wedged ourselves into the closet crammed to capacity with the entire wardrobe of my family. Israel and Manek had raised the floor up to be one of several crude safes constructed throughout the apartment to hide small valuables and family documents. I gag from the gas of mothballs, dresses long impressed with Mama's cologne, fried lard, and the humid flavors arising from wool overcoats that haven't been cleaned in many a year.

"Guess what I am?" mouths Tadek, awakening the genie of his so-called invisibility, believing he could take on the texture of my father's striped suit. The insistent knock resonates from the kitchen and I hear my name called again.

"Forget it, we can't make it work this time," I whisper. "We just have to stay quiet and hope the guy will leave soon."

We hear our front door open and my father offer brave pleasantries to the visitor who replies in civil tones that he had come to see an exceptional boy who lived here. My mother joins in, speaking in what I called her 'parlor' voice she used for special occasions. In the next instant, she is calling out joyously that it was safe to show our faces in the kitchen.

Fredek Lempl sits by the stove with a long wooden box resting on his knees. He is a small, neatly groomed man, handsome in features despite the dense web of minute broken veins that mapped the undersurface of his skin. He exudes immense goodwill and was Pinski's public face because of his talent for exalting any listener, without flattery, to feel that they were the most important person he'd ever met. (His fear of Boris also made him scrupulously honest.)

Lempl rises from his chair when I enter, gives me a short bow and shakes my hand. He sets the box down on the kitchen table with great care, tapping

Betrayals

it firmly and declared, "This is to be presented personally to a young man called Roman Ferber. Might that name belong to the face I'm addressing?"

I nod shyly. Tadek looks equally stunned but nudges me forward. The box, as Manek would explain to me later, was constructed of walnut heartwood, its knots and curly grains polished to an auburn patina. I run my fingers over its upper lid, leaving greasy fingerprints on the carved image of an urn reversed from which a stream of inlaid stars flowed. My parents keep wheeling their smiling gaze between each other and me, my mother's eyes tearing up.

"Open it, Romek," she urges, "it's a present from Pan Pinski, with his best regards."

I feel embarrassed and feel like weeping too. Gifts were from the normal times, from the safe days of another life. We had become outlanders now, edgy conniving people, thinly varnished with the conceits that Torah verses, bartering vegetables from a one-eyed man, and a few lessons from spinsterish teachers, somehow kept us in the stream of the civilized world —a territory we could no longer access. Who offers gifts to such ragged aliens without arousing shame and foreboding that something excellent conferred will eventually exact a terrible price? There had been no presents of any kind given across my family and friends since our troubles began, save for the shared wooden horse and the chocolate bar I had received for evading the grasp of the Rattenfänger Taubenschlag.

I unlatch the metal clasp of the box and raise the lid. What lay within immediately scatters the demons of my bleakness. On a bed of padded red satin rests a gleaming brass telescope with an equally shining tripod at its side. It is of medium size: compact, an easy weight for small hands, and is of such perfection I am afraid to touch it. No one in the kitchen speaks for the longest time, mesmerized by the aura of bright rays emanating from the glowing instrument.

Lempl smiles. "Is it to your liking, little prince?" he asks kindly. He helps me raise it from the box and mount it on the tripod, the legs of which could extend quite high and in several directions. He shows me how to adjust the eyepiece and to manipulate its many settings. "This is a Zeiss reflecting telescope, Romek, one of the finest," Lempl says. "It uses a concave mirror to collect and focus light on a second mirror that in turn reflects very bright images and relays them to the eyepiece."

I put my eye to the glass and my mother's chin filled the lens, detailing minor wrinkles as deep as canyons, right down to the fine crevices of thickened lipstick along her mouth. Tadek was saying, "It's only four hours until it gets dark. Please, Romek, will you let me look through it too?"

The largess of the gift makes me swell with generosity; it is the finest present ever bestowed on me in my short life. I put my arm around Tadek's shoulder and answer, "Sure. We'll be scientists together, discover new planets, sell them to the Germans and move everyone to the Alps. Pani Lydia will help us."

My father pumps Fredek Lempl's hand and pats his shoulder, pressing upon him the family's towering gratitude for Pinski's kindness. My mother is already badgering me that the 'thank-you' letter must be written and hand delivered at once. Lempl dismisses her notion politely and warns Papa in calm tones that the telescope should be well hidden when not in use lest any investigating platoon finding it assumes it's being used for spying and sabotage. He ruffles my hair and says good afternoon to us with a note of emotion in his voice, Christian enough to absorb the glow in being the herald of such delight.

Tadek picks up the telescope's instructional manual and wails that it is all in German and how are we expected to manage our planetary properties if the only guide to our equipment was written by the Krauts! My mother gently shushes him, sits us both down at the table, takes a pen and a sheet of paper and begins to translate the basic points into Polish.

There is more fuss and awe when Hanka, Manek and the Horowitz parents arrive home to see the shining object of my deepest cravings set up on the windowsill in our quarters. Manek thinks it's also suitable for peering down the street to see any action arising from Gate One. Mama too agrees that something so expensive would have to be hidden from any visitors, with the exception of the Rosenfeld sisters. However, everyone concurs that it was a crown jewel of a gift, and would be an excellent source of fascination and entertainment for the boys. I can't wait to show it off to Pani Lydia who, I am convinced, will now transform me with her teachings into an astronomical genius.

When the night finally settles on us, both families become quite festive at the prospect of surveying the stars. Mama makes us kids some ersatz lemonade while the grownups sip careful measures of schnapps from coffee cups. It would be only fair, my father declares, to allow everyone turns at gazing through the lens.

My brother angles the scope nearly vertical to the sky then lifts me onto a chair, saying that I get to be the first explorer. I put my eye to the glass while Manek turns the focus. Half a pastel moon appears above the darkened streets. The treetops disappear and I track my gaze over lunar highlands and shadowy craters. Tadek keeps asking me are there people? Do you see any people? His sister, Gizia, flicks the back of his head with her fingers, "Idiota! How could there be people? You think there's a train that stops there?"

My mother squeals in surprise when she gazes at the firmament, claiming she can see an immense swirl of red fog. Could it be a bomb? You never know, these Germans are everywhere. We all have to look in this same corner of heaven. No, Mama, there's no Luftwaffe buzzing around Venus, assures my father—just star clusters so dense they appeared as fiery light-filled blizzards. Tadek and I spend so much time gawking at the arcing moon

Betrayals

that when finally exhausted and ordered to bed, we have to be lifted into our quilts.

The last thing I feel before my eyes close is that for the first time in many months I am intensely happy.

✺

The forced labor pattern in the Ghetto runs a six day-week with very long hours for all workers possessing a *Blauschein* (the blue work permit). However, on one of the rare rest days (which were never maintained on any regular basis), my father convenes a religious discussion on a warm June afternoon when we can invite a little company and still have a safe margin for guests to return home well before the curfew. The Rosenfeld sisters arrive, primed to debate with a nervous young Rabbi named Avraham Bronstein, who follows minutes behind them up the stairs. Mama dips into her hidden store of good black tea and Luisia Horowitz bakes. I whine about wanting to show off my Zeiss telescope to Lydia but my father reprimands me to keep my wants to myself.

"Now, Romek," whispers Papa, leaning me against his knee, "I want you listen carefully to Rebbe Bronstein, he's a renowned scholar on the teachings of the great *Tzaddikim* (holy men)."

I gaze beyond my father to the tall, thin-limbed man standing in the doorway, dressed in a long black gabardine with wire-frame glasses that had a cracked right lens. He steps into our kitchen with the hesitant gait of a wading bird. It quickly becomes apparent that the Rabbi was not made to be a *magid* (a preacher). He greets Papa in a clipped, dry manner, nodded curtly to everyone else, and retired to perch on the windowsill. The presence of women, especially the keen stares of the cute Horowitz sisters, seems to make him intensely uncomfortable.

Wicked Hanka let her hand brush his as she gives him a glass of tea, causing the Rebbe to startle and retreat from her. Tadek badgers him if it was true that famous Rabbis of the Kabbalah were able to perform the miracle of invisibility?

Bronstein stares at the two of us through his fractured eyewear with the tamped impatience of one regarding the feeble minded. Pani Lydia tries to excuse our fantastical questioning. "These boys have a rich imagination," she intones, "which we don't discourage but strive to direct to more scientific inquiry."

The Rebbe, who had previously heard of our kitchen Cheder, appears to regard her coldly. Her offence to him is not just her assured words, but that this woman, with suspect ideas on the structure of nature, should be charged with the education of young boys. He finally answers us in a reedy, deadened voice, "A person unseen is one who can make mischief against others. The supernatural deeds of the Rabbis would not extend to such evils. Miracles may be granted to the deserving, although too many of them would denote a distortion in the fabric of the universe."

"Couldn't we just have one?" I ask, sensing from his watery blue eyes that our childish petition was no more than a nail in his backside. My heart droops because the happy enthusiasm of this rare afternoon with Luisia's ginger cakes, relaxed smiling parents and our beloved teachers, is about to expire in the dim aura of this sour-faced churl. Everyone takes their seats while Tadek and I sit on pillows by the stove, away from the glare of the begrudger, where we could whisper foolishness to each other.

"According to Dov Ber ben Avraham of Mezritch," Bronstein begins, "it was the task of a man's life to perceive the spiritual dimensions of the material world."

It is the only sentence he would give out because at that very moment I hear the familiar sound of my brother pounding up the stairs at racing speed. His steps coding a threat. My mother instinctively jumps up and shouts to Tadek and me, "Get ready to leave!"

My brother erupts into our kitchen, exclaiming to everyone, "There's a huge sweep coming from Gates Three and Four! You can't move down Krakusa!"

"Who do they want?" my father demands, leaping to his feet.

"Families who've been denied the *Blauschein* (blue work permit) but also other categories. It's no longer an OD matter. The Gestapo has a new registration committee. I saw them turning away people with good skills already on work assignments. It makes no sense."

"You see, Leon, nothing is assured." Israel Horowitz is saying. "The game shifts all the time."

"But our blue cards are OK, so what's to worry about?" asks Hanka.

Manek explains that the sweep is an excuse to reduce the Ghetto numbers yet again.

The end of his sentence is drowned by the crack of distant gunfire. He feverishly gathers up coats for my sister and me and a heavy crowbar. "It's more than just the labor cards," he's saying, "they're clearing out entire buildings and making selections, especially kids and old folks. You should see what's out there! Not just the usual militia but Ukrainians, German and Polish police, ODs, and some new units from the Waffen-SS—all with heavy hardware. We have to split up, Papa and maybe let them come into an empty apartment."

My father nods soberly. He knows not all of us can hide upstairs in the secret attic space.

"Hanka and Romek, come, I have a place for us to go," Manek orders.

My mother takes down the emergency rations bag that hung on the door hook, a canvas sack that was checked every day for candles, bread, some canned food and water bottles.

"Where will Papa and Mama stay?" I ask as the adults whirled around me.

Betrayals

"In the attic," my father says. He pulls me into my coat and I see his hands are trembling badly as he fastens the buttons. Everyone had ignored the athletic departure of Rebbe Bronstein, who, by time I am being dragged out of the apartment by my sister, had already fled. The Rosenfeld sisters wish us a rapid blessing and leave too for the safety of our attic. I don't want to go at all and set off a terrific fuss.

"Tadek?" I cry, struggling out of Hanka's clasp. "Tadek, come with us! We'll take the telescope."

"You'll see each other later, Romek," soothes his father, who rapidly mounts the stairs with my friend, his two sisters and Luisia. Tadek stares back at me and shrugs as he is towed away to the upper gloom.

"No! No!" I yell and cling to the banister rail with a death grip. "I'm not leaving without Tadek and my Zeiss!"

Hanka slaps my wrists hard several times. "Stupid little moron! Get moving or we'll dump you here!" she snarls.

I start sobbing in anger and hang on even harder above the wail of sirens in the streets, shouts, yells, and the crunching roll of armored vehicles. Papa comes running out onto the landing pleading loudly, "Dear G-d! Romek, you must leave with them, now!"

My mother gently plucks my hands off the banister, coaxing me to go.

"Let me get him, Mama," says my brother, cutting in between us. "Come. Hold on to me, Romek," he says gently. "I'm going to take you somewhere safe."

He lifts me up and sweeps me out of the apartment.

11

Blood Will Have Blood

IN AN INSTANT THE THREE OF US ARE DOWN THE STAIRS and out on the sidewalk, darting through terrible shouts and hundreds of people running. I see a woman fall heavily and two men behind tread along her back. A couple races along with a line of many children behind them, the youngest hollering pitifully. A terrified girl with a baby in her arms turns in the middle of this raving human stream calling, "Jakob, where are you, Jakob?"

A wiry old man overtakes us. I see him sweating and crying hoarsely. He drops down on a stoop and begs his two sons to leave him there. They obey without protest. We hurtle past a boy's bloody form face down in a shop doorway, his head pillowed on his left arm. Behind the glass of the door, a woman gawks back at us but ignores him.

I glance back down the street at the immense torrent of people behind us; rapid gunfire overhead swerves their direction blindly. Several tanks and military jeeps with mounted machine guns pursue them. They lumber dinosaur-like, followed by marching rows of Polish police and heavily armed soldiers, driving the terrified herd ever forward to the Ghetto's main gate. We halt to a hurried walk in the thick of the mass.

"Manek, where to now?" Hanka yells.

"The Wegierska Street sewer! We have to get out of this crowd," my brother orders.

We break for it and dash into the entrance of a building connecting to a spacious courtyard where people have left in such haste I see, through the open windows of a kitchen, chairs overturned, and a table set for lunch intact with steam still rising from a bowl of potatoes. An abandoned dog by the stove cowers away from us in sorrow. We exit back into the clamoring streets and run frantically for several blocks only to hear the tanks getting closer. My legs feel boneless. I can't keep up. My brother and sister are twin engines of speed; they lift my heels off the ground in their towing.

An alley leads us to the junction of Josefinska and Wegierska where Szymon Weintraub, a close friend of my brother, beckons and waits above an open manhole in the sidewalk, its metal ladder visible. Hanka descends it at once; Manek lowers me down into her arms. He and Syzmon follow, hauling the heavy metal cover into place with Manek's crowbar. My legs ache, my eyes are salted and stinging. The rumble of the tanks thunder overhead and the shouts eventually grow distant.

Blood Will Have Blood

We are in total darkness, a blackness made denser by dripping water and the horrendous stench of human waste. Far away, I hear the tidal swish of the river.

"You must move everyone further in," says Szymon to Manek.

My brother rustles around in the rations bag, "First we need to light the way."

A match flares, candles are lit and he hands one to each of us.

"Where are we going, Manek?" I ask him. He grins and ruffles my hair.

"To hunt for alligators," he replies.

"It stinks in here!" I complain.

"It's a luxury compared to up top," says Hanka softly. "Romek, I'm sorry I slapped you. Let's be friends, huh? We're going to be down here awhile."

She puts her arm around my shoulder and we all start inching forward along a narrow brick track just above the foul rivulet.

"About three hundred meters in," advises Syzmon, "will take you to where the conduit branches off in two directions. Use neither. There's a sort of corner bank there where you can sit down. Don't wander about. You never know who else is camped down here. Stay away from the storm drains. Limpet mines are hidden by the grilles and gunboats wait on the river for anyone who survives the big bang. I'll let you know when it's safe to come out."

The two men shake hands and we watch as Szymon's candle flame shrinks down into the gloom and his footsteps fade away.

It takes us a while to reach the sewer's junction. There is just enough room on the tiled walkway for Manek and Hanka to sit with me huddled against my sister's knee. From the opposite bank of the sewage flow, I hear a faint rustle, like the sweep of a woman's long dress crossing a carpet, an unpleasant sibilance that comes and goes.

"Are there really alligators in the water?" I nervously ask my brother.

I press into him because there are odd motions in the gloom. A splash hits the sewage, then another. Hanka raises her candle and I see the water-slicked heads of several huge rats swimming like Olympians against the stinking surge. We both cry out, aghast, as her light shockingly reveals hundreds of their tribe, parading along the water pipes directly above us! They are swift and everywhere at once, their eyes glinting with malicious intent. Manek takes the crowbar from underneath his jacket and strikes it repeatedly on the bricks. The noise resonates down the tunnels and the rodent squadron turns as one squeaking body and take off into the shadows.

Hanka's candle shakes but her voice is firm. "Romek, remember when we break out the food, you cannot spill crumbs anywhere."

"It's OK, I'm not hungry," I assure her.

✤

On the stage of mayhem above us, members of the Jewish Police in my family are all being called to active duty, my Uncle Arnold among them. He is forced to give block-by-block residency reports to Hauptsturmfuhrer (Captain) Walther Mueller (a mercurial protégé of Wilhelm Kunde, Commandant of the SS Special Units) on how many Jews could be arrested from each street while still leaving enough to maintain the labor force. (My uncle had previously prepared for him a detailed survey of the number of skilled workers in the Ghetto.)

However, this day's roundups mean that Arnold had to work directly with Mueller's unit and keep a count on the arrests and eliminations. As my uncle explained later to my father, he was able to access the schedule for the time our building was going to be searched. It was a hunt in which Arnold was compelled to make a big noise in the arrest of neighbors while leaving my parents and the Horowitz family undisturbed in the attic crawl space.

Mueller deploys over a hundred and fifty men in an assault line that ran laterally across the Ghetto from Gates Two, Three and Four. The troops search the streets in the immense forward drive toward Gate One, to either shoot or round up any escapees and stragglers who had avoided the first sweep. Feigel Birkner brings the Captain information that some eighteen families are hidden in the cellar of a house on Lwowska Street.

"Shall I march them out, Sir?" offers Feigel.

Mueller ignores him and orders his ordnance team to come forward. Why waste time? Clusters of model 24 stick grenades placed all along the lobby gets the job done. In a volcanic flash, the façade of the building drops away in a cloud of yellow brick dust to reveal all the rooms to the street, like a large open doll's house. A fiery column from the ignited gas supply finally explodes the house skyward. No cries are to be heard from beneath the burning stones.

✤

The river waters soften the boom from Lwowska and I come awake at the terse murmur of the after-blast vibrating through the sewer walls. Then there's just the lap and swirl of the fetid stream. The network of slimed corridors is considerable; one could walk the sewer for several kilometers and traverse the entire underbelly of Podgorze. I find the place full of ghostly sounds, solitary footsteps far away, and the faint drift of indiscernible voices. Manek says those in concealment down here try to avoid each other in case the face they meet in the gloom is that of a collaborator. He stirs at every noise, his awareness at the simmer. We have to limit our conversations to whispered necessities, Syzmon had advised, because, although the Germans were never keen to enter these arteries of waste for fear of disease, they would sometimes lower a listening device down the vertical wells to track fugitives.

Hanka pulls out a small writing pad from her jacket and from the time we sit down to rest, we pass notes back and forth in the candlelight. My clumsy scrawl repeats the question, "Talk now?"

Hanka's written reply, "Not until we say so or I'll feed you to the rats!"

Before he blows out the candles, Manek writes a single command, "Sleep!" I'm wide-awake and stare up into the darkness, guessing at what's buried in the twenty-five meters of brick and rock over me: old shells, dog and fish bones, sunken boat hulls, lost rings, coins, and washed-down garbage. I wonder if the sewer runs under our apartment house and imagine the three of us coming home up through the cellar drains.

As Uncle Arnold would later describe him to us, Captain Walther Mueller, young in his promotion (twenty-eight), was a farmer's son from upper Bavaria, whose earnest Catholic mother earmarked him for the priesthood. Although drawn to the rituals of the mass and the luminous mysteries of devotion, it was rumored by his gossipy adjutant that he had crept reluctantly through his few years as a temporarily professed in the Benedictine monastery of Andech.

Chafing under the rule of silence and the enforced celibacy, he abandoned his monk's cell to enlist in a brigade of the Waffen-SS (a militia known for their hellish ranks of former criminals, ex-Einsatzgruppen and Russian prisoners of war). Removed from the refined air of the monastic life and the gentle guidance of his confessor, Mueller buried beneath his military ferocity a key principle of Benedict's rule: that the daily choices one makes become the lodestar of a destiny.

I pull the thin blanket up to my chin and, despite the hard bricks beneath us; it seems I'm floating in this lavatory darkness. From the layers of earth and stone above us, I pick up the random vibration of what must be many vehicles. Manek whispers that, according to Syzmon's estimate, the numbers being held captive in the yard of the Optima factory must have reached four thousand. By now, my parents and all the Horowitz's should be face down on the attic boards, and in our apartment the carved box with my beautiful telescope lay well hidden behind the pipes under the sink, beneath the plumbing territory of the cockroaches.

In their forced entry, the soldiers would often feel deflated finding nobody home. "Bloody wily Jews, got out ahead of us, like vapors in the night." Uncle Arnold and the Polish police sergeant would argue about the dismal report they'd have to make, "No pick-up was possible at this address, the building is empty. We ripped out the wainscoting, broke down the closets. Could be a whole village behind the wallpaper, or more likely silver plate and hidden rations. We took whatever was of value, a little compensation for the unit's disappointment."

Above us on Czarnieskiego Street, Mueller's platoon score over fifty wayward Jews, many of them battered and disoriented from being hurled bodily down the stairs of their tenements. The Captain rails at Feigel Birkner and does the very thing German military edicts forbid. He puts a gun in the hand of a Jew and orders the OD and two of his Waffen sharpshooters to get busy!

Feigel, skilled at such eliminations, is all rote obedience. He walks down the line of unfortunates, putting the handgun to his neighbor's heads, including his own uncle and cousin. Just before the last bodies fall, a woman turns and faces her executioners to demand, "I want to look at the ugly shit that's going to have my life! I want to take that face to hell with me, so which one of you pricks is it going to be?"

Her superb insolence fells a dazzling blow on Feigel's efficiency and momentarily unnerves him. This is not how it's supposed to go. Her words loose a flood of defiance in her sisters who grab her by the hand and the five women take off down the street. Mueller himself gives chase, shooting them in the back but is amazed when the sassy girl rises up, gushing red from her wounds. She manages to stand for thirty seconds to say, "You!" before the pavement claims her.

At one point in the blackness of the sewer, I panic to see over the arc of Hanka's elbow a cluster of red dots, like dancing red eyes across the foul stream, the fig odor of cigarette smoke following on. A match is struck and quickly extinguished but in the few seconds of the flame, I glimpse a line of dark figures moving along the opposite bank of the cesspool. I hear the clatter of a rifle butt hit against the tiles. These human steps have a light military beat to them but these striders are not Germans. Manek's palm finds my mouth and covers it hard; its urgent press signals that we are to remain as still as the dead.

Up top, the gates of the Optima factory are so congested with the delivery of hundreds of captives that the line to enter stretches all the way down the street. A cordon of soldiers urges them along. The people shuffle forward eagerly, thinking that safety awaits them inside. If normalcy had been the order of the day, the queue would have appeared to any unsuspecting onlooker as citizens patiently waiting for an outdoor festival to commence.

Mueller and his hounds ride by in open jeeps. It occurs to the fallen novice that the subdued orderly column is ripe for the picking. Save the Reich's budget on ferrying Jews to all points under heaven. The vehicles halt and many of the families drop flat to the sidewalk because the Captain and his machine guns are busy trimming away a hundred or more people from the end of the line.

Uncle Arnold is at the factory gates with his lists and is astonished at the gunplay. The duty guards are equally flummoxed, having received orders to arrest but not to shoot. A senior Gestapo officer in the guardhouse is utterly incensed and shouts a protest. He comes roaring along the gutter, by the fractured prone mass, in the sidecar of a motorcycle, weaving among and over the wounded, yelling at Mueller to call off his firepower immediately because he has to report the total number of prisoners to the SS General of Transports. "How dare you screw around with my quota, you crazy G-d-damned bandit!" The officer kicks hard at a dying man and screeches, "Do you think I can put rotting meat aboard the trains? Take that excrement you call a detail and bring me back live bodies to make up the shipment or I'll be seeing you in Kunde's office!"

It's been several hours since we entered this chamber of cess. Manek and Hanka wake up and, although we can burn a candle for a short while, we still have to write notes to each other and maintain silence. I hand a dispatch to Manek that I have to pee badly. He scribes back that I've come to the right place. Hanka walks me a little way down the brick path and I make against the wall. I turn my back to her when she needs to go. As I wait for her to finish, I see a candle beam moving way down at the far end of the junction. The light tremors for a moment, a dark figure turns, and then is gone.

Riding the surface of our refuge, Captain Mueller and his men roll down Limanowskiego Street still shooting stray Jews as they run. Uncle Arnold, riding in the open truck behind them, pulls his cap over his eyes to avoid the sight, numb with shame. The radio in the Captain's jeep crackles with news from his forward search team. "Yes, there are more of them, Sir. Multitudes like lice, like ants. We've emptied attics and cellars for over five hundred square meters. We have about four hundred and fifty prisoners lined up by the Judenrat office. What's the order, Captain, Sir?"

Mueller curses the dolt subordinate over the erratic frequency. "What did you have in mind, Sergeant, taking them on a bloody picnic?"

"We can't shoot them all, Sir? Cause too much bedlam; they might make a run for it. There's just me and a dozen others left to cover them. The rest of our unit is investigating the storm drains along the perimeter. Permission to wait until the rest of the platoon gets here, Sir?"

Mueller angrily snaps off the radio and orders his adjutant to halt the jeep. His aide asks him if he'd like a fresh uniform to be fetched from the barracks. His blood-soaked outfit might give the enemy the idea that he's wounded. The Captain calls him a prissy old tart, afraid of his own shadow. "Do you see any Jewish warriors here? This is a street-cleaning operation, not a battlefield."

He strides off, intent on wiping out the infestation at the Judenrat and to stock up on live replacements for that whining whore of an officer looking to fill his transport quotas.

❋

We have been under streets now for almost seven hours. I try to eat a cheese sandwich with one eye watching out for the rodent swimmers but the rank odor of the place seeps into the bread on my tongue. I can taste the disgusting essence, my stomach spasms and I suddenly vomit all over the blankets we're sitting on. Manek whispers to me hastily that it's OK. He wipes my chin and pours some cold sweet tea down my throat. The malodorous jailing dark, the weird unseen presences, the marauding rats that threaten to bite, the drenching toilet stink that I'll never be free of, and now my wet soiled shirt, all cause me to erupt into a deafening squall of tears.

"I want to go home!" I wail. "Can't we get out of here, please?"

Hanka shushes me, dabs at my tears, kisses my wet cheeks and writes on her pad, "Not yet, Romek, just a little while longer. Please, you must stay quiet."

But I will not be comforted! I sob and howl louder than any professional mourner. My cries are duplicated as the echoed chorus of a hundred miserable kids down the winding tiled corridors, with enough piercing high notes to have attracted the attention of every collaborator from here to Warsaw. What stops my blubbering cold is the distant breaking-glass shriek of a woman's voice, "Shut that brat up or drown him in the shit because there are respectable people down here trying to get some sleep!"

Now, I'm ashamed and more wretched than ever. Hanka hugs me close and Manek decides to speak. "Come on and walk with me, Romeczku," he coaxes, "I'll tell you a story while Hanka watches out for the rats. We'll do some exploring, run a few ghosts off the premises."

❋

The aide to Captain Mueller signals to Uncle Arnold in the truck that his master is taking a short cut through an alley toward the Judenrat not far from Gate One. The Captain orders his men to fan out and he enters the alley alone. A barefoot child, no more than seven years old, emerges from a doorway directly across his path, dressed in a ragged man's jacket that comes down to its ankles. Beneath it, a filthy once-white shift, the sleeves of the coat hang foolishly, well below the kid's skinny arms. The young one is of an indeterminate gender, but possesses a challenging beauty, the face of a little magistrate framed in red curls. The child stands before him and eyes Walther Mueller quizzically, without any fear at all.

The Captain is amused at first, but the calm interrogatory gaze soon begins to nag at his bravado. He reasons to himself maybe the goblin before me is a mental deficient? There is so much tribal madness among these Semites, reaching back to their exile in the desert. It occurs to Mueller that the child is giving off a quiet aura of indifference to being killed, that destroying this small body would be even less grief to its nature than stealing its raiment from a coat hook.

"Who...are you, kinder?" asks the soldier.

The child doesn't answer but takes a step toward him, a small dirty hand extended. Mueller quickly retreats a few meters back. He is startled by a sudden prick of fear. The idea that the child might actually touch him is repellent. For the Captain asserts he is surrounded by practitioners of the blood libel, brewers of the occult, Rabbis who can draw diabolical offspring into existence from an ancient tree of words, from the darkness of the unmanifested. The young one and the man survey each other silently. It's this map of stains on my uniform, he thinks, that's so fascinating to this young one. This small golem is tracing their outline, how many names in every blotch. Can such things be measured? Whose lives do I wear today?

The child stares at him imperiously, fixed, resolute.

"What are you?" orders Mueller, reassuming his iron authority, irritated to be faced down by such a ludicrous opponent. The question causes his eyes to drift to the target sight of the freckled forehead. He unholsters his side pistol. The child does not run, nor flinch, nor plead for anything. Its stone gaze is too much, a weapon unto itself. There is nothing else to be done but shoot the immovable thing. Mueller fires once. The young one falls lightly as a sheet loosed from a clothesline by an easy wind. Out on the street, my uncle would later relate that he and the surprised German adjutant exchanged questioning glances and quickly pursued the bullet's clap.

The alley's walls enfold the Captain, who doesn't hear their concern if he's wounded or not. The three men freeze in an unearthly stillness. Mueller waits some lengthy minutes, unable to leave but doesn't know why, confounded and too uneasy now to step over the small corpse. Arnold and the adjutant see an alley that is empty except for the three of them and a laundered sheet lying crumpled in the gutter. Mueller shakes his head and backs away from them. He exits the lane from its southern end. Arnold marks his diffident hallucinatory gaze as he staggered to rejoin his men. They suddenly stopped their casual conversations of body counts at his look of stark surprise, at the mark of some internal fissure arising within and without him. "We're almost to the end of it, Sir. You need to take it easy."

He doesn't hear them because some wayward tide is coming in fast, flooding the narrow strictures of his soul, busily unbraiding his solidified might, opening a fearful softening in him—the likes of which he has never known.

Mueller and his platoon finally rest their killing weariness on the steps of St. Joseph's Church. Uncle Arnold reports with his lists naming who is now gone from the world and the numbers of thousands who are corralled, still breathing, in the Optima courtyard. The data is critical to Kunde's office. The adjutant asks Arnold to report his figures later but to stand by while he hands Mueller a glass of cognac and asks if he requires a medic. The Captain seems emptied out, an unanchored husk, afloat in some morass. Mueller waves the aide away.

In what would be his final letter home the day before, he had written, "Dear Mother, all we do is shoot Jews, day and night, as we might target crows bothering the corn, we bring them down. This is not work for a soldier."

He opens his uniform to find that their blood has soaked through his shirt to his skin. His chest is totally painted with them, a union of his own making. The alcohol stings as he tries to wash himself clean with it. His head throbs from the bark of the guns, his arms sore from raising the weapon he stills swings in his right hand. The bells of the church ring the evening Angelus, their threshing bellowing through his lungs. The Captain dare not go inside the place. He fears the Child will be there.

My uncle recalled that he and the soldiers waited patiently for their next orders, hesitant to approach him. Mueller stares beyond them and walks away to seek solitude in the tattered garden of the rectory, where even the marble saints are not bullet-free. Although he is on sanctified ground, he feels hollow, amazed that the habit of prayer has been completely excised from him. He can no longer detect his former reflex for it within the splintering disarray he has become. He slides his hand inside his stained shirt and is surprised to find the beat of his life is still allowed. It seems to him now such a wasted generosity.

There is a rustle in the overgrown shrubs. Mueller turns and sees nothing but senses the ardor of the One who waits. The sky teeters and the dried-up patchy lawn starts a slow spin beneath him. He hears the trees roar as they bend beneath the request. What are you? What…are…you? He finally becomes the question; it is his naming although he will never be able to withstand its relentless prosecution. There is a short mercy from the metal shaft of the pistol in his mouth and an unknowable deliverance in its firing.

※

Down in our dungeon of evil odors, Manek strolls with me along the slippery bank. I grin up at him through my swollen eyes, my hand in his, much comforted in my brother's unending talent for transforming any misery of mine into delight. We come to a halt because Hanka is gently calling to us. We turn back to see Syzmon by candlelight, smiling by her side and beckoning. The surface time is here! I start to run to them but Manek grabs me by my shirt, saying, "Slow down, little horse, before you take the crap bath."

Baby rodents skitter over my shoes. I don't mind them now. I'm going home to our apartment, to my parents, to Tadek and my prized telescope. We clamber up to the streets, to their resounding soaked-up losses, to the sweeping emptiness of the avenues with their cordite air, and the distant clamor from the church tower on the Rynek Podgorski announcing the night coming down.

We ride home hidden in the back of a towed farm wagon balanced on bus tires, a shuddering makeshift vehicle hooked-up to the battered car of Zigo Kousevetski, who had waited out the volatile predations in the streets to deliver a load of turnips to the rations depot. Uncle Arnold rides with us in the wagon too. Some rogue captain, he says, had been on the rant all day, hell-bent on filling up the burial carts. Manek looks nervous but Arnold tells him not to worry. The captain has been removed from his duties permanently.

There are hardly any street lamps operating along the main avenue, but I can see by the few that are lit through the slats of the turnip cart the faces of the public dead illuminated for a few seconds. They crowd the sidewalks. We pass by them in the gutters, along pavements, and in doorways, some with their eyes skyward in surprise at their lives so quickly slammed shut, others hunched in recoil against their wounds. Five girls lie face down, all their hands linked together. A passing wind flutters their hair. I glimpse a group of twenty or more by the closed shoe store on Benedykta Street, all stacked up neatly like cut timber, head to toe, the top logs composed of several kids about my age, the line of their small white hands palms out. My sister pulls me away gently, saying, "Romek, give them the respect of not looking."

Uncle Arnold ushers us into our building triumphantly, shouting "Malia, Leon! Your treasures are home and safe but they smell like a pigsty!"

My parents are standing at the top of the staircase to greet us, wreathed in smiles of relief and welcome. Our uncle declares his nerves are frayed from the day and he needs a drink. Papa urges him inside and to go open the bottle on the kitchen table. My mother is wearing a rubber apron and carrying armfuls of old painter's drop cloths that had once belonged to the decorating business of my grandfather, Arye Ferber. She pinches her nose in disgust, hurls the covers down the stairs, and orders us to strip off, make ourselves decent with them, and throw everything we were wearing into the basement. She and Luisia will soak our clothes later in a tub of carbolic soap.

"I'll kiss you all for returning after," she says warmly, and blows us kisses anyway. "You boys can sit there while Hanka comes in to bathe, then it's the two of you for the tub."

"You are a joy to my eyes and your smell is exquisite!" says my father in delight. He came hurrying down the stairs to hug Manek and me fiercely, rubbing our hair, laughing and kissing our faces and saying we were rose gardens of men, fragrant and blooming, and far blessed beyond our poor neighbors now lying in the streets with the life blown out of them. He tells how he and Mama are prepared for the marathon bathing about to commence in the kitchen, using every pot and basin in the place to boil hot water on the stove. My sister is already under the stairwell, struggling out of her filthy clothes.

She reappears, her dark hair loose, classically draped like statue in the paint-spattered sheet. My father strokes her cheek and says how pretty she looks in casual grime. He takes her arm and she goes flapping up the stairs, vents of sewer gas drifting after her. Manek and I strip off, cover our nakedness and wait on the landing outside the apartment.

Tadek sticks his grinning head through the door to stare at us. "Is it true that you took a canoe and went rowing through crap, through rats as big as dogs?" he asks.

Manek laughs and dares him to come outside to sit in our mists. Maybe he'd like a perfumed embrace?

The only washtub in our crowded apartment was a sturdy wooden rain barrel that served for cleaning both laundry and people. (Manek and my father had carried it home weeks ago from outside a disused tavern.) The item was leak-proof and wonderfully deep. Mama, my clean sister and all the Horowitz women had retired to our room to kibitz when my brother and I take turns in the barrel. The kitchen is now a jovial men-only space. Tadek is allowed to offer cigarettes to the adults. Israel Horowitz, my brother, Uncle Arnold and my father are all yammering on about the upheaval we'd just survived and blowing blue smoke for dramatic emphasis.

I'm cocooned in the tub of hot sudsy water, refusing to come out because the cleansing warmth around me feels like such a paradise and dissolves the terrors of the day. Tadek floats our shared wooden horse across the foam, and I sense that he's happy to please me because we are safely back together again. I make a mental note to inflate our adventures beneath the streets when I would frighten the pants off my good friend with elastic tales of the haunted sewer and red-eyed demons.

Papa rolls up his sleeves and sponges me off gently, lecturing that if this were the Mikvah, he would be rinsing my limbs with the crystal flow from some icy spring. "It's essential, Romek, to immerse oneself in the *mayim chaim*, in the restoring grace that arises from living waters, that brings a person to a state of *tahor*, of purity."

My father's face is grave as he explains, "This is especially true of these past hours, because one should not handle the Torah or enter the holy places if exposed to the presence of the dead. You know, little Romek, in centuries past when people only washed once a year and their skin was a corrupt shell of dirt and vermin, it was the Jews who lived through the Black Death epidemics because of the Mikvah."

He goes on to say that what was harder to survive were the subsequent accusations of the goyim that the Rabbis provoked such plagues through their connivance with the malignant angels of the *Shedim*. These demonic seraphim, the Christian priests claimed, hovered above the beds of good Catholics to bring them harm and sickness in the night.

"Are the Germans Shedim, Papa?" I ask him as he rinses my hair with a pitcher of cold water.

Blood Will Have Blood

My father wipes my face and smiles at me, "Not all Germans," he says. "Just the ones we have to put up with. But, let me tell you something, sweet boy. Any day now, they are going to have their tuchas kicked out of Krakow, on the end of an American boot! Wait until the Yanks invade, the Krauts will be wetting themselves to get back to Germany. You'll see all those brave Marines marching down Florianska, and so many of them will be fine Yeshiva boys from New York and Brooklyn, with Polish grandfathers of blessed memory who once prayed in every synagogue in Krakow."

"Your father, Romek," comments Israel, not unkindly, "has America mania and Roosevelt is his new Moses."

"I'm telling you, Izzy," answers my father, sending soapsuds flying through the air. "The days of this occupation are numbered. Hitler will never hold it together against the Yanks. We can't just surrender to the idea that nothing will change. It takes the promise out of any future, and I won't let the man in Berlin rob my children of that."

My father puts on his stoic face, determined to protect his cherished reed of hope. Tadek is shaping cones out of the sinking foam of my bath in a distracted fashion. The water is now uncomfortably cold and I want to get out but have an odd feeling of not wishing to be naked before the men on the edge of any rising pessimism. Luckily, my mother comes striding in from the other room at that moment and immediately asks, "Why isn't that boy dried off and in his nightshirt?"

✼

Pinkoza Ladner is a distant cousin of Israel Horowitz, a man everyone knows in the Ghetto by the impossible nickname of Pinie Koza (Pinie the Goat). He is an affable unassuming soul who, my father would say, was guaranteed to be among the favored of heaven because of his quiet devotion to clearing the streets of the dead. Pinie got help from another of my OD uncles, Samek Weiner, who has sent him Yankel Gorowski from the Judenrat office and two dimwitted boys in their late teens who needed some legitimate employment to avoid the transports. Yankel has to be cautioned against pilfering the pockets of the deceased and the other two from gawking at the nakedness of any dead females they might handle.

For a man with any conscience, the work of an OD is a daily poison alleviated only by the most subversive fictions. My uncles make daring lists of the dead, matching their names up with equivalent forged ID cards. Rarely do the Germans check to see if the face moldering on the sidewalk matched the photo staring out from the newly manufactured Blauschein. This leaves a number of recycled cards with new photographs to be issued to the living that otherwise would have been allocated to the selection lists.

Pinie Koza surveys his unlikely morgue crew and complains to my uncle that "This wasn't much to work with, Samek, this is no upstanding *Hevrah Kadisha* (burial society) we've got here. Wouldn't you rather be sent to the grave by the devil?"

My uncle pats his shoulder kindly and advises, "Just give them a spade, my friend, and make them good *Shomrim* (watchers over the deceased), we need to clear the streets before these citizens bloat up and fester their gases over the living. If there's one thing that puts the fear of G-d up these Germans, it's the first whiff of typhus."

The burying man takes my uncle's words to heart and instructs his feckless team as they sit behind him on the former lumber cart pulled by two sturdy chestnut drays. "This work is a grace," he lectures, "remember it as such, especially in these times. The dead one is addressed with all politeness as "the Met", and, if we were doing this properly, we would ask their forgiveness for any indignity we might inflict upon their lifeless form."

Yankel is hardly impressed with Pinie's reasoning and complains loudly. "Forget the nice white gown, the fancy psalms, cutting the tallit fringe, and don't try to soothe these lost with petitions for their eternal rest. What's to rest? Who will repay their taken days? Believe me, Goat Boss; they'll be pounding against their tomb lids for justice for generations to come."

The horse-drawn cart trolls the Ghetto for the next two days, hauling the dead to the cemeteries of Jerozolimska and Miodowa Streets. Wherever the cadavers congregated in number, both Ghetto residents and the German military were diverted to other routes. The Judenrat have sent more workers to drape the swollen corpses with old sheets soaked in bleach and vinegar and to recover their clothing for delousing and recycling. When the sheets run out, the maggoty remnants of the "Mets" are doused with lye, wrapped in layers of paper and bound with string. Such shrouding gave the streets at night the bizarre appearance of an ancient Egyptian excavation.

Pinie Koza and his men tie scarves around their faces and continue to clear the avenues. With each body lifted into the cart, Yankel Gorowski persists in his random and cursing rage on behalf of the departed that the Goat Man comes to understand it as an unpolished tribute, a rough and wart-ridden holiness in and of itself. So, thinks Pinie Koza, it's not the Kaddish but we'll take it, because grace has the peculiar wearing properties of water on stone, and Yankel the schnorrer is smoothing out very nicely.

From the deep culvert that runs beneath the closed bathhouse on Josefinska Street, they bring out the body of Rabbi Avraham Bronstein, who'd left this world from a single bullet to the ear earned by arguing with Mueller's men. Next to him, they discover the thin form of a woman garbed in a summer dress, on which no wounds could be found, (who had actually expired in the damp channel from a swift and merciful stroke). Pinie Koza notes the woman is not young but still attractive, and even in her terminal state gives off a reserved scholarly air. A pair of starched white cotton gloves hung from her side pocket, a lady-like gesture on a hot afternoon when one must hasten into exile. She had the tapered muscular fingers of a former pianist, the slender and learned hands of my teacher, Ester Rosenfeld.

Blood Will Have Blood

❂

Manek tells us that the selected sat in the Optima courtyard for two days, a peculiar marketplace of the whispered bribe, the light-handed betrayal overlaid with apprehension and the wooden frozen state that the waiting induced in all the detainees. No one was allowed any luggage or change of clothing and no food but a little water. They were guarded mainly by personnel from Symche Spira's political section, a new breed of OD spawned by shifting SS policies; men heady with the freedom to extort, to defame, ready to kill their own on a whim, who sought to become the perfected mirror of their masters.

Down the lines of prisoners they walked, the ODs Forster, Spira, Susser, Wertal and Pacanower, their manner rather like bookies at a racetrack, betting with those who carried anything valuable that freedom could be had for the right price. Spouses, parents and grown children, the new identity cards in hand, stood anxiously at the gates of this people depository, also with money or jewelry to see if they could purchase their relatives. And so went the bargaining.

My name is Riva Fishbein; I have two thousand zlotys for my husband, Mattius Fishbein. He is a skilled stonemason and valuable to the Reich. Please can you find it in your heart to release him? Here is his new Blauschein. Mattius is allowed a brief minute with Riva and is freed to be assigned to building more barracks just down the road at the new labor camp of Plaszow now under construction.

A fine-faced boy of eighteen steps forward. My parents are Dr. Emmanuel Widowski and Dr. Gutka Widowksi, both are dentists; as such they can maintain the health of workers needed for the war effort and will treat the teeth of any German military if permitted. I can offer you a collection of my grandfather's gold coins. He was Professor Henryk Neumann, a renowned numismatist of ancient Roman currency.

Spira sees the leather case open with the gilt of the coins shining as offered by the Widowski's guileless son, Berek. The OD severely questions what is a Jew doing with such treasures when the decrees of long ago ordered that such precious things be surrendered? Please, Sir, they were on loan at the time to the Department of Archeology at the Jagellonian University. The coins' documents of provenance and a letter with the University's logo prove the boy's truth and save him from being put against the wall. Spira, much enriched, sends him home, walking earnestly hand in hand with both parents who were blessing the day they conceived him.

Fourteen-year old Yehudith Blatt sits with her widowed mother, Lyuba, and her only parent's boyfriend, Herman, a parasitic lover, a leech, a complainer, who is always first to eat more than his share of their meager rations. He secretly pimps the pretty adolescent to the Ukrainian guards in exchange for his freedom alone, claiming she is a troubled child and well seasoned as a whore.

A corporal drags the sullen Yehudith to a worker's outhouse north of the gates. His shift is over in fifteen minutes, he barks in bad Polish for her to wait and to be surely naked when he returns to unlock the door. The girl, nervy and full of vitriol, doffs not one garment. She stands high on the toilet seat, spits on her palms and quietly levers the slates off the lavatory roof to climb up and slide snake-like out in the bright sunlight across the roof's beam, above the waiting faces far below, and in through the factory window to surprise an elderly machinist in his repair duties. The man, without a word, hides her beneath the turbines until it's all over.

Herman suffers mightily with a thrashing from the disappointed guard who has to lie to his sergeant about the escaped kid, while Lyuba comforts herself that matters are righted in some way and, while realizing she may never see her daughter again, that Yehudith will certainly live to see this time dissolved.

The Pharmacist Pankiewicz, with Manek's help, sends over food and medicines to comfort the elderly and the hospital patients who had been dragged from their beds, still fevered, sutured, infected, and those rising to health.

Manek unknowingly hands salts of cyanide to eighty-year-olds, Maurice and Jana Binder, the toxin hidden in a box of chocolates given to my brother by their oldest son, Lukacz, who came by it through his labors at the Wachs lamp factory on Lwowska Street. The Binders thanked my brother graciously, called him sweet deliverer, wished him a thousand years of joy, but were sure not to offer him any of the ganache truffles. Jana combed her hair, put on her lipstick and her best shawl, Maurice his silk bow tie. They ingested the chocolates after making their whispered prayers and sharing a final kiss. They will be found later, thought to be sleeping, clutching each other tightly against the south wall of the yard. Pinie Koza and Yankel will have to lift them in the burial cart as a one body to save breaking the frail bones of their embrace.

On June eighth, shouts announce the order for the deportees to move out. The Optima gates open and the mass of prisoners are marched to the waiting boxcars standing at the station in Prokocim. The thousands of travelers packed into the wagons start an unraveling in the weft of a vital tapestry, part of the once-breathing fabric of our community, in and beyond the Ghetto. Among its brightest threads were:

Mordechai Gebirtig, composer of Jewish folk songs,

Abraham Heinemann, artist and painter,

Clara Rossen, architect,

Alfred Gutmacher, violinist and Klezmer exponent,

Bianka Gutmacher, soprano,

Gumpel Singer, goldsmith and engraver,

Blood Will Have Blood

Menisha Kohn, embroiderer of Torah mantles, parochets and kittels,

Shulem Spitzglas, diamond cutter,

Haskiel Kops, stonemason,

Moishe Beck, bookbinder,

Rabbi Izydor Teitelbaum, historian and theologian,

Leiba Blume, midwife,

Genia Klein, schoolteacher,

Avram Hadel, typesetter,

Amelia Werfel, playwright

Oren Hadel, printer,

and Viviana Eckstein, poet.

12

The Narrowing

WHILE BORIS PINSKI IS STILL GENEROUS WITH US, we are running out of things to sell him. My father trades him six Pelikan fountain pens, the rare Stresemann's from 1929, for several hundred zlotys and cartons of cigarettes that we can barter on the street or with one-eyed Zigo for food. Boris is always solicitous with Papa. He comments with deep respect that, would to G-d, if he could have had a male parent with the noble heart of Leon Ferber, his life would have run on quite a different rail.

It was rumored in the Ghetto that Boris was the issue of an assault on his mother by a bishop well positioned in the Catholic hierarchy of Krakow. A situation, Mama says, that might account for his schizoid swings between his intense devotions at the altar rail, his skewed sense of justice, and his disturbing reflex for easily murdering people he simply hates. Boris negotiates with my father for any remaining wealth that we have, saying that he cherishes our family so much that he could smuggle us out to Sweden, or even to Palestine--at a very affordable price. Is he game?

Papa graciously declines the offer, mindful that such a business offer comes from a confirmed strangler, and explains he won't allow the Reich to drive him from his homeland. News had filtered in, says Papa that the Germans were getting the crap knocked out of them in Russia and G-d will surely move the generous hearts of the Americans to bring their army to Krakow.

Boris affirms that the proposition is always open, but don't wait too long, dear friend. Consider it while you're still standing; consider Pani Mala, and your excellent children, especially that young boy who has his eyes on the stars, who deserves a future where no fear can reach him. Have no doubt, Leon; this Ghetto is no more than a waiting room. Do you ever wonder why the Germans expend so much forced labor and money on the rail lines to the east?

❦

I learn more of the world's sharp infestations, especially the tarsal claws of lies that grasp and cling. All four parents and even Lydia Rosenfeld impute to us that her sister, Pani Ester, has escaped Krakow with the stunning fiction that she's gone to Paris to join the French Resistance! Tadek palms his open mouth and is wide-eyed with admiration at the news. What a woman! Ester is our heroine of the hour. "Please always think of her that way," urges her sister with a wan smile.

Of course, I don't buy this for a minute, since having eavesdropped on Uncle Arnold whispering to Manek that a woman's body that might be Ester was taken out of the culvert beneath Josefinska Street. I say nothing to Tadek about this and support the lie of the adults.

The Narrowing

"She's probably on a most secret mission," my father advises. "Discretion is everything in these matters, Romek."

Pani Lydia has to move from the basement across the street because the place was cleaned out of the older folks in the Optima action and, having escaped that sweep, she is afraid to return. Uncle Samek gives her a tiny maid's room in the back of his building and he and Papa help her move her few meager possessions there. That's how Tadek and I came into ownership of some of Ester's books. We argue over the copies of the children's editions of *A Tale of Two Cities*, toss a coin and I end up with the version in English that pisses me off no end because I can't read the damn thing, only stare at the illustrations.

Yet, when I hold it, I'm ill at ease. The foreign words are incomprehensible but I see Pani Ester's name in the flyleaf and a dedication to her from her long dead Frenchman written in elegant Polish, "For Ester, the most precious gift of my time on this earth, who has given me a far, far better love than I have ever known. Your devoted Edmond."

I take the book to the top of the staircase and sit in the dark to think. I turn the soft leather binding over and over. A slight smell of lavender arises from the pages, Ester's singular fragrance. And it comes to me as sure as my own breath that she's not part of any Maquis brigade blowing up German depots in France. She is here, riding the cart of the Goat Boss to the Miodowa Street cemetery. I weep a little, hug the book, say Kaddish for her and then go and ask the one person I know who would always tell me the truth, my brother, Manek. For once, he is evasive.

"What will you do if it turns out that the lady is dead?"

"Tell Tadek and everyone." I declare.

"Will that be such a good thing, little man?" Manek asks carefully, "Especially for those people who may already know?"

I say I'd think about it, which is precisely what he wants me to do. I sleep with her book under my pillow and would wake in the night against its engraved covers. For Ester came to symbolize much of the Ghetto dead to me, a figurehead of refinement, learning and style that embodied the river of lives washed away by the selections. But for Tadek's sake, I enter into the lie that she was busy driving the Huns out of Paris because it seems to me to be the best way not to have people weeping and davening all over the place.

The next morning I carry the Dickens book into the kitchen and pompously announce to everyone that I intended to learn English. My father winks at Mama and applauds, saying now when the Yanks and the British army finally entered Krakow, I would greet the liberators in their mother tongue. Tadek whispers to me that if this ever happens, that I was to be sure to ask General Eisenhower where his father could buy a red Cadillac and if it could be driven across the occupied zones.

Ewa Urbanowicz explains in detail to my Aunt Cyla (who gossiped the tale to my mother) how she had avoided the round-ups by hiding with Jaroslaw Graczewski in the Schoenholz's mansion. My aunt almost fainted at this dangerous information. The Advocate and his Frida were enjoying a holiday in Carinthia, where they hoped not only to obtain more excellent Austrian Riesling from a slain man's cellar, but to file papers with the SS Commissariat in Klagenfurt and lay claim to the confiscated vineyard. Frida had a pastoral vision that after the war she and Dieter would retire to the peaceful hobby of viticulture. (The original vintner, Berusch Mannheimer, his wife, and three sons had died defending their wines but not before a dozen members of their clan were sent to Dachau.)

Ewa shocks Aunt Cyla with the lubricious tale of her lying naked across the satin luxury of the Schoenholz's bed, sipping the stolen Austrian vintage with the adoring Jaroslaw, who made a lumpy, sallow-skinned nude. The two were on a deliciously wicked campaign to stamp every place that Frida held precious in the house with their unending lusts. The bed of the Advocate and his spouse was a vast raft with a gilded, carved headboard made in Nancy, and appropriated along with the rest of the stunning Art Nouveau collection of Esau Zetterbaum, a wealthy architect long expired in Treblinka.

The bedroom where Ewa and Jaroslaw frolicked was in a suite set apart from the rest of the house. The Polish housekeeper, Lyra, had left for the night and had temporarily handed off the keys to the chauffeur. Jaroslaw set his cravings for Ewa and comfort on the broad stage of the Advocate's mansion. In every room whose door he could open, he was king. He raided the caviar, the smoked venison and other delectables from the kitchen and hand-fed his Semitic love wild raspberries and ate chilled peaches off her smooth belly.

But the thing he sought to feast on most was their planned tour of desecration. He had the naked Ewa stretch her heavy marbled thighs across Frida's embroidered chaise, roll her luscious self on the velvet sofa, and drink from the fine cut crystal engraved with the family's crest. He cajoled her to rest her melon-shaped butt in the Advocate's chair, wearing nothing but the Frau's mink stole, sitting beneath the red Swastika flag above the desk where lives were signed away. Exhausted by too much food, sex, and their extravagant sacrilege, the misaligned lovers finally fell asleep in the damp satin sheets. Draped across the Aubusson carpet lay a lilac chiffon and black velvet cocktail dress where Ewa had thrown it, a gift from a cousin.

Jaroslaw banked every image of his Jewish goddess for those trying days when he'd have to cringe at Frida's crow call that she needed to be driven somewhere in the next two seconds, or on meeting the somber figure of Advocate Schoenholz in the beige-carpeted corridors with the request that he take these papers to Wawel Castle at once, to be signed by the imperial hand of Governor Otto Wachter himself. A matter most urgent, the

The Narrowing

relocation of a thousand Polish workers for the coalfields of Westphalia, and put the dogs in the car because they're pissing all over the tapestries in the dining room.

Jaroslaw carries the soft leather file that contains the random reorganization of destinies. As he walks away down the mirrored halls to collect the neglected Schnauzers, he smiles to himself on thinking that there is no place in the entire house that has not been rubbed against, caressed by, or sweated on, by the sumptuous Ewa.

※

Two weeks later after the summer deportations, death itself lay down to rest its gorge. The streets of the Ghetto have settled into a melancholy calm, save for the constant drifters that narrowly escaped the selections. They wander from the Judenrat office to the crowded hospitals searching for any news of loved ones taken. Their hope is ferocious, their quest unceasing. They carry sheaves of papers, old ID cards of their relatives, marriage certificates, and entire photo albums. Look here, this is Michal, my husband and I on our wedding day, and this is Rachaela, our firstborn, please, have you seen them? And there, just behind the bride, are Michal's parents, Liliana and Viktor. Please, you must know them? They went to the Optima yard together.

Women carry small photographs tied with string around their necks or pinned to their coats. They walk the Ghetto hoping that someone will recognize the faces they wear. Several men and women keep vigil at the Prokocim depot listening for the far wail of a train and the clicking dance of wheels over the lines that lead to the east. They stand staring into the empty horizon along the burnished tracks as if they can magnetize the one they ache for back into the world.

Whenever Pinie Koze and his burial cart appear in the streets, the seekers clamor around him holding up the photos and pleading, please look. Did you bury my Georg? My Szaja? My Ascher? He offers comfort and patiently considers every question. When the answer is yes, he is always honest and says the *Met* (deceased) now abides in the splendor far beyond this earth, so please, go sit Shivah and honor them by refusing the *Shedim* of despair.

Often the bereaved don't leave immediately because the Goat Man gives off some tenacious serenity that makes his leathery ugliness beatific, a charmed aura of steadiness they need for their sustenance before they can return to their shabby dwellings and the iron silence of the absent.

In the late summer of 1942, the Ghetto boundary is redrawn to eliminate the area south of Limanowskiego Street, effectively cutting the community laterally in half. Residents on the abandoned southern border are forced to move. The new demarcation is defined by a barbed wire fence running the length of the odd-numbered side of Limanowskiego, with Gate Two being transferred from Wieliczka Street to the crossroads of the main avenue and Wegierska Street. The main avenue is like the Red Sea divided without the benefit of a heavenly tidal wave to drown the enemy. Torrents of the populace scurry through the new Gate Two from morning until the night curfew, hauling trunks, valises, boxes, wheelbarrows of coal and firewood, arms full of clothing. Carts are scarce and bicycles only carry so much.

I notice a mother and father pushing a huge bedstead across the tram track on which rode their three young sons. This same bed, with screeching metal castors that could be heard for blocks, was seen making endless return trips to and from Rekawka Street, with a grandmother, many chairs, luggage, and several pieces of other furniture. After the fifth foray, the couple's oldest boy, an enterprising type about my age stood outside the wire loudly advertising the services of the short-distance bedstead and two sturdy parents who will move your stuff for a few zlotys, will even accept food as payment.

It takes several days for the south side residents to move into the many dwellings vacated by the deportees. Where three people dwelt in one room, you now had nine. In some buildings, upper corridors were suddenly at a premium. We know of five families with a combined number of eighteen kids who agreed to live communally along the top passageway of their building. They would only sleep in the tiny two room-and-kitchen apartments allocated them but created an elongated common room that looked more like the lobby of hotel, chairs of all styles lining it from the landing to the far wall. Rules are laid down that there was to be no drinking, shouting or carousing in the public space. This works well for a time until some nameless spoiler from the floors below starts stealing the chairs to use them as firewood.

✤

The narrowing of the Ghetto brings many complex effects, both bad and good. Several of the abandoned shops now outside the wire reopen with new proprietors, many of them Aryan, that delight the black marketers. When the far wall comes down, we are permitted to view, for the first time in many months, the rest of Podgorze. Likewise, many Poles come to the wire to see what is happening in the Jew Zoo. For the most part, they are friendly and call greetings but dare not risk any prolonged interaction with us except at dusk when all sorts of illicit trading commenced.

After the duty patrols pass by and just before curfew, the night air above the fence becomes thick with flying food, canned goods, loaves of bread, jars of condiments wrapped in rags so they wouldn't break, and money pulled along in brown paper bags strung under the wire to a secret cashier on the Gentile side. A shadowy figure silently tallies up our purchases in the hidden darkness of a doorway and then yanks on the string to relay the change home. Under this devious scheme, I acquire my first pair of new boots in two years.

As my feet grew, my old shoes had become torture. Israel Horowitz had slit open the sides and sewed in extra panels he'd fashioned from upholstery leather. But not having enough sole to stand on gave me a penguin-like gait and caused women in the street to suggest to Mama that I might have

The Narrowing

rickets. Now, Manek makes me stand on sheets of old newspapers to cut out the shape of my bare feet and then goes shopping at the wire. He returns the same night with a pair of shiny new boots that I insisted on taking into my quilts with me so I could sleep in the tannin odor of their leather. The boots fit me like a second skin, but it is days before I can bring myself to wear them in public. Newness in anything, especially clothes, makes me awestruck; I want to preserve them forever.

Mama and I return home from the rations depot one afternoon when a magnificent Citroen sedan starts to trail us. "Walk fast, Romek," orders my mother; thinking it was an official Gestapo vehicle. "Don't look back. Wait till they call an order."

We are still quite far from our apartment and my new boots squeak like mice trapped in a church organ. My mother's fear transmits down to her hand that held mine—but to run would invite the raised rifle. The silver car cuts across our route and halts beside us. Thankfully, no Swastika flags are flying from its hood. The back window opens to reveal the hairless pate of Boris Pinski sitting behind his driver, Fredek Lempl. "Good day, Pani Mala and my little stargazer, get in and let us take you home," urges Pinski with tender concern.

He opens the door and we climb into amazing upholstered luxury. Pinski opens a small valise filled with chocolate bars, wine, boxes of Havana cigars and two bottles of brandy. "Sometimes, I like to personalize my deliveries," he says. "So much nicer for the customer, to see the face behind the sale, don't you think? Speaking of which, do you know this person?"

From the loaded valise, the black marketer pulls forth a photograph. Mama and I stare at a man's long face, huge Semitic nose and eyes with an almost Asiatic fold. "No, I have never seen him, Pan Pinski," answers my mother. "Is he missing?"

"Not that I've heard of," says Boris gently. "I ask you because he wears the insignia of an OD but it's a mystery that I'm unable to find him sitting in an OD office anywhere. He appears to be on permanent street duty."

"Is he your friend?" I ask, wanting to be helpful because, in spite of the wicked stories that whirled around Boris, I feel safe now to be in his presence, since he has shown true regard for my father, and we constantly benefit from his impetuous generosity.

"No, my little brave," says Boris. "More like a business acquaintance."

We pull up in style at the corner of Krakusa and Josefinska Street where Tadek and Bella Abramowicz playing hopscotch in the sidewalk stopped to gawk as Mama and I get out of the car, heavily laden with gifts of tea, cocoa, French soap and a Cuban cigar for each of the fathers and Manek.

✻

Our fathers go out on the landing to smoke and become two living news outlets of several disasters. Tadek and I, pretending to fuss around with our cockroach kennel under the sink, eavesdrop through the door crack to be entertained by such jaw-dropping gossip as that of known collaborators, Lionel Feldstein and his wife Tereska, recently found tied together and floating in the Vistula, that an arms depot in Ludwinow was robbed in broad daylight of crates of rifles, an unknown number of grenades and several Panzerfaust anti-tank guns, and that a senior Polish captain of the resistance had hung himself in his cell at the Montelupich prison rather than betray his compatriots.

Tadek's father begins to pace the linoleum to rouse himself into a debate with Papa. A cloud of fragrant cigar smoke drifts in from the hall and we hear both men speak for the first time of the end of the Ghetto. Leon, listen to me. It's coming, you'll see, they're cutting down the residences to make the dissolution easier. We're sitting on good real estate here, better for the Krauts if they would ship us to the Ukraine or to their factories in Germany.

Israel? You worry too much.

I'm sent to Aunt Cyla's to hide more frequently during this time because we hear that kids like me are disappearing daily. I go to sleep often with my shoes and pants on because I never know when I might be hauled down the stairs to be hidden under mountains of potatoes in Zigo's rattletrap of a cart.

Uncle Samek persuades me that one method to attain my revered invisibility is to be tied up in potato sacks for the short rides from our apartment to his residence. My mother rubs my white hands and face with soot. I step into a sack, another covers my head, potatoes are flung in with me to give the right texture and the sack is tied with rope. Samek carries this burden over his shoulder down the stairs, walking backwards and holding on to the banister in case he should stumble with his heavy load that would crush both boy and tubers.

Once aboard the cart, I can actually see a view of the Ghetto streets through the sacking's weave. The pavements are crowded night and day with feckless wanderers and beggars of all stripes, people who live in doorways and under stoops (but who are forced to scatter into sewers and rain culverts after the curfew), mostly country Jews sent in from the surrounding villages and towns. Papa says even in peacetime the city might defeat them. These men and women, who, for generations, had no notion of the world beyond the rural borders of their shtetl, are identified by their pure lilting Yiddish, and the gaze of stupefaction that their eyes no longer survey their tended fields and neat vegetable gardens.

Once inside Uncle Samek's apartment, I'm sprung from the sack to have Ewa Urbanowicz order that I wash the soot from myself immediately in the sink. Ewa is allowed to use the sewing machines in her free time to alter cast-off clothing to fit her beauty queen's figure. Since my Aunt is out fitting a new dress on Frida Schoenholz, Samek asks me to amuse the baby. My cousin, Lonius, yowls with enough vocal power to lift the roof when his father leaves to go about his OD duties, his time spent these days mainly fending off Symche Spira's group from ransacking the rations depot.

The Narrowing

I haul my screaming cousin out of his cradle and bounce him in my arms. He is a solid ball of raging noise. I feel his little body deflate and expand with every screech. Ewa ties a bright rag of red linen into a doll form and throws it at me.

"Here," she says. "Entertain him with this, and shut him up, if you can."

I swing the baby around the room, rocking him, playing finger puppet with the remnant and letting him drool all over my shoulder. Ewa drives the sewing machine in fierce concentration repairing a mauve silk hat. The selvedge is decayed so she has to make pleats in it where the holes are.

"If you wear that in the street, won't the guards shoot at you?" I ask her.

"It's not for wearing in the street," she growls. "Go change the baby's diaper; he stinks like a backed-up toilet!"

Lonius, exhausted from his tantrum, pees on my arm. I walk him over to the kitchen, take a dry diaper from the clean pile on the ironing board, sit the child down in the sink, and quickly haul him out of his stinking clothes.

A large mirror is hung over the faucets and I manage to prop Lonius up on his plump bowlegs so he can bat and squall at the infant in the glass. The hot water surging over his tiny butt makes him chortle with delight. Washing him is like handling an oiled eel but the deep sink contains him. The next minute I look up, I almost drop my infant cousin to the tiles in shock.

In the mirror, I see Ewa Urbanowicz undress to her underpants and throw her work clothes carelessly onto a chair. She seemed not to mind my presence at all. I run more warm water and sponge the baby down all over again. As long as I'm at this task, I don't have to face the half-naked woman strutting around with the white globes of her bare breasts swinging and the humps of her behind swaying, as if driven by unseen pistons. I have never in my nine years of living seen so much of a woman's body.

The re-soaped Lonius pats the suds and squeals at the mirror, pointing a chubby finger at the sight of Ewa, almost as nude as he is. The girl was having a personal fashion show. She stepped into a pair of high heels and draped herself in various bolts of cloth that never quite covered her.

"Hey, Romek, do you think this color is too much?" she demands from across the room.

In the mirror appears a vision of a female ripeness twirling around in a sizzling orange fabric; hair flung back, one breast hanging out. It occurs to me from her voyage across the floorboards that I'm staring at one of the best-fed physiques in the Ghetto. I knew well that Cyla and Samek weren't sharing their rations with her because any surplus, if they had it to spare, was always sent over to our apartment. I must try to wheedle out of her what her food source is.

"It looks very nice, Pani Ewa," I mutter, shampooing Lonius's baby fuzz for the umpteenth time. Her heels go tapping across the floor and there's more

174

rustle of cloth. My cousin starts to whine so I make a circle of my thumb and forefinger and blow soap bubbles for him, believing that I could fill some time in this distraction—the damn woman will have to get dressed at some point!

The next instant a new image of Ewa appears in the glass, a fashionable mirage in a lilac chiffon gown with a black velvet bodice, a mauve hat set at a seductive angle on her dark hair. Both the baby and I grow silent as this cloud of airy fabric, with a stunning girl emerging out of it, flows across our vision.

She too is in some magical chimera of her own, dancing lightly around the sewing machine. Down on the street, there would be the stick-boned women, begging for a few groszy, who would sell a child for a piece of bread, but here, in this moment, was my limited idea of rare seductive perfection.

An unseen man suddenly speaking from the doorway breaks my fascination. "It fits you like a dream," he's saying. In the mirror, I note the blue uniform of an OD.

He strides into view and pulls Ewa to him in a brutish fashion. My mouth drops open as he kisses her roughly. She struggles away from him but he practically swallows her lips and rummages frantically under the chiffon skirts. Ewa pushes him away and nods in our direction. The man looks up and grows angry at the sight of Lonius and me.

I quickly haul the baby out of the sink and wrap him in a thick towel. My "octopus" of fear is back and its light suckers are reaching all along my spine. I sense the newcomer has a wild might, that he's not just another OD with the usual on-the-take swagger, but bears a reflex more predatory. His dark narrow gaze makes a sideways motion, reminiscent of a reptile sizing up a target before the jaws open.

"I thought you'd be alone. Who are the kids?" he barks at the girl.

"Cyla's son and her nephew," Ewa answers, stepping between the man and us.

"They're lucky to still be breathing," he says in surly tones, as if we had pilfered the air.

"You can't be here. You should go!" Ewa demands curtly. She turns to me and says, "Romek, please take the baby to the bedroom and stay there until I call you."

I hurry away with Lonius, grateful to be out of the man's baleful presence. I lock the bedroom door, tuck the baby into his bassinet and listen for a time as Ewa and the OD argue ferociously over something.

I hear him curse her obscenely and yell something about "that pox-ridden Pole across the river." Then a brawling conversation between the two of them ensues. The man attacks with many references to an unnamed "he." When he gets here, this entire Ghetto shit will dance to a different tune! He

The Narrowing

will be the one to change the tide, even the fires of hell will obey him, you won't be so proud then, you lice-ridden whore! You think things have been rough up to now? Believe me, girl, it's been a picnic compared to the chastisement that's coming! He is the blade edge who'll make you thirst for oblivion, and, Ewa, don't think I won't deliver you to him on a plate, you uppity Jewish slut!"

In all of this rant, Ewa answers him with cool contempt and I feel his rage seep across the room. There's an ugly thud of a chair being flung against the wall that feels like a blow and more loud shouting between them. I run to the bedroom window and throw open the casement. My mind won't steer itself, what will I do if this man kills Ewa? Surely, he would come next for Lonius and me? I gaze down into the dark courtyard, there's no way to jump: the drop to the paving stones is several bone-breaking meters.

The baby has fallen into a peaceful sleep through all this mayhem but I have to figure out something with the night and the curfew coming on, how I may have to tie my cousin to my back and clamber over the rooftops before this devil breaks down the door. I could take Lonius and find refuge in the crowded courtyards, and hide until Uncle Samek with his night permit would come to fetch us. Big problem: how do I get away unseen carrying a wailing peeing alarm in my arms alerting the platoons roaming the streets? Nevertheless, good fortune suddenly opened a seam.

The whole apartment shakes from the front door's aggressive slam and the menace retreating down the stairs followed by a terrible quiet. Ewa treads lightly into bedroom, cooing "It's OK for you boys to come out now".

I wrap the slumbering Lonius in a log roll of blankets and haul him onto my shoulder. Ewa stands there, smiling bravely, although I could see her mouth is swollen and bruised and her hands shaking. The shoulder strap of her lilac dress is torn and her hair a wrenched mess but she still oozes an unstoppable glamour.

"You OK, Romek?" she asks tenderly and walks me into the kitchen for lemonade and some kugel. We all sit. A good calm arises among us. Ewa cradles my cousin, singing softly to him. I slurp at the lemonade and it comes to mind that the snake-eyed OD has the same gaze that stared out from the photograph shown to Mama and me by Boris Pinski.

※

Dora Gittelbaum is a formidable warrior in the Jewish underground. I always thought she would be the perfect wife for my brother Manek. She matches him in smarts and daring and misses only a few notches in the humor department. She is not beautiful in a conventional sense but her curved elongated jaw and smooth profile command attention. On the same night, Ewa is fending off her demoniac OD, Dora is out on the Bydgoszcz road concealed in the shadows of the abandoned house with two of her captains and her fighting team waiting for Fredek Lempl to arrive with a case of German rifles (the fruits of the raid on Ludwinow depot.)

This is an unusual delivery because no money will change hands. Pinski is claiming the deal as his contribution to the partisan effort; financed in part by him selling a missing Panzerfaust anti-tank gun back to Fritz Goertner the Flogger, who now works in the Reich armaments office across the river and is a dab hand at retooling documents for the misappropriation of military hardware.

Dora has the hiding place all prepared. She and her father, Julius, a former builder, have created a wooden chute within the chimney space of the roofless living room that can only be accessed via the underside of the false wall recently cemented on the outside of the house. They had mixed the new stucco with peat mulch and motor oil to give it the same dingy pastiche as the rest of the exterior. Dora, Julius and two other women are stained brown with the camouflage mix and smell like a refinery. Their oily reek competes with another odor, a rotting-meat stench that the nearby farm laborers complain of when the wind is high, that causes their herding dogs to scratch plaintively at the earth for the source of the aromatic rot that so beguiles them.

As Fredek would later relate the tale to my father and to my eavesdropping, it was about eleven when he turned Pinski's Citroen into the lane that led to the house. He finds the place from the crippled roof beams that spike the sky, dark leaning masts above the trees. He exits the car and pulls a small firearm from inside his mohair jacket because of the fug that swirls around the property. He senses it immediately. Dora greets him. He silences her at once, gesturing for no talk at all. He fears one of Commandant Kunde's killing platoons has been here. The rest of her team gathers and is primed to flee at the sight of the cocked pistol, except Dora, who whispers the order for them to ready their guns. Fredek leads them to the well where the miasma rises to defeat their gasoline vapors.

His flashlight shining down the well's mouth is reflected back at him in the empty eye sockets of the fifteen or more corpses resting in tumbled layers above the water line.

✼

Papa encounters Rabbi Efroim Geller by the front steps of the Hospital for Infectious Diseases. Efroim unnerves him by having a sudden weeping fit right there on the sidewalk. My father, much concerned, supports the shuddering Rebbe into the Hospital lobby.

"The heart is cut from me, Leon," Efroim sobs as they seat themselves in two wheelchairs because the waiting room benches had been chopped up for firewood. "My beautiful synagogue has been desecrated."

Papa wheels himself closer to the distraught face and queries if the Zucker Temple, on the south side of the Ghetto and now outside of the new wire fence, has been razed.

"No, a worse abomination," Efroim explains. "The Reich's confiscation bureau has converted it into a warehouse for stolen furniture. If you know of any man breathing on this earth who loved his shul more, I will bow down to him, I swear."

"My dear Rebbe," says my father, "there's not a house in all of Podgorze that loss and grief have not raided, and with respect, are missing temple treasures more sacred. Ask the women out on the streets following the burial carts."

Efroim's grief settles at my father's gentle chiding. He lapses into a short bitter silence and looks like a man slowly emerging from a drugged sleep. "You're right, Leon, I made much of my attachment to the place. But you know that a synagogue is more than cut stone. My Belfer used to say that its rooftrees could be raised in every atom of a believer, its walls carved by human intention and its gates lit by devotion."

Here, the Rebbe's tears well up again and he wrings his tallit in remorse. "I'm telling you, Leon, I burn with shame to address Yahweh in prayer. His house has fallen into the claws of the horned one, and I, its most wretched protector, could do nothing when the soldiers came to put the Ark to the axe."

In this moment, my father would lower his face so Efroim could not see his slow smile and the knowledge in his eyes that it was the Rebbe himself who had worn a fake leg cast for a week so he could walk the Torah scrolls of his beloved shul, one at a time, to safekeeping at the Eagle Pharmacy.

"The soldiers threw me into the streets," says the Rebbe, "and locked up the place. Still I couldn't leave and slept by the back door for three nights. Inside I heard a soft motion, the lightness of the Shekinah (Divine Presence) washing over the stolen goods, like the Angel over Egypt, purifying the violent way they were taken. I dared not re-enter, my feet were *trayf* (unclean)."

"You know, Leon," Efroim continues, "for many years my vocation was sealed in the rare air of the Beth Hamedresh spent among white-beards and black hats, trying to squeeze a hundred subtle meanings from the holy texts. Such pursuits were my delight, the jewel of my hours; I thought that's what I was supposed to do with this life of mine. I have never known personal harshness or deprivation and now my head is being held to the fire. Tell me, this great darkness that has descended on us, can you fathom its reason, its purpose? Why does it need to be?"

"I have no answers, Rebbe," says Papa. "I believe it to be a temporary landslide in human affairs. We must keep faith in what is good. Let the situation right itself, as it surely will in good time."

❈

My family gets detailed news concerning the new labor camp at Plaszow from an unlikely source. The relay is Aunt Cyla, who got it from Ewa, who was informed by her lover, Jaroslaw, who I hear third hand, is beating me out in the eavesdropping stakes.

Across the river in the marbled salons of the Schoenholz house, much preparation is underway. We hear that the Advocate is busy signing requisitions for timber, cement, water pipes, steel beams and industrial manufacturing equipment, while his chauffeur sits quietly listening outside the open door of his office waiting to deliver these documents to various contractors reluctantly trusted by the Reich.

The Counselor this morning is in an empire-building mood, for the village of the damned is being developed at Plaszow. Barracks under construction for both the military and the soon-to-be imprisoned, workshops to be set up to implement the lucrative war contracts of factory *Treuhänders* (trustees) such as Julius Madritsch and Oskar Schindler. A mortuary already filled by the thousands of dead from the German slaughter in the Ghetto is now concealed among the innocence of the trees, earthen catacombs that could, with slave labor and stones from the original Jewish cemetery nearby, be given a veneer of concealment and respectability.

The Advocate is so absorbed with his grand plan he calmly rebuffs several irate phone calls from the Armaments Inspectorate office in Warsaw who are continually beset by missing jeeps, stolen air-cooled machine guns, pilfered mortar cannons, and, astonishingly, a factory-fresh Sturmoser tank that lumbered off the supply train from Hamburg in broad daylight, to be driven to points unknown by a soldier unnamed persuasively dressed in German military regalia. The Quartermaster General pesters Schoenholz with squeals for subpoenas and high-level Gestapo investigations to root out and prosecute the traitors in the Wehrmacht who must be in bed with every black market fiend in Krakow.

Jaroslaw hears it all. Tell it to Berlin, the Advocate advises tartly, explain to them how the best trained army in history has a problem hanging on to its weapons in non-combat situations, how Jews can pick up a tank, put it in their tallit and walk it across the river undetected, you raving imbecile! Have you any idea of the number of German vehicles rusting in the landscape between here and Russia? Has it not occurred to you that the Fuehrer's accounting office builds in constant loss factors in the budgets of the garrison commands, balanced to the last pfennig, and such depletions are far exceeded by free labor and products and profits thereof in the occupied zones? Call me when they steal the eyes out of your head!

Satisfied that the arms bureaucrat is trounced, the Advocate slams down the phone to find himself staring into the petulant gaze of Frida, who declares, for the third time that week, that she would rather be drowned or divorced than move to the new camp at Plaszow.

She stridently refuses to live among Jewish degenerates and suffer typhoid-infested prisoners, crude soldiers, barrack discomforts and dining off tin plates. Neither would she ever consider transporting to such a cesspool her precious Meissen china, her Belgian linens and her tapestry collection (all confiscated from the house of the wealthy Goldberg family exterminated in Belzec), the delicate Dutch landscapes by a second-tier painter, School of

The Narrowing

Vermeer (seized from Ira and Senka Perlmann, now in Dachau), the ballroom-size Aubusson carpets, (impounded from the country home of Moritz Sabersky, executed in the Plac Zgody during the June actions) and the eighteenth-century diamond-and-ruby necklace with cabochon-cut earrings to match (confiscated from gem merchant, Tibor Kohlmann after he and his daughter Adela tried to buy their freedom, but who were shot by the rabid Walther Mueller just hours before his suicide).

"No, no, Dieter, darling, I cannot give in to you this time," Frida bleats on. "I've worked hard to build a wonderful home in this disgusting Polish outpost, to ensure an appropriate environment for a man in your position. It isn't fair. You cannot expect a woman of my sensitivities to leave this marvelous little palace for that ugly red house in Plaszow!"

This far into the conversation, the document-sifting Dieter has selectively tuned her out. He has a lawyer's skill of mentally tracking several subjects at once and extracting only what he thinks is useful. Frida, for her part, has the kind of vanity that causes spontaneous deafness. She doesn't even hear her husband when he says "We're not moving. And the red house was never for you!"

Even as he declares it, he's rapidly filling in the appropriate forms for the said property. "The house is to be allocated to a very senior officer. You'll like him, Frida, sweetheart. He's a good Catholic from Vienna."

Frida is about to browbeat her husband some more when they both become aware of Jaroslaw, hovering in the doorway and being circled by the woman's two frantic Schnauzers. The boy's smiling face is flushed with tumultuous secrets and he looks suspiciously happy. Frida coos at him and asks what's on his mind. Has the fan belt on the Mercedes torn again?

"No, not at all, Pani Frida," mutters Jaroslaw shyly, "I wish to respectfully ask permission of you and Advocate Schoenholz for a two-day holiday in the next month. I need some time to attend to my wedding arrangements. I hope it is not an inconvenience."

13

Streets of Fire

IT'S THE MORNING OF SHABBAT and Papa is over at Uncle Samek's apartment with Israel Horowitz and other men who had gathered to pray in a secret minyan. Hanka is across the street with Tadek's mother and sisters on a long line of women waiting to have her hair styled by Glinka Czerny.

Glinka sells her coiffeur's skills for food and her service list reads like the menu of a bad café. Color treatments: half-a-loaf of bread, a permanent wave: canned fruit with a three-can minimum, a henna treatment: a good quantity of powdered eggs or sugar. Glinka also does delousing but that task demands a high tab of fresh vegetables or real coffee. Beetroot currency is not accepted. Hanka will pay for her new hairstyle with five potatoes.

On this particular morning, there is the promise of onion and potato latkes for breakfast. Tadek and I are in the kitchen, juggling rejects from the potato supply in an excellent relay to each other. Mama, who was busy at the stove, would soon deliver the pile of fragrant pancakes to the table. All is well until I miss a catch and the spud bounces smartly off my mother's derriere. She shrieks, Tadek gasps, and immediately flees the kitchen for the hallway, leaving me to face the deadly rays of punishment firing from Mama's eyes. She picks up the potato missile and snatches me by the collar, waving the root close to my nose.

"This is not a toy!" she rebukes. "Are we such millionaires that you should throw food around on Shabbas like it was garbage? What a *shande* (disgrace)! Go sit out there with that other *chamoole* (jackass) and wait for your father!"

Her commentary fuels my swift ejection into the corridor where Tadek squats sheepishly by the banister. I stare at the slammed door, tortured by the siren scent of fried onions. "Five minutes," assures Tadek, grinning at me and holding up as many fingers. "She'll be out with something on a plate, kvelling (gushing) over her little Romek."

"Let's not be here then," I say, knowing that our temporary disappearance would drive her wild with anxiety.

※

On the third floor of our building, an apartment had fallen temporarily vacant. The previous family of Naftal Bratkiewicz, his wife Itka, and three young children had barricaded themselves in the place for several weeks, the parents refusing all orders to report to the Plac Zgody during the selections. Their open defiance astounded the entire Ghetto; everyone feared they would provoke an avalanche of reprisals. The family was commanded to turn themselves in to the Jewish Police.

Streets of Fire

The Bratkiewicz's were intractable, declaring in a tart reply that they would have no dealings with the ODs and the Judenrat, all cowardly betrayers of *Yiddishkeit* (Jewishness) in Naftal's estimation.

Such a barefaced refusal caused a manic rage among the Ghetto's German command. Unterscharfuhrer Horst Pilarzik laid blame everywhere and beat the OD Symche Spira in the face with his pistol butt. For each tooth-cracking blow he endured, Spira silently vowed he would visit the same ten-fold on the lawless head of Naftal. Even the Ghetto's commandant, Wilhelm Kunde, feared complaints to Advocate Schoenholz, who might phone his cronies in Berlin with the worrying news that the regime in Krakow was losing control. Kunde quickly issued orders that the family be executed publicly at Gate One upon their immediate arrest.

When Spira burst into the apartment with his Ukrainian platoon, he found not one of the Bratkiewiczs left alive. The three daughters, aged one to five, were blue from suffocation, their mother and father enfolding them in a bloody embrace. Since the stench of their mortality had already permeated our stairs, our parents could hardly soften the story with benign lies. Yet the adults muttered secretly among themselves, arguing all opinions on the matter in whispered tones. I collected grains of their conversation with the practiced indifference of a deaf rock while sitting at the kitchen table, pretending to read.

Papa had sent a hurried plea to Uncle Arnold and Pinie Koza to come and remove the corpses from the third floor, but Spira refused to let any funeral matters begin until the Ukrainian guards tore the place apart, looking for anything of value. Pinie, my father and my uncle had waited nervously in our kitchen with the front door double locked, until the sounds of axed wood emanating from the third floor quieted down.

Pinie kept his eyes closed and swayed gently, sending a prayerful plea through our ceiling for the *Mets* (deceased) not to look upon this earthbound grossness. Once the *gonefs* (thieves) had left, Tadek and I stayed in our apartment under the watchful eye of Salka and Gizia while the mothers and Hanka went upstairs with the men to wash the dead and wrap them in the burial sheets.

They found the bodies of the family powdered with brick dust, broken glass and festooned in coils of stripped-off wallpaper. Naftal's wife, Itka, bore the print of a mud-caked boot across the blue cretonne blouse she'd worn for her final day.

"It was Pan Bratkiewicz's idea all along," I'd heard Salka gossiping to her sister. "But can you imagine the mother agreeing to such a thing?"

After the bodies were finally taken out to the burial cart, our two fathers put on their tallits, stood in the center of the destroyed home and intoned lines from the Book of Samuel: *Lovely and pleasant in their lives and in their death, they were not divided.*

Then there was the letter found in Itka's pocket, seeking no redemption but offering a soft declaration of intent in the dead woman's neat hand. Luisia, Mama and Hanka took it into the bedroom to read it but Tadek and I heard every sad word that my sister recited.

※

It was in the Bratkiewicz's former tomb where Tadek and I decide to hide out after the flying potato incident. The apartment's door panels are splintered open, not hard for a boy's hand to reach through and turn the bolt from the other side. The two of us creep into the fetid odor of shattered masonry, old wallpaper glue and the absent dead. We burn with a curiosity for some clue as to the shape and power of Naftal's decision.

Papa and Manek had nailed up the broken windows with timber from an old table. Now, only narrow plumes of October light enter. Debris is strewn everywhere, the tiled stove is gone, several chairs and a credenza have been carried out to the waiting truck. One of Spira's ODs had waltzed sportingly down the stairs wearing an old mink coat of Itka's, an item alone that would have earned her a bullet to the head. The walls of the apartment have been cleaved open and exposed right down to their laths. From somewhere, I hear the soft trickle of hidden water. Tadek is pulling me to the door.

"I don't like it here, Romek. Let's go."

"Are you scared?" I taunt at the look of disturbed amazement in his eyes.

At nine years old, we are both well seasoned to atrocities. Nevertheless, homicidal parents are something new. Such a notion is a thorn in my mind—to think that beneath my mother's warm eyes as she bent over to kiss me at night there might be brewing the means to my end. It could hardly be possible? Not even if I hurled acres of potatoes at her.

Tadek's face comes close to mine in the foul gloom. "Their Papa, how did he kill them?" he whispers.

"Does it matter? They're still dead."

"It matters, because, Romek, if it was one at a time," he says hoarsely, "the others would have had to watch and wait for their turn. How could they do that, how could their Mama just hang around and not run or fight?"

"You dope, they were just kids, and their Mama went along with it."

The question chills me, however, not that I have the wisdom to answer him. I go over to the ruined mattress where rivulets of dried blood blemish the striped cotton to look for clues. It is punctured with aggressive bayonet rents and its stuffing fluffed out in dirty bunches. At its head were two equally ripped-up pillows. One of them holds a tiny bloody palm print, next to it, a larger image almost smudging the first; a woman's splayed fingers sheltering the child's hand.

Streets of Fire

I put my living palm on the place of both and Itka Bratkiewicz's loving slaughter rises up to me. I hear the words from her last letter clearly, as if she was still narrating the events of a week ago.

"I sweetened the dried berries of Belladonna with the last of the sugar blended with wood alcohol. I had the children ingest the mixture first and held each one of them close as they drank. They appeared calm and content to take their magic medicine, as our eldest, Dwora, called it, like the princess in the storybooks who changed herself into a seahorse to voyage far across the world. Isn't that true, Mama? Yes, indeed, my precious, I said, as I rocked her, this is what such royal girls drink, take a sip and close your eyes. I'll keep watch for the gentle tides to take you down beneath the cool green waters, where the great ocean beasts sing of one so rare as Queen Dwora. A bony rack of a child, she slumped back against her sisters, so easy and light-footed does the life step out of her. Kunde cannot have her now or any of them. I have forbidden it. I'll strike G-d in the face if I have to and dare any retribution!

Earlier, I had recited to all the children another tale, a journeying story, and told it well, of a morning to come when we would arise together in a far different terrain from this lightless place. We didn't want the girls to suffer, but even when their lips were dry and shrunken from the cup of venom, nothing was as swift as we had hoped. I put my ear to their chests, listening to the thin skein of heartbeats of the two remaining, so strong from my Teibele whose will, even at age three, was hammered in iron. Even baby Stefania had that sly ploy of failing infants, of rationing the air. I gave her the Belladonna in her milk but still she stayed anchored and undefeatable in her small bones.

Naftal, sweetheart, quickly now with the pillows, let nothing remain awake for the ravening that will come up the stairs. Finally it was done—without any struggle. We laid them out side by side with tiny Stefania between her two sisters. Our turn was much easier. I take the finely honed blade and sawed at Natfal first, the ligaments of his forearm thickly corded. He did not even utter a cry when I had to do it several times over and the blood sprang. As for my hopeless limbs, it was like tearing tissue paper. I looked upon my girls in their fading and was beyond much sensation. Naftal and I kissed and lay down on the bed, lingering for some minutes on this side of breath. We curved around our lovely nestlings, already far along the road. We recited the Shema and asked to be no more. Amen."

Tadek and I stand in the enfolding stillness of the room, its iron quiet punctuated by dripping water, the determined ship of the Bratkiewicz lives now well over the horizon. I feel blunted and confused. The family's absence has an inexplicable immensity I have never experienced before, as if a wild comet had blazed through the apartment and out the other side, the vacuum it leaves still faintly humming and smoldering from such a heated transit.

But there are familiar steps suddenly approaching. Tadek smiles in relief, preferring another possible chewing out, rather than this useless adventure in missing ghosts. My father's face appears in the busted door panel. "You boys shouldn't be in here. You are to come downstairs to eat lunch at once," he says firmly. "Then, Romek, I want you to pack enough clothes for at least five days. Manek will be taking you back over to Aunt Cyla's in the morning."

"Papa, how did you know we were here?" I ask.

"Maternal radar, your mother has a thousand eyes. Thank G-d, the woman doesn't work for the German navy. Come on, hurry now."

My wardrobe is not exactly that of a prince. In fact, the mothers, on laundry day, devise an orderly recycling of the few pants and shirts that existed between Tadek and me, who are the same size. (This doubles our available garments and deflects any rough fighting between us.) Since we can't knock the daylights out of each other, Tadek and I sometimes face off in the hallway and hurl stupid potty-humor insults at each other. He threatens a spell that will force me to lick toilets for a thousand years. I shoot back, may his *tuchas* (backside) drop off, that this same tuchas should leave him and roam around by its two-cheeked self, ashamed to say that it was once attached to such a dumb schmendrick as he! We would make pencil drawings of the little tuchas, gave it a cartoon-like character and a narrative. Tadek named it "Mottel", after a boy he once hated in his former Cheder.

We write Mottel the Tuchas into the most scatological dramas, giving him a weapon of whistling up farts so powerful to blow German soldiers clean off their feet and send them whirling through a merciless tornado, wailing for their Mamas. Whenever Mottel wants to impress a pretty girl, we sketch a rose in his crack and have him declare that his two blushing cheeks were a vertical smile for her eyes only.

The parents often allow Tadek to sleep next to me in my family's room and we carry on the adventures of Mottel under the quilts. Sniggering insanely long into the night with tales of our miniature hero conducting a symphony with his baton carefully placed, singing opera—in all flatulent bass notes, Mottel at the bank with only one place to keep his wallet, Mottel gets fitted for a pair of pants with no legs...but where should the tailor put the zipper? We keep spinning out the stories, whispering lunacy in the dark, partly because I knew it makes Hanka crazy. She slaps at our quilts and orders us to be quiet, but more than once, I've seen her bare shoulders turned away from us, quivering with laughter.

There isn't much time for humor in the coming days.

My mother packs a few things in my rucksack. Her face is strained and somber. She folds my ancient nightshirt that now bears a huge cotton patch sewn into the backside, a cut-down sweater of Manek's and my brown boots that I wear infrequently to preserve their fineness. When she isn't looking, I grab some of my Mottel drawings and a pencil and hide them in a side pocket of my only luggage. I leave our apartment wearing Tadek's green corduroy pants, walking between Papa, Israel Horowitz and Manek, sheltered deep among the men of the work detail, led out by Uncle Samek.

Streets of Fire

I remember it keenly because Tadek was still asleep when we leave and I never did say goodbye to him.

The gray streets are calm in the early call-to-work hour: a few open jeeps here and there, the curfew soldiers with their heads slumped, snoring loudly to the widening sky, their guns laid over their knees or resting on the jeep's hood, almost daring any rebellious hand to reach for them.

Several lines of laborers thread their way to Gate One, escorted by the ODs, their boots on the cobbles striking a hollow clatter. My Uncle Samek slows the line down when we near his apartment house; the men of our detail draw closer together. He nods a signal to my father, who immediately pushes me inside his overcoat while Manek stands in front of us. In the next instant, I am swept up by the two of them onto the stoop and through the front door where Aunt Cyla stands waiting in the vestibule. It is all done so rapidly that, when I look back, my brother and father had rejoined the work contingent and were rounding the corner to the main avenue.

Aunt Cyla is a consummate artist when it came to concealing me and her baby son, Lonius, and had arranged a number of options. These included a huge disused water tank on the roof of her building, where two planks were deliberately removed above the laterally placed iron hoop that circled the base. From directly below, it would appear to any searching eyes that the tank was broken open and seemed to be empty. Manek and my uncle had fashioned a false bottom about a meter and a half deep, just enough for a body or two to squat in.

"Come," says my aunt, "I have a warm cozy little nest for you and Lonny, but not on the roof. I want you two close to me."

What she has is a deep trench cut into the crawl space beneath the floorboards directly next to her bed. My Uncle Samek had made it spacious enough for two adult bodies to hunch in, so my infant cousin and I are less of a claustrophobic fit. The hinges to the planked door are concealed in a cut bevel and the door's inner surface is lined with thick felt to temper any sense of hollowness from a boot tap or a curious knuckle. My tailoring aunt had cleverly placed buttoned flaps in the felt that, when opened, allows for airflow and affords a limited view of the room through several small knotholes. The door boards line up seamlessly with the rest of the floor and no one would ever suspect a dwelling place lay beneath them.

I manage to sit up in this barrow and Lonny can stand with enough space to take at least a three-step scoot before meeting the wall. Within this floor coffin, I drift in and out of sleep with Lonius, tucked into his blankets next to me, a warm chubby sprite that often sleeps with his eyes half-open and his tiny starfish hands splayed upwards, as he if expects some boon to be bestowed upon them.

In the evening, Aunt Cyla feeds and entertains us both in the kitchen while Uncle Samek sleeps off his last shift. When it was time for me to enter our floor cave, she provides a chamber pot, a water bottle and a flashlight.

Lonius, she hands in after me with his quilt, a wool rabbit and his feeding bottle. In these hiding episodes, my cousin's scrunched-up face develops an odd waxy sheen. Sometimes I get scared in the night because no air seemed to be traveling through his tiny body. More than once, I bang on the timbers for someone to please open the planks, Lonny isn't breathing right!

Aunt Cyla pulls up the floorboards in an instant and thrusts him inside her gown to suckle at her thin breasts. Mother's milk arouses the baby from what seemed like a centuries-old stupor, causing him to grow pink and utter snorts of contentment. Having feasted well, he returns from a silent, almost marbleized child to a screeching little shitter.

"What's wrong with him?" I complain. "The freaky kid sleeps with his eyes open."

"Romek, darling," pleads my aunt. "He has a little something in his milk, so he snoozes a full eight hours. You don't want him wailing all night."

Her eyes indicate the bottle of prescribed narcotic on the kitchen shelf with the golden bird of the Eagle Pharmacy on its label. I think of the slain Bratkiewicz girls, murderous mothers, and Lonius lying next to me, half cranked out of his skull after barely a year in the world. From the gossip between my mother and Luisia Horowitz, I'd heard that some babies are such perfection that heaven issues them a return ticket back to the angels, should they decide that their earthly expedition is not worth the trip-hammers that litter the highway of human existence. I fear that Lonny might mistake wandering along the Luminal road as paradise beckoning and decide to keep on going. Who would believe that I hadn't rolled on him and squashed him like a plump beetle?

"Don't worry, Romek. This child," my aunt says, with her marvelous smoky laughter, "is indestructible".

She tosses the baby high into the air and he yodels with joy at his soaring. There goes our Lonny, flying above the light fixture, spinning down to be caught with instinctual accuracy into her welcoming arms. The fling-me-to-the-ceiling game goes on for some minutes. I watch their easy gladness, and the more their shrieks of delight fill the room, the more I'm compelled to ask, "Auntie Cyla? Lonius is an OD's son. I'm an OD's nephew. Why do we have to hide all the time?"

She sits down and rocks the baby close. Her words are carefully measured.

"In the beginning, Romek, we had some privileges, extra rations, protection from the arrests. Then the big sweeps started. Your uncles and your father bought off certain men at the Judenrat, and some of the higher-placed officers in the platoons who would warn us to keep kids like you hidden. Now, the regime is changing, those safeguards are running out and there are no guarantees...for any of us."

"What's going to happen? What will they do to me and Lonius?"

Streets of Fire

My aunt sighs, shifts Lonny to her right knee, and beckons me to into her arms. "They will do absolutely nothing to you and Lonny, because there are so many people, Romek, who love you both so much they will always stand between you and danger. We have to live through this, waiting for the time when it's over, forever, and it will be soon. I promise you."

She kisses me and speaks with such conviction that her words loosen the deep bite of fear that lives in me. I want to ask her why Lonius was born at all. Why let such a small helpless thing come into being in this awful place? But I sense the question already tore at her and that she has secretly turned endlessly beneath the crush of its wheel. How do I protect this tiny life when there's no escape? I have no defense against the edict that Lonny is the seed of an ill-fated race and, for that alone, is condemned to be felled from his nest as surely as the fledgling is taken by the hawk.

❦

The next few days run as one dark malevolent tide. On the evening of October 27th, the Ghetto is a ground of dread. Uncle Samek warns us that several armed platoons of Sonderdienst (auxiliary police units of ethnic Germans) have arrived in Podgorze to combine forces with the Ukrainian units, the German military columns, and the Polish police. From the shadows of my aunt's apartment, I have seen hundreds of soldiers amassing in the streets just beyond the Ghetto's perimeter. Samek says trucks are neatly lined up, three meters apart, flatbeds becoming machine gun placements and floodlights placed along the wire by Gate Two, (although there is some question as to whether they can be switched on if needed, since our grid supply was always minimal). Tanks are parked over the manholes of every sewer point and the Vistula's bank laced with numerous trigger mines sunk into the mud.

The number of men and arms seem of such a foolish scale, an overblown might more suited for a Napoleonic battlefield than scaring the crap out of a people already cowed and long depleted.

"Who do they think can fight them?" queries Aunt Cyla.

She assures me of everyone's whereabouts: Mama, Aunt Halina, Cousin Sonia and Uncle Arnold's wife, Lorcia, are sheltered in one place that won't be searched, Arnold's apartment above the OD headquarters. The Horowitz sisters and their mother are working outside the Ghetto, and Tadek is with them. Hanka is staying out at the airport with her labor detail. Boris Pinski has organized to keep Manek, Papa and Israel Horowitz across the river in one of his safe houses.

"Why couldn't I go with Papa?" I whine bitterly.

"Because," Cyla explains, "we were lied to, it was said we should be prepared for a culling of old and sick people but OD families were to be left in peace. We had no clue that they would send a giant to crush a mouse."

The curfew had been lifted temporarily as a lulling measure, causing many of the Ghetto dwellers to scatter to prepared hideouts, more traps than protection. Those who had no safe refuge drifted helplessly through the streets most of the night, not daring to raise their eyes to the siege of military at every wall, fence and gate.

We pass these hours in safety, my cousin voyaging peacefully on the waves of his chemical sleep, and me in an exhausted daze from staying alert to every sound from the floor above. Aunt Cyla pulls a chaise into the bedroom, so she can rest just beside our sunken bay. "You must not come out, Romek, until I say so," she advises softly.

Soon, I hear her light snoring and beyond that the sound of what seems like far away drumbeats, one, two, three, pound and stomp. The drumming resounds, first to the north of the street, then I hear it closer, to the right of us, episodes of intermittent gunshots. I turn to my right and my baby cousin is inert, asleep. His half-open eyes give off a weird glint. I ask him softly, "Can you see me, Lonius? Shall I tell you a story? There was once a tuchas that walked the world by itself. Its name was Mottel..."

Many voices above us, they come and go all the daylight hours. My uncle's apartment is a way station of desperation. I listen carefully through the wood to the voice of a male visitor named Levi Zeitlin, an unemployed shoemaker.

"Can you believe, Samek, who is in the streets? The Gestapo bigwigs, the Jewish affairs men, Heinermayer, Malotke, Hasse, Ritshek, and officials of the labor office, the cream of the Krauts glaring out at us from the open Daimlers. You'd think they were going to the bloody opera! And that donkey's arse Sturmbannfuhrer Haase is parading all over the place with map experts and the housing plan. The order went out that once the labor details had left for work; those remaining should go home, pack a few things and return to the main square. Everyone had to get out of their apartments by ten or eat the bullet. I know we all can't stay here, but please, Samek, the water tank? Just for my wife and the twins? She's a little woman and the kids are so skinny you could fold them up in an envelope."

I sense my uncle's hesitation. A woman's light step crosses overhead, I see a narrow swirl of dress through the cracks and Aunt Cyla is saying to a girlish face, there, please don't cry, my husband will take the three of you upstairs to the roof.

I lean over and whisper to my comatose cousin that we are now four kids in an invisible residence. I wish Tadek was with us, Lonny, I'm running out of Mottel material. I need to pee and shout up a request to come out. Lonny's diaper is rank and I can't manage the gymnastics of changing him in these confines. The baby is awake, kicking his fat little heels against our hatch. The planks are lifted and Cyla's face appears with her usual radiant smile.

"How are my sweet angels?" she greets us. I hand her up Lonny the crapper and climb out into the broad air of the room, which seems to me in this minute as spacious as a meadow. The baby hangs over my aunt's shoulder and grabs at a hat half hidden on shelf above the sewing bench, a mess of mauve silk. The infant coos and stuffs the item in his mouth.

"Look! He's eating Ewa's hat, Auntie," I say.

Cyla whirls around and pulls it out of Lonny's gums. "Who said this was Ewa's hat?" she queries.

So goes the interrogation, as if there wasn't enough *tsores* (woes) out on the streets, it's now seeping in to the room, right up to my eyes. I tried to explain I had watched Ewa sewing it, so it must be her hat, no?

"Romek, the last time I saw this hat," counters my aunt, "it was walking out of here on the head of Pani Weingarten, one of my best customers.

"Maybe the lady threw it away," I suggest, "and Ewa found it and walked it back in?"

"Roman, Beile Weingarten took such a hat with her to Sweden, she bought it to wear on the trip with her family. How could you see Ewa wearing it?"

Oh, no! I thought my aunt has a secret window into my skull, to where images of the semi-naked Ewa come spilling out of my guilt. Ewa, wrestling her plump backside before me into the lilac chiffon dress and somehow, Mottel the tuchas enters the vision; with tiny pink hands, he gallantly reaches up to help the girl close the side zipper.

I decide: better tell Aunt Cyla that Ewa was already dressed—that'll work. It's not the same hat, I lie. Ewa's hat went with a purple dress that had a black velvet thing around the middle. I smile weakly, because now my aunt's face is drawn tight and she's making strange swallowing motions with her mouth. I have a sick feeling that the sharks of blame are circling. She kneels before me and puts her hands on my shoulders, squaring my gaze to hers. This is what adults do to get you to confess to something you haven't done, or when they want to tell you news that you don't ever need to know.

"Romek, did you actually see Ewa wearing a purple and velvet dress with this hat?

I nod a mute yes, speculating that maybe luscious Ewa and I will go to hell together, led by my wonderful aunt, both of us jeered along by the ghosts of the Bratkiewicz kids and Mama who will stone us with potatoes as our cart of remorse trundles by. "Why not ask Ewa about it?" I suggest.

"I can't very well do that," says Aunt Cyla, "she's across the river, about to marry some dumb *sheygets* (a gentile male)."

The next level of disaster cannot be more fitting. An immense sheet of red flame suddenly lights up the street outside and the thunderous bellow of an explosion rocks the entire building. I sway without will and fall heavily. My aunt starts screaming her son's name in a crazed chant and drags me underneath the kitchen table. Lonny is crawling over by the sink. His mother snatches him by his diaper and squashes us both beneath her slender frame. We hear shouts, orders and the repeated tattoo of machine guns. Next, the grinding winch of the tank gun as it swivels around to another target. Aunt Cyla utters one word, "Again!" and smothers us against the floor. This time I feel the detonation vibrate through my bones as the building across the street shatters in a fireball. A brick-scented heat fills the kitchen and I see the glass in the apartment windows swell and bubble inward from the blast wave but the windows mercifully hold.

A heavy quiet ensues, then more yelling from the streets, people shrieking in unison, the usual running steps and screams! It's an hour before this tumult subsides and just when we think the worst of it is over, there comes the sound of the front door down in the lobby being forced open! Men have entered the building! We hear them crashing up the stairs.

Cyla hauls me to my feet and with a single glance orders me into the floorboards. Lonius is hollering up a storm! She stuffs a feeding bottle into his howl. In less than ten seconds, we are both back in the darkness under the floor. Keep drinking, Lonny, I pray, keep drinking! I stroke his fuzzy head and rock him, anything that he shouldn't betray our presence. He gives a little mew and suckles lustily on his bottle. Heavy boots are overhead followed by the bass tumble of Russian mixed with Polish.

A fresh voice above us: it's Symche Spira himself, questioning Aunt Cyla, who is charming in her defense. He's asking in mock sympathy as to why she didn't hear the announcement? All ODs and special status categories are suspended for the day, and where are her husband and the rest of her family? Everyone must make their whereabouts known to the authorities.

I hear her quickly cross the floor and sit down at the sewing machine, to the dress panel sitting under its needle. She starts up the clacking beat of the treadle. "My husband is on duty, with Commandant Kunde at the Plac Zgody," she says in pleasant tones, "and I have a gown to complete, a special order for Frau Haase. You must know her, Pan Spira, the wife of the Sturmbannfuhrer from Berlin?"

Spira is instantly impressed. He plucks at the watered silk with his assassin's fingers; it's of a quality fine enough to support the ruse. Something must be resolved quickly because she hears his Ukrainians stomping across the roof, passing by the wrecked water tower where the young woman and her twin girls rest in paralyzed terror. Aunt Cyla drives the sewing machine faster, its treadle shuddering loud enough to cover any cry of the infant in the floorboards beneath Spira's feet. She knows this man cannot be sent away without some pay-off—it's always expected.

He gives her a grimace of admiration. She is beautiful and quite alone here, and he could do with a little diversion from all those broken women being dragged through the streets. Then there is the husband, an OD too, which could be messy, but Spira would say the bitch encouraged him, even lifted her dress to him.

Streets of Fire

Cyla silently picks up the relay of his lust. She sews a sleeve and marks Spira's slight build; she notes her heavy tailor's shears nearby that I had seen her sharpening that morning. Through the floorboards, I catch their dazzle on the wall as she cuts a thread. She would kill him if necessary, for Lonny and me, but she would never survive the Ukrainian guards on the stairs. They're out there guffawing over cigarettes, dumb mastiffs waiting for their next order.

Through the gap, I see Spira hesitate. On the mantelpiece, Uncle Samek had left a pair of gold cufflinks in a small porcelain dish. They were nothing special but ideal for now. Both Spira and my aunt's eyes travel in the same minute to their glitter.

He picks them up. She radiates the gifting. "How perfect! Please, Pan Spira, I know my husband would want you to have them." He feigns surprise and bad modesty.

"No, I insist," she says, "take them; they will be so appropriate for you."

All the while her legs never leave the machine's treadle, blessed be the noise and dear G-d please get these horrors out of my home. Spira glows like a schoolboy with sudden good marks. He bends to kiss my aunt's hand and she waves him away gaily. He bows and the door finally slams behind him.

Not until the roar of their jeep fades away does the sewing machine fall silent. I give a light tap on the boards and ask if she's OK. She gets up, I see her hands shake a little but she walks over and for the second time that day frees the baby and me from the floor.

"Can we stay out now, please?" I ask, rocking Lonny in my arms. He flops around like a sweet little drunk, although he's still conscious.

My aunt hugs and kisses us both fiercely. "Yes, my gorgeous prisoners, you are up to stay! Let's cook something nice to eat. Set the table, Romek, tonight we have guests." Her finger points to the ceiling, "Ladies in hiding are coming to dinner!"

❋

In a time when betrayal and losses of all stripes is as assured and regular as blinking, Boris Pinski had long ago made a promise to Eli and Guta Nasielski to seek the truth about their missing daughter, Beile Weingarten and her family. Papa said many Ghetto people were derisive at the vow and they laughed at the very idea. My father silenced the bitter tongues, exclaiming, "Who else will give these parents justice?"

"What can you expect of this Catholic schlemiel and all his money?" argued Israel Horowitz. "It's the soldiers; they obviously found the Weingartens trying to escape and shot the lot of them. In a forest of slaughter, what's a few more corpses?"

Why bother with their deaths any way? The elderly Nasielskis are long gone in the box cars to the big lager at Auschwitz. However, Pinski, himself a part-time assassin and a failed Christian for sure, had traveled the Bydgoszcz road to view the odorous mess in the well and, as one that knew the map of human treachery intimately, he declares to Dora Gittelbaum and her father, "This is not the work of the Waffen-SS."

Regarding the varying decomposition of the fifteen bodies, these people were killed at different times. The massacred Jews are hauled out of the conduit and what remains is burned behind the ruined house. Dora and Julius prayed. Boris joined them, shuttling his rosary through his remaining fingers. With his thief's vow, he silently petitioned the Virgin. *I confess, Holy Mother, I am far beyond the reach of all human and heavenly good but are we not adrift in an ocean of evil deep enough that we should add to its rising waters? Let the wicked be punished in thy sight and these innocents know they are avenged for all time.*

It is the hat that sings out for Beile—the one my Aunt Cyla had made for her when optimism still had some currency. Hats don't walk unless escorted by a head, says Boris's driver, Fredek Lempl. In the pocket of Beile's dress, they find the silver hatpin that Cyla had given the woman as an accessory. The circle of viciousness continues to ripple outwards, the little war within the greater conflagration.

My aunt gives the hat to Boris on one condition that he's not to punish Ewa Urbanowicz in any way. He makes an honorable pact and tracks the purple dress to Ewa, and, saying nothing, returns the matching hat and offers his Citroen sedan for her forthcoming wedding. He approves very much of the betrothal of the luscious girl to the Catholic chauffeur. How useful Jaroslaw and his Jewish bride will be. His little messenger doves and his business entrée into the acquisitive hungers of Frida Schoenholz. Boris considers, with some satisfaction, the amount of trading that awaits him with the German Frau, but first a matter to settle.

Fredek Lempl related a confidence to my Uncle Arnold (shared because of past favors between them) that enabled him and Pinski to finally discover their quarry on the Ghetto streets. They greet him with a bottle of single malt Scottish whiskey, a rare gift for Feigel Birkner and an invitation to business.

"One must be discreet, Pan Birkner, you'd best taste it in the car," persuades Fredek, "we have an excellent source from a contact in Kalingrad. We can supply you as much of this product as you can handle."

Feigel assumes he has been well favored by the gods; it's his kind of enterprise. The Zeus of illicit business waits for him in the butter-soft leather of the Citroen. Pinski invites him to sit down in the back seat and already has a full glass of whiskey from his own personal decanter resting between his feet. He slaps Feigel on the back and warmly urges him to taste the unopened bottle. "I assure you, you will never again in your life drink anything as smooth and as potent as this brew."

Streets of Fire

Fredek cuts the cork on the flagon and pours Birkner a tall shot. The OD raises his glass cheerfully and empties it in one gulp. The two other men take deep drafts also. The whiskey lights a mellow fire in all of them. Fredek replenishes the OD's glass repeatedly but ensures his own refill comes from Pinski's bottle.

"A toast to…absent friends," rouses Boris with a broad grin.

"And who are these lucky companions of yours?" asks Feigel, his voice slurring.

The black marketer reaches into his Italian cashmere overcoat and presents him with a sunlit photograph of Beile and Witold Weingarten on their wedding day.

Feigel tries not to react but sputters in agony, the insides of his throat are beginning to melt. A corrosive acidity burns his esophagus and his stomach feels as if he's being knifed from within. He coughs violently and examines the empty glass in astonishment. Boris and Fredek stare at him with a feral curiosity. Boris glances at his gold watch and waits. Vapors of sour almonds rise up Feigel's gorge, his legs begin to thrash, his lungs shutting down—it takes him at least seven minutes to expire from the potassium cyanide. The last thing he looks upon is Beile; her beauty of long ago framed in a veil of Brussels lace and white jonquils.

✻

Tadeusz Pankiewicz had explained to Papa that he remained alone in his pharmacy during the tumultuous selections of the Ghetto's narrowing. Having warned his staff to stay home, he lowers the shades and places a sign in the window advising that any one in need of medicines should ring the shop's bell. Outside, it's a fine morning with a surprising return of summer's heat. The cobbles of the Plac Zgody are a ready oven to sear the feet of those who had been rounded up unshod. Pankiewicz can hear the pitiful chorus without.

Arresting thousands of innocent people and having them sit all day soaking in their own terror provoked in the soldiers and the mercenary police a frenetic urgency. He had observed this before at other selections, a rising hysteria that something more must be furthered to nail down the heady imperative of their authority. Can it be they sense the fragility of its threads? How else should they find a necessity in the beating of elderly men, in the random shootings of young women, in the spontaneous rigors of exhaustive bloodletting?

The pharmacist startles yet again at the rise of agonizing screams beyond his door. In this hour, Pankiewicz can hardly find his usual deep reserves of valor, not today. He knows that outside he will find his colleagues and good friends, learned men and women taken up despite their armbands that classify them as essential workers. The arrestees include skilled physicians such as Sigmund Leinkram, Leon Gluck and his wife and daughter, Doctors

Fredrika Ameisen, Amalie Goldman and Rachel Molkner, and his kinsman in science, the pharmacist Magister Immergluck.

At the end of it all, Pankiewicz will keep his emporium open most of the night, readying himself for the little he can do in the time of lamentations. Many will return from their work detail to find themselves alone, motherless, widowed or instantly orphaned. Empty rooms will possess them, walls will compress their grief, where are my own? So much blood on the staircase, can it be theirs? See, the doors broken open, the shattered gates that let the demons in; sorrow upon sorrow.

The pharmacist takes down his drug compendium, adjusts his brass scales, and searches busily among his apothecary jars. He measures various powders into his healer's mortar to mix a remedy that will soothe all hurts, a calming potion to give the organism a chance to stabilize, regroup and endure.

He works with diligence and invention, pushing back the needling certainty that there exist in his time such gross afflictions for which no medicine will ever be found.

PART III: 1943 ~ 1944

14

The Traveler from Vienna

ACROSS THE RIVER, Ewa Urbanowicz was made to dress for her wedding rehearsal in the pantry of her intended Catholic in-laws. Jaroslaw's father, Karol Graczewski, took an immediate shine to the girl's gaudy voluptuousness, finding excuses to brush against her while whispering a slavering hint that he would be a much better man in the marriage bed than his feckless son. Ewa swallowed her nausea at his salivating gaze and his seedy conspiratorial smile.

Paulina, Jaroslaw's pitiless shrew of a mother, saw no favor in his future bride at all. In her eyes, happiness was a vulgar luxury, kindness a manipulation, and any hint of fleshly pleasure a betrayal of her distorted purity. That she had once been impregnated was an accident of Karol's drunkenness in the first year of their marriage. Beyond that, they cruised through a swamp of mutual indifference and stacked-up resentments, usually heaped on their boy and on the world without.

The arrival of the war and the German occupation in Krakow was of no real disturbance to the Graczewskis, just a deeper shade of dark among the bleak tints of the somber existence they gravitated to. Besides, they now had a front row seat for the annihilation of all that they so long believed had menaced their entrenched Catholic superiority—the city's Jews. Paulina was firm in the opinion that faith had sent the Reich to deliver them from the infidel, and the Black Madonna herself would exalt the Polish race to the very footbridge of heaven once the nation was finally wall-to-wall Christians. To further this cause, she regularly ratted out Semitic neighbors who had managed to live outside the Ghetto by posing as *Geshmat* (converted), and she would watch with tremulous satisfaction as the soldiers kicked and clubbed elderly Jews into the waiting trucks.

No split-lightning beauty as Ewa had ever graced the miserable custodian's lodge of Jaroslaw's parents. Their home mirrored their souls' grayness: cold granite paved floors, crude dirty white walls bordered by fingers of green mold seeping up from the skirting boards overlaid by the perpetual stench of bad drains. The family's heavy mahogany furniture was violently ornate, possessing a density that gave off a haunted, unpleasant aura. The entire house was a quarry of perpetual shadows, the daylight forbidden by dark moth-eaten rugs and stifling brown drapes. Outside, a parched garden spawned many cabbages, one of the few plants to get a roothold alongside the thirsting roses that died quickly in the early summer from neglect.

Ewa stood in her silk slip on the stone floor of the Graczewski's pantry, combing her bleached curls, the yellow hair pleasing to the guards at the checkpoint. The girl happily twirled before the pocked mirror. True, she hadn't much attachment to Jaroslaw, but was drawn by their sexual gymnastics and his rock-like commitment to transforming their lives. In a

The Traveler from Vienna

few days, they would be beyond Krakow and in Finland where, Aunt Cyla had advised her, boats left frequently for the USA filled with escapees helped by the Jewish Aid Society in Helsinki. Besides, Ewa had grown confident in her beauty; any man would come to her aid for some heated promise of her. In time and in a different setting, it would be easy to divest herself of the lummox Jaroslaw.

Jaroslaw had sold his parents a watertight fiction that Ewa was a fervent Catholic from Zakopane, a daughter orphaned through an unfortunate auto accident by rich parents who had left her a significant dowry. (In truth, she had been orphaned by the Christian zeal of a vicious pogrom in her mountain village and her father sold to the transports by a collaborating priest.)

On the stained table in his parent's kitchen, the now former chauffeur laid out a fortune in jewelry pilfered from the wall safe in Frida Schoenholz's back parlor (who herself had acquired them in the Reich's edicts of confiscations). Jaroslaw, astonished at the abundance of dispossessed currency and diamonds that overflowed Frida's secret repository, had helped himself to an early wedding gift.

Before his parents, he'd lovingly fastened a choker of emeralds set in platinum around Ewa's neck and crooned how well they shone against her yellow hair. It could be said to be a righteous moment that the dazzling green stones resting above her breasts had, in a sense, come home. Their first equally beautiful owner having been fitted with a necklace of hemp in Auschwitz after she'd boldly slapped a senior officer for his obscene mauling.

His mother's and the girl's eyes met in a collision of the same urgency: best get them off the slut and to the pawnbroker first thing in the morning, considers Paulina. Ewa, seeing the greed ignite in Paulina's eyes, decided that all this finery should be secretly cashed out with Boris Pinski immediately and a safe passage to Finland bought for the two lovers that very night. Bugger this wedding, she thought, we'll deal with such formalities when Jaroslaw and I are breathing the clean air of the Steppes, far away from these small-minded Poles, to a place where I no longer have to be blonde.

Ewa had left her unlocked suitcase in their gloomy front parlor and Paulina suspected maybe the girl was concealing more wealth for the taking in her luggage. While the bride was busy perfuming herself in the pantry, her future mother-in-law had her claws raking through Ewa's meager possessions: two cast-off but well-repaired dresses of my Aunt Cyla's, a few old blouses, one good pair of shoes...and hidden deep in the arm of her patched coat, a small album of family photographs. Paulina had a punisher's keen intuition of what she would find before she even opened the leather case.

There Ewa's ancestry is laid out in the yellowing prints. The girl at thirteen, already disturbing in her candid stare and moist full lips, garbed in a black velvet dress with a delicate collar of Viennese lace. She is seated in a photographer's studio, before a painted Italian landscape, her legs primly crossed showing off her new patent leather shoes. Beside Ewa stands the bearded man who is now ashes in Treblinka, but whose image will trigger the girl's equally fiery destruction and finally give voice to Jaroslaw's long-buried hatred for his parents.

The image spiked Paulina in the heart with triumph as she stared at the portrait of Rabbi Julius Urbanowicz, his arm around his pretty daughter, a tallit folded across his shoulders, his gaze fierce and commanding in this celebratory hour of Ewa's bat mitzvah. As a serial betrayer in such matters, Paulina knew well how to handle the situation; that it was best to send word and the indisputable evidence at once to her contact at the garrison's barracks. Poor Jaroslaw, thought his mother, to have fallen so low under the Semitic spell, how much better he will feel in the end.

Manek shows up at Aunt Cyla's the next afternoon to bring me home and we left together in the company of Vera Zeitlin, a nervous, thin woman with red-rimmed eyes, and her four-year-old twin daughters. My brother kindly avoids her questions of her husband's whereabouts and instructs her to go to an address on Krakusa Street where Dora Gittelbaum and Rabbi Geller will give her and the children permanent shelter. The Rabbi and her rescued father-in-law will have to tell her that Levi has been executed along with thirty other men against the river wall near Solna Street.

My brother is unusually quiet as we walk. His face looks gray and sleep-deprived. A hollow calm pervades the streets with the dead now cleared away. Their passing is evidenced by the dark red pools collecting in the gutter to be lapped at by abandoned dogs. Several trucks speed by covered with heavy tarps, and my brother pulls me into his overcoat, urging me not to look. Nevertheless, I do.

I see a line of human arms, blood-strewn and bruised, hanging from sides of the vehicles and the plumes of women's hair blowing in the wind as the convoy races along the hard top to Gate One.

"Where are they taking them?" I ask Manek.

"I told you not to look!" he rebukes, gripping my hand tighter.

"So I looked, so what? I know what they're carrying."

"And does it make you feel like a makher (big shot) to know?" asks my brother.

"It doesn't make me feel anything."

We continue on to Josefinska Street and I'm struck by the fact that after all the mayhem, and the trucks bleeding with the slain on their way to the mass grave at Plaszow, those who have survived find some life anew in the small rounds of everyday actions. Knots of people dot the sidewalks, and I hear

The Traveler from Vienna

their noisy accounts of how they have managed to keep their souls inside their bodies during the great cruelties.

Well, I prayed a lot, declares one man, every hour I had hope on my lips. God favors the voice of the righteous carried to him in humility, answers a woman with a traditional wig and the staid demeanor of a Rebbitsin (a rabbi's wife). Next, another takes up his tale. Spira and his thugs were so busy flogging our neighbors, they stupidly told us to wait our turn along the wall by the Judenrat. So, who waits for a flogging? Look, I said to my brother, Zanvele, they are so focused on their wickedness, they will never notice if we just walk away. If they follow, they'll either shoot us or we'll fight them to the end. Zanvele and me, we strolled off to hide on the roof of our building.

※

Broken wood slats, old suitcases and bits of odd furniture litter the sidewalk to our building. The air is infused with a burnt-iron odor mixed with the smell of foul drains, dog crap and brick dust. Manek and I clamber over the shattered remains of the front door. The interior of the apartment house appears as if a gargantuan claw has reached deep into its core and torn out the structure's innards. The banister of the first floor staircase has been axed to kindling and battered apartment doors hang askew from their hinges. My rising fear increases because the plaster dust beneath our feet is a sticky reddish muck, the walls perforated with bullet holes and random steps are missing from the stairs.

"What about Mama and Papa?" I plead.

"They're fine and Hanka too," Manek assures me.

Nevertheless, matters are hardly right because from our floor, I hear a grieving so loud and sharp it makes me nauseous. At the edge of such moments, I wait with my stomach roiling for the explanation of who is dead, who is taken, or who may have destroyed themselves. Bursting into our kitchen, we find Luisia Horowitz on a chair, rocking back and forth, howling like a dying animal. My mother, her face wet with tears, is holding on to the woman and they sway in time together. My arrival seems to increase Luisia's distress, she flings up her hands at the sight of me and screeches, "Oh, Romek, dear child, thank G-d that you live!"

I look anxiously toward my mother, who blurts out three words, "Tadek is lost!"

I'm rooted to the tiles, my tongue bunches up behind my teeth, I can say nothing, thinking that Tadek is up to some mischief by lagging behind his mother and will come through the door any minute.

"Then we'll go find him, Mama," I say stupidly. "Won't we, Manek?"

I grab at my brother, who makes me sit down at the table, "No, no, we won't, little warrior. I'm sorry; it's not possible," he advises. "Pinie Koza saw him at the railway station; he was with a hundred other kids the soldiers put aboard the trains."

At his words, Tadek's mother tears at her clothing and convulses with screams. Manek and my mother immediately help Luisia up and take her into the Horowitz's quarters to lay her down on the bed where she strikes her head with her fists and recites over and over, "It was a few seconds, I looked away...just a few seconds, when I turned around the crowd had swallowed him. It's as if he had been swept into the ocean. G-d forgive me! Who can live with this?"

Mama wipes Luisia's face while Manek makes her sip something from a dark glass bottle. He closes the door but says to me softly, "Wait just a minute, Romek, and then I'll come to you, OK?"

I sit at the table alone, feeling utterly numb and abandoned and fantasize that Tadek, who was gifted with a solid amount of chutzpah for a ten-year-old, would somehow escape from the deportee's train and find his way back to our nest. I reach for my drawings rolled up in a tattered bundle in my pants pocket and unfurl them on the sticky oilcloth. I take my pencil and draw Mottel the tuchas with a sword and a gun in a little chariot hauled by two armored cockroaches, next, a crude image of Tadek with a shield and spear ready for battle. However, Mottel is wise and I sketch him pulling Tadek away, saying, "Leave the field, young master, your best friend awaits your return on the second floor landing...come away home!"

The daydream comforts me as long as my pencil moves over the grubby pages but then my tears start to fall in great salty gobs blurring Mottel and his courageous enterprise into a gray mess. The knowledge is so acute that I will never ever see Tadek again, not on this side of life.

I weep uncontrollably, even as my father steps into the kitchen and immediately gathers me up into his arms.

"I know, Romek," he says. "I know. You need to be courageous now for Tadek and his family."

I press my face into the stubble of his neck and his tenderness makes me grieve even harder. He sits down with me on his knee, squares his gaze with mine and says, "Look at you, just a few years from your bar mitzvah,"

"Will I live so long? Will they take me away too?" I answer between my barking sobs.

My father shakes his head and pulls me closer. "No, Romek, I won't allow anyone to take you away," he declares. "And you will live to become the man worthy of your parents."

He lifts his tallit from beneath his jacket and drapes it around my shoulders. I nod mutely and dry my eyes with its fringes. The shawl is old and threadbare, and like him, saturated with prayer, bound by worn threads that still held together.

"Papa? I want Tadek to come home!"

"Roman, he cannot. You must accept that. If cutting off both my hands would bring him back, son, then I would happily raise a knife to my flesh."

I am not to be comforted. Manek returns from the other room and Papa and he take turns rocking me while I sob through the Shivah hours of that awful evening. They both say little and when they do speak, it's in small futile utterances such as, "There, lamb, be soothed. Don't let the hurt make you bleed so."

Despite my own wailing, I can hear Luisia still grieving in the other room, both of us one long plaint of misery. Her two daughters and husband Israel, equally heartsick, have returned home and are all huddled around her, bound in their mourning. Eventually, Mama comes back into the kitchen, lifts me up from my father and carries me into bed with her. She anchors me tightly in her arms and urges me to sleep. Soon I feel her breath become light and easy and am lonely against her large, soft body. An hour later, Papa climbs into bed beside Mama and me while my brother and sister slide into their quilts on the floor.

"We're all here, Romeczku," murmurs Hanka. "All of us, together."

I lay sealed between my parents in the thick darkness, miserable yet cosseted. I waft in and out of sleep. My waking moments are ploughed with confusion and anger. Knowing he slumbered like a felled tree, I whisper gross blasphemies to Papa, directly into his right ear. "If the Almighty is so powerful, why is it that Tadek cannot be found!? What's the point of having a G-d who is so useless and a Messiah who's in no hurry to get here?"

I listen for any motions in the street and wish I could get up and rest next to Manek. When I finally give in to sleep, I enter a seam of dark as oppressive as a tomb, only a small spark of awareness flickers across my mind; this is what the cold plunge of death must be like, to be as nothing at the end of a vast and futile sorrow, and to awaken in the abyss.

✻

The traveler from Vienna ordered the military's Daimler to halt at the corner of Targowa Street. He quickly set his broad frame down on the sidewalk, swift enough to prevent the Master of the Ghetto, Wilhelm Kunde, from opening the car's door for him. He marched at a belligerent pace through a lightly falling snow, deliberately ahead of Kunde and his Unterscharfuhrer, Horst Pilarzik. Little dogs and master hounds, he thought, at their clipped steps behind him. We shall see who will rule here, he confirmed to himself. The traveler is exhilarated in the bracing cold of this morning, after his success in clearing out the ghettos of Tarnow, Lublin, and Belzyce, and in the latter, siphoning off over seven hundred Jews for the Belzec gas vans, sending the questionably lucky five hundred survivors who could pay him to the Budsyn labor camp near Krasnik.

Thanks to SS Polizeiführer (SS Chief of Police) Julius Scherner, who had fondly ignored the traveler's past financial conjuring, Krakow is the diamond of his career in the Aktion Reinhard (the planned extermination of all Polish Jews). By now, Commandant Kunde is at his side, explaining how the Ghetto had been compartmentalized into Sectors A and B. The Viennese presses on down the street alone, a scanning raptor. He quickly notes the number of courtyards to be sealed off, how many tactical squads to be deployed along the rooftops, the order of tanks to be positioned at every crossroads. An early morning sweep to be sure; create a channel down the main avenue with an impregnable cordon on either side. Clear out Ghetto A first; remove the most useful through Gate Two, keep the streets free so the platoons could easily maneuver, then drive the remaining vermin out.

The night hunt would follow. Let the quiet settle long enough for the hidden to believe in their petty victory, when the floorboards would come alive; attic trapdoors open and wallpaper split asunder against the pressure of bodies freeing themselves. It was his way to implement such matters with the utmost speed, fear being one of his most effective engines. They never learn, these Jews, easy to trap as flies in a gluepot. A bloody show, the shouts, the pleading, but at last, a quiet resignation on which they believed their survival depended, and there we'll be, he thought, waiting to mop up the last of them.

The traveler turned back to see Kunde smiling and talking with a dark-haired, well-dressed man; he beckoned the traveler to come meet him. The Viennese hesitated to shake what he thought at first was the hand of a Jewish OD but Kunde introduced the stranger to him as the pharmacist, Tadeusz Pankiewicz. Pilarzik explained that Kunde's friend was a Catholic also. The pharmacist gave a short bow to the new Untersturmführer and uttered a courteous if formal greeting. He noted the broad shoulders, the face full of severe authority, dark blue eyes whose whites bore the yellow tinge of early liver disease. Pankiewicz also detected the odor of amines on the man's breath; similar to the chemistry of endocrine storms he'd once studied in violent epileptics and patients with fevers of the possessed who cut their own flesh. His gaze examined the man's skin tone and facial mannerisms. The pharmacist intuited he's in the presence of a highly intelligent psychopath, and would soon learn that he has gazed on the venom of death, in the person of its arch serpent, Amon Goeth.

※

Our street is depleted yet again of several neighbors; disappearances that, for once, are not provoked by the gun or the selections. Witold Zelkowicz and his family from number fourteen have departed, Andreas and Marta Reznik from number eight, plus Marta's five grown brothers, along with Dr. Yerahmiel Gruber, a dentist who traded food with Mama for a little periodontal work (sometimes performed with a terrifying mix of crocheting needles, watchmaker's tools, and the last items from Dr. Gruber's dwindling equipment). All these people have gone "upstairs."

It must be true because my father tells me so. I take his words literally and wonder how many friends and allies of my parents can possibly troop along our landing and head for the attic, silent and unnoticed. Curious, I even mount the staircase to the hiding place and knock on the false panel, hoping there might be some kids of my age concealed there. Without Tadek, I have become desperately lonely.

"Hello? It's OK," I explain to the somber wood. "This is Romek Ferber from the second floor. It's safe. You can come down now and visit us, if you like."

Hanka hears my reedy pleas and comes to fetch me home. "You little mug, there's no one up here."

From her, I discover that "upstairs" really means down the road, at the Plaszow labor camp. Hundreds of Ghetto dwellers are assigned there daily, even Jews who work in the Aryan sector of Podgorze. Several prominent OD's are also relocated to the camp, including my Uncle Arnold and Mama's brother, Wilek Chilowicz and his wife, Marysia. Their jobs in the Ghetto are quickly filled by others hoping to gain safety for their families. I think at first that going "upstairs" sounds interesting until I hear my father and Israel Horowitz whispering together of how the new "Hund" is making the work camp a shooting range.

The parent quartet has many low-voiced conversations in these weeks, fervent conspiratorial talk that ceases abruptly whenever I enter the kitchen. I am ego-ridden enough at ten years old to think that the adults are swapping evidence of my latest sins, misdemeanors unknown to me. Worse still, without Tadek to urge me on, my powers of invisibility and eavesdropping are waning. My brother says it's because enchantment is like electricity, it needs a good operating circuit. His words make me weep in secret for my lost friend. Magic is no good alone. I drift about the apartment like a listless ghost amid the adults who seem in a constant state of low-simmering anxiety.

Our ceiling pantry is almost empty. We eat soup for days on end, often a limp variation on the one we ate the previous day. There are dark shadows under my eyes that look like they've been gouged out with a meat hook and Manek wakens me several times in the night because I've been sobbing in my sleep.

One afternoon, without warning, the daylight before my vision closes down to a single pinhole and I slam to the kitchen tiles in a dead faint. The last thing I remember is my mother crying out for help. I'm packed into my parent's bed and a message with a list of my symptoms is sent to Dr. Leon Gross, a prominent Ghetto physician now also "upstairs." Uncle Samek comes to visit with a written but distant diagnosis from the doctor. I hear Mama whispering to Hanka that I have a vitamin deficiency and that I am suffering from a severe depression, which I misinterpret as my body having endured a surface collapse somewhere, like the deep sink holes on the Rynek Podgorski caused by heavy tank traffic.

My condition somehow brings the adults out of their hushed secrets and I become the darling of their attention. Hanka and the Horowitz sisters read to me anything I demand. Manek obtains chocolate bars and a few small hard apples that my mother stews with some powdered milk. Israel Horowitz helps my father bathe me in the sink and rubs my runty limbs with lanolin. Papa makes me ingest quantities of cod liver oil laced with a little whiskey and molasses—the taste is more than unique. Tadek's mother stays on the sidelines but one afternoon she comes to see me in bed with a pile of neatly folded clothes, his former wardrobe, all ironed and pressed in her arms.

"These are for you, Romek; I want to see a boy walk in them again. Better wear them before you reach your next growth spurt."

I am alone in a swathe of quilts, the door shut against the two families. Our bedroom-cum-living space has a heavy silence, grubby curtains, and the gray sky outside dulls the ceiling paint. I feel stronger but I'm not letting on yet that I'm better. While I'm in my parent's bed, little is expected of me. Enclosed in this room, I can be quiet and solitary and have time to imagine that my city and these streets are in some other country, a place where life is as it used to be. In my daydream, I'm back on Waska Street, sharing Moniek Hocherman's new bike that we both can't ride yet. We take turns weaving up and down the cobbles on the contraption. Neither of us can travel but a few meters without toppling over, but we skim along the street, hollering in exhilaration, knowing the fall is coming regardless.

My image of the two of us breaks apart. Moniek is long gone, and now Tadek is gone. The memory of them is one seamless loss but I must not cry or Papa will be in here again with his worried smiles and the cod liver oil.

Hanka reads me a story about a boy who is given a magic ring, and by this item he can wish himself into many distant lands, some not even on this planet. I want to shape such fantastical places for myself but my imagination falters and the best I can do is conjure me reunited with Tadek and Moniek, all of us together happily living on a farm that mirrors the Tomaszow's former property in Borek Falecki.

We boys are now important landholders, each one owning a fine dappled Percheron horse and it's always summer. Our days are spent doing as we please, and the parents call us only to come into the house to eat. I stroll beneath pear trees swaying from the weight of their golden fruit, and a handsome collie with a soft white ruff trots beside me. Her name is Bella. She is my dog exclusively and my mother does not forbid her (as she would in reality) from resting on the pillow beside me at bedtime. Bella possesses a heroic nature and it's her duty in the night to guard me loyally from all dangers. I sleep well in her calming presence. I have spun this tale to myself several times but couldn't quite make it stick somehow.

There has been talk of the Ghetto being closed down, and that we too shall soon be moving "upstairs." I get out of bed and pull on some of Tadek's clothes. From outside, I hear the stamp of boots, loud shouts and dogs barking, the afternoon change of platoons from the various gate points. There is a clatter from the kitchen and the pitched voices of the two mothers arguing over what to prepare for supper. I feel sad that I have no

The Traveler from Vienna

real Bella to come and rest her head on my knee and watch the darkness while I sleep. I can't remember the last time I felt safe.

✻

A brother (and another uncle) on my mother's side, the OD, Wilek Chilowicz had been appointed head of the Jewish Police unit that will keep order in the new camp of Plaszow. Wilek would soon complain of the demanding nature of the warrior from Vienna, giving us every detail. But for now on this chilly morning, all he can do is stand by and watch Amon Goeth press for details among the compulsive ministrations of Advocate Schoenholz.

"Are you certain there are enough latrines?" asked Goeth. "While I've no wish to induce a sense of luxury in our tenants, I can't have the place awash in excrement. We'll soon be maintaining enough shit as it is."

The three men stood on the steep shoulder of a snow-patched hill in Plaszow with Goeth fretful about the efficiency of the plumbing installations. Advocate Schoenholz was more than ready to counter the man, rotating blueprints of the latrines, bathhouses and sewage lines at arm's length. "We share your concerns, Herr Commandant, but the necessary health regimens have been well considered. As you can see, the sanitation plans conform exactly to the standards of the *Militärische Hygene Agentur* (the Agency for Military Hygiene)."

But only just. Amon knew that the hundreds of prisoners working the deep quarries in the camp were secret shitters to a man, since the bare whisper of typhus or dysentery would be cause for mass executions. These prisoners buried their waste with the efficiency of house cats, hiding it deep in the cavities left by the hacked-out granite blocks they hauled across the frozen grassy dunes. The warm winds of summer might betray their toilet habits, but by then such excavations would be filled in and sealed permanently.

"The water pipes are scheduled to be in working order by next week at the latest," Schoenholz advised.

Herr Commandant smiled winningly at Schoenholz. The Jew Chilowicz he barely regarded and he found the bespectacled Advocate an unending tedium but one who could be relied upon to detail every beam, nail and brick. "As you can see," droned the legal voice, "the men's barracks are complete, the electrical supply to the fence bordering Wielitzer Strasse is now active, and I have reports on the operational status of the printing shop, the central storage facility, brush factory, foundry, the paper products plant, and the administration building."

"Well done! You know, Schoenholz, you should have been elected the Mayor of some city," lauded Amon, but not here, he muses, not in my rough little kingdom still waiting for an extension of the railway line from the Krakow-Plaszow station.

He tracked his gaze over the camp's stark hills, at the barracks still no more than bare pine frames on crude foundations, at the Ukrainian guards offering a chorus of cursed orders to the lines of inmates toting planks up the steep slopes, the yellow wood a cheerful gold in the otherwise monochrome landscape. Christ, he considered, how many men does it take to supervise these ants. What lousy deployment, needs to be reorganized immediately, the prisoners run on automatic anyway, always in motion, the fetching and carrying offering a safe hypnosis, or so they think.

The Reich's engineers had complained of certain provocations, unnecessary delays. "It's hard to lay up the walls or get a roof positioned, Herr Commandant, with a work force of broken arms, and these bloody Russian gladiators waling into the carpenters and bricklayers with rifle butts and truncheons any time they're bored."

As it was, Schoenholz had needled him endlessly about the slow progress of the camp's completion, a problem partially solved by Amon ordering a twenty-four hour work push or else. Polish laborers reinforced the day shift while Jewish inmates toiled during the darkness. Herr Commandant thought it most amusing, that he wouldn't have to look upon many Jewish faces (at least for now) when he made his fear-inducing rounds in the light of day. We shall be infested with them soon enough.

Still, as my Uncle Chilowicz complains to my father, the Ukrainians had a rabid appetite for excess—unable to maintain discipline without causing a few daily homicides, a tendency that irked Amon to a fury. He was the lord of life and its terminations. There shall be none before me in these stakes, he'd asserted. He had no love for the black-shirted guards, illiterate and crude, so settled in their moronic brutalities inherited from generations of ignorant feudal serfs. To him, they were so far beneath any German soldier. He had to tolerate them until Himmler sent him his elite cherished Totenkopfverbaende (SS Death's Head Units).

"Not to worry," he had assured the engineers, "we will soon curb the enthusiasm of these Ukrainian degenerates." As a gesture of good faith, he'd shot one of their sergeants himself, a vodka-fuelled blond boy from Chernivtsi. Better that than have Schoenholz dropping ledgers on his desk, demanding triplicate paperwork, and whining to Berlin about the rising costs of construction.

"And the house, Herr Commandant?" the Advocate is asking him in obsequious tones. "It is to your liking?"

His face was close to Amon's and the military man regarded the washed-out gray eyes, thin gold-rimmed glasses, the white doughy skin with green veins visible along each cheek, pursed lips jutted in calculated expectation. He reminded himself never to make a friend of this civil servant so devoted to scrutiny.

"It's superb. I particularly appreciate the view from the balcony. But where you have truly excelled, my dear Schoenholz," said Goeth, "is in the wellbeing of my horse. He is more contented in his new quarters than I've ever seen him. Is that not so, Chilowicz?"

The Traveler from Vienna

My uncle concurred quickly while the Advocate, unruffled, adjusts his rolls of blueprints and heavy files and comments, "I'm happy to hear that. Soon he shall have equine companions to add to his comfort."

From the hill, the three men smiled down on the new stable far below, built close to the site of the former Synagogue, and located on the foundations of a funeral home, adjacent to the old Jewish cemetery, whose broken headstones provided a pavement marking the route to the German offices and residences.

A prisoner named Zozislaw Kepner, a skilled glazer required specifically for this shift, was pushing new window frames balanced in a wheelbarrow along the well-written pathway. He raised his cap to the dead, stepping as lightly as he can over a grave marker naming his kinsman, Rabbi Kepner, an eloquent firebrand, who once debated with czars and rightist bishops, and was expelled from Moscow for speaking out against the Kishinev Pogrom of 1903. The bones of his erudition, along with the earthly remains of others from the ravaged cemetery on Jerozolimska Street, were now strewn over the marshy ditches below the new security fence on Panzer Strasse, causing the local dogs to pace frantically along the high voltage wire and whine with yearning.

✺

I'm back on snooping duty and attempting to sift all kinds of rumors that abound. I track a secretive discussion between my father and Manek how the Judenrat are keeping the steady stream of Ghetto dwellers flowing "upstairs," that a long line of human flea farms stretches down the block from the delousing station on Josefinska Street, their cleansing a preparation for moving. Other signs of migration are empty apartments and furniture congregated in the courtyards. Pieces labeled as rare and of a fine antique quality are sent to warehouses in various parts of the Ghetto, while others are carelessly hurled from windows to shatter on the cobbles. The hungry gleaners from Ghetto B are soon to come in waves and bundle up the shattered timbers for fuel.

I imagine Podgorze being cut away from the world by a giant pair of scissors. In what firmament will we fit next!? Even with all its lunacies and terrors, we have adapted to living a hushed and cautious existence for the last two years. I am settled in this cramped apartment and can't comprehend being moved on yet again. I feel an odd pride for my family, we have been menaced but not taken, we have schemed for food and not starved, and we haven't been struck down by the tuberculosis or the typhus that came stalking behind the roundups. True, we are missing Tadek, the stalwart friend of my adventures, but we have prevailed.

It's in our nights that I churn my fears and sense the inexorable lurch of the Ghetto towards a vast uncertainty.

"Romek, go to sleep," urges my brother.

15

Plaszow Spring

ON A MARCH MORNING, an order signed by Obergruppenführer Julius Scherner is issued to the Judenrat of the Podgorze Ghetto. All persons are to evacuate Sector A by 3:00 pm to be marched to the Plaszow labor camp while those occupying Sector B are to report the day after to the train station. Several hundred German and Polish police surround the Ghetto walls to curb the fantastic uproar aroused by a clause in the decree. No children under fourteen permitted in this relocation. Crazed parents rush to surrender their kids to relatives and friends in Sector B. The police along the inner perimeter willingly let many mothers cross the barrier but few are allowed to return to Ghetto A.

The truck with the bullhorn trolls down Josefinska Street and sings out in Polish that children age ten and under are not allowed to enter Plaszow. I take this as excellent news and proclaim cheerfully to my parents that since I cannot go, nobody has to move at all. Isn't that great? My mother stares at me, her eyes narrow.

"G-d help me. I have a moron for a son," she complains. "You're coming with us, so start packing!"

Manek has shined my boots splendidly and hands them to me. "Put these inside and then add your feet next, OK?"

He next gives me two thick wedges of poplar wood, deep heel cups planed and lacquered to a bright sheen. I place them where he indicates and force my feet into the boots to find myself immediately taller. My father smiles and tells me I look quite the man. My brother pulls me into one of his old jackets with wide shoulders, rolls up the long sleeves inwards and rams a cap with a broad peak on my head that shadows my face.

"You will march in the middle with Papa and me on either side," he says. "Keep your face down and your gaze to the concrete until we are beyond Gate Two. If any military asks your age, you will answer clearly that you are fifteen. If they ask for your blue ID card, you will show them this."

My brother hands me the all-important labor ID card and I see that I have aged five years in a photograph deliberately worn and creased, but am disappointed to learn that this Roman Ferber is a brush maker. "I don't want to be a lousy brush maker," I protest. "Can't we say I'm a buffalo hunter or a landowner with many orchards?"

My father moans and throws up his hands in despair, and my sister, always the bulldog, seizes me by the shoulders and shakes me! "This is not a game, Romek! It's either a live brush schlepper or a dead buffalo hunter! Do you want them to take you away from us?"

Plaszow Spring

The desperation she's giving off scares me badly. I promise her meekly that I'll love my lowly occupation and I'll be the tallest, smallest person who doesn't speak much. We're allowed to pack only a few changes of clothing. I search under the sink for my Zeiss telescope to find it gone. Mama puts her arm around me and says with regret, "Don't look for it there, my angel. We sold it back to Pan Pinski for some rice and vegetables."

Oddly enough, the news does not upset me. I'm too intent on our new exile.

The Horowitz family leaves the apartment ahead of us while my father gathers us together in our room. "Hopefully, this will be our last removal," he says calmly. "In the place we are going to, the only nation we will have is each other; purpose enough to live for, G-d willing."

He holds my hand tight and in the next minute, we walk out of the place and are down the stairs, joining the huge throngs of people on Krakusa Street. The moment brings an unexpected separation. Hanka is not going with us. We kiss her many times before she has to stride off to join a waiting contingent who labor at the Krakow airfield—all exempt, for now, from relocation. She bends over me and says tenderly, "Be good. The next time I see you, I'll be looking at a young man, not a whiny brat. I'll find a way to get letters to you all."

I cling to her for some minutes and feel a tremble in her shoulders. She kisses me some more and pulls away quickly at the shout of the OD for her to get in line. Their unit moves out immediately. Uncle Samek and Aunt Cyla are waiting for us on the avenue now packed with thousands of people. Cyla has a large black holdall slung across her back and is carrying a basket with bread she'd baked, some cheese and a thermos of milk. She has made herself somewhat dowdy, but I can see a good dress and a wool coat covered by a ragged old raincoat of her husband's. She offers me some hard candy.

"Where's Lonius?" I ask her.

"Oh, we shipped him on ahead," she says, smiling at me.

"How did you do that? Did Ewa take him already?"

My question stops her smile immediately. "Ewa is elsewhere," she replied.

Before I can ask her anything more, platoons of soldiers come marching from the side streets followed by jeeps carrying senior officers. Manek and my father pull me into the center of the multitude. Mama gets behind us with Aunt Cyla. We are to stride out, four across, and my father is pleased to see Rabbi Geller join us Ferber men. Whistles shrill and the mass surges forward down the avenue toward Gate Two.

Although it is still March and old snow lies in grimy piles along the gutters, the day is warm and humid and I soon become a melting swamp in my adult's jacket. My father is craning his head to see above the crowd. He makes a signal to Uncle Samek who leans into our line and warns in low tones, "A dozen soldiers either side of the gate up ahead. They're looking for old ones, kids, and people faking good health. Whatever happens, keep moving. A few more meters and we'll be on the road south."

A jeep rolls by, cruising a little slower than our walking speed. I glance over to see, standing in the front passenger seat holding on to the windshield, a very tall German officer in an overcoat decorated with many medals. Seated behind him with the air of traveling dignitaries are two huge dogs, Great Danes that bark furiously at the multitude. The officer's gaze is predatory, his motion swift, he's pointing at mainly older men and women. "You!" he beckons. "Here, come here!"

The chosen brim with shock and bitter terror; a little further and they would have passed by this vulture. The soldiers pull the unfortunates out of the line and order them to stand with the hands above their heads. The rest of us walk on in silence.

Where the main avenue curves around to Wielitzer Street, our route is set south toward the Plaszow camp. This bend of the road represents a new border of vileness that defines for me how protected my previous two years had been—until this particular morning. From this moment forth, there are to be no safe places, each minute I breathe seems to bring its own new dangers. The march slows down as we reach the Ghetto's exit. My Uncle Samek looks nervous and moves into the line with my mother and my aunt.

Up ahead two young couples with young children are arguing solicitously with a Waffen-SS wearing a medical armband. He pushes them back inside the wire, shouting at them to return to the Ghetto at once. This triggers an order for the guards to come spot-checking and interrogating marchers at random. I look upon a boy of about seven who is pulled roughly from his mother's hands. She grabs onto her son, gets slapped but does not let him go, then the two of them are hauled away together, the woman falls and is pulled by her long hair with her child sheltered on her belly to protect him; her back slammed repeatedly against the cobblestones. From somewhere behind us echo the thunder of rifles, screams, and anguished cries.

In the noise and mayhem, another mother dashes out of the line and back towards the Ghetto, the heavy lump hidden in her coat being a two-year-old girl. I watch her running, the small girl bouncing and screaming on her shoulder when the soldiers fire on them. The woman appears to take a wild leap into the air to catch her falling daughter, whose head is now a bloody red mess. The two go down together and lay still on the sidewalk.

My father turns my face forward. "Romek, don't look, you mustn't look." His whole body is shaking.

"Leon," Rabbi Geller whispered softly. "You can't let them see you comforting the boy. It might betray his age."

Manek eases me gently away from Papa and says, "Keep your eyes ahead, little man, we'll soon be through this."

Plaszow Spring

Another order is called through a bullhorn for the marchers to step to the left for the arrival of a military limousine bearing the Sturmbannfuhrer Willi Haase, SS Chief of Staff and Police for the Krakow District. There is a lot of yelling back and forth in German. Deep inside our immediate group, my mother is able to whisper to us a rapid translation. The three-cornered dispute is between the Waffen medic, a red-faced lieutenant who keeps looking into the empty barrel of his hand gun, and the important Haase, who refuses to get out of his car but is demanding to know why all the disorder and what bloody fools are running this checkpoint anyway?

In our march to Plaszow, I drift into some kind of numbing fog with strands of mournful and indignant conversations washing over me. A man's sour voice from beyond my right shoulder, "I gave Lilia every zloty I had. It won't matter, she'll whore herself out to anything that breathes. I can see her now, just before curfew, calling across the wire to the soldiers, saying she's a maligned Catholic and if they come to the house on Janowa Wola, she'll show them her baptismal papers—and a good time. I could break that dirty bitch's neck! Decked out in the rags she strips off the dead. What woman follows the cemetery cart, looking for a corpse in her size?"

"Who commanded you to be with such a pretty sinner, "answers an older male voice. "Ugly schmuck, you're lucky a dog should raise his leg to you."

From another man just behind my mother I hear, "Remember Berele Habermann, the jeweler? What a fool, hid hundreds of wedding rings from the Krauts. No wonder they shot the whole family. What's to die for? It's just geld (money)."

A wife's voice barks at him, "Pitzele, your mouth is good for nothing but garbage and it's overflowing already!"

Next the educated drawl of someone I can't see but it sounds like a university girl whose tone is haughty and assured, "My stepmother Fradl, may she perish from her vanity, greed or both, crossed to Sector B to retrieve four strands of pearls from Aunt Balbina. She was to return with both aunt and the pearls, said the necklace was owed to her. Can you imagine? Such a thing will barely buy you a crust of bread."

Men and women on the sidewalks stare at us; whole families bundled up in winter black wool. Some faces betray their fear that where we are in this moment, they could be tomorrow. Grandmothers with cheeks of cured leather, shrunken lips collapsed inwards, hard-faced pitiless men, raggedy young wives too malnourished and dispirited not to agree to the group disdain, fearing the thrashing they'll get at home for the disobedience of empathy.

I glance over at the pained face of one well-dressed man who stands hand-in-hand with a fine-looking boy my age. The boy smiles and waves to me. My gaze connects for a few seconds with him and his refined parent, and I feel it would be safe, even commendable, to know them. The father holds the truth of our story in his eyes. Nevertheless, a hefty woman next to him caws out, "The war is over! The Judas people are leaving! Now we will have peace!"

The military escort is hardly impressed by her bid for an armistice. They swing their rifles away from us to fire several shots into the air. The retort scatters our Polish audience rapidly into the side streets. Some sections of the march break into applause but a shouted order quickly silences it.

✳

In the backpack I am carrying to the Plaszow camp I have two changes of underwear, another pair of pants, a sweater that once belonged to Tadek, some socks and a weighty tattered primer, "Native Animals of Eastern Europe and Russia, Volume Two: Predators of Carpathia and the Taiga " by Anatole Zedkedy. The book has extraordinary, large-plate engravings of wolves tearing at bison and Siberian tigers leaping across the tundra in dramatic displays of sharp-toothed magnificence. The volume had been a treasured gift from my science teacher, Lydia Rosenfeld, and the only book I was able to grab in the leaving of our apartment, sliding it into my backpack with its heavy linen-boards facing outwards.

As the afternoon is wearing down to fading light, I have become a piece of weary bracken floating between my father and Manek. My feet hurt and the dread of our destination adds to my hunger and exhaustion. As we get closer, I note the chimneys of the barracks, the new roof slates of the workshops, and one extremely steep hill with smoke rising above several manned watchtowers. Beyond the electrified wire fence, there is a large red villa with a balcony.

One would imagine that the practical effort of moving several thousand people through a single entrance into the camp would have required the usual order and strict efficiency of our jailers. Instead, the short haul from our turning off Wielitzer Street and entering Plaszow's main gate became several meters of startling barbarity. There's great hollering and I foolishly think that the people up ahead are dancing! Hundreds of them are weaving in a frenetic shoving waltz, dashing to left and right under Russian shouts of, "Move in, damn you! Hurry up! Move in!"

The Ukrainian units are angrily bludgeoning people through the gates! Swinging their clubs in a deadly caustic rhythm. I see Uncle Sam clutching at Aunt Cyla and her backpack from behind, his face drawn with terror. My mother too moves closer to Cyla, protecting her right side. We are almost at the gate. Papa grabs me by the collar, pushing my head under his arm, shielding me with his coat; his shirt is damp with sweat, muscles corded up. He expects to get hurt.

A dark uniformed figure appears above me, a sharp-boned face, fine green eyes but the lips are pulled back in a hostile bark. Papa cries out in anguish as the man strikes him hard across the shoulders. Yet he asks politely of the brutish presence, "Please, Sir, a little patience, we'll do as you ask, but the child here…"

Plaszow Spring

I didn't dare look up but heard the heavy slap of my father being hit in the face. Manek shouts something defiant and tries to stay the next blow but is hammered in the back of his knees by another black-shirted devil. He slams to the gravel and Mama is crying out to him, "Get up, Manek! For G-d's sake, get on your feet!"

With my brother half bent, my back is exposed under my father's elbow. Papa is now dancing the pain step, twisting me and himself this way and that. A great throng of people are screaming and knocking against us. We are in a wild hurricane of yelling and squirming bodies. The Ukrainian's eyes rage at me above the hefty club he swings against the sky, it thwacks across my spine but meets the heavy book in my backpack. My mother is screaming something incomprehensible! I'm shocked that I feel a powerful reverberation rather than bone-breaking agony. Breath leaves me in a whoosh but Papa grabs me and throws me into the waiting arms of Rabbi Geller to be sheltered in his black gabardine.

We actually move out of beating range but I call out something stupid like, "My book! My book is broken! Papa, where's my Papa?"

I hear my father shouting, "Push forward quickly! Get beyond them!"

There's a great surge from behind us. I can't see anything. My feet are off the ground, flying in the wings of the Rabbi's sour smelling overcoat. The daylight returns and Geller hands me off to my mother. She's panting in relief and smoothes back my hair. Manek comes staggering up behind us and quickly herds me and the rest of the family down the walkway paved with the broken remnants of Jewish tombstones. I look back and the beating waltz is still in full tilt at the gate. One man dares a kind of running tennis game against the Ukrainians, skipping out of hitting range, laughing in their faces and athletically fielding each blow with the skilled angle of his suitcase.

By now, it is early evening and dusk is rolling across the sky. We catch our breath under the eaves of a long building that houses the communications center, to be stared at by an anxious Polish clerk wearing earphones, his thin neck laced with switchboard cables. Samek chats with him through the window. The man nods kindly but says, "It's fifteen minutes before the big count. You'll be in serious trouble if you're not in the line by then. Sorry, but I can't be seen talking to you." The man quickly retreats to attend to the clack of his teletype machines.

"Let's regroup for a moment, everyone," Samek pants. "Are you hurt, Leon?" he asks my father who murmurs a denial through his bleeding lips. Aunt Cyla has the shakes and my mother holds her up while my uncle and Manek remove the heavy knapsack from her shoulders.

"Open it up, please!" Cyla pleads in a desperate whisper. "Let some air into it."

"Maybe you should wait until the barracks are assigned?" asks Papa.

"Wilek will make sure there'll be no prying eyes." assures my mother.

Uncle Sam cradles the backpack with great delicacy. My mother unzips it carefully just a little ways. Deep inside what I think is at first a large pink doll wrapped in shawls is my baby cousin, Lonny, the infant of the chemical sleep. A small human log ferried through the gunfire and the Ukrainian gauntlet, to arrive in this moment amazingly unscathed. He yawns as if the tumultuous world around us was one planet over from his father's broad arms. I count three of his new teeth and the sight of his weird gnome's face floods me with pleasure—he always looks like a miniature old man in a diaper. He closes his eyes and snores complacently.

"The kid's a brick wall," says Manek, stroking Lonny under his chin.

"Close up the bag a little and cover his face," advises my father gently as new inmates hurrying along the path stare curiously at our group. By the gate, I see my uncle, Wilek Chilowicz, talking with the guards. He nods to us, but waits a while to approach so as not to arouse suspicion that we are family. I have a short spark of delight that Lonius is here, my tiny war companion, and I am whole, saved from hurt by Anatole Zedkedy and his second volume. Mama smiles and says thank G-d it was one of the writer's longer works.

We are ordered to form lines of ten by gender in the Appelplatz, a large square bordered on three sides by the barracks. We take our place with the other prisoners but through their elbows, I spot Uncle Chilowicz walking behind the German intake officer with two other OD's, one of whom is Uncle Arnold. Wilek's wife, Marysia, and a team of uniformed women are counting the female inmates. Deep in that cluster, my mother, aunt and infant cousin are hidden. A relieved silence falls on thousands of people who stand for several hours in the chilling evening as group-by-group are assigned their quarters. With Wilek present, my family has the small privilege of not waiting too long. Barrack numbers are called out and the assignees zoom out of the crowd on the double, eager to get indoors.

When it's our turn, we congregate in a side avenue of wooden barracks with the uncles. Arnold reads us a document written in German that sends our womenfolk to the female residences and we males to separate quarters. I panic to see my mother walking away with the other women.

"No! Not yet!" I call to her, and she hurries back to me for a minute.

"Stay with your father and brother, Romek," she orders roughly, but I could see her sternness wasn't real; her eyes were lit for me.

"Take me with you, please?" I beg her.

"I can't, Roman. If I do, the soldiers will never believe you're a young man of fifteen. I'll see you every day, as much as I can, I promise. Now be a mensch and don't complain."

Plaszow Spring

She kisses my cheeks several times and walks away, off-loading the bag of Lonius from Cyla, who is exhausted from carrying all that secret baby flesh the distance from Krakow.

※

Night in our barrack, the overhead lights are switched off but the east end of the building is lit by a candle set in a tin can resting on the coal stove. Our group includes me, my father, Rabbi Geller, Manek, two teenage brothers, Emil, Krystof, and their only surviving parent, an optometrist named Michal Porhoryles. We are a cozy enclave of low-voiced chatter below the tier of bunks. The Porhoryles boys are former students of the same Gymnasium that Manek once attended and seem to know him.

All of us are packed around the tiny blazing grill of the stove, which warms our fronts while plumes of chilled air hover at our backs.

The windows are blacked out against the RAF Mustangs and the US Air Force that make frequent reconnaissance swoops over the camp at high altitude, causing Amon Goeth to scream at their fuel trails and aim his rifle uselessly at the sky. "If you ever see them, don't look up, Romek, whatever you do," my father whispers to me in his secret joy at the late evening drone of the Roll-Royce engines overhead, the British fighters escorting the deeper bass notes of the American B-17 warhorses. "The Krauts don't like it. Those British and American boys will soon be dropping their payload over Germany."

"Can we go home then?"

"Not yet, little man, not yet."

We speak softly so as not to wake the many sleepers, already snoring in different notes up and down the bunk line. The boundaries of conversation are comforting and equable, each of us interested in entertaining the other men in some fashion.

"Will you read to us, Romek, from the book that was your armor?" asks Papa.

"You mean…for everyone, out loud?" I ask, astonished. I usually read to my father when we were alone. At such times, I could stumble as much as I wanted to and still be praised. Rabbi Geller comments that "Romek will lead the way" because I have a library of one and few, if any, books at all would be allowed Plaszow's inmates, (although Uncle Samek had said there were two book depositories in the vast complex of the camp).

"But what do we do, Rebbe, when everyone's heard my stories?" I ask him.

Rabbi Geller taps his forehead, "There are many kinds of books, little scholar. Those that dwell in the imagination are an endless treasure. We can keep ourselves knit together with memory making, by stories from our mother's kitchens, from gossip heard in the marketplaces, and the holy scrolls themselves. Every soul is a library, and a salve to the madness that might eat at our minds in this place. Read to us, my boy, and then we may be able to take up your tale too."

I rest against my father and open the Ukrainian-dented boards of Zedkedy's Volume Two. "Wolves in Poland feed mostly on ung...ungulates," I begin with my voice shrill and utterly self-conscious. "Hunting occurs mainly at night and in early morning on pastures close to forests where domestic animals remain without supervision. The massive molars and powerful jaws of a wolf can crush the bones of its prey in six to eight bites. Their biting capacity is...680...680 kilos of pressure per 2.54 centimeters."

I stop because I'm feeling sorry for the moose and imagine the 680 kilos of fangs closed around my scrawny thigh. Manek is on cue with a cheeky song about a cunning Taiga antelope who outwits an old wolf by crooning like a female in heat. The men laugh uproariously and even the Rabbi titters at the risqué chorus. Next, Michal Porhoryles spins a true account of a client of his, a wealthy shortsighted countess having her poodle dined on at a family picnic by a wolf pack that released a stolen brisket from their jaws in favor of a live prey. Rebbe Gellar, of course, scrambles through his vast memory of shtetl legends. "Things of this world are not always as they seem," he intones. "One must be careful, gentlemen, in examining what appears to be true at only first sight."

He goes on to make me crazy with sadness from his story about a Russian prince who returns from hunting to find his son's cradle overturned, the infant missing and his faithful dog with blood around its mouth. Believing that it has savaged the child, the prince draws his sword and kills the dog. He then hears the cries of the baby and finds it unharmed under the cradle, along with a dead wolf that the noble canine had defeated.

I feel tears rolling down my cheeks by the time he finishes telling it in his grand dramatic style and am yet again embarrassed before the men. My father stands up and says, "Come, it's time to sleep, for all of us."

I get a hug from the Rebbe and a confusing order to grow a tougher skin while still having the capacity to bleed for others.

"It's just a story, Romek," comforts Manek. "You can make up your own ending where the dog wins, shoots the prince, and he and the baby live happily ever after."

We disperse to our bunks, three or more each allocated to one narrow pallet, and the misery of head-to-toe sleeping. However, it was for me the most wonderful arrangement. My brother, father and I shared the top bunk above the Porhoryles men. Wedged in between two of them, each with their arms around me, I feel cocooned and secure (for now). Safe from the Waffen-SS in their upholstered beds, from the searchlights and the watchtowers, from the burning meat stench oozing out of the fires on the tall hill, and from the Austrian man and his feverish angers, who slept an unholy rest in the red villa.

Plaszow Spring

Uncle Chilowicz has entered my age into the camp records as way beyond ten but my parents think this ruse will wear thin once I let loose with my duck-quack of a voice. Therefore, Mama orders, no lip flapping on the barrack avenues unless it's necessary. I am not to be outside alone without a family member in case the Ukrainian or German militia questions me—just the thought of interrogation is terrifying. I also require a job since my non-working status guarantees me a fast route to the deportee transports.

My uncle assigns me to help in some fashion in his private barrack where Manek is working as his secretary. To be alongside my brother pleases me very much but then I too get an assistant of my own: my cousin, Wilús, the six-year-old son of my mother's sister, Frania and her husband Henryk Schnitzer, who have been assigned from the Ghetto to run the Madritsch clothing factory in the camp. Their function as managers has given them an extra margin of secrecy to hide their child from the deportations. However, he still has to be a shadow in daylight. (Kids of Wilús's age and mine are known as "camp hamburger," easily devoured by selections.) The sight of this cousin's cute little kisser doesn't please me at all. He is a querulous boy, a spoiled, whiny gnome of obstinacy whose stock response to any instruction or request is "I don't want to!"

"Whatever you do with him, Romek, make it fun," advises my brother. "Any arguing or loud fuss might draw attention from the day patrols. We don't need Goeth coming around looking for targets."

I come to understand Plaszow as a huge and intricate kingdom of almost biblical make-up. Certainly, slavery was back in style, as surely as the Jews had laid bricks for the Pharaohs. Here, they labor at a variety of occupations that come with attendant beatings, endless overtime, and personnel reviews frequently rounded off with arbitrary death sentences. Despite all this, industry is humming in the camp. It has a furrier's emporium, labs that test the mineral rocks from the quarries, a foundry, six tailor shops serving the output of military uniforms, locksmiths, tinsmiths, watchmakers and a shoemaking family that produces fine handmade boots and shoes for very German foot marching around Krakow.

Part of Uncle Chilowicz's responsibility is to see that order is kept among these different tribes of workers. He also has the unenviable task of being a sales connection for Amon Goeth, whose ironhanded governance involves the illicit sale of camp supplies on such a scale that even Boris Pinski had stood aside to let Amon have all the grocery end of the black market. More revenue fills the Commandant's pockets from the treasures that were repeatedly spread across the desk in the Chilowicz's living room.

I become a sorter of plunder, sifting jewelry from the satin pouches of affluent Jews, confiscated from their private safes and bank deposit boxes, from once-elegant homes and from the booty found in the false bottoms of suitcases just before the selection trains pulled out. Under Manek's supervision, little Wilús and I end up arranging brooches, bracelets, earrings and other valuable pieces according to color, size and category. Later on, the Hassidic brothers Friedberg, former jewelers and goldsmiths, will come with their loupes, magnifiers and grading scales to report the value of the glittering fortune.

The jewelry sorting is an absorbing tactile duty for two kids and I don't hear one cantankerous word out of my cousin once I have organized various games around the shining bounty.

We learn from my brother how to distinguish a star ruby from a garnet and sapphires from blue quartz and sort through bright falls of gold, including necklaces and all the wedding rings for which Berele Hermann took the bullet. We group cascades of pearls into color and size allotments and spell out our names on the black felt cloth with the molded gold nubs, the gilt crowns from a thousand Jewish mouths now silenced. Since I am reasonable at arithmetic, it falls to me to count these dental fragments into units of one hundred and place them in small leather sacks for Mojesz Friedberg, the goldsmith in his family, who will measure the carat weight and test the metal for its purity.

The hazardous sin in this, my first job, is dropping anything on the floor where loose diamonds are concerned. At the end of the day, Manek turns on all the lamps above the sorting table and hands me a flashlight so Wilús and I can search on our knees for any lost wealth buried in the carpet or hiding in the cracks of the floor timbers. With my eyes narrowed, I try to discern anything gleaming, but I don't understand what the big deal is because come tomorrow, the treasure trove of today will have a solid pedigree written up by the Friedberg brothers and be dispatched to an anonymous destiny only Amon Goeth and my uncle know of. By morning, the sorting trays with their raised edges and black cloths will be piled high with another mountain of dazzling loot and we will begin our hypnotic task all over again.

For our safety, Wilús and I camp out in the living room of my uncle's private quarters, bunking down on the carpet at night under layers of army blankets. There are no soldiers to threaten us and the food we receive is so much better than the meager rations permitted other inmates. Leaving us with a water bottle and a chamber pot, my aunt, Marysia Chilowicz, turns the key in the living room door in case we're tempted to wander through the premises and out into the betraying beam of the searchlights. Lock-down in the camp commences around 8:00 p.m. and any shadowy figure caught in the barrack lanes thereafter guarantees a storm of rifle fire. One lone prisoner shot in dark means hauling everyone out of their bunks to the Appellplatz for a head count and punishing investigations.

Wilús moans and cries in his sleep, wetting me with his tears. I wake him from whatever monsters are crowding his dreams. "Stop crying. What's wrong?" I ask him.

"I don't like it here."

Plaszow Spring

"Nobody likes it here," I say.

"I want to be with my Mama."

"You can't, you're stuck with me."

"That's what I don't like," he sobs.

With his delicate heart-shaped face and full red cheeks, my cousin is an ideal portrait of those cherubs etched in the corners of ancient maps that blow the winds across the earth through their plump jowls. Nevertheless, distracting him to happiness is a constant concern. Wilús has a wail as shrill as the morning reveille and no sense at all that we are utterly dispensable to our captors. Sometimes at night if I hug him for comfort, he will resist and hit me.

"Shall I tell you story? I know a good one," I offer during one of his rebellions.

He stops blubbering at once, his eyes brighten and he nestles close to me.

"There was once a brave dog who saved his best friend called Baby from a dangerous wolf..."

The narrative is loosed like a hare in meadow to enchant my small cousin. Mottel the Tuchas make a return performance in my imagination, being in allegiance with the canine hero. The baby's father becomes a ruthless bandit and the enemy of all that was good, so I orphan the child to inherit some rich kingdom in Siberia and even have Mottel bring the wolf back to life by means of a magic song. In the finale, Wilús is sleeping so quietly his breath is only discernible by the way it lifts a frayed thread from the blanket.

From the far distance of Krakow, I hear the air-raid sirens faintly blare and die away and I imagine my father in his bunk, hoping it's the RAF squadrons zooming over the Vistula to bomb the Germans out of Warsaw. The plume of the camp's searchlights sweep by the window but I cover my face to sleep and say to Mottel, who still dances in my mind, that we need some new story material, a little slapstick perhaps.

16

Dodging the Devil

THE NEXT MORNING'S BOUNTY is a slew of watches that we hold to our ears to see if they tick and pre-sort what's working and what isn't; our sifting boxes are labeled men's and women's timepieces, silver and gold. We have some jewelry today too, mainly necklaces and earrings. However, one leather case holds a spectacular diamond tiara fit for an opera star. I ram it onto my greasy, flea-ridden hair and admire my reflection in the window.

"You look like an ugly lady," jibes my fresh cousin. "Hurry up, I want to wear it."

I place the coronet on his brow and intone, "I now crown you Prince Wilús of Plaszow."

He cracks up giggling; the heavy item slips down his small head and becomes the most expensive collar he'll ever wear. He parades before the windows, checking himself out in the glass: the sunlight spatters us both with reflected shards of brilliance. I am startled to see another figure visible in the panes and turn to see a very tall man standing in the doorway! No visitors are allowed in the room when we were sorting, and at first, my heart turns to stone because I take the person to be Amon Goeth, but the man smiles in a manner that calms me instantly.

"I heard there were young princes here," he greets us cheerfully, "and among all these treasures, I think they shine the brightest."

Manek comes in behind him, they shake hands warmly; the man leans against the windowsill and ruffles Wilús's dirty hair. The visitor is nattily dressed in a well-cut double-breasted suit with a mohair trench coat resting on his shoulders. He has well-carved features, light blue eyes and bears himself with an easy self-assurance. "So what do the princes have for me today?" he asks, smiling again at us but mainly addressing my brother.

"Cartier, Vacheron, Audemars Piguet. What did you have in mind, Herr Schindler?" Manek asks him.

"Something good-looking but hardy," says the man.

"We have a fine Girard Perregaux, slim 24-carat casing, two-tone dial, it would suit you well," my brother answers with a sales clerk's persuasion, although the item will be free. He lifts the gleaming timepiece from its satin box and hands it to the elegantly dressed stranger.

"What happened to the former owner?" he queries. "You know how superstitious we border people can be." He catches my eye, grins, and says, "So young man, what do you think?"

"I think it's very beautiful…you should wear it in good health, Sir." I reply, his fulsome presence making me shy.

"My kid brother is developing high taste at last," comments Manek and pulls out several papers from the files. "The provenance indicates the item is from Shmuel Reznik and Sons, an upscale watch and clock store on Florianska Street. They once stocked my father's pens. The Rezniks got out to Canada as early as 1939, sold most of their inventory for a passage through Finland."

"Well done for the Rezniks," approves our visitor.

My brother fastens the watch on Oskar Schindler's wrist. Schindler pulls back the sleeve of the wool overcoat and it gleams discreetly against the four-button sleeve of his cashmere jacket and his diamond cufflinks. He stands up and his huge hand shakes the grubby, limp fingers of Wilús and me.

"I know Manek or his uncle couldn't run this operation without men like you," he says kindly. "You boys stay safe," and he walks with my brother out into the barrack avenue.

I watch them go through the window. Several soldiers who pass the big man salute him but look askance at the familiarity of his arm resting lightly on Manek's shoulder. Schindler doesn't even regard them, there is boldness in his step, and he gives off an aura of being impervious to danger. His comment on the Rezniks was the first time that I'd ever heard a German applaud Jewish escapees.

※

Wilús and I have a true encounter with the descendants of wolves.

One Sunday afternoon when there is no jewelry to sort, Wilús and I grow bored with making paper planes from Aunt Marysia's old magazines. I have a notion to visit my father at his work. It takes me half-an-hour of bribes and threats to get my cousin to go with me. (There would have been hell to pay from my uncle if I'd left the stubborn little nit by himself.) Apart from a single OD sitting in the front office, ignoring us and filling out a mountain of paper work, we are quite alone. Once I get Wilús inflamed by the daring adventure, it's easy for us to slip out of the living room window and drop down into the barrack lane. Papa is on an extra shift in Plaszow's printing shop, where we will surprise him.

I have not breathed outside air for almost a month, let alone walked down the camp's streets. It feels so good to stroll in the open sunlight. Wilús catches my festive mood and kicks a stone down the alley as we head towards the Bergenstrasse and Building 92 that is the papermaking and printing center. I remember seeing a few soldiers pass along the alleys but we hide in doorways and wait until the road ahead is clear. What is unusual for such a fine spring day is the stark quiet, the absence of inmates grouped for a gossip on the barrack steps or sauntering through the lanes to barter whatever they had for cigarettes.

A voice comes to Wilús and me, seemingly from above, from out of the clouds. "Get indoors!" I think I hear it say but don't pay it any mind. Then my name is uttered. "Romek! You and the kid! Get off the damn street!"

Wilús and I look around, there are no guards to see, no ODs of the whipping type, no Ukrainian guards to play tennis with human heads.

"Look up! Up here!"

We raise our surprised eyes to see Emil Porhoryles lying flat against the roof of Barrack N33.

"We going to the print shop to see my dad," I call up to him cheerily, strolling on with Wilús's hand in mine.

"Don't! You'll run right into them. Goeth and his men are walking his dog from the Appellplatz. They just turned into the Bergenstrasse."

From over the rooftops, I hear a hound's insistent barking and Zedkedy's text returns to haunt me, broken moose femurs, 680 kilos of biting force. I pull Wilús around and starting running back the way we came. "No! No!" Emil hisses from above, "You'll never make it. The dog will out run you. Get in here!"

I make a swift detour with Wilús up the barrack step...to find the door locked from the inside! Emil has now scrambled to stand and listen in a skylight beneath a chimney. All of our eyes are on the wide empty gap that is the T-junction of this alley and the Strasse. We hear the voices of subordinate officers answering their commander in German with layers of Sunday pleasantries and Amon Goeth cooing some foolish indulgence to his dog that makes his men laugh raucously.

"Wait there! I'm coming down to get the door," Emil calls to us.

We wait...and in the voices coming closer and the dog's eager whine, I live the broadest stretch of forty seconds to grow a terror so immense that it was, in itself, devouring. Wilús is staring up at me, sensing that there is no bravery to be had here. His lip is trembling; he looks like he's about to cry and I need him to be silent. I stare at the door as if my eyes could melt it and then look over to the vacant gap. I hear the crunch of boots and the scrape of dog claws on the gravel...coming ever closer! The door blessedly flies open, a hand grips my shirtfront and Emil is pulling us both inside. He shoots the bolt as quietly as he can and we all hide under the nearest bunk.

They are here, in the alley. The sound of the bolt in the metal chute was smooth enough but discernible to the hunter who even now licks and howls with intent along the stoop. I hear the click of its nails on the porch, its wanton breath on the underside of the door. We cover my cousin's mouth and urge him not to make a sound.

Dodging the Devil

"They won't come in," whispers Emil. "They think our group is on the Sunday stone-breaking shift."

Except another besides Emil is not—a man dismissed from a quarry team at noon because he can hardly stand from enteritis. It is this unfortunate on his way to the latrine with his guts cramping who we hear screeching pitifully for any kind of human help, who will bear the sharp pressure of the jaws that tear into his fleshless hips, puncturing a renal artery. The piercing screams outside are never ending and Wilús starts to tremble beside me. I cover his ears.

The man stumbles but tries to escape, his bowels let loose and he bleeds a fountain along the stones, the odorous flow driving the pursuing hound to ancient and instinctual ecstasies, strings of red-stained saliva flying out from its open muzzle, it looks back once and growls an alpha signal to its human pack. Come, now, run for the moving prey to be brought down with the killing bite, the sport is well applauded by the uniformed onlookers. Goeth waits several minutes before delivering a mercy bullet to the dying enteric.

An officer among the company with the clipped humor of a military school graduate comments that in the forests around Weimar, church edicts say one can no longer hunt on Sundays. I hear Amon Goeth laughing and asking the commentator in Polish to find him some damn Jesuits among the prisoners for Rolf to stalk, as a punishment for such prissy clerical arrogance.

❊

Although we'd heard that Goeth was a father himself, he had zero tolerance of children. Not just Jewish kinder but any person under sixteen was automatically disdained. I'd observe him on the Appellplatz during a random selection of the unemployables among us, usually luckless folk at either end of the age spectrum. Manek would ensure that I appeared as adult as possible but hardly detectable among the inmates in the back lines. Seldom did the disorderly angers of the warrior and his day-officers reach this far. They were usually paid out arbitrarily on the poor bastards visible in rows one through three. Goeth would take a youthful chin gently in his gloved hand and shake his head with pitying invalidation of the clear gaze that dared not meet his own. He indicated to his adjutant carrying the list. "Take this one, these two, no, not that one but these three."

The man standing next to me whispered in bewilderment to his companion, "I don't get it. He chooses both the sick and the strong. What is it that he's looking for?"

For certainly those who stood there under arrest had no individual substance that reached him. They were as weeds to be cut down, but their reflective surface is still, for the moment, human. This was their burden to him, to have this nettlesome determinant ever present.

Journey of Ashes

My first career as a handler of gold and precious gems lasts exactly ten days due to Goeth's mercurial blood hungers. The Commandant is taking a more than a keen interest in the rising amount of wealth being processed in my uncle's quarters. Both Manek and Uncle Chilowicz fear that the sight of child labor might suggest to him inefficiency, and my cousin and I, little pilferers to be disposed of. All too frequently, Wilús and I are suddenly snatched away from the glittering riches on the sorting bench and pushed into a closet whenever Goeth comes bellowing through the front door of the office, eager to sift his manicured hands through the loose diamonds and elegant watches.

My uncle's pretty wife, Marysia, could delay him charmingly, but only for a brief time. The warrior was always polite with her, even flirtatious, but he kept strictly to the Reich's prohibition against sexual mingling with Jewish women, although, as Manek said to Papa, he punished them mightily for such rules that thwarted his lechery.

In our stifling concealment in the closet, with Wilús wedged under my arm, my hand clamped over his mouth, I would catch snippets of dialogue from the Commandant's surprise visits. My uncle's defense was always to deliver good news.

"You should see what I've saved for you today, Herr Commandant. Such splendid treasures that would make a Czar envious," he would exclaim.

My uncle was careful of the warrior's moods and was well attuned to his reactions. He knew instinctively when to flatter, when to deflect rising anger, and when to distract with some dazzling luxury. Whatever connivance of goods, money, and willing Polish whores from Krakow that could be made to orbit around Goeth appeared to soothe the beast. The artisan Mojesz Friedberg was often present at his inspections of the wealth on the sorting tables.

On this particular day from within our hiding place, I heard Goeth require sharply of the terrified Hassid, "Which of the vermin are you?"

"*Ich bin der Goldschmied* (I am the Goldsmith), Herr Commandant," Mojesz answered in cautious German, and his trembling hand opened wide to offer an exquisitely wrought cigarette case he'd refashioned from the smelted gold fillings. Through a crack in the closet door, I saw the glitter of the slender box etched in superb detail with a classical hunting scene. Sapphires blazed in the eyes of the slain hart and the embossed figure of the hunter, precisely carved, stood out forcefully in his muscular aim of the bow; the fleche of his arrows outlined in tiny white diamonds. Mojesz had even added Amon's initials, delicately engraved with undeserving majesty in a heraldic frame of ivy leaves down in the lower right corner.

Goeth raised the item to the sunlit window, turning it over in his palm several times. In our dark refuge, my young cousin squirmed against me so much that I feared he would propel both of us through the door of the closet and out into discovery.

I could see the confusion in Goeth's face; the gold case mirrored a hypnotic pleasure in his eyes. I observe him totally disregard the artisan, he was as invisible as the wind, although his artistry has just moved him a few notches up the survival ladder. Manek said to me later that Goeth had a grudging admiration for Mojesz's art, and might parade him at one of his frequent dinner parties, debating what mistake of nature is this? Such remarkable talents settled in the race of Christ-killers, can you imagine? What can heaven be thinking?

However, in that moment I saw the warrior glance over Mojesz's head to my uncle. He gave Uncle Wilek a brilliant smile. "Exceptional, my dear Chilowicz, exceptional!" he declared. Buoyed by being the proud owner of the museum-quality piece, Goeth strode away, saying how he must show off this latest finery to his good friend, Oskar Schindler.

My uncle waited for the imposing bulk of the man to disappear down the barrack lane then freed us from the closet. Wilús complained that he was hungry and needed some clean clothes because he peed during the entire episode. We both stink of him. "Better get him washed up, Romek, and you too," said my uncle, and explained that for such a narrow escape, we'll need to be relocated elsewhere in the daytime hours. He left me to wrestle with Wilús, who kicked me hard and bit like a ferocious girl as I struggled to strip him of his wet pants.

Later that night, I asked my Papa about the Friedberg brothers, who quartered themselves down the far end of our barrack and didn't mingle much. "Such a proud dexterity they have," he said respectfully. "You can read in the history books, Romek, how their ancestors were highly skilled jewelers for generations, who went to their graves with gold seamed into the scars on their arms. Many are listed among the members of the Goldsmith Guild of Bocholt as far back as 1445. Jewish artisans working precious metals at that time were forced to assume Germanic names to practice their art. We should be grateful that such talent still lives among us."

❊

My tetchy little cousin is soon relegated back to the Madritsch uniform factory where his father is the supervisor, and where Wilús is small enough to be easily hidden among the bolts of cloth during any selection. I find myself promoted to the position of *Bürstenhersteller* (a maker of brushes) and am sent to the brush workshop run by a genial man named Marius Koslowski.

This small products outfit is in a new barrack, lit by skylights and windows that face the sparsely grassed slopes of a hill called Chujowa Gorka. The room smells of resins and is quartered by a series of wooden worktables, a shallow well running down the center of each contains cutting and combing tools, nails and studs, pine brush handles, hammers, glue, metal bands, braids of horsehair, boar's bristles, bundles of coarse grass fibers and the belly fur from Moravian goats. There are a few other boys and two or three women, but it is mostly adult men who labored there. They patiently teach me how to knot the animal hair correctly and how to mount a good head of trimmed straw onto a broom.

I like working with the horsehair best because the material was strong and silky and still holds the oaty smell of the long-dead animal. Once, with a quick sadness, I have to wash blood off a ruddy mane, no longer to be lifted by the wind. I pull hanks of it through the refining combs until the fibers run free of any tangles and I have the glossy lengths secured. Marius helps me guide the material across the trimming blades, cutting it to various lengths for clothes brushes of different thicknesses, short thick-knotted tufts for polishing army boots, or laying sections down alternately with pig bristles to produce a man's clothing brush. The toil is absorbing and peaceful; it makes the time pass quickly.

My forewoman is Leokadia Weiss, a radiant beauty who is wonderful to look at, with full lips and dark blue eyes set in the frame of her jet hair. I worship her and am reduced to a blithering loon whenever she leans over me to correct my work. It is Leokadia who helps me make a nailbrush for Mama from boar's hair bristles.

The evening I finished it, I proudly run from the workshop to the camp kitchens to give to her but am caught by my father, who flies into a sharp temper at finding me alone outside in the dusk. "Roman! Why didn't you wait for your brother or me? I won't tolerate this disobedience!"

"But I can find my way, Papa, really, I can," I protest.

"Foolish boy! Have you any idea of what could happen to you in the short space of a hundred meters in this place? Do you want to crush my heart altogether? Do you?!" and he shakes me like a wet dog until I lapse into a honking storm of tears while trying to explain in short bursts that I had a special gift for my mother.

My father is right, or course. Kids and young women out alone are always targets for the soldiers, many who resent having their military roles reduced to jail keeping. They grow bored and their tedium can turn to resentment and brute force at the cause of it. Somebody has to be punished. The Waffen-SS takes their cue from Goeth, their superior. They applaud his tearing through the camp, firing on prisoners at random from the saddle of his horse. If we are lucky, we hear the drumming of the Arabian's hooves several meters away before the warrior himself appears, standing in the stirrups, reins flying loose, rifle sights raised, a rictus of glee on his face.

I have made a new friend in Stefan Ginter, the son of our Blockelteste (the barrack Kapo), a boy my age who bunks not far from us. Stefan has a whole tribe of relatives in Chicago, who, before his family was dispossessed in the Ghetto and sent to Plaszow, would write to him and his parents frequently before the mail was censored then forbidden. Their letters inflamed the imagination of Ginter junior with vivid descriptions of American westerns.

Although he has never actually seen the movie, his hero is Roy Rogers in *The Carson City Kid*. "He rides just like Herr Commandant, but he doesn't really kill people," Stefan tells me and proudly shows me a tattered flyer from the Savoy cinema in Evanston. It carries a dramatic photo of the smiling cowboy dressed in fringed buckskin astride a rearing Trigger. Although I can't read English, I love to handle this worn leaflet because it arouses in me a warm yearning. It has an aura of American moxie, with its flamboyant copy (as translated by Papa) that exclaims, "A horse, a hero and a Colt 44!"

Maybe it was idea of Roy Rogers and his Palomino riding the range in *Silver Spurs* that inspired Stefan because always had a sixth sense about the distant whinny of Goeth's mount and would whistle an alert to me and other boys in our clique that it was time to get under cover.

One afternoon, we both gamble on a bad risk and hide underneath the foundation of one of the barracks only to have our faces sprayed with gravel kicked up by the death horse as it sped by. I saw sparks flying out from the steel shoes but covered my terrified face too late with my cap, thinking this could never happen in Carson City! I lay there picking pebbles out of my teeth, not comprehending fully that the retort coming from the punished soil was the loud clap of spent bullets. When the mayhem and the tumult of screams died down, Manek came to fish us out and lectured that the roof was a better place to hide than the dusty crawl space, because Amon's dogs would often come hurtling after their master and were hunters of vicious prowess.

"They particularly like tender boy flesh," my brother warned us.

I only once dared to approach Goeth's horse at rest in his well-appointed stable.

There is no guard here in this quiet hour. Stefan and I sneak in to visit the animal because we are eager to see if he could be related to Trigger of Hollywood. I just want to look at him because of his magnificence. Both Papa and Manek had assured me that Goeth might slaughter a hundred Jews a day but he would never raise his whip to the soft muzzle that snorts its breath at me. The horse is speckled from its dark legs up, with a blunt gray brow and the muscular curved neck of his desert breed. I reach to stroke the neat forest head and he makes a graceful step, shaking his mane but his dark moist eyes don't swerve from my own. His luminous gaze speaks to my skewed sense of the fantastic; there is no offense in me, it says, even when my purity is pitched against the monster on my back. I live in the power of motion, for the earth that flies beneath me. The ways of men are outside my realm. I am not of them.

"It's not his fault, Stefan," I whisper. "The things that Goeth makes him do."

"Naturally, idiota—when did you last see a horse shooting a rifle?" says Stefan and hands the innocent some grain from the feed bin.

I slide my hand under the animal's deep chest to feel the engine of his giant heart thrumming and consider silently, oh, how we could go forth, this amazing creature and I, the two of us daring to ride far away to where there is no spoilage of others, no tearing open, no blood to run. I hold the insane notion for a second…what if I stole him? Gallop on his broad shoulders to the gate, his equine force clearing the electrified fence in one mighty soaring leap! The soldiers would never dare shoot at us because it's Goeth's horse, with a dizzy Jewish boy clinging to his mane, the two of us flying high over Krakow and beyond, to the Carpathians and the green freedom of the forests. The animal stands patiently, one resting hoof arched, staring at me. I disappoint the dream when I get to the part where Goeth hangs everyone in my family in reprisal while I'm riding towards Russia.

A voice behind us hisses, "What the hell are you two doing in here? Trying to fit your necks in the noose?"

We turn to face the anxious fury of Goeth's groom, a lean strip of a lad about fourteen years old, who spends many fraught hours polishing his master's tackle and grooming the horse endlessly, lest any minute imperfections in both sign his daily death warrant.

"Oh, my G-d," he moans. "If he finds you anywhere near this animal, he'll kill us all. Go, now!"

It's no use us explaining about Trigger of Hollywood because the young groom is pushing us out of the stable, all the time wheeling his head around to see that the three of us are still alone. The horse looks on, unperturbed. He is not of us.

Although there are strict prohibitions against prisoners visiting each other's quarters, on certain Sundays, Manek is able to smuggle me into our mother's barrack. Because of her kitchen assignments, we celebrate these rare hours with some of her secretly baked kugel that she rations out. My Aunt Cyla is billeted next to her with Lonius, who is now over a year old, and who sleeps in a suspended cradle sewn from frayed blankets tied to the struts just above his mother's bunk.

I'm astonished to see so many other small children in the place. Most of them are sullen and withdrawn, having been trained that they must never yell or run, or ever play outside. Others are delayed in their growing by the scant diet. In some cases, the women allow them to be somewhat active at night in the barrack, taking shifts to sleep and supervise them. These infants are among the human detritus of the camp. They have no work capacity and are allotted no rations so their mothers share, barter or steal food for them.

Cousin Lonny is one of the healthier infants. He's sprouted a thick wedge of hair, and scoots about now on his sturdy knees and even utters a few words. He laughs a lot at the bear-like toy my mother has sewn for him. I play with him for hours on end, tossing the raggedy animal ahead of us and sending him tottering down the aisle at crawl speed. Later, while Aunt Cyla styles

Mama's hair, I lie on her bunk with Lonny astride my chest, drawing on sheets of old newspapers more escapades of Mottel the Tuchas, while reciting the story loudly with sound effects. The baby boy wrecks my performance. He chortles merrily, tears up my efforts and shoves the pages in his mouth. My mother thinks this is not such a good idea since she doesn't approve of Mottel anyway.

"Romek, enough already, don't be teaching Lonius any bad words," she says through the hairpins in her mouth.

"Why not? Is he missing a rear end?"

"Can't you make up stories about something that doesn't belong in the toilet?"

"Like what?" I ask her in true curiosity.

"Oh, how about the tin soldier tales you and Moniek Hocherman used to swap." she suggests. Aunt Cyla winks at me over wrapping Mama's hair with cloth strips to curl it up. "Draw Lonny stories of angels, the kind that helps little ones become good children and mind their manners."

"He would never believe me." I answer, more to Lonny, who was lying face down on me, fast asleep. I'm amazed by how much heat his young body radiates. I have a small stove on my belly.

This Sunday afternoon imprints deeply. I remember someone nearby painstakingly teaching her boy to read and write his name, Lonny's gurgling laughter, and the women applauding him or talking softly with each other, trying to keep their fearful offspring entertained, swapping cast-off clothes.

"Take my Reuben's sweater for your Adela, it doesn't fit him anymore, and here's a dress that will suit your oldest girl."

"Please, does anyone have any cold cream? Tekla's skin is as dry as parchment." My aunt suggests chicken fat for Tekla's eczema and her infant sister's bad diaper rash but my mother says that I'm to go and ask Manek to get some zinc ointment from Aunt Marysia. On my way out, I hear a faint dry weeping from six beds away, and a woman pleading, "No, Ziri, not yet, we'll eat later. You just have to wait—it's no use crying like that".

Mama, who can no longer look at the wizened, malnourished three-year-old under the blanket, offers his grandmother the rest of the kugel.

My family and immediate friends eat reasonably well during the time of my mother's work detail in the camp kitchens. Of course, the food supply in general is greatly reduced by Goeth's ransacking. He has my uncle cream off a certain amount of goods from the supply trucks the minute they entered the camp's gates. The remainder are allocated in a seventy-to-thirty split, with the lion's share going to the military units and the meager leftovers being boiled down to some gruesome slop for all the prisoners, usually accompanied by bread the texture of shoe linings.

Mama is well tolerated by the German kitchen staff because she can translate their orders easily, is an ace cook and is called upon to prepare robust meals for the Waffen ranks and their officers. She always makes more than is needed so we can be the beneficiaries of her largesse. It's a risky business for her but her brother, Uncle Chilowicz, finds ways to have her move leftovers safely across the compound. My father ensures that our immediate bunk clan is also covered by her generosity; this includes Stefan Ginter and his father, Rabbi Geller, the Porhoryles brothers, and my grandfather, Arye Ferber.

Grandfather Arye is a man of a restrained and discreet demeanor. A skilled housepainter, he is also well-read and spends many hours in high-minded discussions with Rabbi Geller. When their views lock, they would both sit in the long silence of chess players, chewing over each other's opinions but neither conceding a move. Papa says it's going to be interesting to see who colors whom with their wildly different beliefs: Rabbi Geller with his shtetl philosophies or my Marxist grandfather, whom I adore. Arye was in his seventies when we were all removed to the Ghetto, then to Plaszow, and I ask him the same perpetual questions that I constantly badger my father with. "Why are we here? What do they want with us? Why can't we just go home?"

Arye smiles and lies lovingly to me, "It's but a short time now, little Romek, you'll soon be back on Waska Street. You'll go to a fine school for older boys, and your father and I will build you a bedroom of your own by the rear terrace so you can see the chickens from your window."

"Will you paint it any color I want, Grandpa?"

"Of course, child, what color would you like?"

"Orange," I declare.

He pulls heavily on his pipe, "Hmm, pick again, Roman, pick again."

Then he sinks into himself as if hypnotized by the fragrant blue smoke that gathers over him. His lit tobacco (an illicit supply) always smells like burnt figs.

My grandfather had lived most of his existence in Krakow. He had made a good business as a housepainter and raised nine children when the Germans came and manacled his family's life. The sheer astonishment that outside forces could have so massively disrupted everything he had ever known never left him.

"It's as if, Leon," he would say to my father, "I was abducted in my sleep to awake in some far away alien country. This is not my life but I have no idea how to get back into my old skin."

What concerns him most was the forced separation from his wife, my grandmother, Salka, whom he had slept beside for over forty years, and who now lay alone in a sorrowful slumber in the women's barracks. Arye pines for her, and while Manek and my mother arrange secret visits for them to see each other, both aged lovers find it hard to bear that their long life together has come down to this, imprisoned in this grotesque place. My mother and Aunt Cyla swallow the fear daily that Salka might be ordered to the Appellplatz and condemned to the fate of those elders deemed as useless eaters.

17

A Murderous Shade of Blue

THE MEN'S LATRINES OF THE CAMP are in an elongated, barn-like structure with rows of open toilets down its span. A few dirt-encrusted sinks at the far wall is the one place where we can wash ourselves in the fetid, brown flow that trickles from rusted faucets. As far as the toilets are concerned, there is absolutely no privacy and men have to relieve themselves in full view of each other. The guards rarely patrol here unless an official search is called.

I sometimes hang around at the decent space of a few meters and listen in fascination to the Goeth scandals the crapping inmates tell one another. I was still an Olympian eavesdropper with hearing that would make a panther jealous.

"He's like a goat in heat, has a different woman every night, he even wears his holster in bed, hanging from his nakedness," claims Witold Bjeski, a shallow young tailor.

"Witold, you're a bare-arsed fool!" argues Menachem Kindler; a carpenter in his sixties who is seated next to him. "Do you think women confuse a gun for the best part of a man? The lousy prick must fear the assassin's bullet every minute he breathes."

The grizzle-bearded elder raises his eyes to the fractured roof and intones, "G-d of Moses, take from us this gross evil, this unnatural thing passing as a human being!"

"Curse your mouth," yells a former Yeshiva student from the row behind, "for uttering the Holy Name in this filthy place!"

"Curse away, you dolt!" shouts back Menachem. He stands and beckons to me, leaning a crepe-skinned hand on my shoulder. "What example do you set for this young boy here? Who dares to forbid Yahweh to walk in any quarter of his universe?"

The carpenter leans into my ear. "Is your father preparing you for your Bar Mitzvah, child? Does he mind your religious instruction?"

"Oh, yes, he does, Sir," I answer, eager to make a friend of the garrulous elder.

"Remember, not all men who claim holiness earns the right to it," he orders, jerking a yellowed thumb in the direction of the biblical scholar, who was moaning with constipation.

"You will ask your good father," continues Menachem, "to teach you *Psalm 139* and mark the words: *If I ascend up to the heavens, you are there; if I make my bed in the depths of hell, you are there.* Understand, my boy?"

"Yes, Sir, I will. Excuse me, Sir, but are you a Rabbi?"

A Murderous Shade of Blue

The old man fastens his pants and laughs raucously, "Heaven defend me! No, I am the bane of the black hats! One must keep faith honest, ask the right questions, and always question the righteous."

Menachem winks at me and I warm to the energy beneath his lively irreverence. "Don't I know you, lad?" he asks. "You're the son of the mensch who works in the paper-making shop, Pan Ferber?"

I nodded with eager pleasure. I'd often heard Manek say that Menachem was a respected artisan who labored in the wood shop, building items listed in the orders received from the camp's central office. Among his tasks is the repeat mending of furniture smashed by Goeth in his drunken tirades that Menachem would repair as good as new, often reinforcing the items against future outrages.

"Come, dear boy, let us discuss a little business," the carpenter is saying to me.

He walks me down the aisle of toilets to the swamp-scented sinks. There we strike a bargain. I'm to ask my father for any surplus paper dropped from his cutting bench and hand it off to Menachem, who believes well-exercised bowels are the key to a healthy survival. In exchange, he will offer me bags of wood chips three times a week to heat our barrack stove, as much as I can carry from the carpentry shop without incurring any suspicion from the guards. The carpenter instructs me to divide the kindling in half; fifty percent for the men in my barrack and to keep the rest for myself as barter currency.

With the wood, I am able to work some peculiar transactions around the camp. Some of the shavings I trade for cigarettes and swap the smokes with Leokadia Weiss for warm socks. Though new, the hose were all single feet, of different shades and various sizes, yet Papa and I match them up as best we can. We keep a few pairs to wear and barter the rest with workers at the quarry for a sack of stones to block the rodent highways underneath our barrack floor. Still, the infestation is invasive and Pan Ginter orders that every rat cornered has to be murdered on sight. This I am not able to do at ten years old. I am too easily undone by my sentiment toward animals.

※

I awake in the anemic light to the surging tap of rain against the grimy windows, alert to the charcoal gloom without and within. All around me, gray-skinned men in our barrack slumber badly under patched gray blankets and old overcoats. Papa lays snoring with his back to me; my brother is positioned head to toe with his feet against my face. I am comfortably pinned in their male warmth up against the wall.

A skittering motion along the bunk rail, and I see a tiny darting rodent halt and delicately comb its ears, eyes glistening, claws new and pink, with infant skin showing through soft drab fuzz. I whisper to him to run lest the men awaken to come battering at him with staves and shovels. Under my straw pillow is the famous life-saving Zedkedy book. However, when the junior rat sits back on his haunches and raises his miniature hands to me in an almost human gesture, it seems so wrong to even consider crushing this nonchalant creature with a book devoted to zoological wonders.

Manek chides me later that I should have wrung his neck before he could spread disease, words which have me flummoxed since it occurs to me that this rodent was out of a health scare job forever. An entire zoo of epidemics stalked Plaszow; tuberculosis, scabies, deadly influenzas, untreated wounds from floggings, poisoned kidneys, jaundiced livers. Many elderly prisoners, starving and impatient to be liberated, bring their tortured selves to an end on the electrified fence. Sickly babies who managed to be born in the camp make a lightning visit to this world, and finding it a horror, depart at once for the next. As for adding to the killing, what good is that?

My namesake, Roman Ferber (a younger brother of my father's), who worked in the camp's paint shop, received orders to restore the shop's peeling walls. Trained by my grandfather always to be meticulous in his craft, Roman the First laid down two coats of color the delicate tint of robins' eggs. The job was done with a dedication beyond fear, the results flawless and pleasing, and the clean up impeccable.

When Amon Goeth came to inspect the work, he asked my uncle where he had gotten the paint. Roman politely explained that the blue product was all that was available. It wouldn't have mattered if my uncle had layered the walls with Egyptian gold, for in Goeth's mind the imagined sins of prisoners, if left unchecked, could easily inflate to potential rebellion. The warrior circled the room and pointed at its south end. "Look, over here, *Meistermaler* (Master Painter)." Roman the First leaned in to where the imperious gloved finger aimed but saw no drips or smudges. Blue was the last color of his final minutes; Goeth inexplicably shot him in the back of the head.

My father helped Arye Ferber carry his son's body to the cemetery house for washing and the incantation of prayers. Uncle Chilowicz fixes matters so Roman the First can be buried in the Jewish cemetery in Podgorze. I'm not permitted to go but Papa and my mother get a pass to attend the burial.

My grandfather's mind is undone by this loss, he looks at me in confusion, pulling me into his knee, lovingly calling me "little Roman," saying when I grow up I shall be the heir to his paint business.

That April, my grandmother Salka died in her sleep in the women's barrack. Arye was allowed to come and wrap her in the winding sheet. He spent time kissing her hair and crooning over her face, which had assumed a pearly, youthful aspect. Another voyage was made to the graveyard and Papa fears that his father, having had the heart pulled out of him twice, will soon follow Salka and his son to the afterlife. The gaping pit in his spirit takes him deep into its silent recesses; he speaks to no one for several days and answers my greeting rarely. It's as if the man has become a stone. Rabbi Geller tries to counsel him but Arye will not be prayed over or comforted by anyone. Papa advises we should let him be and recognize that what we fear to be a damaging retreat or oncoming insanity is the heavy lifting of nature gone to do extreme repairs on the iron soul of my grandfather.

In all this, I forget that my father has lost a brother and mother in the space of a few weeks. I don't see him grieve openly but he spends his spare hours in intense conversations with Rabbi Geller and Manek in the chilling dusk outside the barrack. Another loss under discussion is our friends, the Horowitz family, which we have never encountered ever since we entered the camp. I hear Papa say he fears the worst for them since the young daughters and the parents were soon separated to be dispatched to different lagers. Now Tadek's absence is complete and his family is no more. The men talk incessantly until the curfew siren goes off, and it's time for the dark of Plaszow to release its dangers.

For many nights after these events, my mind is a tearing sadness of willing this and wishing for that. Let there be no more deposits in death's account; the greedy bastard is a millionaire in tortured flesh. His wealth is grossed in bones and mounting. I look for my brave infant rat every place. Long may the willful vermin run under the floorboards, let the molds loose their creeping spores, let the fly lay down her thousand eggs in the eyes of prisoners before they're closed forever. Life has to be good for something! I cry out fiercely in my sleep and hysterically awaken into my father's ready embrace. He rocks me slowly; his voice is soothing, "Shush, my *Shepsele* (Lambkin), be calm. We must endure, Roman, we must. This is not forever." However, I cannot stop weeping because now love is stabbing at me with all its doughy mercies.

❀

By the summer, I have commenced my third career of my childhood and finally moved over to the Papierfabrik shop (the paper and printing factory) where I can work alongside my father. The operation prints the camp's letterhead and creates special stationary for Goeth's administration office. Output is divided between two departments: the noisy printing floor for the typesetters and the inky presses, the other, our cutting room, where endless rolls of paper come cascading off huge metal cylinders. I find myself the only ten-year-old in a team of fifty very efficient adults.

"What we make here, Romek, is very necessary," Papa lectures me, "for the German war effort. As long as we perform our work well, we will be safe. So I expect your work to be flawless, however simple the task."

I actually have a job I enjoy because, like the brush making, it's calm and absorbing. Our brusque good-natured foreman, Ben Geisehals, has me producing hand-made envelopes using a cardboard matrix. I carefully fold the pre-cut paper and then glue the sides down, but cringe inwardly if I mess up because my father's eagle gaze rarely misses any mistakes. (However, my failed envelopes were not entirely wasted; they also went to Menachem Kindler's toilet paper supply.)

Except for the very elderly, sick, and disabled, kids under fourteen-years old in Plaszow are labeled as "worthless eaters," totally disposable; a definition that enforces roundups of young ones in actions swift and unannounced. When I walk the barrack lanes with my eyes scanning for trouble, I imagine seeing through my shoulder blades and any shouts and running feet drives me into hiding in a second.

Manek would get notice of the kinder sweeps hours before the troops started sifting for kids throughout the camp. Whenever I see him appear in the doorway of the factory, I know it is time to go hide. We hurriedly collect Stefan from his job in the poultry barn, and my brother escorts us to the used clothing warehouse, so as not arouse suspicion. There, my Aunt Cyla and my mother are waiting to bury us in layers of men's coats next to Wilús, who is still young enough to regard our concealment as an amusing game.

We kids lie for hours surrounded by the itchy odorous cloth. It comforts me to peek out of my fabric casing and have a view of my mother's shoes, even as she walks away. It's hard to describe the experience of being hunted. I can't say that it heightens the permanent sense of danger we dwell in—that condition is the norm. I always trust to fate that I will not be found. Once in seclusion, I will myself to become undetectable and compel my muscles into absolute stillness.

Many other parents took extraordinary measures to protect their children. In my mother's barracks, there was a pretty adolescent girl of thirteen with long dark braids named Hermina Munschowa who had come through the Ghetto and her first year in Plaszow as an older teenager fit for work, until she was felled by dysentery and a German orderly named Werner Scheldorf in the camp's infirmary discovered she was a circumcised male. The medic terminated the sick lad, now known in the grave as Herman Muschowa, with a benzene injection directly to the heart, not so much because he was a son of Moses but because the man was so affronted that the boy had posed as a female.

One of the Kapos cut the braids off the dead Herman/Hermina and brought them into the barrack, determined to punish the liar of a mother. He walked down the line of bunks, before the blank gaze of the inmates, whirling the glossy hanks in his hand but not one woman cried out, or stepped forward to claim kinship with the lost son.

I knew a feral orphan in Plaszow, fifteen-year old Teodor, wild as a captive jackal, who barely spoke in human tones, but his deranged ferocity seemed to shield him. Teodor was the sport of the motor pool soldiers, who would fire shots at the boy, forcing him into a cruel dance, but rather than running away, he would dash at them head on, snarling and laughing in the heated cordite air. The bullets never found their mark. The boy had no barrack assignment at all. Goeth had murdered his parents on the family's first day in Plaszow and he'd gotten lost in the administration records of the thousands of inmates.

A Murderous Shade of Blue

Teodor was perpetually covered in granite dust from sleeping in a chute in the stone quarry. He moved across the compound at will, a grimy ghost darting and quick. If you met him alone, he would snarl and snap his teeth open and shut, as he did at me in one scary encounter when I was taking a message to my brother. I eventually understood this was Teodor's signal he used when begging for food. Since I had nothing edible to give him, I offered up a metal button hanging loose from my jacket. He took it as if he'd been handed him a rare diamond, holding it up to the sky and bellowing with joy.

There is very little to amuse us after the workday is over. Often I am too exhausted to study or have Papa help me with any of my lessons. I want to fool around like a normal kid. Stefan, me, and fourteen-year-old Lolek Norenberg, the son of a shoemaker, along with some other boys, often sneak into an empty barracks in the evening before curfew and tell each other dirty stories about girls and other sexy stuff of which we only have a half-witted knowledge. It is here that I fail at my first attempt at smoking. I choke and sputter from dragging on one badly rolled cigarette passed among us. Lolek draws pictures in chalk of naked women on the barracks wall, but they turn out so unappealing as to appear monstrous and cartoon-like. I manage to compete a little with my Mottel tales, but after the first wave of guffaws, the older boys tease me, saying that Mottel the Butt is only good for little kids and bedtime stories.

Late one night Manek and my uncle, Henryk Schnitzer, awaken my father and me with an emergency—we are to come at once to the camp hospital. Once we are outside, I see Uncle Chilowicz handing the soldiers of the curfew cartons of cigarettes that delight them so much they shake his hand vigorously and make pleasant-sounding noises in German. With the two corporals taking the lead, we march safely across the Appellplatz posing as a late work detail to the back door of the hospital. It is opened by Dr. Josef Nussenfeld, the former director of the Jewish Hospital in Krakow.

The physician ushers us into a laundry room bathed in candlelight where we find Wilús lying on a makeshift table in the arms of his mother, my Aunt Frania. The kid is sobbing a chugging cry of distress. He reaches for me immediately, grips my neck, and I feel a tautness lighten in him. A huge red swelling with an ugly yellowish dome at its core projects out of his left ear. The doctor says he has to cut something away and it's important that Wilús not scream. Dr. Nussenfeld has prepared two cotton gags heavily soaked in sugar water and quinine. He speaks kindly to me. "Tonight, Romek, you will be my assistant, put this in your mouth. Tell your cousin how delicious it tastes and to bite down on it."

I stare at him and fear that something medical is about to happen to me too until Manek whispers, "Play it to the hilt and Wilús will copy you, you'll see." I stuff the cotton wadding between my lips, chew a little and swallow the sweet bark taste with a phony relish. Wilús, his face wet and swollen, points at me and demands, "Romek...give me too." I stop up his small mouth with a similar plug, urging him to get his teeth into it.

The doctor paints the foul ear lump with benzocaine, explaining that other than the quinine, this is all he has to ease the procedure. He nods to the three men in the room and they press down gently on the boy, their shadows elongated up the darkened walls. Aunt Frania and I are holding Wilús by his head. My lips are burning from the weird medicine and I don't want to be standing this close to what will happen. The scalpel rises in the candlelight, a rapid one-two slash, the blood spurts and runs fast. Dr. Nussenfeld calmly blots at the wounded ear and cuts again. I look away. Wilús flinches and moans, his body seizes up with all his strength, but his mother lovingly tells him that he and Romek are in the invisible place where no one can find us.

Next, I hear a soft sucking sound from the syringe drawing up the disgusting ooze into its barrel. Then it's done. The good doctor is packing the small ear with a padded dressing and binds up the child's head. Manek offers my cousin and me apple cookies, most likely filched from Amon Goeth's pantry. His mother rocks Wilús close, but he spits the gag out on her shoulder and points at me, "No talking, Romek, no talking." The turban bandage makes him look like a tiny magician but he manages a pained smile and, through my quinine nausea, I realize a rush of true admiration for my gutsy little cousin.

❀

As the months progress, deportees from ghettos and camps across Europe are sent to be warehoused in Plaszow, until the boxcars and trucks can filter them to other lagers in Southern Poland and Germany. We are a lateral tower of Babel, with thousands of transit prisoners from Holland, Greece and Hungary. The array of languages spoken on the Appellplatz prompts the questions I continue to pester my father with, "Why are these people here, they're not Polish, and some of them are not even Jews? Just how big is this war anyway?"

Manek says that this massive shunting of humanity all over Europe is due to the Germans' diminishing victories. They literally don't always know what to do with the great number of people they have in harness.

"The foreign faces on the Appellplatz," says Papa, "bring us good news, Romek. General Montgomery and the UK Allied Forces have landed in Italy. I hear the British and American airmen have rained fire on Berlin for several weeks and the Red Army has liberated Kiev."

"What about the Yanks, Papa, are they coming to get us out of here?"

"Soon, my boy, soon, now that Eisenhower will be running the show as Allied Commander."

"Will they bring the big Cadillac that Tadek always wanted?"

A Murderous Shade of Blue

Manek answers that he's not sure, but asks me if I would settle for a US tank and Amon Goeth in chains.

The winter of 1943 lays siege to the entire camp. The brute Polish season brings days of unending blizzards, the hoarse wind a knife in the mind, temperatures so low it hurts to breathe, ice lacquering the interior walls of the barracks, no way to ever get warm, and sleep that is not sleep but a barely-conscious zone sealed in by a bitter, relentless cold. These punishments encroach on people who already skate the edge of starvation, illness, and other daily terrors. Rabbi Geller strides the aisle of our barracks, wearing every garment he owns and breathing out a small fog, asking heaven how it is possible to add more darkness to the darkness?

A chink of light is given to our family, a single blessed name called out one Sunday morning. My sister Hanka has arrived in Plaszow! A transport of the airport workers' detail is down at the front gate, and here are two signed passes. "Papa and Roman can go there and futz around as if they're helping Uncle Chilowicz process the intake," offers Manek, since our relative is checking all the paperwork. My father whoops and hollers and the men in their bunks break into spontaneous applause. Not all of them are clear as to the reason for our joy, but the mere sight of any happiness is so contagious, I swear it seems to raise the meager heat in the place. Manek hurries off to inform Mama and to arrange a bed for Hanka in her barrack.

Within the layers of barbed wire, the new contingent of prisoners is small and there's no military escort. I scan the line of faces for my sister. She's not here! She's not anywhere! Then she is...I see her...by the fence! After all these months, she looks to me like a real grown-up, the way women appear to boys my age when they're someone's wife or even schoolteacher. She's wrapped in a tattered heavy coat but carries herself with a steady confidence. Beside her is a tall, handsome man who holds her elbow, guiding her chivalrously over the wire alley's thick ice. My father whispers I must wait until she's safely inside the camp and then we can all be reunited. He quickly wipes away any approaching tears before they freeze on his cheeks.

We hurriedly follow the prisoner intake line over to the fur factory, where Hanka and Juzek Lipschutz, the gallant escort, will work from this day forth. Juzek leaves us to go to his barracks and the foreman, Immanuel Lieberman, a furrier from Makow, turns a blind eye while Papa, my brother and I embrace Hanka, showering her with a thousand questions, talking over each other, our words raining down on the lovely face that has been missing from our lives these many months.

Hanka: "Romeczku, you little bear, how you've grown!"

Me: "I'm almost eleven but on the Appellplatz, I'm fifteen."

Papa: "Romek works with me in the stationary business, isn't that wonderful, Hanka?"

Manek: "Papa and short-shirt here are quite the executives. Every order Goeth writes complaining to Oranienburg that they're spoiling his killing sprees is written on paper made by his prey—I wonder if he realizes that."

Hanka reaches into her coat and pulls out some small ragged photographs. She smiles radiantly and says, "No one hunts the men I love, now that I'm here," and hands around pictures of our father, Manek and me from a sunny afternoon long ago. The crumpled images show us standing on Krakow's main square, the Rynek Glowny. I see myself, a real boy then (not my prisoner self), bony-kneed and awkward in short pants, surrounded by pigeons with my arms outstretched, a human perch for the cooing masses.

In the photos, I'm faking a turgid grin because I'm brazening the secret fear of wings so close to my face. Papa is smiling too and scattering crumbs to the birds while Manek waits with his hand on my shoulder for Hanka to click the camera. It's actually us standing there in 1938, but it's as if I'm looking at strangers from the far interior of a dark tunnel. How was it that we were once these people? How was it we are caught up in this present that has no edges, in this place where the future does not exist, where we dwell as ghosts in our own skin?

✻

The camp hums with rumors of dangerous shifts in the regime. The isolation ward reports a typhoid outbreak that sparks a panic in the entire inmate populace because the slightest symptom means vaccination by the bullet. The fevered dead are sewn into sacks and buried in quicklime or burned on the killing hill of Chujowa Gorka. Traces of events also drift into the camp from the now-deserted Ghetto. Certain OD men left behind to clean out apartments of any hidden wealth are lulled into false comfort that soon they will be compensated for their dedicated service, free to leave Podgorze, and settle anywhere in Krakow. Skeptical souls seek out imaginative forgers such as Wadylslaw Wichman of the RPZ (the Council for Jewish Help) on acquiring foreign documents to flee Poland. Some are successful in escaping; others are promised travel permits to Argentina by the Gestapo but disappear mysteriously on the road to Warsaw.

I witness my parents' wretchedness on hearing the news that Pinie Koza, the saintly burial man of Miodowa Street, and his wife and children were executed soon after the Ghetto's liquidation. Those in our barracks who had been comforted by Pinie's noble ministrations gathered with Papa and Rabbi Geller to mourn. Although I am not old enough yet to be counted in the minyan, my father encourages me to join with the rest of the men in prayer: *In the heart of thy chosen servant thou didst plant the seeds of duty and compassion, O G-d, and in the morning he did bring you the blossoming of his soul for your eternal glory.*

A queasy victory comes to us through the execution of Symche Spira and his family. According to Manek, Spira had been the most loyal turncoat of the Ghetto overlords, Kunde and Haase. He was a rigid orthodox Jew, but without any honor or sense of sanctity, who exercised his petty hatreds against the more cultured of his kind, and sent many to a brutal end through his venal career as a thief, blackmailer and collaborator. Stripped naked and summarily shot, his ambition was reduced to cinders on the mount of burning.

Ironically, it is this well-organized death chain coupled with the Nazi bureaucracy in Oranienburg that slows Amon Goeth's trigger finger—even beyond his orders that Plaszow is to be converted to a concentration camp. Killing is to be more professional and calmly expeditious. Oskar Schindler lectures the Commandant in a fraternal way that any random shootings of workers from his Emalia factory might give the *Treuhänder* (trustee) cause to complain to the Department of Economic Enterprises. "It's not a thing I would relish doing, Amon, but I can't afford the loss of skilled laborers."

My brother had been in Goeth's office delivering paperwork to his secretary, Mietek Pemper, and overheard the discussion with Schindler oiling the wheels of his argument with a fine cognac.

"Oskar, you old bugger," slurred Goeth. "You are a contradiction in fine mohair. Those desk fairies in Germany have no idea what it's like to run a piss-pot like this. It's a constant bloody circus!"

Manek watched from the shadows of the hallway as the Sudetenlander helped the melancholy Commandant out of his jacket and settled him motherly into an armchair.

"You drink too much, my friend," advised Schindler.

"It's the salve of kings," boasted Goeth. "It takes the edge off. Besides, it's entirely your fault, Oskar. You're murdering my liver. You corrupt me constantly."

Schindler smiled ruefully, "I don't think you need much encouragement."

Then, as Manek told it to our father, Goeth fell into a kind whining despair, about his wife in Austria whom he no longer loved, and his children whom he found tedious and demanding. Here he was, a soldier in his prime, trapped in this vale of shit, having to take in more prisoners than the place could possibly hold, and move others out in coordinated relays. Then there was the Ghetto dead, thousands of them all simmering maggot soup festering beneath the lush woodlands surrounding the camp.

"Can you imagine?" the warrior protested sourly. "Those pen-pushing shits in Section D have spewed out the lunatic order that I should dig this trash up and burn it. I tell you, Oskar, it's too bloody much. What do they expect? That moldering Jews will leap out of the grave and start bitching about how badly off they were?"

"Amon, I think you need a refill and a nice girl to keep you company," Schindler soothed him, "before you start your excavations."

The skin of the forest floor is peeled away and the dead of Podgorze are thrown up from the earth like a massive potato crop, to be re-exterminated on Chujowa Gorka where cremation pyres burn for days on end. Special units of live prisoners hollow out the mass graves, their faces wrapped up against the slip-sliding flesh that rents and shreds from the bones to come away in their hands. The remains are ferried to this market day of fire on wheelbarrows and handcarts, and what refuses to stay whole is collapsed into sacks for easier conveyance to the flames.

Neat pyramids of wood are balanced in rows against the smoky sky and rivulets of kerosene run down the coarse grass, the odious crackle of skin opening, the pungent smell of hair frying, and, all the while, workers, numbed to their hideous task, grab at the bloated bodies with rakes, turning them over so they'll reduce on their uncooked side. The vast cremation casts off a bone-made snow that tastes like soap and spoiled pork. This human rain descends on inmate and soldier alike, and is carried by winds across the Vistula to settle on the shoulders of the carved saints in the bell tower of Krakow's Cathedral.

Goeth screams at his adjutant to solve the damn pollution problem! He orders his groom to lay down hay in one of the storage warehouses and re-stable his beloved Arabian there; that it might cease to whinny and fret at the coating of discarded lives scattered over its lustrous mane.

As for the cremation crews in the barracks streets, Manek has given me his "don't-look" command, but I do look, not just for the human dross being hauled to the hill, but because of the sharp lament that rises as many recognize former neighbors, relatives and even enemies. On the ramshackle carts, I see Ewa Urbanowicz, her naked beauty withered and brown as if she had continued to age underground, having been buried in the forest's bog whose tannins had begun to cure her skin. She rests on top of an uncircumcised man that Aunt Cyla recognizes as her Catholic husband. I discover one-eyed Zigo from the rations depot and watch a man kick and curse at his blackened wretchedness for each time Zigo had cheated him. I also sight the love of my ninth year, Bella Abramowicz, being wheeled past us, who I identify only by her amazing golden hair.

The warm weather of the spring of 1944 spawns an increase in all kinds of pests: rats, body lice, scabies and giant cockroaches that swarm athletically through the latrines. The camp is also packed with over twenty-five thousand inmates, a mobile fluid populace that is added to by transit shipments and selections more than it's decreased by disease, killings and transports. Goeth demands more budget to badly feed and house the overflow. At so much per head, his own personal coffers are much enriched. A new infamy menaces us: a great dilution of current residents to accommodate an incoming shipment of thousands of Hungarian Jews.

A Murderous Shade of Blue

It is announced that throughout the lager there is to be a health action, a *"Die Gesundheitsmaßnahmen"*, a ruse for weeding out those too frail and too redundant to live. The Commandant crisply orders Dr. Leon Gross and that travesty of medicine, the SS physician Dr. Blancke, to make selections from the barracks.

Goeth's loud criteria: "List the totally expendable but feel free to improve upon the definition. I want a record of every elder over sixty, sick and pregnant women, children under fourteen and all the disabled. Weed through the labor contingents; get rid of the useless and the malingerers. I want the infirmary emptied totally; we'll terminate the infected here and hurry along the bastards who dare to be tardy in their dying. Infants are automatically for the trucks, and clean out any political shit lazing about the detention cells. This is not a bloody spa!"

His orders ill frame my destiny for an entire week and scrapes at all our nerves. I can't go to work but hide again in the clothing warehouse. I join my small cousin and other children under the benches for several days, sheltered beneath mountains of garments raided from the destroyed ghettos of Tarnow, Lublin, Belzyce and Katowice. We are protected by an excellent lady named Helena Serafinska and her staff, who live there, sorting garments on racks and in bins. My mother manages to slip in daily from the camp kitchens with food for us kids in a cardboard box labeled "*Mäntel Der Frauen*" (women's coats).

Wilús, Adela Susser (a smart girl of eight), and I are given small tasks to keep us from fretting and nagging at the women with our fears. We collect laces from hundreds of men's shoes too worn to be useful, tie them in pairs, put the old shoes in sacks for fuel and pack the laces into boxes by type and color. I make comfortable beds for Wilús and me on the crude planked floor from several heavy wool coats, many bearing the label of "Zelkowicz Bespoke Tailoring, Lvov." I put my feet into a pair of men's velvet evening slippers bearing the monogram "R." I pretend they were made just for me and go la-dee-dahing around the benches in grand style, making the women and the other kids shriek with laughter.

I'm convinced the ghosts of the dead live in their former clothing. Many garments are filled with smells that conjure an image of the lost wearer; a tweed jacket with suede elbow inserts exudes tobacco and a man's lime cologne, and there he is, a university scholar of ancient letters and high-flown thoughts. I see Pani Helena take a green satin evening dress and lay it carefully on her cutting table to make a repair to the side zipper. The gown looks like it's hardly been worn; the neckline is sculpted with turquoise sequins, a repeated design of peacock tails that glitters at me. I imagine it swirling from the shoulders of a very rare woman and reach out to touch its gleaming opulence but Helena nudges my hand away lightly.

"No touching, Romek. This is very special. I have to deliver it to the Red House, for one of Goeth's ladies."

"Maybe the pig-Meister will bury her in it," comments Avala, another seamstress.

"Whose dress was it anyway?" I ask.

They hesitate and shoo me away to play with my cousin. I saunter off but linger by tall sacks of a thousand shoes to listen in on their tale of the emerald dress.

"Did you see the label? The House of Worth, in Paris," comments Helena. She beguiles Avala of the gown once belonging to Viktoria Rajinsky, a statuesque beauty of twenty-three. She had come to Krakow at eighteen to marry her betrothed, a well-heeled lawyer, Eisev Blodnik, who was murdered for protesting the violations visited upon his exquisite young wife during the confiscation of their home. The Waffen officers used her badly. The girl was allowed to take few items of clothing with her on her arrest. She was shot at the gate in Plaszow because the guards thought her mentally defective. The dress was ripped from her suitcase and carried to the warehouse in a fit of disappointment by my Aunt Marysia, who lacked the stature and the shape to justify the splendor in the garment.

Music from the loud speakers drifts in from the Appellplatz and I hear the woman who sorts and grades hats telling Helena that she's never seen so many nude men in one place, and how her husband, G-d keep his soul, would be blind with shame for her to look upon such things. The women too! Can you believe it? Hundreds of people, all as nature made them, running past the inspection doctors at full speed, literally for their lives! Helena comments that these Germans have no class: exposing a woman to her father, a sister to her brother, such ugly immodesty. Oh, Magda, check that hatpin, would you? I think those seed pearls are real.

✻

My father stands naked before a barrage of eyes, the doctors seated at long tables whose gaze is blunted from scanning all this flesh and the indifferent clerks with their typewriters rapping out lists of erasure. The sun warms Pap's bare torso, his broad chest is impressive and his muscles fairly solid for a man of fifty-two. They will pass him back to his labor unit and Manek too, whose twenty-year-old physique is more than approved. Dr. Blancke pulls the next card from the file and requests "Roman Ferber, aged fifteen, Papier Fabriker. Step forward!"

My father salutes the man formally and admits in all seriousness "I regret to tell you, Herr Doctor, Roman Ferber is deceased."

"We have no record of that here. What was the cause?"

"He died in the typhus outbreak, Sir."

"If I find that he is suddenly resurrected," says Dr. Blancke evenly, "he will have a second chance to visit the grave. Do you understand?"

"Yes, Sir," agrees my father, "but the cremation detail carried my son to the hill to be burned with the others. I was witness to it."

On these liar's words, Manek noted, real tears welled up in my father's eyes, because if not dead now, the specter of my possible demise held fast to him. My Uncle Chilowicz had made an expensive deal with Goeth to exempt at least eight kids from my clan during the selection, including myself. We were to remain in the barracks but this arrangement had no purchase with the Ukrainian units who were sent to search at random and corral every young one they could find.

Since I'm "dead" on paper, I'm no longer on the daily roll call but have to hide up in the rafters of our empty barracks every morning. On this day from where I'm perched, I hear a terrible howling erupt up from the Appellplatz, orders shouted, music played. A minute later, Menachem Kindler came bursting through the door, "Romek, Romek!" he urges. "You must come down right away! They'll be searching here in the next half-hour."

He caught me when I leapt into his arms. We hurried to an open side window, and the carpenter lifted me through it. From there it was a frantic dash through the barrack alleyways.

"Where are we going?" I stutter.

"The *Hotel-Scheiße* (Hotel Shit)!" Menachem declares.

We dart our way through long streams of people, clusters of congealed fear, hurtling in different directions, trying to dress in stumbling haste. Then we are in the men's latrine and my stalwart rescuer is lifting up the heavy beam with the toilet holes cut into it. Below I see a deep trench of flowing excrement that gives off such total rankness that it outbid my memory of the putrid dead. I stand on the edge, hesitant, my stomach twisting up badly.

"Get in, brave friend," orders Menachem. He lifts me under the arms and lowers me into the pestilential darkness. "Grip the ridges on the side, make sure you get a foothold, and, for G-d's sake, don't slip."

I balance on a narrow ledge; the walls feel slimy and wet, and the odor is throttling. The beam is slid back into place and the only light we have comes in from the dump holes above us. I say "us" because I find it's pretty crowded down here. "Hello, Roman," whispers my friend Stefan, who is holding on to my cousin Wilús. Lolek Norenberg and some other boys are here too. I can make out the faces of several girls who have their dresses tucked into their underpants so that their skirts would not be fouled. I try to smile but outside the terrible shouts begin again. My cousin lets out a yelp and I signal him to be silent.

Helena Serafinska, Avala, and a contingent from the warehouse are ordered to collect the still-warm rags mounting at the edge of the Appellplatz. The women encounter an immense sea of bewilderment as hundreds are driven to opposite sides of the plaza, many trying to snatch a shirt or a blanket to cover their nudity. Helena is fully clothed and comprehends the doubled-edged vulnerability of bare skin against relentless circumstance. Trucks are backed up to the square, the dirty canvas drapes open and waiting.

Helena would later tell of how parents were driven back and hemmed into a crucifying anguish, surrounded by troops who stood facing them elbow-to-elbow, ready to charge at the howls of grief that picked up strength as the children and other rejects were herded to the transports. Over sixteen hundred souls will be shipped to the big lager at Auschwitz; among these were some two hundred and sixty-eight children, maybe more.

After it is over, Manek brings me to Uncle Chilowicz's quarters to be stripped and bathed. My clothes, embedded with the latrine stench, are burned at once. Helena sends over a small man's jacket too loose in the shoulders and pants whose waistband came up to my armpits. This outfit arrives with two clean shirts that did actually fit. The neatly pressed clothes voided any aura of the desperation that besieged me and gives me the semblance of an essential worker. Hanka comes to walk me to my mother's barracks. I notice my sister's face is swollen from weeping but I am too scared to ask her for whom she is grieving.

My deliverance bears bitter fruit. I stand at the edge of a cluster of eight or nine women whose pain appears to weld them all into one body. I see my Aunt Cyla flopped against my mother, who is dabbing at her face with a cold wet cloth because one of her cheeks is bruised dark purple from her brow to her chin.

"What happened? Did the soldiers hurt her, Mama?" I ask but the question falls away from the circle. No one hears me.

Cyla is clutching Lonnie's rag bear and waving it manically before the women. "This was my son's. You know him, my son?"

My mother kneels down and tenderly embraces her.

"Hanka, what's wrong with her?" I petition my sister's back, but she shushes me with her hand. What I see is a woman, who appears like my aunt, but her eyes are fevered, and her head lolls out of control. I grow very afraid that maybe she's about to die right there between the bunks. Fragments of whispers swirl around her. "They came in…we had the boy well covered up but he began to cry. It happened so fast, she fought them like a tigress, they knocked her down. Took him…the baby, they took him!"

I go and sit on a lower bunk nearby and decide to wait until they notice me. I hear Helena trying to make it right, telling softly how when Lonnie was hurled onto the truck, she saw him land in the lap of mad Teodor who was sitting next to a skinny girl. Lonnie was screeching at full volume and Teodor, who was instantly delighted at this flung bundle, wrapped the infant in his jacket and gave him his knuckles to suck on. Lonnie quieted down, and the thin girl smiled, dried his tears and put her arms around both of them, saying I'm going to tell people, Teodor, that you are my husband and this is our baby, then we can be everywhere together. The instant young

A Murderous Shade of Blue

father cackles through his blackened teeth and rocks my stolen cousin joyfully, saying how much he looks like Teodor's own mother.

Dr. Elizabeta Kolmeny, free from the selections because of her medical experience, walked out of the chaos and climbed aboard the truck. She sat tall and imperious among her small charges, even as she was threatened with a flogging, called a stupid bitch, and ordered to come down at once! She calmly refuses and demands of the stumped, unnerved sergeant to either shoot her there and then, or show some damn efficiency and get this transport moving!

I try to picture them all, my one-time hideaway companion, sweet, quirky Lonius who was about to become a real boy, the nice girl who is barely twelve and crazy Teodor—with one protector to share among all those dirty kids bumping down the road to Auschwitz. Dr. Kolmeny will spend the distance, checking teeth, cuts and bruises. She makes a thorough note of who has ringworm, lice and possible measles, smiling and reassuring the children, because she's convinced that she must operate with all her healing skills, as if everyone will be alive tomorrow.

Aunt Cyla is hollowed out, emptied of all needful instincts save one, a pull in the blood that makes her inhuman in the sense that she doesn't feel the savage blow to her ribs when she demands of the Waffen-SS officer a seat on the next truck to the big lager. The Captain has no time for such idiotic whimsies; the single purpose ablaze in Cyla's slender frame becomes a manic irritant, a power that must be tamped down at once. She is unstoppable in her request, it's the only thing left for her to want beyond the return of Lonius.

Her husband, Samek can bear no such protest. He has become one of the partially dead. His infant son is gone, tearing away from his father critical bits of his soul never to be retrieved. He is sealed in the belief that nothing good will ever be possible again. His wife's plea to be sent down the road doesn't even disturb him. Go. See. You won't find Lonius. Fearing that some soldier will shoot her out of hand for her wolfish and unrelenting demand, Uncle Chilowicz reluctantly arranges for Cyla to be on next Sunday's transport to Auschwitz.

My aunt will eventually become the totality of her desire, living through her eyes all that time in the camp. She passed herself off as a kindergarten teacher that she might wander freely among those in the Kinderlager, gently upturning small faces, asking everyone what is your name. Do you know a boy named Lonius? Requiring of other mothers, my boy Lonius, should you see him, tell him I am here.

However, the young one's essence remained hidden from her, down in the ashen mud; down among the secrets only stones know, in the smoke plumes that constantly striped the sky. The more the truth concealed him, the more she sought. The child finally became his mother's lifeline, braided around her by his long and eternal absence to be reborn as the soft fuel of her survival.

18

The Journey from Plaszow

AFTER THE TUMULTUOUS SELECTIONS OF THE SPRING, a strange vacuum sprouted in the camp. Goeth complained bitterly that it was getting harder to maintain the fiction of Plaszow's once-large population and justify the amount of incoming rations for people who were no longer alive. Despite these dilemmas, he had accumulated a substantial fortune in siphoning off the Reich's resources. However, a significant threat dwelt right on his doorstep. My Uncle Chilowicz was a walking dossier of the Commandant's many convoluted black market deals.

For the prisoners, the daily excitement that nourished us as much as any stolen bread was news from the Polish resistance in Krakow that Germany was losing the war badly. Yet to think on how a singular death from hurt and illness is repeated in a million similar stitches in the broad fabric of catastrophe, how tightly these threads knotted together in Plaszow's summer of 1944! There, in one corner of this vile tapestry, are woven such annihilations that would stamp my life forever.

It's a late August day in 1944 and on this sun-glazed morning with the air already humid, Manek walks me to the papermaking factory. My brother is looking spruce and well-shaven, and I tease him that he must have a hot date with his girlfriend, Lilka. He smiles but admits nothing. At the workshop ramp, he squeezes my face between his hands in affection, kisses my forehead and says to me, "OK, Romek. Do good work." I watch him as he walks away briskly in the direction of the Chilowicz's quarters. He turns once and waves; his gesture full of cheerful bravado.

I remember at the time having no courage or sense at all for anticipating certain events that fell without warning on a person. Even as one is content, in the darker unknown the wheels of disaster are churning. Who will be caught beneath their deadly revolutions? Out of the swirling horrors come the most absurd questions: where was I on that day, or at that hour?

I was folding paper for a ten zloty bet and laughing with my father when the world fell away...

Across the camp my Uncle Chilowicz and his wife Marysia are in the building materials shed, meeting an SS man named Sowinski. Marysia is careful how she walks because a fortune in diamonds taken from Goeth's plunder is secreted in the thick seams of her uniform. Such expensive alterations are also well concealed in an extra inner lining inside my uncle's jacket, with more of the glitter in his pockets.

At this hour, my mother is over at the Madristch factory with Helena Serafinska, working alongside Mattias Groenski, a pattern cutter. All three carefully concentrate on carving cloth into parts of uniforms: sleeves, lapels,

The Journey from Plaszow

collars and so forth. The fabric is excellent blue serge, imported from Frankfurt. By the time Mama has prepared the vest panels for the machinists, her brother, his wife and several others are concealed inside the empty tank of a fuel truck, lurching along with a millionaire's cargo towards the main gate.

By now, Marysia had packed away her OD's diamond-loaded uniform in a small valise and changed into in a simple but expensive summer dress with a narrow-fitted linen jacket. She tolerated the stink of diesel and old wood inside the tank. To her it smelled of freedom. By this time next week, she thought, she and my uncle will be rich on the shores of Finland, and the week after, enrolled customers of the Bank of England. She intends to seek out a final refuge among well-meaning London Jews who long ago saw the wisdom of anglicizing their names. Marysia envisions a sedate carriage house in a redbrick mews in South Kensington. She vows that once in the country of delicate civilities, she will burn all her clothes that stink of Poland, and will require an entire new wardrobe from the made-to-order department at Harrods.

I have many envelopes to fold and glue today because I have a bet on with the typesetter, Gerek Kasmarek, that for ten zlotys, I can produce three hundred by the end of the afternoon. Gerek is about my brother's age and often lets me watch him set the metallic type within its printing blocks. He brings me my pile of pre-cut envelope sheaves and dares me to get busy! It's a provision of the gamble that I cannot waste one sheet of paper—Papa is keeping careful tabs on me to see that I'm fair with Gerek. We stare at the clock above the door, and at exactly ten-thirty, our contest begins!

In this window of time, Hanka is over at the furrier's workshop, and having a bad allergy to beaver fur from the coat she is repairing. Her beloved man, Juzek, asks the shop supervisor to move her to a bench where she can handle a set of women's lamb's wool coats, taking apart the black garments to be retailored for German soldiers at the front. Delightedly, she's seated alongside Juzek's work area, giving the lovers a space to exchange light-hearted flirtations.

One asks then, who is happy and who is safe in this hour?

Down at the front gate, Amon Goeth was waiting for them, Sowinski being his creature. He found a defunct pistol on my uncle but was more annoyed by the shimmering hoard he discovered in his pockets. Uncle Chilowicz was dumbfounded at their betrayal and silenced into submission by the bitterness of it all. Marysia was totally disbelieving, but with a whore's instincts, tried to charm her way to survival. There was nothing too venal or disgusting she would not have offered to Goeth, including her husband's head, in order that she might live.

For her final minutes, she smiled and wet her lips under the impression that Commandant was about to indulge himself with her behind the truck. Goeth was all business and efficiency—he alone put his pistol to Uncle Chilowicz's head. Marysia died next before she had finished the sentence, "My dear Amon, we could have such a good understanding…"

Their bodies were driven back up to the camp streets and laid out for all to view as a lesson to others against such larcenous escapes…with space left for three more.

By now, I have folded and glued a hundred and eleven envelopes, setting them to rest all crisp and pure in their wooden tray.

At around noon, my cousin, Wilús, in the ironing room of the tailoring shop, is standing naked in a tin basin of hot soapy water, shrieking with delight because he's being bathed by two affectionate females, Helena Serafinska and his steady playmate, Adela Susser. All three of them get a soaking from the revels that become necessary when scrubbing my cousin. Wilús wants Adela to strip off and jump in the water with him but Helena says that's not proper for a young lady. She rolls up Wilús in a dry sheet and stands him upright on her sewing bench to dry him off. Adela brings his clothes and he submits while she lovingly dresses him as if he were her favorite doll. Helena lets her play the little mother, watching both children with a hesitant pleasure because it is a short reed of normalcy in this time of hounding disaster.

Amon Goeth cornered Wilús's parents, my Aunt Frania and Henryk Schnitzer, behind Madritsch's factory. My uncle fiercely protested his innocence and for the moment it appears the Commandant is listening with a sympathetic ear. "Yes, I do understand," he agreed with low-voiced politeness, "You're not at all like that Chilowicz rabble. But you must be aware that a man in my position must take all precautions."

He stopped up Henryk's speech making by shooting his wife immediately. She dropped to her knees, astounded by the chasm of silence that yawned open to meet her. She looked on at her husband's shocked gaze and his mouth forming the shout, "No!" Her last thought was that she must make sure to see her son Wilús, to see him…before an immense stillness envelopes her. Her husband at least got to curse Goeth loudly one time before he suffered several bullets too. The Commandant had no idea that their line will continue well beyond him in the still-damp little boy now napping peacefully on a pile of old wool sweaters yet to be unraveled.

Inside the uniform factory, my mother is not yet aware that she has lost her brother and a sister in the space of three hours. The shots are muted by the rattle of a hundred sewing machines and the fiery hiss of the steam presses. She moves peacefully between cutting out sleeves and delivering the correct number of pieces to the busy tailors.

By three in the afternoon, Gerek comes by my workspace to see if he was going to be poorer in the wallet be the end of the day. I boast that I am now up at two hundred and twenty-eight envelopes. "Better count your zlotys, Gerek, and get ready to pay up," I tell him proudly, although my elbows and wrists are tingling with fatigue and I keep running to the sink to wash the

The Journey from Plaszow

glue off my aching fingers, all the while announcing to my father and my workmates, "I'm winning! I'm winning!"

However, who is happy and who is safe in this moment?

Towards the end of the workday, the door to the paper workshop blows open and a rough-looking man I'd never seen before strides over to our foreman, Ben Geisehals. He whispers something, causing Ben to grip him by the shoulders as if he is questioning the man in severe doubt. I'm up at envelope two hundred and ninety-four when I notice Ben beckon to my father. The three of them huddle together for some time and I can only see my father's back with the arms of the two other men covering his shoulders.

From this precise moment, I abandon the envelope Olympics and the ten zlotys no longer matter because the three men bound together in urgent conversation are emanating a very strong badness. I see my Papa gasp and shake his head. Ben's mouth is drawn tight; he pats my father's arm in the comforting way when nothing can be done about a situation. The men and boys around me are beginning to whisper and cast furtive glances my way. My father's face is white, as if an illness has suddenly come upon him. He walks over to me slowly; his voice is hoarse as he says, "Romek, get your jacket. We have orders, everyone has to assemble."

The men gather outside the barracks in lines of two abreast and are marched forward by the OD escort. I grab my father's hand. It feels dry and leathery and he seems not to notice my fingers linked in his. I want to ask him many things, the questions appearing to transmit silently out of my chest to him. He stares directly in front of him as he explains. "Roman, Manek has been taken from us. He's gone."

"Gone? Gone where, Papa, on a transport?"

"No, child, I'm sorry to tell you that...your brother is no longer alive."

Manek, my golden brother, my protector, my warrior is taken from us. Is taken... from me? In the space between my short painful breaths, I can't find any means at all to even ask how such a thing is possible.

Rabbi Geller delivers the story. There was an announcement made over the speaker system ordering Manek to report to Goeth's office immediately. News had already reached my brother that his uncle and relatives had been killed, and he knew that any confrontation with Goeth would be disastrous. It would also have been totally out of character for Manek to offer himself up meekly. I believe that he was not, in his last moments, on his way to submit to Goeth for any reason. Despite the efficient trap that had snared the Chilowiczes and the Schnitzers, my brother would have had a fallback plan. He still knew many people outside the camp, especially in the Polish and Jewish resistance groups, but he would have avoided sharing any escape plans with his family, because of the emotional toll on my parents.

I believe that Manek was but an hour or so away from freedom, brought about his way, or else he would have suffered at the gates along with our aunt and uncle. He must have refused to go with them, realizing both their fellow Jews and Goeth's henchmen had marked them for revenge. (Marysia was particularly hated because of her reputation for flash-point brutality to female prisoners. My uncle had also accumulated a small fortune, along with Goeth, in ransacking the wealthier inmates of the camp.)

Manek had left word with close friends at the electrical workshop to give his fond regards to his mother, to his girlfriend, Lilka and to offer his gratitude yet again to Oskar Schindler. Hurrying his way down the steep barrack street, he'd run headlong into an SS man, Unterscharfuhrer Zdrojowski, who, eager to please his Commandant with apprehending one of the named escapees of the day, grabbed my brother roughly by the arm. Manek instinctually hit him full in the face! Zdrojowski pulled out his gun and fired twice, killing my brother instantly.

Things of random, the wrong turn made, stepping out of cover a minute too soon, being seen, not being seen, fate spinning on the split second, either treachery or deliverance rising up to meet us. How do these circumstances collide? Who is to say what forces draws them together? Like fish to be skewered, we dart and hide, we swarm and flash along troubled waters, hoping not to be chosen for pain or loss, hoping to make the next upstream place of no harm. There is nothing to be done. Except endure.

❋

A train lumbers through winter gloom, its wheels groaning over iced tracks. I can tell whenever we reach a hill and begin to ascend. The engine pitches forward in a mighty grinding effort. In the gloom of the boxcar, the men seated on the far side are suddenly raised up higher than the travelers in our area. My cousin Wilús and I sit against the wooden wall, wedged between my father and my Grandfather Arye. Our car is the standard ten meters in length, constructed from rough-hewn timbers, one of hundreds requisitioned from the former Polish rail system.

Earlier in the day, the SS transport agent, Kasper Horst, had cursed loudly on reading the manifest that detailed only thirty *Jüdische Lastwagens* to take us away, and not the usual fifty or more. He'd stood before the assembled prisoners at the Plaszow rail depot, turning the pages of numbers and routes on a clipboard, denouncing his lousy job and carping at his unhappy corporal about the rolling stock blown to shreds the week before by the partisans in the forests of Babia Gora.

No one dared to snigger, but you could feel the spark of smug redress transmit throughout the lines of prisoners.

In our leaving, my father had made sure we were the first to board the train so that we might claim a corner space and sit as comfortably as was manageable. I've become a partial armchair for my cousin, who has his skinny butt in my lap and his legs draped over Grandpa Arye. Papa instructed us to keep our hands off the uneven planked floor, away from the ingrained quicklime that could burn the skin. The floorboards are piebald;

little islands of dirty white interspersed with a darker ruddy stain. "The lime is a precaution, Romek," he explained, "a method of disinfecting the place."

The situation is far from sanitary. We are eighty bodies packed into a space designed to hold half that number. A large oil drum is located at one end, a makeshift toilet where all these travelers relieve themselves—if they can reach it in time. My father says if I don't think about it, it won't affect me, but my nose and the foul stench still collide no matter what thoughts wander through my mind.

The train surging up a hill arouses the men near the loathsome drum to shout and hang on to its rim, so the contents won't slosh over on them. When Wilús and I have to go, Papa calls out for Menachem Kindler to help us. The crusty old reprobate rises out of the crowd, his matted white hair flowing around his shoulders, and shouts like a preacher, "Gentlemen, please make a mitzvah for these beautiful boys; relay them over your shoulders."

I see Wilús passed from man to man and Menachem balancing him precariously above the drum, helping him with his pants. Minutes later my cousin is buttoned-up and parceled back to us, the men ferrying gently him on their upturned hands.

We are a day out of Krakow and this is a mystery ride. No one has told us kids exactly where we're headed, except that we're going to work for Herr Oskar Schindler at his new armaments business somewhere in Czechoslovakia. This is Manek's legacy to me and my family—through his easy friendship with Schindler he was able to have our names placed on a list of essential workers the *Treuhänder* (trustee) needs for one of his factories across the border. Despite our fears that Goeth would continue to hunt our clan down after the shootings, Schindler himself got urgent word to my father for us to join this all-male transport while we still lived. Our rescuer declares that the women of the merciful list included Hanka and Mama who will soon follow us.

Leaving had been hard and a relief at the same time. The mound of Chujowa Gorka shelters my brother's cremated bones. He will have no other grave but that barren hill. I had wept at the thought that we were abandoning him, another nameless pile of ashes blended down among the silt of thousands, fading from the world's memory.

So many things happened after the killings. Weeks later, Amon Goeth went missing, reputedly having gone to Vienna to visit his family. There were murmurs that he would never return. A blessing for us—we feared that he would not stop erasing Ferbers, Chilowiczs and anyone else he thought privy to his extravagant pilfering. The Reich ordered that Plaszow was to finally be closed and its inmates dispersed to other lagers.

In late September, the leadership was taken over by a milder commandant, Hauptsturmführer Búscher, a man of poorly developed brute imagination or any other kind, who, brimming with official process, was appointed to wind down the operation. Plaszow in its end time is mainly a domain of women, German military, some Polish police, some unclaimed kids and a few elderly folk. My father reassures me that my mother and sister would join us in less than a week.

Trusting nothing, I ask, "They will come, won't they, Papa?"

"Believe me, Romek. You will see them in a few days."

"Do they shoot people where we're going?"

"Not in the least! Herr Schindler is a different kind of German, a civilized and righteous man, a friend to Jews."

"Will Commandant Goeth be waiting for us when we get there?

"Thank G-d he will not."

Before our departure, my mother and Hanka wore out my cheeks with a torrent of kisses outside our barracks. They inflicted the same on Wilús too, who was wailing in full voice for his own parents. The boy was frantic. My grandfather had to pry his desperate fingers off Hanka's skirt because he was sobbing and refusing to go without seeing his Mama. My mother rocked him until we had to report for the transport detail. Uncle Samek tried to get Mama and Hanka a day pass so they could come to the station to say goodbye. He was still trying to have the paperwork stamped by the time we were marched out of Plaszow's gate.

In the boxcar, my family and I stood behind a pack of men some ten deep. The noise outside was a collision of shouts and pleas. Grandpa and Papa lifted us kids up onto their shoulders that we might look for Hanka and Mama on the platform. I was hoping to see them, air-kissing their affections over the heads of the two thousand or more men being bullied onto the train. The square of daylight framed by the entrance is shrinking as the wagon fills up. Two soldiers gripped each side of the portal and yelled at us to move further in. Somewhere a whistle was blowing. They hauled on the doors and slammed us into darkness. I saw steam clouds pass the single barred window in the center of one wall. The train grunted and heaved. We were moving.

My mother and sister never showed.

Papa tells me our wagon has made many such journeys, indicated by the number of small chinks that perforate the walls, where other travelers have stabbed at the wood to suck in plumes of fresh air. My grandfather widens the hole above us with a loose nail. Now we have a personal breeze in our corner, just above my father's head, from a slit that also lets in rain. I put my dented tin mug to the gap to capture any moisture and was rewarded with a gray trickle of water spotted with coal grit from the locomotive. We sip at it anyway.

The Journey from Plaszow

The engine hauls us through the beginning of another Polish winter. Sharp cold wafts in from every gouged nook diluting the gross fug that hangs over all. The holes also announce the morning; narrow slats of daylight stream across the car. Hunched under my father's arm, my hand on his bony chest falls and rises with each breath. So much muscle has fallen away from him recently; the belt of his pants is pulled several notches tighter. My face rests against the warm tier of his ribs, a safe place to dream.

"Get some sleep, my boy," he whispers to me.

The men around us jostle for space with low-voiced mutters and snapping complaints; they lean into each other, as if the wall of sour-smelling clothes will fall entirely if even one shifts. The train's clacking lulls me into a passive drift, through layers of the previous weeks that had wavered us between hope and disaster. No refuge is to be found from Manek's annihilation. I carry an unceasing echo of him; it lies down with me, it rises up with me. It's surely no ghost but some turmoil in the web of familial flesh. He is with me and yet when I reach for him, he's no more than a distant figure totally uncoupled from us. I asked Papa about it and he said this is how it is, Roman, these tenuous cords of love—we're left holding the frayed end.

The pictures that memory keeps throwing off—even if I don't want to look at them—come wheeling fast before my eyes. Manek on that last morning; us two walking together, his nonchalant grin; my cheeks cupped in his affection. The even set of his shoulders that bespoke cool assurance as he walked away. He'd raced into his adult state so far ahead of me—always in easy ownership of himself, a hopeful scholarly youth, a former warrior of Zionist resistance, now a staunch survivalist in Plaszow. All these merits and more lay deservedly upon my brother, the laurels of small victories on the last day of his life.

There is to be no reconciling my final image of him with the vileness of his wasting. It was one of those rare moments when we were forced to cross paths directly with Amon Goeth. The rigid corpses of my relatives, along with my uncle's deputy (a man named Mietek Finkelstein), were dragged from the gates and laid out in a half circle on the main road by the first set of barracks. The public address system blared that all inmates were ordered to come at once to look upon the dead as a warning against any dark impulses to insurrection.

From every workshop, quarry, depot, and warehouse, prisoners trudged toward the viewing in total silence. Whatever judgments many may have held toward the Chilowiczs, if Goeth's chattel man could be so easily wiped out, the inmates now feared a mass blood-letting and more retribution. The military escorts weren't that organized for such a speedy reaction of compliance, they quickly raced to fall in alongside the prisoners filing robotically through the barracks lanes.

My mother was ashen-faced. She could barely focus her gaze, her hair and skin had taken on a strange sallow hue, she staggered and was held up by Hanka and her boyfriend, Juzek. She appeared to me as one who had journeyed to the country of death to discover its borders closed to her and confused at finding herself still in existence while her oldest son and kin lie there in the mud—their flesh rent and disarrayed. My father advised me that I am to be steady and calm for Mama's sake. "Don't show fear or any disturbance. You can weep all you want later."

"Manek wouldn't cry," I said.

I look up to see Amon Goeth seated on his dappled Arabian at the edge of the crowd. He's wearing an impeccable short-sleeved white shirt, epaulettes of rank on the shoulders and insignia above the breast pocket. I stare because I'm looking for signs of the slaughtered on him—Menachem Kindler says you can't shoot people that close-up and not be warmed by their blood. However, this is Amon's morning. He'd prepared well for it: a cup of Bavarian chocolate, fresh cream from the Plaszow dairy, maybe a shot of bourbon, the relief of his compulsive butchery, then back to his villa to shower away the offal of death and into pressed jodhpurs and the starched shirt laid out precisely (on pain of a beating) by his Jewish maid, Helen.

The horse is jittery and stamps his hoofs at the odor of kills wafting his way. His master speaks soft words to him, pulls on the reins, makes him prance back daintily; turning the huge brown eyes away from what Goeth would later write up in his report to Section D was a planned rebellion. I see... Manek...his jacket totally soaked and crimsoned, his head too, which is slumped away from us and inclined to Aunt Marysia, who is totally unrecognizable except for her manicured hands. It seems barely credible to me that my brother is not alive. "Let's run to him! Fix his wounds, please, we must!" I whisper to my father and start to pull away but he clasps me tight by the hand, hauling me back because Goeth is watching us keenly over his shoulder, wheeled around on the saddle while his horse gazes elsewhere. Papa hisses, "Romek, please, you must keep silent!"

I don't want this moment but my eyes betray me and will glue it inside my skull forever. Rabbi Geller and some of the men from our barracks shuffle behind us reciting the Shema. Goeth barks an order to one of his brigadiers, who turns and shouts to the mourners to shut that rattle up or join the executed! To further our obedience, the Commandant had the ODs position placards just behind the slaughtered on which is written the irony, "Those who violate just laws can expect a similar fate!"

⁕

I became obsessed with asking the adults around me where do the dead go? "Where is my brother?" Some faces turn away from me in silence, as if I might contaminate them with the question. Others snapped at me because they too were missing a sibling, a parent, children shot at the Ghetto wall or sent to the killing lagers. Why should the Ferbers be any different? Having asked him only once, I dare not repeat my all-consuming query to my father for fear of wounding him, and my mother was completely unapproachable, locked up in her grief. She would come at me with sudden effusive affection,

The Journey from Plaszow

hugging me breathless, saying, "My Romek, sweet Romek, you are still here, still here."

I sought out Rabbi Geller, who I thought, with his learning and inclination to great mysteries, would help me search the immense beyond for Manek. He gave me a delicate non-answer that no good man is wasted under G-d's law, all living things that mirror his glory return unto their Creator. We must trust that divine order knows well its own purpose. "That doesn't help," I sobbed. "I want my brother! I need to know where he is! I want to hear his voice! I want to be able to say things to him!"

It was Menachem the carpenter who brought me some comfort, weighing my questions with serious contemplation. "I do know, young Romek," he finally answers, "that the highway of the dead is busy with such comings and goings all the time. Do I believe that Manek's fine spirit is alive in some fashion? Yes, child, I do believe that he dwells in the afterlife. Mind your prayers, as any good boy should, say a loving word to your brother. Be sure and let me know if he answers you."

The boxcar allows no space for us to walk or barely move but my father encourages us kids to stand every few hours to take the numbness out of our legs. He makes up stories to entertain Wilús and me, but we soon tire of them because he repeats plots already told. Besides, my cousin is still an inconsolable mess, whining constantly for his parents, though it has been carefully explained to him by my grandfather that they too are now in heaven.

In the belly of the train, the darkness offers refuge for my silent conversations with Manek. At first, I'm more mind-tied than tongue shy; I'm an eleven-year-old boy talking to dead relatives. However, I petition my brother; Dear Manek, this is me. Please get Wilús to stop crying and making us crazy over his mother and father. He doesn't know where heaven is or how to get there, and is dazed at the idea that he has to live to be an old man before he can set off on the journey. If you see Aunt Frania and Uncle Henryk, tell them to fix Wilús in the head so he'll quiet down and let us take care of him. Papa and Mama miss you very much, so does Hanka. Thank you. I love you. Roman.

I listen for a reply, nothing definitive; just the snoring and wheezing of eighty unwashed men on the rails to another country. Nevertheless, the asking doesn't feel so bad. Maybe it takes many conversations for Manek to hear me. I have time to get it right. Our train backs into a siding cut into the flank of a hill outside Kedzierzyn, where it sits for half a day. From our air hole, I see trees crisped by the first October frosts, their boughs glistening and swaying under a lively wind. We're facing a broad screen of verdant evergreens growing above a network of several rail lines. I see a man in a cap by the signal tower pulling a lever to switch the rails. The tracks shudder into position. Many voices around me are asking, "Where are we? Are we in Germany? Isn't this the route to Dresden?"

Outside comes the martial stamp of boots on gravel and orders called. The wagons are to be opened for fifteen minutes to empty the latrine drums and for the water buckets to be filled. Kapos only on the ground! The doors grind open in their metal slots to let in a torrent of viciously cold air. But we welcome it, loosening our foul-smelling warmth to its bracing chill and the good tang of pine resins.

By the slant of the sun, Papa says it must be about mid-morning. He lifts me up so I can see the pleasant vista outside. We have stopped in a shallow valley. The dense forest snakes its way across fields and along the ridge of a small mountain. Between it and another hill I announce that I can see a church steeple and the red roofs of several houses. To the west sit terraced vineyards, their grape bushes tied up against sturdy posts for their wintering.

The traveling Kapos disdain to unload the latrine tub and, after some rapid quarreling in Yiddish and Polish, Menachem and three other men are allowed to remove it, dump the contents into a ditch, and return to the train. On the way back I see my old friend raise his cap to several mounds that line the embankment (the graves of previous mobile prisoners who made their final stop here). Our fifteen minutes of sunlight is short-lived. A distant rumbling grows close and a well-dressed SS officer down on the tracks ordered all the boxcars to be closed and locked. Once again we're shut up in semi-darkness. I take up a position at the spy-hole because there is a rush of speculation among the men that a battle payload is coming through the valley. Wilús starts moaning that he's hungry. I lift him up to the nook so he can look too and he reverts to a nosy boy eager to get a glimpse of the world without.

What passes before us are over thirty flatbed cars bearing damaged tanks, broken anti-aircraft guns, eight-wheeler trucks and jeeps, iron testaments to battles lost, their metal hides badly fractured, their gun ports missing. I narrate for Wilús what we're seeing and that gets my father all excited because across the boxcar the men have formed a short pyramid up to the one small window with the metal bars. An emaciated lad of about eighteen, Rafael Flüsser is the top lookout who can see more and reports on the commotion outside.

I'm describing all of this to Papa who gently nudges me and Wilús away from our viewing point to see.

"It must be over for them," he says. "They're going home...to Germany."

"Does that mean it's over for us, Papa?"

"Maybe, Romek, maybe."

Dear Manek, time is not here. Not in our wagon, I don't even know what day of the week it is. Do they have weeks where you are? Papa has a dry cough, says it's the fumes from the engine and the latrine bin that has him breathing shallow. It makes me secretly afraid. The transport Captain warns he would take any sick prisoners behind the coal bogey and give them the

The Journey from Plaszow

bullet. What if Papa is so ill they make him leave the train? Grandpa would never let him go alone and we'd never leave the two of them. You can see how this would turn out. Wilús is doing much better. Grandpa has a special way of talking to him. He tells the kid that his parents, may their memory live forever, have instructed that the three of us should be his new family. Wilús seems to like this plan. I actually got him to laugh the other day.

I found a few crayons in my knapsack, mainly blue ones, and a cedar pencil, the lead still sharp, that I'd "borrowed" one time from the desk of Uncle Chilowicz. Papa and Grandpa let us use their backs as stools so we can sit up at the wagon's wall and draw funny pictures. Mottel the Tuchas has returned! I drew him fighting a monster called "crap man," an evil troll who lives at the bottom of the latrine bin. Wilús giggles at the story, but wants to put a captured princess in the drum too. Papa says that's not such a great idea. Can you hear all this, Manek? I miss you a lot. I wish I could see you. Don't forget us. Roman.

❊

Birds wheeling above us, tumbling kestrel hawks that nest in the secret ledges of the Carpathians. Their hunting screech awakens me. My eye to the air hole, I can't look up that high but sight the arced shadow of their wings against the steep embankment. They hunger for field rats and fox kits who warren in the dried-up ferns. Wilús wants to know where we are. I tell him I think Poland is long gone and that the station signs have become another language, mostly German, but the kid asks have we reached America yet? Isn't that were we're going, Romek?

The men of our car grow argumentative. Some pray in anxious tones, reciting from the pages of their dog-eared Siddurs (prayer books). One group runs a kind of dice game with two, four and six-holed buttons but no one dares to bet their bread allowance (three hundred grams a day) and fantastical debts are devised. They play for money they never had or will never see again. One man bargains his house long confiscated or half the reparations he intends to sue the German government for. Another ransoms a field where, he claims, is buried the religious silver of his ancestors. My ears prick up at an animated discussion of Amon Goeth led by Kalman Sacher, a former optician who knows my family. From what is said it appears that the kingdom of Goeth is now over forever.

"Vengeance finally found that piece of drek!" declares Kalman. He goes on with the tale and the other men also ferment bitter opinions against their former tormentor.

"Arrested at his father's home in Vienna," Kalman narrates, "rich folks who own a publishing house and are so-called people of culture; all that privilege and Amon, a monster at his mother's breast, can you imagine? They stuffed his lousy keister in the prison at Breslau, going to be a blaze of a public trial. The Reich bosses will nail him for every pfennig he stole, they found over eighty-thousand Reich marks in his apartment, place was like a damn delicatessen; hams, foie gras, smoked venison, all kinds of canned goods, whiskey, cognacs, French wines."

"Maybe he planned a career in the grocery business after the war?" says another.

"Are you kidding me? Can you imagine his ugly puss grinning back at you over the smoked fish? Too bad his aide Chilowicz is dead, and his bitch of a wife too, would've been star witnesses."

"Oh, you really think a German court would believe testimony from a Jew?"

"Not so loud, show a little respect, those two young boys and their family down the end are kin to the departed."

The train halts in the night. I hear the luff and rumble of other transports passing close by and the steady howl of an air raid siren way down the tracks. I poke my rare pencil through our spy hole and cry out when I lose it as it hits against a stone wall. We have stopped in a tunnel. The sky outside is threaded with the drone of engines. Our train doesn't move for two or more hours. The locomotive lets out occasional wheezes of steam, an exhausted beast at rest. There are fearful mutterings among the men, whispers of the horrendous. Why are they keeping us here? Are they going to kill us? A loose-fleshed Russian, Leonid Borosov leaps up, his voice gaining octaves of panic. "This is how these bastards do it! I know their methods, in the middle of an empty place, some bare field, so that just eyes can't witness, first the clothes come off, then the open pit. They have an execution platoon, gasoline trucks and ploughs waiting to tidy up the job!"

My father nudges me aside, stands up, and calls out with authority. "Sir, please, calm yourself, I beg you, don't frighten these children."

Curses and protests rise as hands and feet are stepped on. A stench of sweat and rotting cabbage drifts our way. I stare up at Borosov's dark form looming over us, and feel my father reaching for the man's hands; he's speaking in a manner that once soothed me when I was little. "You mustn't let fear overtake you. It'll suck the heart out of everyone."

"But we must be ready, when they open the doors. This time we must be ready!" Leonid fearfully insists.

Papa, holding on to him, asks Leonid quietly whenever was the other time? The big man is shaking and mentions a place near his former home in Kiev called Babi Yar. Shame and dread rise out of his stink but he says nothing further. Papa advises him to come and rest beside us. His soft words slacken the shadow of the man and they both sit down. The Russian slaps my father's shoulder gratefully but the threat has been lit. Other voices rise, inflamed by it.

"We're moving east, maybe to the gassing lagers inside the Ukraine."

"This man is right; they mean to finish us off! We should do something!"

The Journey from Plaszow

Menachem Kindler shouts louder at them for their foolishness; that any mother's son with half a brain could tell from the easterly slant of dawn light that the train has been traveling to the west all this time. Why is it his cursed misfortune to journey with witless Jews unable to discern one compass point from another! His irritation is lost in a great thunder that suddenly explodes over us, the car shakes violently; coupling hooks clatter in their connecting hasps. Someone cries out that the wagons are on fire! More shouts of fear, prayer and outrage, fists beating on the locked doors! I fall hard against my father because the train convulses and shoots forward out of the tunnel. Streaks of flashlights dart back and forth on the tracks; soldiers are yelling and guiding the locomotive on with tungsten lamps. Pillars of illumination tower between earth and sky—the broad beam of searchlights piercing the clouds, but they will not find the phalanx of Lancaster bombers now roaring away to the Baltic Sea.

Dear Manek, it's been quite a night. Our Polish engineer had to loop the train around our set route for least ten kilometers. Grandpa Arye translates from the German yelling on the tracks that the British RAF has blown up the supply lines at Jelenja Gora. The men in our wagon have gone from wetting-their-pants terror to cheering the King of England and calling down blessings on his mensch, Winston Churchill. We have nothing to eat, except the bread ration. Maybe food is not a thing you can make happen but, if you can, we'd like a big pot of soup, very thick, maybe chicken? Eggs would be good too and Wilús wants raspberry cream pastries and chocolate bars. Oh, and some soap please. Papa says we're dirtier than mud-rolled dogs. My eyes are closing. Wherever you are, I wish I could be with you. Roman.

I do see my brother, so vivid is the dream that I feel the heat of the sun on both of us and when I take his arm it's as solid as my own. It's a summer day; my family and I are sailing a yacht on the lake at Rabka-Zdrój. Mama always liked coming to the spa town, she believes the mineral baths are beneficial to children. Hanka is stretched out on the deck, oiled up and ready for tanning. Papa and I are fishing from the back of the boat when I hear a shout. There's Manek calling to us, stepping lightly over the waves. No one else seems to notice him except me. He looks handsome and well turned-out, dressed in his tennis whites with a yellow cravat tied loosely at the neck. He smiles and beckons for me to come, to step down and walk on the lake. I yell that I'll have to swim to him but he says not so. Then he is at the bow, his hand in mine, lifting me down to the lake's surface.

"Is this a joke," I ask my brother. "You want me to fall in, right?"

Manek laughs uproariously, "No, Romek, you pin-head! It's just like ice-skating."

We link arms and glide across the glittering waters, my feet scudding the wavelets without getting wet. I ask him if he is OK now, no more bullet wounds. He looks at me as if I have a slate loose. I start to sink beneath the swift current but he bears me up saying, "Take one step at a time then another, the rest is easy."

19

Shifts of Fate

SHARDS OF ICE HANG from the single ventilated window of our boxcar, the wood frame rimed with frost. The men jostle each other for positions at the lookout holes, tense and expectant that the journey is ending. The train chugs slowly towards a towered gateway flanked by single-story buildings on either side. My Papa and his father are in urgent furtive conversation, not always a good sign. I pull at my father's coat sleeve.

"Is this the Schindler factory, Papa?"

"Maybe, Romek, I'm not sure."

"Will they give us something to eat? I'm very hungry."

"I know, child. I've listened to your stomach for the last twenty kilometers. Such a churning, when you get a meal, I want you to eat it slowly."

Along the line of the transport, boxcars are crashing open; men are shouting, dogs barking, and a voice through a bullhorn jarring enough to be broadcasting from a deep well. It demands that everyone is to get out and on the ground immediately. Our wagon is unlocked and we tumble forth onto a wide graveled siding. The grubby insular safety of the last three days is totally gone.

We are still in Poland, in a lager named Gross Rosen near a town that Grandpa says used to be called Rogoźnica. This camp seems very flat with many buildings stretching off into the distance. Everyone from our transport has been pushed into three barracks so new, there are no bunks, nothing except bare boards on which large sheets of heavy brown paper had been spread, for easy clean up, as if we were dogs that would make a mess in the night. There are too many of us to lie down and stretch out on the paper mats. We sit up with our legs around each other, in a herringbone arrangement, each man leaning against the breast of the one behind. Papa slumps against Grandpa, I lie in Papa's arms and encase little Wilús who is placed at the end of our line because of his size.

You should see us here, Manek. Stacked columns of men knit in foolish order by our limbs and the stripes on our uniforms, the way Moniek Hocherman (you remember him) used to pack his tin soldiers, fifty to a box. Papa has lectured me on the colored triangles worn by permanent inmates: red for the communists, purple for the goyim called Jehovah's Witnesses; the men with the pink triangles on their striped pajamas are harmless but the real *Shedim* (demons) are those who wear the green and black triforms.

"What's so bad about them," I ask my father.

"They are the spilled bowels of Poland's worst prisons, Roman. Men deformed in the soul who are given free rein by their captors to commit the foulest brutalities. You are to avoid their eyes and any contact with them, do you understand?"

"Yes. Are they Jews too, Papa?"

Do you know, Manek, what he tells me? Regrettably, some are Jews, but all are depraved, pitiless, and full of darkness. Papa says like the German militia, they dwell outside the laws of G-d. Our father is scaring me, Manek. Please take care of me, of all of us. You must because I saw a green Triangle crossing the Appellplatz this morning, a big thick-bodied man with gray moss growing on his teeth. He was dragging a person bound in a sack from the head to the knees, screaming and writhing. Every time the prisoner in the bag would cry out, the Triangle would laugh horribly and club hard at the fabric, causing the bones to ring. We were made to watch this. The sack began to leak blood and soon the one within stopped shouting altogether.

There are women somewhere in the camp; we have seen a truckload of them being driven down the main avenue along with some thin, wasted men caked in white powder, over-worked specters from the stone quarries. Papa, Grandpa and the men of our transport argue desperately among themselves because the list of the workers for Herr Schindler's factory cannot be found and the Germans won't let us leave without it. I'm scared they'll send Papa and Grandpa to the mine here where Menachem says they assign the *Nacht und Nebel* (night and fog) prisoners; those who toil for a quick death and are sealed alive beneath the granite stones when the rock face is detonated.

An audience is needed, the Commandants ordered—for a football game to be played on the wide apron of a field, pocked with shallow holes caused by the mined-out reaches of granite. Several thousand inmates line the field's boundary, stamping their ill-shod feet on the frozen turf. Even some women are among the onlookers who are mostly men, gaunt in the cheeks and reddened eyes sunk into a permanent unease. I'm standing with Papa and Rafael Flusser, Wilús is holding hands with Grandpa Arye. Someone fires a pistol at the field's south rim. Figures stripped to the waist are running, three dozen or so, in our direction. Behind them comes a contingent of green triangle men, a great army of them, making the odds at least four to one.

"Dziadzius? (Grandfather) Where's the football?" asks my cousin.

There isn't any, of course, because the targets to hit and kick are the half-naked! In some evilly comic ballet, they come speeding and yelling down the field, the pursued leaping and dashing every which way to avoid the swinging clubs of the Triangle gladiators. If a victim collapses, a swarm of them falls viciously on the man, batons chopping at him, hammering a whimpering red mess into the scant winter grass. The turf is already dotted with bloody convulsing bodies. If the runners make it to the end of the field still upright, their reward is their breathless life. Armed guards stand along the perimeter, relaxed and chortling at the spectacle while we onlookers remain stunned.

My father is hollering at the top of his lungs, "Despicable! Stop this! Stop this!" Others along the fringe of the crowd are inspired to take up his protest. A cluster of Triangles halt, wheel around at this daring chorus and charge the watchers twenty meters down from us. The prisoner line breaks and the panicked section streams off in many directions.

There's a great noise from the north end of the field and a sight that caused my father to bellow to heaven for help. My champion and defender, Menachem, is among the hounded! The strength in his old legs has taken him almost to the finish line when a Triangle slammed him hard between the shoulders. Rafael Flusser tries to shield me from the sight in his ragged coat, but I knew the carpenter's familiar roar and I look. He's swung around and snatched the club from his startled aggressor. The audience is hailing him to run! My grandfather lifts Wilús up into his arms and turns them both away so the boy won't have to see anymore of this.

A short distance and he would be across the goal posts of the living, but Menachem doesn't move an inch. You can see it in his face, a superb madness blazing for the end of all that is intolerable! He turns, demonic with rage, driven by a righteous power, swinging the club like a claymore and hacks open the skull of the Triangle attacking him. The man falls into his arms, brains spraying out behind him. The crowd's voice soars in hysterical applause. Two amused corporals by our group raise their rifles but do not shoot because a surge of the destroyers come for Menachem. He bellows curses at them and splits their bones, one after the other, until three of them fall bleeding and moaning at his feet. I'm screaming his name when they finally bring down the old lion but he dies with his hands clawed tightly around his enemy's throat.

※

Dear Manek, if you see Menachem in heaven, say "hello" from us. I'm sure you two will be the best of friends, he always thought well of you. Let him know if there's any good timber where you are. Papa says he was a fine carpenter, proud of his trade, and never content just to idle the hours away. Good news! We are finally getting out of this terrible place. A new list has been made for Herr Schindler's factory since the old one has gone missing during our journey, a document ordered by the military here and typed from memory by a former Plaszow OD, Marcel Goldberg, who once knew Uncle Chilowicz.

Papa tells me that Goldberg is either everyone's enemy or friend. Many men insisted they were on the old list and therefore their place should be automatic. Others argue to toss off the names of those who can't afford a bribe. Goldberg is alternatively solicitous to those who know enough of his past to hang him. To others he tries to be a subtle auctioneer of places on the list. He vacillates between servility and absolute lordship over it. However it turns out, he will be a rich overseer of the living at the end of it all. Papa, Grandpa, Wilús and I have kept our places on the list, influenced by Manek. Goldberg has fond memories of my brother and says that Manek always treated him decently but I think he's afraid of what Schindler will say if we don't show up at his factory. Still, because of my brother, we will ride the train across the border to relative freedom and I thank him mightily.

Papa says now he knows you are within the gates of heaven, Manek, because of the miracle you have made for us of our continued journey. I hope to meet you every time I lie down to sleep. Wherever we travel, stay close to us. I miss you, Roman.

We're back on the train, all several hundred or more Schindler men, reducing our original transport almost by a third. I do like riding the train. Thus far, our mobile prison has afforded us a rugged safety. As long as we are moving, not much threatens us. There's much more room in the wagon now and Wilús and I can stretch our legs out, lie down fully, or even walk among the other travelers. The mood among our company is genial. My father would say "festive," even when we pray for Menachem. Papa wants me to take a lesson from my old friend's final battle.

"He was a man of great pride, Roman, whose head would not be bowed."

"Then why did he want to die, Papa?"

"Everyone has their limits, child, and one must make a decision of what to do in such awful situations. Menachem chose to fight."

"I would have run, Papa, all the way to the finish line. "

"I would hope so, Romek. I would want you to live, no matter what happens to us. You must promise me that you will do that? Promise me you will!"

"I promise, Papa."

The distance to Brinnlitz is two days and one hundred and sixty kilometers. Rafael Flusser had magically conned some extra bread ration for our car and was generous in sharing it among the men. Grandpa says he's a fine well-mannered boy, orphaned by the Ghetto selections but who has older brothers in the Polish resistance. Rafael is smart too, and wants to be a geologist, if, after the war, he can take up a scholarship at the Jagellonian University. He draws a map for us on the wall of the car with my crayons, showing our route across Sudetenland to a town called Zwittau that sits in the border armpit of Germany and Czechoslovakia.

I'm excited because I'm about to leave Poland for the first time in my eleven years. Wilús still thinks we're going to New York and cheerfully informs the men that's where his parents are now living, New York City, in the country called Heaven. He proudly announces he knows a lot of people there already. Rafael offers to teach him some basic geography, but Papa gently advises him to let the child dream. Any lie is worth the smile on his face.

The men sing in fine voice, cheerfully offering each other undying friendship; promising to make introductions to unmarried sisters and issuing endless invitations for when the war is over. "You'll come to my house, meet my mother, I think she's still alive, G-d let it be so. She makes a brisket so tender you could weep."

"You too, dear friend, I want to introduce you to my cousin, Basia, ripe as a plum, never married, a very particular girl but you I know she will like."

My grandfather slips his arm around his son and whispers in delight, "Listen to them, Leon, to the conversations of men who know they will live!"

The morning of the second day and, for us, it might have been the first day of Creation. The train clatters slowly into the station at Zwittau, Czechoslovakia, around five a.m. The sky is a waning dark; the mountains above the town are silhouetted by the creep of warm light edging their flanks. We are the only commuters of the hour at this depot. Porters give us an offhand glance but civilly greet and salute the military escort from Gross Rosen who, for once, are not brutal in our disembarking. We are ordered into lines of four prisoners across and marched into the streets, to cover the blessed six kilometers to the Schindler factory.

We stride through a community of tidy sedate houses, well fenced and well kept, with a sense of dedicated order. I see manicured gardens; flowerbeds mantled with pine boughs and rose bushes hooded in sacks by some careful gardener to keep their summer juices from freezing. Rafael comments here lives the strict Lutheran bourgeoisie, who offered their Hitler youth to the Volksturm to assist in the ruination of Europe. We pass a local garage. On the wall is a painted slogan, "*Halten Sie die Juden aus Brünnlitz!*" (Keep the Jews Out of Brinnlitz!)

Too late for that, we are here. We are alive!

Manek is with me in this hour, I sense his nearness, marching with me as we approach the new camp. True, it has the standard watchtowers, barracks and a guard house festooned by barbed wire but on the ramp, grace awaits us. Do you see him too, Manek? The very tall man wearing a Tyrolean hat that looks lost on his broad frame, his smile is that of a card player with a winning hand.

Schindler raises the ludicrous headgear in a benevolent greeting, "Welcome, gentlemen, come inside, we fired up the boilers, bread has been baked and there's freshly made soup, that's what these young boys are sniffing at. You must be hungry after your long journey."

His easy manner and civilized welcome bring tears to the eyes of some men, so long have we been treated as if we had no human stamp at all. He opens the door to the factory and urges us to enter, that we should be out of the cold and into the warm yeast-scented safety.

On his left wrist I see the fine Girard Perregaux timepiece.

Do you remember, Manek? The watch you once gave to Herr Schindler so long ago in Plaszow.

Shifts of Fate

❃

Today, I am nothing but a mouth; I'm on a food vacation!

In the last few hours, I have eaten four bowls of a rich turnip soup, a buttery dish of surprising substance and flavor, many thick slices of freshly baked brown bread, three hefty servings of semolina pudding with honey and raisins, all washed down with several mugs of black sugared tea. Even though I've opened the buttons on my pants, my guts are drum tight.

The fine supper and its abundance have slowed me to a dead halt. I'm lying on a pile of straw, wrapped in several blankets. Wilús is curled up next to me in a heavy sleep and snuffling like wind blowing under an ill-fitting door. We rest in an unfurnished dormitory that runs the upper length of Schindler's factory (a former knitting mill belonging to a Jew named Hoffmann, long sucked into the turbulence of the disappeared). In fact, we boys have been warned to keep our hands off the disused looms on the main floor, stacked on their sides, their innards spewing dust-caked wool threads.

Downstairs I hear the men in drifts of discussion about how to pour the new cement floors needed to absorb the weight of the machinery to come—huge molds to produce artillery casings. Although it's only four in the afternoon, the other kids and I are in bed because there's nothing for us to do except eat, play, and eat again. Frau Emilie Schindler and her husband have decreed a no-limit policy on food for the children and Papa says it's our duty to add heft to our puny bones. Frau Schindler had mentioned to the fathers that anyone under fourteen should be examined by the former Judenrat physician, Dr. Biberstein, to ensure that we have no illnesses that might obstruct our development. It was the first time I'd ever heard a German grown-up (other than her husband) speak kindly that we had a future to grow into.

Later that night, my Papa, Grandpa and Hanka's boyfriend Juzek, who is here too, climb into the straw beside us. I nestle against my father. We are warm, not hungry, not now. It's a strange sensation, this absence of want in the belly. I pester my father, who is patient even as he's drifting off to sleep.

"Papa, can we stay?"

"Yes, child. Herr Schindler says the Germans are suffering defeat on all fronts. The Russians have already invaded Eastern Prussia."

"Will Mama and Hanka come soon?"

"On the very next transport that pulls in from Plaszow."

"Then we'll all be together?"

"Together...yes."

The next morning there's creamy hot oatmeal and fresh applesauce for breakfast. Some of the boys eat with their eyes constantly on the move, as animals at a waterhole fearful that they might be driven off by predators. Frau Schindler offers us second helpings and the waterhole types are too meek to speak up, but she piles the delicious concoction into everyone's dish anyway. There's a German military unit living in the barracks by the wire, but Herr Schindler has forbidden them to enter the factory without his permission and he's not issuing them any invitations.

Within these walls, we have a rare freedom, to eat and rest, to work at human pace or even at a snail's speed. The installation of the huge metal presses is constantly delayed while the civil engineers and workers measure and argue amiably about every screw and nail. I have a sense of time comfortably slowed. Many men no longer have that hurried apprehensive step, of scurrying away from danger with their gaze lowered under their caps. Here there is lightness in every face I see around me. It may be a temporary holiday from fear, because, as Papa says, the factory is still regarded as a sub-camp of Gross Rosen, and Herr Schindler has warned us to look busy if the bosses from the Armaments Inspectorate Office ever show up.

Wilús, the other boys, and I fill up our days with short foot races where the course is the entire length of the upper dormitory. We play-leap-the-straw pile, tell dirty stories about girls we've never met, have fake contests of marbles substituted by small pieces of coal and conduct several card games from a deck that's so tattered and faded its markings are barely readable. We cheat, we fight, we wrestle; a thirteen-year-old boy named Lazlo makes Wilús shriek and I have to knock him down until he apologizes. His father pays my Papa off with a small exquisite block of mint chocolate for my cousin. Wilús, the little fink, refuses to share it. He becomes a favorite with Lazlo and the bigger boys who let him ride their shoulders while they gallop him around our living quarters.

PART IV: 1944 ~ 1946

20

The Camp at the End of the World

I CAN'T REMEMBER MY FATHER doing any real work at the Brinnlitz facility, not because he was loath to but because casual disorder lay over the entire Schindler enterprise. It was a place stillborn. For the short time I was there, I recall there were curious gaps in the manufacturing processes. Bins of shell components sat around, their caps waiting to be riveted before being shipped on to other factories to be filled with fuses and high explosives. Herr Schindler took an impish delight at the haphazard output of his business and was away from the place for long stretches of time.

It was during one of his absences that our stay of barely seven days in this industrial paradise came to a terrifying halt.

It's the early hours of the morning. Wilús and I are cocooned under blankets but my father's sleeping pallet is empty. I hear a commotion from below, voices layered, the clipped bark of Unterscharfuhrer Josef Liepold from the big lager at Auschwitz, followed by the nasal authority of an inspector from Section D and the urgent whispers of our men.

"It's only ten or twelve, such a small group, can't we say no to them?"

"Herr Schindler would refuse! He'd kick their arses into the yard!"

"But did you see the papers—the official stamp from Oranienburg?"

"Somebody get Dr. Gross in here, maybe we can say the kids are not well?"

Liepold reads the unholy order aloud, a dozen children or more to be scoured from each camp in the Gross Rosen network, those inessentials, fake little munitions workers who would never cap a shell in this lifetime, who have no place or purpose in an armaments plant.

I get up and drag my cousin into his pants because my father is calling for me to come to the main floor at once. His tone has that drift of exaggerated calm he always uses to soften a bad situation. Wilús and I clatter down from the dormitory loft to find a group of boys and their fathers herded up one end of the workshop. One man says to Liepold that Herr Schindler is going to be pretty steamed about all this. The German retorts that the *Treuhänder* (trustee) better not bitch about much, given the lousy output of this factory and the breathtaking concessions made by the local SS office. *Do you think our tolerance has no limits! Get these transports organized!*

In an instant, the good soup, the tasty bread, and the comforting sense that from here in Brinnlitz we would commence a final journey home as a family united evaporates. It's a cheater's trick. There will be no remaining.

I stare at the two officials with the power of the rubber stamp: Liepold, thick-waisted, his importance pushing at the welts of his leather coat, next to him the adenoidal inspector, pencil thin and all efficiency in his well-cut civilian suit, carrying a briefcase gorged with letters and writs. Why so few of us to go, always a sinister thing to be singled out. Hanka's fiancé, Juzek, is standing with my father. I hear Papa say that he'll travel with the two boys. Juzek, who has a special affection for Wilús, says he will go too, that he can easily pass for the boy's father. Papa insists there's no need for them both to suffer this journey. He'll be the one to leave with us. However to where? The thought stabs my mind then I utter it, reedy-voiced and desperate.

"Where are we going, Papa? Who is going?"

My father pats the dirty stubble of my hair and evades my gaze. "We are ordered back on a train," he explains, "you, me and Wilús."

"Why, Papa, what for?"

"It seems that men and children are required for a medical unit at the Auschwitz lager. A Doctor Mengele has need of us."

"But we're not sick, Papa, why would he want us?"

"I don't know, child, but we have to leave right away."

"But what if Mama and Hanka come here and find us gone?"

"Don't worry, Herr Schindler will tell them about our new location."

My father's evasions are so wildly transparent. I can never tell him how much they terrify me, that we need to stay put, and if we are not here when they arrive, my mother and sister will be pinned by the same bitter sorrow. I feel swamped by a sense of futility, by the rotten demon of having no say to be in any place by our choice alone!

In the accumulated awfulness of leaving Plaszow and entering this very hour, I finally understand the terrible deadness in our living that pursues us in a hundred different ways wherever we go. Tears surge up in my eyes, but I don't want to cry in front of Papa and the other men. Grandfather Arye volunteers to go with us too but Dr. Mengele's orders are specific: children from age five to fifteen and one parent only. Certainly, he wants no men over sixty and any lie about my age is useless now. My grandfather holds Papa's head between his hands, strokes his cheek tenderly and says, "We'll see each other soon, you and the boys. I know this will be so."

Then he bends down to me, kissing me several times and instructs me that it's time for me to become a true warrior.

"Like a real soldier, Grandpa?"

"More like a person, Roman, who believes that even the most difficult things can be changed."

"I don't know how to do that."

"You will learn and you will prevail. Take good care of your father and Wilús."

I'm shaking as I put on my coat. Wilús is pestering me, tugging at my sleeve, saying he wants to go back upstairs and sleep some more. Before he can start whining, my father takes his hand and says, as if we're preparing for a vacation, "Come on, Wilús. Today, you will take your first ride on a real passenger train."

Outside, the darkness resists a thin seam of light to the east. No one speaks as we march out of the gate in the punishing cold with only two soldiers to escort us. The compound is shrouded in a bleak silence. No movement in the barracks from the German platoons still dreaming of victory. Wilús and I are lifted into the waiting truck bed. Its frame is bare and open to the frost. There's only room for the fathers and boys to stand up. The engine roars and we lurch down a sandy ramp to the road.

I grip the rail to stare back at the shadowy hulk of the factory, barely visible in the loosening night and think how Frau Schindler will have no boys to feed when she wakes up. Wilús is fretful and shivering. My father tightens his scarf and pulls him up onto his shoulder mail-sack style where he promptly falls asleep. Everything is a hideous lopsided dream. I was there. I was safe. Even the straw bed comforted me. Now I'm out here, in the cold air with tears stinging my cheeks, shunting once again down the ugly road of uncertainty.

※

We're seated altogether in a third-class wagon of the Polish State Railroad, on hard wooden benches befitting our lowly tariff (paid for by the Reich). We travel in clothes shiny with months of dirt and sweat, and our group emanates the awful piss-reek of unwashed wanderers, (although the other passengers were not that much further up the grooming scale).

The faces that stare back at me are mainly leather-skinned, unshaven farmers, sullen black-garbed women, and railway and factory workers in patched overalls and creased overcoats. They give us the once-over, shrug and hold their tongue against the easy insult for a dozen *Zydzi* (Jews) in harness to two German soldiers. Some of the women even smile at me, but I don't dare to respond because my stomach yearns for the coal-streaked baked potatoes they're eating, roasted en route for them, so they say, by the fuel gaffer in the fiery embers of the train's furnace.

My father comments discreetly to another parent about the invisible barrier between them and us; that we travel as felons, in the company of soon-to-be free Polish citizens, in our own country. We have no food and such adult opinions don't help my ravenous hankering.

Wilús, who got the window seat, has been chirping to the Galician countryside for the last fifty kilometers, exclaiming loudly at every bony cow and horse startled from its grazing by the locomotive's wail. The boy's pleasure delights Papa and he even makes me smile when he suggests that, should the train mow down the nearest herd of Holsteins we can cook and eat some steaks. "Can we, Uncle Leon? I'm very hungry."

The Camp at the End of the World

The two guards are the most peculiar German military I've ever encountered. The younger man seems shy but friendly while the older one is positively uncle-like in his good nature. A practical plainspoken man, he seemed shame-faced to admit when we boarded the train at Zwittau that he had orders to take us to the big lager at Auschwitz. He made me very fearful at first with his startling kindness and careful manners. I kept waiting for him to scream and kick somebody, for the usual livid craziness to show itself, the familiar blood-raging evil that caused Amon Goeth to blow holes in prisoners from his balcony while sipping a glass of sherry.

In our journey of unending hours, my father calls this officer "our German."

"He must be a devoted Catholic," Papa claims, "to have the compassion to buy us coffee and refreshments for the kids out of his own pocket at the station stops."

My father is so moved by these gestures that he shakes the man's hand as if they have been lifelong friends. "Our German" allows us to get up and walk around; he doesn't reach for his rifle every time one of the boys whispers he needs to use the toilet at the end of the carriage. He's very courtly to the Polish women seated nearby who eye him with distrust but he talks to us easily in good Polish about his family back in Germany. He even offers to carry letters for the men to their own womenfolk. I ask my father if this soldier is so terrific, why doesn't he just set us free?

"His superiors would shoot him for shirking his duty," Papa explains.

"Maybe they'll shoot us for nothing. Why don't you ask him? He likes you."

"Ask him what, son?"

"To let us go home."

My father stares out of the window at Poland passing by. I can see the struggle in his eyes reflected in the glass.

"That's not possible, Romek, not yet," he says.

✻

"Our German" and his corporal march us from the drab railway depot where the station boards still carry the Polish name, *Oświęcim* (Auschwitz). The road ahead stretches through flat farmlands, level as a board, fields cleaved by winter winds overlaid by the smell of old manure and decaying roots. We trek on and I note the spire of an old church, the slate turrets of a duke's castle and the Sola, an apology of a river, no more than a thin skein of black water stilled by freezing. Along the gray air, somewhere out of the dimming horizon, a full orchestral waltz is playing.

"It's Strauss," declares Papa, his head at a listening angle.

The ghostly music continues to pour out of the empty sky yet there is no concert hall hereabouts. Crows striding in furrows cackle at the violin surges. Before us, I see many dark low buildings extending forever to the horizon. It's not another town, just on the scale of one. I sight the electrified fence that surrounds the place and the watchtowers; the music seeping through the barbed wire is louder now. We descend a long drive and there's a sign wrought in beautiful metalwork above the gates that reads *Arbeit Macht Frei (*work makes you free*)*. The Strauss mystery is revealed to us at this entrance; there sits a full orchestra of ragged men in dirty striped suits before a conductor, a black jacket over his prisoner's garb, wielding a baton.

We are so mesmerized by their performance that our marching step is undone and we crash into each other. "Our German" herds us back into an orderly block of chilled travelers and leaves us with a fussy uniformed clerk. I drift sideways away from Papa, fascinated by a scrawny prisoner slumped on a chair by the gate, still and patient, as if waiting for a late visitor. His eyes bulge open and stare straight ahead and he smells bad. In his blue-tinged hands, he holds up a sign that reads, "Here I am."

"How come they just let you sit there?" I ask him. "Are you the gate man?"

Loose music pages suddenly waft across me. A clarinetist from the orchestra dashes from the musicians' benches to gather up his score under a shower of curses from the conductor. The clarinetist, a square-jawed man, indicates the seated watcher. "That's Spitzer, the piano tuner," he says. "Poor bastard thought he could just walk out of here. Best get back in line, boy, or they'll swing you too!"

❋

My early weeks in Auschwitz-Birkenau had a disordered motion. Time was sawed into isolated blocks, scaled to size by how good or violent the days were. Many were shadowed in useful forgetting, others deservedly obliterated.

After the intake count at the gate, a new escort ordered us into a small barracks, separate from the other prisoners, and locked us up for the next twenty-four hours. Frequently, a key scraped in the double doors to open on a new face every time. One was a labor detail man looking for strong backs for ditch digging, a single dismissive glance at us and he departed chuckling. Next, a medical orderly in a white coat with a clipboard enters. He demanded we stand at attention and put all the kids down front. He scanned us for exactly ten fear-flooded seconds, shrugged in disappointment and he too left.

A Kapo named Milosz, sporting the purple triangle of a Jehovah's Witness on his striped shirt, came to us late in the evening with his assistant to distribute soup, bread and two buckets that served as toilets. (Milosz was unusual among camp inmates in that he had a full head of hair, oiled to perfection in crested waves. It was said that he lived, for now, under the protection of a senior officer from the supply depot.)

The next morning we were all marched to the other camp's citadel, Birkenau. There, an orderly whipped us through stripping our clothes off and pushed us into a bathhouse that was joyously true to its function. (Papa

The Camp at the End of the World

had been assured by Milosz that the camp's once busy gas chamber had now been converted into an air raid bunker but was reluctant to believe the man.) Nevertheless, we showered in scalding water and the older men got a total body shave. Next, we endured a slathering with a delousing liniment and my shorn head, pitted with lice bites, turned a bright red from the stinging chemicals.

When it was my turn to head the clothing line, I was issued striped pants coupled with a random shirt and an over-sized jacket. These garments, so the *Blockführer* (Block Leader) said, were lifted off the backs of the dead before they were buried in the field behind a now-defunct crematorium (although there is still a burning pit for those who die in disease). (In all the ludicrous brutalities of the last three years, I was constantly dressed in cast-offs from those long gone to the next world and wondered if I'd ever live to fit into the next size up.)

However, nothing prepared me for the brass nib of the pen that speared a number into my left arm, down into the layer of muscle, making me shake and scream and scream! The blood and ink gushed in a purplish swale and my tattooist, a surly Pole, slapped me around the head for crying out, and hit me again when my father, suffering the same labeling nearby, begged him for pity's sake, he's just a boy! It took both Papa and me to hold Wilús down when a calmer man from the numbering detail etched the white twig of his forearm. My cousin shrieked pathetically, and in his terror, pleaded with us not to let the stranger kill him! I wept too and said we would live, please, Wilús, just try to bear it, a few minutes more, so we can live!

The struggle was so terrible that I heard Papa, who had the boy tightly clasped in his arms, whispering prayers in the child's ear. Wilús passed out, his teeth clamped tight, gray spume foaming at the corners of his mouth. My father carried him away quickly down the waiting line of prisoners, rocking him as he walked. I hurried behind them, hoping that my cousin has survived the ordeal but I heard him give a low sob as he rose to consciousness.

Once we were assigned to our barracks, Papa cooled our written arms with snow scooped from the windowsill and bound them with torn rags before the *Blockelteste*, (the barracks leader) a bad-tempered Slovak called Pan Stasiek, roughly ordered him to depart to his own quarters. My father kissed us and strode away, leaving me there with Wilús, and me trying to push back the awful loneliness of his going.

✻

We are housed in timbered structures some thirty meters long by ten meters wide, furnished with rows of wooden sleeping platforms in three tiers. Two walkways on either side the bunk avenues lead to a stove of meager heat at each end of the barracks. Thinking it would be warmer near the roof, I try to commandeer a top bunk for Wilús and me. Two brothers, older boys, Melchior and Czeslaw Rosenheim, are already nested there on the straw pallet. Their ancient grandfather Haim, who has the bunk below, stares at us in toothless disapproval. Melchior, aged thirteen, smooth-faced, with a feminine demeanor, is also hostile at our arrival.

"May we sleep here, please?" I ask. I have to petition them while perched on the edge of the high bunk with Wilús hanging off my back.

"What about the kid, does he pee the bed?" demands the snippy thirteen-year old.

I want to hit him, tear off his girlish lips, but I grovel because I need two things desperately: a place to hide Wilús during the day and to make at least one friend I can count on to keep him safe.

"No, he's a very clean boy, we both are."

Czeslaw, the older one at sixteen, nudges his brother, "Come on, it's not like you're giving up a palace."

The old grandfather cackles up at me through sunken gums. The fly of his pants is laced up with string and his frame is shrunken but I notice his hands are huge and muscle-corded. He hunkers back down on his bunk, cursing his unseen sleeping mate. All four of us boys lie down on the narrow wooden platform and arrange ourselves in canned-fish mode, head to toe. I curve my body around Wilús for warmth and am comforted to find myself face to face with Czeslaw, who seems a reasonable type.

We whisper our histories in the dark. "Are your parents here?" I ask him.

"No, the typhus got them in May. We came here from Lodz, after the Ghetto was liquidated."

"How come the old man is still alive?"

"My grandfather's a bookbinder, had his own business. He can still sew a good cover. Commandant Schwarzhuber likes to keep him around to repair any rare volumes that show up off the transports. How come you and that small cousin weren't ordered to the *Kinderheim* (children's home)?"

"What Kinderheim?"

"The barracks three alleys over where they usually send any kids under twelve."

"I'm fifteen," I lie.

"But he's not." He jerks a thumb at Wilús, who was snoring lightly.

"Where he goes, I go!"

Czeslaw cuffs my shoulder lightly. I sense from his voice he's smiling in the dark.

"Well said! I like a man of conviction."

"Is it nice, the Kinderheim?"

The Camp at the End of the World

"Dr. Mengele likes it. The way a *Shochet* (kosher butcher) likes a chicken under the blade. He goes there to harvest kids for his work. Has an endless supply of them."

"Does he hurt them?"

"At every opportunity but you'll be safe as long as you don't draw attention to yourself. You know the drill. Keep your eyes down, make sure you find work to do and, for G-d's sake, don't get sick."

Czeslaw turns away from me to sleep against his brother.

The barracks at lights out: men and boys shut away from the terrors of the day, entering into a narrow galley of short-term safety and the calm of the night. We could be sleepers anywhere, sealed in the cold darkness. I play a game with myself I deem as hopeless hope, that I will open my eyes tomorrow and be any place but here. I mentally lean into that blurred and mystifying space my father calls the future. Wilús twists away from me and wakes up. He raises his head suddenly and whispers that his lost mother is here, visible and floating above the barracks stove! He points down the aisle and his finger tracks back and forth.

"See, there she is, Romek, right there!"

"No, no, she isn't. You're dreaming, Wilús."

"But it's Mama! I know it's her!"

He giggles softly and calls to her and I feel his heart under my resting arm speed up at some bidding of whatever maternal wraith was adrift in the gloom of the barracks. The Aunt Frania I cannot see. Who is to say whether or not Wilús has found a face in the darkness he loved so well? I can no longer tell the ghosts from the living.

✦

Morning. The barracks swarm with men reluctant to march out into the raw weather but fearful enough to struggle into rags, urged on by a strident klaxon blasting an alert. Wilús cannot go. Aside from the predatory Dr. Mengele, the guards frequently make small kids race through the wire alleyways in their cardboard shoes. "Run, Kinder, run!" they shout. At the last fence the small, bewildered figure in the distance turns and waves, thinking they've won the game and flops over from the sharpshooter's bullets.

The count of several thousand men and women on this morning is going well.

I stand in the back line between the Rosenheim brothers, hoping I will catch sight of my father among the men from his contingent. Czselaw nudges me, indicating I should glance to my right to check out today's *Lange Männ* (Long Man). I see a tall inmate standing with a proud rigidity supported between two others, his cap pulled well down over his bone-white face, his eyes half-open. Each of the barracks usually has one a week; a corpse that has cooled in the night, but who is dragged out just the same, whose number is shouted out, saving us all from endless recounts in the merciless cold.

"You don't have to be alive to be here," Czselaw explains, "just be here. The clerks need to square their head counts, or else."

From his bookbinding days, Haim Rosenheim carries in his mind a vast library of pages and regales us at night with many outlandish tales, adulterated and patched together from original stories. "Do you know, Ferber boy," he calls me, "the Talmud says the Angel of Death is full of eyes, that he carries a long sword tipped with a bitter potion to stop the tongues of men from arguing with him in their last hour? He exempts neither king nor beggar from his harvests."

"From the ash piles by the ponds, it seems that he visits us all the time, Pan Rosenheim," I answer.

"One might say he's a prisoner too, easily commanded by the wicked," he says.

"Like these Germans that keep us here?"

"Do you think these soldiers will live forever? He will find them in the end."

"I would like him to find them now."

"Then you too would be his master?"

Czeslaw chides the old man to lighten up. Haim dribbles, pinches my cheek and declares I have all the makings of a fine heathen.

Nevertheless, he is real, the unholy Angel with the long sword that silences. I have looked upon his baleful form.

Because of a slew of recent deaths from influenza and a horde of *Lange Männer* filling up the burning pits in the far woods and marshes, there is to be a count of every ambulatory prisoner in blocks A through D. We line up for many freezing hours by the railroad track standing in the numbing haze of hunger, cold and robbed of sleep. It's a morning of visiting military stars from the Auschwitz administration.

Several generals in precisely pressed uniforms, exuding pink-faced cleanliness and severe disdain, roll by in open jeeps. I note a handsome officer standing up in the front of one vehicle, very dapper, dark hair and a dark complexion. He's wearing white gloves and clutching a large box of chocolates under one arm, its gold satin cover embossed with fake violets. He waves regally at us, his gloved hand an elegant foolishness among the mud ruts, the oil-stained snow and the filthy, ragged prisoners.

Melchior chuckles in contempt and says it's, "Uncle Pepi."

"Don't ever look at this man, Romek," Czeslaw whispers to me, "you don't want his eyes on you, checking out your age."

The Camp at the End of the World

"What's with the chocolates, are they for his Frau?" I ask.

Melchior sniggers and bites his lips to hold in another seizure of humor.

"They're for the poor little buggers in the Kinderheim."

I take a step to the left to hide behind the man in front of me, well away from the Nazi officer and his gilded box. Twenty minutes later, the same jeep rumbles a return towards the main road from Birkenau with "Uncle Pepi" seated in the back, his arms around two seven-year-old girls, newly arrived inmates, still healthy, both the pretty mirror of each other. I see the officer smiling at them, stroking their hair, with all the light-hearted fondness of a father. The twins settle into the curve of his embrace, their gaze luminous with trust. The Angel of Death has many eyes.

My cousin, Wilús, is barely tolerated by our *Blockelteste* but mostly ignored. The boy is allowed to stay all day in our barracks unharmed because my Papa continuously pays off the man in some fashion. Wilús, his eyes shining at me through his reddened lids, is truly brave whenever I have to leave him alone and join the labor team. (He's of an age where I might have to revive my lost art of being invisible.) While we are apart, my cousin will take a birch broom, too tall for his height, and attempt to sweep the long barracks aisles, a task that Czeslaw has arranged to prove the child's usefulness. However, with his appalling diet, the job exhausts him well before he gets as far as the north stove.

A handful of prisoners are often confined to quarters after the morning count, usually men rank with diarrhea or dysentery but too terrified to confess it, lest they be ordered to the *Krankenbau* (a death-churning infirmary) on the Auschwitz side. They stay close to the slop bucket and are willing baby sitters for the small boy who spends the afternoons above their gassy odors, sleeping in the high bunk.

I learn to smoke and trade in the currency of a slim amount of tobacco I mix with defrosted blackened grass and old dried tealeaves from the kitchen dump. I'm not good at inhaling, but there is a wonder in the awful taste of this mixture, rolled in tubes of newspaper, that blunt my hunger. (The *Blockelteste* in Papa's barracks allows him a real cigarette now and then, a source for its own dilution.) I produce these skinny bundles of ersatz nicotine late at night and trade them with some of the workers in the Canada block, a place as close to heaven as the camp would ever come.

The Canada warehouse is the land of plenty, a storage facility of everything robbed from the exiles on the transports. I have never seen so many multiples of everything in my short life. Haim Rosenheim would take me with him whenever he was called on to inspect rare books that needed sewing or to help in sorting through fine Italian leather luggage on reserve for officers. (Haim is also part of the camp's funeral teams who ferries the dead from the infirmary and those who have died in their bunks to be cremated in the ash pits.) One thing I am convinced of from the similar warehouse in Plaszow is that clothing, like some homes, could be haunted.

The more abruptly the destroyed were ripped away from the world, the louder their phantoms clamored in their linens and elegant French shoes.

On the Canada shelves are thousands of pairs of women's evening slippers, hundreds of sequined gowns, summer frocks once worn to elegant cafes, bowler hats by the meter, and piles of neatly folded tallesim compressed by layers of failed prayers. In one corner stacked to the ceiling are bales of women's hair, destined for submarine insulation. I beg Haim for a few pieces of kid's clothing for Wilús, whose pants are threadbare, who has no muscle anywhere to stay warm and I ask for extra sweaters for us both. There will be no risk of lice in what I find. The women packing the children's stuff to be sent to bombed-out civilians in Germany have carefully washed and ironed every garment.

"Do you think, Pan Rosenheim," I ask the old man, "the kids in Germany hear them?"

"Hear who, Ferber boy?"

"The voices of the dead...from the clothes."

"Since when did garments speak?"

"How can these not?"

"Child, you're as mad as a goat. But that yet may save you."

❊

A young man in my father's barracks, Witold Obwarzanek, falls in love and unknowingly ignites a family reunion. His lady, Otylia Leiser, is an occupant of the women's barracks that stand across the railhead tracks, fenced in by electrified wire. In the late afternoons, Czeslaw and I work by the high voltage barrier on the pretense of clearing snow accumulated in the shallow trench beneath it. We have no shovels, just two battered tin trays borrowed from the Birkenau kitchen. There's a steadiness and honesty in Czeslaw's nature that reminds me of Manek, in the way he watches out for Wilús and me. He measures with his forearm a safe distance to the killing fence and warns me to reach no further but to kneel and scoop the snow back towards me.

"Never do this when you're tired or ill, Roman. There's many a fevered schmuck that's grilled himself from stumbling too far across the ditch."

On the other side of the wire, the faces of women appear at their barracks window. I call them "moon-girls" because of their shaven heads and their lean-dog features that give them a raw, alien aspect. There is a parade of waving hands and many smiles—and the women become pretty in the moment. Czeslaw stands up and whistles back at them.

"Do you have a sweetheart over there?" I ask him, hacking into a block of dirty ice.

"Sure, an entire harem, look around you, boy. We're in the land of romance."

I have no clever reply but he's grinning at me and brushing snow off my shoulder.

"I mean it, Roman, truly, and it's not just an itch in the pants. Fools of every description rush here to have a first or last love. You know why?"

"No. I don't know any girls."

"The Krauts have stolen time from us. We have no next week, next month or next year, just this moment. Sup it up and be thankful."

Witold Obwarzanek was wealthy with minutes and insane with passion for the wasted beauty, Otylia, who rode the open truck every day with other women to labor in the rubber factory at the nearby Buna-Monowitz camp. I heard that Otylia, tall and squared-jawed, had the misfortune to enter Birkenau as both a Jew and an active communist. She had survived at least a year on her skills as a chemical engineer.

I was scheming for a way to visit my father when Czeslaw hauls me out to the wire late one afternoon. It's some hours before curfew and groups of men stand around in shabby knots on the snow-covered rail lines, sharing illicit cigarettes. I'm looking for Papa when I sight a skinny blond man being helped into a deep barrel that's surrounded by a wide circle of prisoners. On the other side of the fence, the women cluster noisily around one spot where the wire sags. Someone has deepened the trench there, creating a snow ramp. Czeslaw looks over at me and gives me a thumbs-up. Suddenly my father is at my side and hugging me.

"Come away from the crowd, Romek," he says. "The guards don't like it when prisoners group together. There could be trouble."

"What kind of trouble?"

"Come, so we can talk and visit a little."

Our conversation is drowned in a great cheer that rouses up from either side of the fence. The barrel begins to roll down the snow ramp under the live wire and comes to a trundling halt at the feet of the women. Several of them quickly push it along the icy path and into their barracks. In the next minute, the barrel-pushers run back out, slamming the doors shut, giggling and nudging each other. A languid smiling face appears at a window, Otylia, then Witold. They give everyone a grateful wave then drop the sacking that serves as a curtain.

The men, including Papa and me, on our side of the barrier watch this farce with cautious amusement. Czeslaw says the punishment for amorous visiting is time closed out forever. I reply the only thing that romanced me was the next meal. Papa thrusts a heel of bread into my pocket but he's listening to loud shouts coming from the women's compound. A voice is calling my name! My father looks around, startled and is immediately afraid.

Czeslaw reads the situation at once and beckons. Papa hurries me into the middle of the men and they instinctively close around us, but the call for

"Romek!" rings above the crowd then my father's name is shouted. Through the dark elbows of the men, I catch a full view of...my mother! She's running by the trench, and with Hanka following! I scream out their names and burst through the protecting arms. Papa dashes after me and the four of us are racing along opposite sides of the lethal barrier like scalded rabbits, hysterical with joy. Mama is yelling at me, tears streaming down her face.

"Romek! My Romek! Stop already. You might fall and kill yourself!"

Two meters of snowy ground and several thousand volts separate us, but we halt and shout our affections exultantly across the short chilly distance.

"My beautiful men, I kiss your dear faces," yells Hanka.

Our parents exchange loving absurdities. Mama asks my father how much weight has he lost, how are his bowels, is he ill, well, in-between. How did we get here? Where is Oskar Schindler? What happened to our train for Brinnlitz? How was it we were re-routed here? When it came to me, both women gush at how tall I've grown, such a handsome boy, a real heartbreaker! Look, Hanka, can you believe the fine head of hair on Romek? (I had the appearance of a sickly dwarf in a man's cut-down coat. Scabies had laid crusty, bloodied tracks on my cheeks and my hair stubble was already rampant with lice.)

Everyone talks at once and my sister literally shimmers with happiness at the news that her lover Juzek is safe at the Schindler factory. "Romek," she says, "I have something I've been keeping for you."

She throws a brown paper sack over the fence into the snow. I scramble to get it, hoping it is something to eat. Inside the crumpled bag are several tin soldiers, given to me by Moniek Hocherman in 1940, at the time of our exile from Krakow. I waved the recovered gift at Hanka in triumph.

Our reunion is halted by the siren blasting out the curfew; orders rasping over the loudspeakers for all prisoners to return to their barracks immediately! The men scramble into marching formation. The women's *Blockelteste* appears at the door of their quarters and shrills their yard with her whistle. Papa shouts instructions for Mama and Hanka to take great care of each other.

"We'll see you here tomorrow and the next day!"

Mama is throwing more kisses, and yelling love, love and more love! Her delight is unbounded as Hanka hauls her by the arm to the open barracks door. "Listen to your father, Romek, be a good son," are her last words to me. In stolen Kraut time, we had all of fifteen minutes together.

By the next day, they were gone.

※

For many days to come I call for my mother and sister across the wind-blown rail tracks to the women's fence. The women stare back at me as I shout Mama and Hanka's names repeatedly. Crazy kid, we are many mothers and we have Malia's and Hanka's by the hundreds. Who is that boy? Is he someone's orphan? No, I think there's a father here too. Then he's doing better than most young ones. At least he's not having his eyes dyed blue by that dirty butcher claiming to be a doctor. Little mensch, they chorus back, there is no Mama or Hanka Ferber here. Go inside, it's too cold for these questions.

They must be somewhere here. They must!

I realize that I'm not looking at the same faces that stood there by the wire last week or the week before. Mama and Hanka are not in the infirmary, nor are they in the punishment cells on the Auschwitz side, where offenders are made to stand in a coffin-like space in total darkness for days on end. Papa doesn't get involved in searching with me in case he finds them among the frozen dead in the sick bay barracks where the untreated diseased are left to starve.

When their corpses are delivered to the smoldering pits, they're stripped and, if not reduced to rags, their raiment collected by us boys to sort for the laundry crew in the Canada warehouse. This task of gathering up these clothes is made more dangerous by a vicious Kapo named Meilech Bronner, who comes upon me and the other boys with a bamboo cane to thrash our backs. His punishments make no sense because the pain and fear disorders us; we scream and scatter from him and the work. Czeslaw speaks quietly to the man, "We're doing our job, please let us labor in peace." The challenge of reason seems, for the moment, the right cure and Bronner strides off looking for other skin to whip.

I spend hours turning over the women's clothing in case I see something that Mama or Hanka might have worn. Haim Rosenheim tries to reassure me. He takes my face between his meaty, wrinkled hands and stares at me in his intense, manic way. "If I should see a good mother and a lovely girl with eyes like these," he sputters, "I would not forget them. Be assured, Ferber Boy, no one who resembles you has gone beneath my shovel of late. The women of your house are alive!"

I'm far from comforted because the wily old buzzard will say anything that roams through his mind. I question all over the place. Other inmates think it a fool's errand. You can tell by the incredulous looks and the mocking questions they rain down on me. Child, you're missing two women out of several hundred thousand absent. You should be so privileged to find them. We are a kingdom of washed-away, gone-forever sorry buggers. Our natural state is who is here, who is not, and who will be lost tomorrow.

My father questions carefully around the compound. The best source is often the *Dachdeckers*, men sent from camp to camp to fix slates on the roofs of the barracks. They watch from the chimneys as the transports come and go. How can they know Mama and Hanka among the hundreds of women driven by the guards and their dogs into the wagons? Papa hopes the two have been moved, as promised by Schindler, to his factory at

Brinnlitz. I want very much to believe this, but he'll never convince me. He has no proof.

I watch him walk by the fences, talking to the gate musicians, the ditch diggers, the returning labor details, trying to discover who is on earth still. His method terrifies me because I know he will give me the happy excuse, hammered from some misshapen concern that a fairy tale of their survival is somehow good for me. My father lies with intense love.

There is no giving up on finding Mama and Hanka. Haim wanders from bunk to bunk in our barracks, nudging, cajoling and finally mentioning their names, muttering possible theories with no truth to them at all. I sit by the stove with my cousin, whose puny bare knees are mottled red from the dying cinders. The boy is utterly happy to be warm and is always interested in the peculiar doings of adults.

"Why are the men whispering, Romek? Are we going on a march?"

"No, it's just grown-up stuff. Watch you don't burn your shoes."

He kicks at the coals, one bootlace already smoking and whips around as someone sharply exclaims Malia Ferber...from Waska Street? It doesn't take much to set Wilús off.

"Is Aunt Malia coming for us? Will she bring us things to eat?"

Now I have the fiction. It's so easy. "Mama and Hanka have gone home," I lie. "They're getting the apartment ready for our return."

"Why didn't they take us with them?"

"The bedroom needs repainting, the one you'll share with me."

"I get my own bed, right?" pesters Wilús.

"Yes. And you can have one of our chickens as a pet."

"Can I eat him?"

"No, you can't eat *her*, but you can have her eggs for breakfast."

The boy's face fattens from delight. He giggles and I feel I've struck gold in the ghastly chortle that shows his graying teeth. The skin of his bony cheeks is dried out and shedding. My tiny spectral-looking cousin instills in me a hundred terrors. What if he can no longer hide here all day in the barracks, what happens if he becomes sick or someone hurts him? What if "Uncle Pepi" comes for him? What if someone pushes me to do very bad things so that he can sit here by the stove at night, what if?

In the winter days of 1944, allied aircraft swooped in waves above the Auschwitz-Birkenau complex, en route to military targets in Eastern Poland and the edge of Russia. Sirens screamed out on a sullen afternoon. Birkenau's loudspeakers ordered every prisoner to line up along the rail line. Thousands of men and women, who must have seemed like ants to the astonished pilots, scurried frantically to get into position. The guards observed us from their foxholes and their cement bunkers (including the former gas chamber) as we were herded along. We remained in silent rows for hours on end; the camp's administrators know the dense mass of humanity warded off any aerial attack. Lulled by the drone beneath the clouds, none of us dared to look up (such glances were thought highly treasonable).

The sky above the camp became crowded with box formations of American B-17 planes leading an escort of P-51 fighters flying low, their empty payload doors still open. A work detail returning to Birkenau was ordered off the road and into the woods. No shots would be fired. The flash from the tree line is too risky. The platoon captain offered a whispered joke, *Fleisch-Anzüge* (meat suits), and commanded a dozen prisoners to form a shield in front of his soldiers. The maples, snow-bent and desolate, will not protect them. The Jewish defense rise without reluctance, silently relishing a small triumph; the drift of burning oil from a direct hit on the Buna-Monowitz factory is manna to their noses. A bunkmate of my Papa's, Solly Leutkiewicz, was among them. He sent his prayers to the smoke-stained clouds: we are here, G-d of Abraham, rain down your righteous fire and end this place forever. Bring us our second exodus.

As December slowly eroded away towards the New Year, the camp became greatly disordered. Huge bonfires of files and paperwork were set alight in old oil drums on the Auschwitz side. In Birkenau, wheelbarrows packed with the devil's history came hurtling along the gravel paths by the railroad tracks, followed by the incinerating detail carrying cans of kerosene. No one dared admit to reading or speaking German. Neither must one have squirreled away in memory, or otherwise, the deeds of hell in these latter days. I heard a bullet echo from behind the barracks—another fool of a linguist gone to heaven, with camp records hidden in his pants. We watched as the military trucks filled up with German units going home to what are surely their decimated cities. No winds of victory will blow after them.

Refuse is scattered throughout the compound, stinking hills of it stacked up high everywhere. Latrines overflow because the septic system is clogged with human ashes. The unburnt dead are careless where they drop; new snow outlines their one-time bones. Unless there's an order for their removal, the winter will keep them. Earthen tanks, full of water reserved for fire emergencies, are totally frozen.

I'm hurrying one morning between the Canada warehouse and Papa's barracks with some socks I've filched for him. Intent on getting out of a persecuting wind, I have the sudden sensation of a girl's smile floating up to me from the incendiary sump by the former gypsy barracks. *She* is here, adrift on her back, her mouth open as if calling to me merrily, delicate white hands upturned, captured under the frozen skin of the water duct. I walk over to where the girl rests in the dirty flume to stare down at her because so few of the dead held on to beauty in their end days. She hangs there gracefully. Hello, I whisper, have you been lying there long? I rap my knuckles on the thick ice, causing the long tendrils of her rags to sway. That she might rise up suddenly is terrifying. I back off and continue on my trader's way.

I returned the next day to see my ice princess, but the sump had been drained of water and her too.

❂

A person who has never known constant hunger can never understand how the lack of food, and the getting of it, spurs the imagination. Finding something to eat daily surpasses all my other wants. I fantasize about every luscious edible under the sun and drink melted snow as hot water to ward off my nagging stomach. Our meager rations provoke a dull kind of despair. By the afternoon, it is hard to summon up energy for most tasks required of us. Hunger also sharpens my sense of smell. I can easily tell when some of the men have found onions or turnips to eat; their bodies give off specific aromas.

Wilús and I must have more rations and I'm too under-employed to live. I need another job—something more to our advantage than the random snow clearing, running errands for the men, or raiding the kitchen dump for tealeaves to make ersatz smokes. The trash piles are a moldering pantry of decaying food, wormy potatoes, and chicken bones with rare flesh on them. I find fruit there I don't recognize as an apple because it's encased in a thick green coating and partially frozen. I carefully peel back the fungus and bite. The cold shocks my teeth, but the juice is sugary and I eat the brown mushy pulp with gusto. There on the food dump, it comes to me that a temporary career in the grocery business would be a good thing for my cousin and me.

Czeslaw retrieves a heavy cookbook from the materials assigned for burning and tears out the pages that we might use them as toilet paper. He hands me Part 2, which details recipes for special occasions. The colored illustrations offer up images of elaborate wedding cakes, cream-filled tortes, fruit pies, hand-made chocolates and marzipan candies. I read the section to Wilús at night who can usually be distracted by a good story. I tell him that a great table of these culinary marvels will be waiting for us at home once we're free. "We'd better be good and ready, Wilús, to know what to choose." He points in delight at the drawings, exclaiming he'll have six of everything on the page.

I speak to our *Blockelteste*, Pan Stasiek, whose tolerance for kids has a thin margin. "Sir, please sir, I'd like more work as well as the snow clearing."

He grins at me with contempt but he's curious. "What do you have in mind?"

"Well, Sir, taking the food trash away to the landfill on the hand carts. You could come with us and take the first pick of everything we find, this way you could move through the camp more easily since you'd have to supervise us."

The Camp at the End of the World

He laughs at me in an ugly snide way, showing small shark-like teeth behind a thin seam of his lips. "Bags of bones, hauling rot? Seems fitting, you won't last a week."

But we do last, and some of us even flourish. Love, or something like it helps us, in the form of Irena Szabo. Very few women and girls hold their looks together under the rigors of the camp, but Irena Szabo has her own privileges. A husky, brood-hipped Hungarian beauty whose dense brown curls no razor ever touched, Irena is an opinionated Catholic *Yente*, who serves as the kitchen boss in the women's compound. She has the high-risk habit of not lowering her eyes before any German military but strides about the place with entitlement in every step. She has kept most of her Venus shape beneath her striped uniform because of her easy access to rations.

Pan Stasiek has an insane desire for the woman and, beyond all reason, she seems to favor our Slovakian Kapo. He is uglier than a robber's dog; a plain-faced, squat man with dark bitter eyes, and a jutting lower lip that is always wet, his lower teeth having been loosened in a barracks fight. However, the boy-drawn wagons give Stasiek temporary sainthood before his lover. We stand humbly outside the kitchen door, hanging on to the cart shafts while he pleads for us. "I'm helping these poor children, Irena; look how thin they are," he says. "For pity's sake, sweetheart, maybe a little bread?"

Irena drags our Kapo away after ordering us to load up the food trash while she and Stasiek are busy molesting each other in the root pantry. We could hear the potatoes bounce and thud against the door as the disordered piles fell about the randy pair. Meanwhile, my team also raids the bread supply as well as the garbage food, but not too much; propping up the stacked loafs on their steel shelves in such a way where they appear orderly and undisturbed. The same goes for the bins of turnips and withering carrots. If it is edible, it is ours, at least in careful measure.

Once I have Wilús fed, I spend my baked currency on other needs and become a trader within a wide bartering network. Inmates will sell anything for sustenance. If their pockets are empty, they will plead to sew my clothes or repair my threadbare boots. A tubercular schoolteacher named Ascher Pais offered to teach Wilús and me grammar and math every other day for half a loaf per lesson. Papa thoroughly approved of this idea, but the man died in his bunk before we could begin our tuition.

People pay me in sugar cubes, cans of condensed milk, odd socks, blankets cut in half, playing cards, real cigarettes, salt, extra soup rations, whole cabbages and, on rare occasions, sausages that were thrown over some deserted section of the Birkenau fence. Dutch and French prisoners often have access to chocolate and medicines. I have to be careful because some inmates drive hard bargains, but if the deal is struck in our barracks, I might push little Wilús forward to soften them up with his winning smile.

Another ploy is betting for food—I play card games such as "66" and "Red King" with the slick confidence of a casino hustler overlaid by cute-boy innocence. Low wins equal one slice of bread; a full house might get you half a loaf or more. Czeslaw becomes my cashier and ensures that no one bullies or cheats me. He stands by with a bread knife crudely fashioned from a sharpened door hasp to distribute winnings. Often my ultimate prize is just getting someone to volunteer to stay in the barracks and protect Wilús during the day.

One night, I score several newly baked loaves from Irena's oven and decide to take two of them to my father while they were still warm. I pad along the wooden aisle of our quarters with my boots in one hand and the loaves stuffed into my shirt. It is close to curfew, but I'm confident I can make the round trip to Papa's barracks if I'm speedy.

The searchlight sweeps across the alleys. I wait until the beam passes, then I'm through the window and outside. I reach back and drag an old blanket after me to wipe out my footprints. It's a dry, cold night and I need not to crunch on the snow cover. I hobble along on the blanket, creating a messy track that looks like a giant slug has passed by. When the searchlight beam scans again, I'm a stationary dark lump covered by dirty wool in the shadows.

In this stop-and-shuffle manner, I reach Papa's barracks and tap on the window. I have a view of a scrawny, half-naked man seated alone on a bottom bunk, sewing buttons onto his filthy striped jacket. (The penalty of even one missing would be the bullet.) I catch sight of my father, sitting across from him, his gaze fixed on nothing. I tap again on the window. He looks up as if he's been stung but signals to me that he'll come outside. We meet in the darkness of the eaves of the barracks.

"Good G-d! Son, what are you doing here?"

"Hello, Papa, I can only stay a few minutes. I've brought you something to eat."

I hand him the loaves of bread, feeling taller in my boots because I can *feed him*. I wait patiently for his delight, words of praise for his blanket-dragging bandit.

My father stares numbly at the crisp golden loaves, then at me, his face stricken as if I had offered him a stone.

"What's wrong, Papa, are you ill?"

"Just a little, Roman, nothing much to worry about. Tomorrow we should see if Mama and Hanka are working in the laundry on the Auschwitz side."

"But, Papa, we already asked there."

His gaze wanders beyond me into the darkness.

"Yes, Roman, we did...ask already."

"The bread is fresh, Papa. You should eat it."

"Thank you. I can't, child. It's Shabbas. I'm fasting...for your mother and sister."

The Camp at the End of the World

"Please. They would want you to eat."

"They would want that we should find them. I'll give the loaves to Pan Greenberg and his brother. Come on, I'll walk you back. We should hurry, before the patrols start their rounds."

"No! Papa, I'll find my way by myself."

"Romek, that's foolish, there's only a few minutes to curfew."

"No! I don't want you to come with me!"

All my generosity has drained away and I'm angry. But I really don't want to leave. I want to stay with him, to repeat cleverly what men have been saying, that the war is fading, any day now it will stop, a giant exhausted wheel chocked by its own long and wasteful span. We *will* go home, Papa, you, Wilús and me. But I say nothing, waiting for him to soothe the scalding hurt rising in my chest. I could demand to stay in his barracks all night but it would mess up the morning head count and could cause dangerous ructions.

My father appears weak and distracted, in an odd state of surrender.

"Go on back, Roman. Get some sleep."

He turns away from me quickly, as he might to a stranger and I can raise no voice to him for pleading. When he reenters his barracks, I watch him stride down the walkway, nothing more than a fading dark figure in the window's crackled frost. Turn around, please, please, I hope. My eyes prick and burn. I see the watch beam in the sky coming this way. I shroud my head with the sodden blanket and can't move for several minutes.

I stumble along the open road by the railroad tracks, no longer caring if a searchlight might find me, my breath blowing ahead in smoky puffs. Along the sharp night air, I hear the muffled conversation of the guards in the watchtower. Either I am truly invisible or they simply pay me no mind. I flip the blanket over the open sill of my barracks window with the notion that I can climb in silently.

I'm part way through the window, eyes down on the floorboards when a sharp claw grabs at my hair and wrenches hard at my scalp. The surprising pain is so excruciating but I can't yell because a foul-smelling hand is clamped over my mouth. Pan Stasiek hauls me off the floor and effortlessly carries me down the aisle to his room. "One sound and I'll hand you over to the guards! You deceitful little shit! Have you any idea what they'd do to me if they discovered you out there?"

I have no air to answer him. It leaves me when he slams me against the wall by the side of his bed. He swings me to my feet by my jacket collar, his sallow face up close to mine. I can smell schnapps and onions on his breath and the cheap brilliantine in his hair.

"This time, I'm not going to kill you," he warns.

I can't utter any gratitude for this small mercy because terror is making me witless. The man locks his door. He pulls off my jacket and orders me to raise my shirt and drop my pants. It's not so much what's coming that sickens me but that I have to be partially naked before him. He hauls a thick leather belt out of his trouser loops, pushes me down against the bed, his knee in my bare back. I hear the wide brass buckle clunk hard against the wall.

"Arrogant little bastard! I won't have you running around just as you please!"

The first blow is a sharp flame up my spine. The second drives the breath out of me. I stuff my jacket sleeve into my mouth, so I can bite down hard and not scream. I will not cry for him. After the fourth or fifth lash, it seems I no longer have a body. I am merely a passive surface where I can hear the belt bite into numbed skin, from a far seam of distance, a dark funnel of nothing into which I sink farther with every strike.

✼

I'm riding up near the ceiling of the barracks, face down on a procession of many outstretched hands. Czeslaw is whispering to be careful, a little higher now. Go slow, over to the right. Behind him, Wilús is staring up at me, walking hand in hand with Melchior.

Haim is on our bunk with his arms outstretched and I'm hoisted and slid onto clean straw. The old man forces a spoonful of warm tea into my mouth, "Lie still, Ferber boy, don't turn over, whatever you do."

The raw red plain that is my back is slathered with fresh snow, an icy balm that slows down the burning. I am to be represented by the dead at roll call and am left in the bunk to be nursed by Wilús, who claims the men have told him that wolves tried to eat me in the night but were driven off.

"Romek, they just bit you a little, but they've gone now," he says sweetly. "Shall I read you a story from the cooking book?"

He waves the cuisine pages at me and I ask, "Just show me the pictures instead Wilús." In truth, he has learned to spin some great, albeit meandering tales from the recipes where he can ramble on endlessly.

Outside, in the drenching rain, Solly Leutkiewicz and two other inmates, who clean out the deceased from the infirmary, stagger-walked a *Lange Männ* (Long Man) into our line and ram my cap on his head. The counting clerks, balancing clipboards and large black umbrellas, hurry down the ranks, cursing the weather and barking out numbers with less than their usual zeal.

I hear that Pan Stasiek is avoiding our barracks with the excuse that the bread mixer in Irena's kitchen is in need of repair. My wounds seep, gluing my shirt painfully into their bloody gorges. Haim cuts the fabric away and sponges my back with stolen antiseptic as carefully as any mother, while Melchior is sent on a mission with loaf currency to trade for bandages and clean clothes from the women in Canada. He returns with three shirts, wearing one concealed beneath the next to arouse no suspicions. "They are washed and flea-free," he says, "Put one on, Romek, it'll make you feel better."

I decide to never ever tell my father about Stasiek's beating, partially out of anger, but also because I know that Papa (a great believer in right conduct, no matter what) would probably challenge the man in the crisp manner of a schoolteacher reprimanding a lout, an act that would endanger us both. My abuser now behaves toward me as if his offense has never happened, but the other men turn away from him whenever he strides down the walkway.

The flesh on my behind and lower back is slow to heal. I sleep on my stomach and Wilús has to tie my bootlaces because to bend over is agony. In the rare moments when I see my father, I walk like one whose joints have seized up and have to clench my fists against the sensitive nagging of healing skin.

It is a useful distraction from the creeping distance widening between Papa and me; a trench that I fear will soon become impossible to bridge. He seems not to inhabit himself and makes small talk robotically, I sense pieces of him are disappearing before my eyes. Wherever my mother and sister are, the best of him travels with them. When his memory can no longer hold them afresh, he lapses into a stone-faced silence where neither I nor his barrack friends can reach him.

The garrulous Solly Leutkiewicz follows me out of Papa's barracks one early evening, puts a friendly hand on my shoulder and assures me that my father's emotional ruin is just temporary, that sadness of such magnitude over his missing relatives is to be expected in these times.

"But don't you worry, Romek, I'll watch out for him. In just a week or so, the Russians will ride through those gates. Once your good parent gets a taste of freedom, he'll be a new man. I'd bet my last zloty, if I had one, that the two of you will surely find the rest of your family. You do believe that, don't you, son?"

21

A Bitter Liberation

WHAT I REMEMBER ABOUT TIME: from the Ghetto to Plaszow, from Gross Rosen to Brinnlitz to Birkenau, all of these places misshaped time for me, each in its own way, and not because I was just a boy in that era with a child's impatience. I lived by the mental clocks of the imprisoned where one can never say, "Next week" or "Next month…I will go to such a place, or do so and so, and so on."

In the Krakow Ghetto, there was waiting time, the golden moment to be outdoors for an hour or so. In the Plaszow camp, time was punctuated by hiding, shrill minutes of terror, and hard spikes of anxiety. Gross Rosen was a short transit of concentrated terror, time there did not move at all. Schindler's Brinnlitz factory was a joyous calming time. It held the promise of freedom but one that broke apart before my eyes. Now in early 1945, the years of organized barbarity are also collapsing and I dare not consider what time will bring tomorrow.

Haim Rosenheim has old-bones wisdom. He whispers to us kids with the intensity of prophesying, "There is a motion in the heavens, my young friends, lights and thunder. G-d is on the move! We must be ready for anything."

He's not far wrong. Red sprays of cannon fire dart across the sky from the northeast. The men say that Russian tanks have reached Zamosc and have liberated the town. On the Auschwitz side of the complex, it's rumored that any livestock, diseased prisoners and many of the platoon dogs have been shot. Restlessness pervades the entire camp; a sense of something momentous is brewing that comes replete with new dangers.

Every day, German units are ferried away in trucks, with a winding trail of camp inmates listlessly marching after them. Our rations have been curtailed, and when the boys and I go out with the carts on the scavenging detail, our haul is mainly sodden potato peels and bug-ridden flour. We make foul pancakes from these weary ingredients and a small amount of precious lard, all fried on a tin plate on the barracks stove. "Salt them enough," I tell my cousin, "and pretend you're eating my Mama's latkes."

One morning in mid-January, there is a great rousing in our section of the camp, the speaker system is blaring orders in Polish and German. Several thousand prisoners are ordered to assemble immediately along the embankments of the railhead. The soldiers are counting men into lines of ten and us kids into separate clusters. Czeslaw says they're grouping people by age and physical strength, the sickly ones and the young at the back of the pack, easier to pick off.

A Bitter Liberation

Convoy clerks scurry towards our group, their eyes already scanning us and shouting. "*Sechzehnjährige Jungen hier!!* (Boys of sixteen line up here!) *Alle fünfzehnjährigen Jungen hier!*" (All boys of fifteen over here!) "*Jetzt! Bewegen Sie sich!*" (Now! Get Moving!)

As cattle pouring through a field gate in many directions, my group whirls back and forth in confusion and fear; such a great number of us have lied about our ages to join the labor crews and live, causing a visible deficit among the truly younger boys. The soldiers and clerks come roving through the liars, yelling and slapping heads and bullying the more youthful-looking into some loose terrorized arrangement.

Above these ructions, I sight my father across the rail tracks, assembling with his barracks' contingent. He's waving discreetly for me to come to him. I wait until a dense block of prisoners march by and dash through the end of their line to where he stands.

Papa hugs me and announces, "We're leaving, Romek. Go get Wilús. Both of you will walk with me and Solly."

Up ahead, the guards are blowing whistles and marching away the men from the barracks next to his, a huge swathe of ragged stick figures against the dirty snow, shouting and pushing through the open span of the gatehouse. It is watching this frenzied disorder of disappearing prisoners that awakens in me a sudden and startling refusal, as if someone is at my side whispering urgently in my ear...*if you want to live, don't go with them. Don't go!*

My father is staring down at me, waiting for my obedient reply. I haven't much time to explain to him, "Papa, please don't make me go, you stay with us instead, OK?" because the guards are yelling hysterically, pushing and beating the crowd forward, the lines are breaking up, disordered and meandering.

"Roman," starts my father urgently and makes a grab at my shoulder, but I do the unthinkable. I pull away from him! I see Wilús standing across the track, holding hands with Czeslaw, a small hesitant dot in all the mayhem, waiting for me. The ugly foreboding speaks to me again. *Turn away! Do not go!*

"I can't go with you, Papa. This marching is not for me," I say to him, as gently as I can. My words are a whip in his face, his mouth drops open. His hand is still extended toward me and I see it tremble badly.

"Roman, everything will be fine," he pleads, "we're going to Germany, to work. You'll learn a trade, this time it's different, I promise you. They need us to rebuild the country. Now go get Wilús, and hurry, please!"

Gunshots retort from somewhere out on the road. There is more yelling and orders as a thousand other men join my father's group, an escort of several soldiers alongside them. His companions are cursing and pushing at him viciously; they have to move forward before trouble breaks out. Their line surges forward.

"I can't go with you!" I call to him. "I'm running away!" Then, Papa and I are separated by an avalanche of marchers.

The crowd swallows him totally. He is gone!

I hear is his loud shout, a request that will echo all my life. "Romek, follow this line, I'll find you, no matter what happens, I will find you!"

I have to get to Wilús fast because I see him standing utterly alone now, blubbering pathetically and grabbing at passing adults. Some meters to the right of him, all the Rosenheims are being marched away. Melchior is supporting his grandfather, who looks as white as death. Czeslaw staggers after them, his face bruised and bloody. He waves to me but points to my cousin. I'm across the tracks in an instant and scooping up Wilús in my arms.

He weeps accusingly, "You left me, Romek! Everybody left me!"

I assure him that he's safe and that it's just the two of us now. I tell my cousin to make no noise, keep his head down, and stealthily edge us backwards into the barrack alleys. Wilús, whose powers of rebound always amaze me, forgets his tears. He grips my neck and smiles, entering into the game. For a hungry kid, it feels to me like I'm carrying an anvil.

Suddenly, we are alone, out of sight of the chaos and the marchers. "Where are we going, Romek," he whispers as I set him down in the snow.

"To find something nice to eat, OK?"

I need to get us inside, any place at all. Out here, we could easily be discovered and driven back into the roundup. We're several streets away from our old barracks, and other than Birkenau's main gate, I have no idea how to get us beyond the wire.

"Look, Romek, it's snowing," says Wilús, utterly delighted to catch the increasing snowflakes in his mouth.

"That's just great," I say, "just great!"

I can see a blizzard swirling in from the distant highway and the long line of bleak marchers disappearing beneath its veil. Ahead, there's a line of well-kept barracks, with paved walkways and curtains on the windows, unit designations painted on signposts, the living quarters of the German platoons. The barracks are the most immediate shelter to hand against the coming snowstorm but I'm afraid to move for fear the nearest one might be occupied by soldiers. There are shouts and whoops from within the nearest one.

"It's other kids," chortles Wilús, "not big people."

A door bangs open and a boy of about thirteen appears. He's wearing a captain's leather overcoat that drags along in the muddy slush and holding a huge can of corned beef in his hand. He catches me devouring the item with my gaze, he grins and gestures for us to come inside. "Hi, my name is Liev Speiser. There are no military here," he calls out with a restored glee. "It's safe. They've all gone, dragging their keisters back to Germany."

The barracks within is one enormous pantry, the stores of the German commissary. A quartermaster's desk and a leather armchair are angled across the entrance and it's seductively warmed by a wood stove blazing away. Four other boys and a handsome girl with a stitched wound across her forehead are standing around it, eating from cans of food with their fingers. The girl encourages us to take whatever food we want and makes much of my cousin. She pours syrupy peaches into a tin cup for him and invites him to come and sit next to her to dine. "Hey, little angel," she says, "You look like you need some fattening up."

Wilús, such a showman, climbs up against her, easily drinking in this affection. The other boys are all asking me at once, "How come you weren't taken, who's the little guy, your brother? Is your Dad on the march or up the chimney?"

I'm more interested in eating than answering the barrage of questions, but I tell them that we've come from the prisoner barracks and how we have no family with us.

The Commissary houses avenues of pinewood shelves that stretched the entire length of the building, each rack marked for its category, *Dosenfrüchte, Fleisch, Tee, Kaffee*, (Canned fruits, Meat, Tea, Coffee). A row of muscular hams suspended from the ceiling sway in greasy unison as someone slams the door shut against the weather.

The girl's name is Beata and she tells me that just next door was the platoon's sleeping quarters, now empty of military. I get a quick stab of fear —the "what if" kind, what if the soldiers return to find a lice farm of a Jewish kid slurping juice from a liter of their canned blueberries? Besides, I consider (foolishly) that maybe Papa had escaped from the prisoner line and could be looking for us.

Beata hands me an empty sack that holds the fragrance of real coffee beans. "Here, pack as much as you like. Go on," she urges, "don't worry about the soldiers, they'll be the hunted ones now."

I start down the racks, eyeing what is practical to take, nothing in glass jars except some jam to eat with rye biscuits. My good little bandit, Wilús, helps me, picking sugar and condensed milk from the shelves he can reach. He discovers powdered chocolate in foil packets, tears them open and pours the contents down his gullet, glazing his chin a light bronze. I select a few loaves of bread and we stuff some of the dried fruit cartons in our pockets after I fill the sack.

We waited until the barracks lane is deserted to leave the food store. A few voices and the distant growl of truck engines still echoed from the railhead.

"Look what that nice girl gave me, Romek," says Wilús, dragging a huge ham in a mesh cloth across the floorboards.

Liev says, "Enjoy. You can be kosher again after this mess is over."

Beata kisses us both and hands us a couple of blankets, winding one around Wilús and tying him into it. We make our goodbyes and take our leave because the rising plan I have to return to our former Krakow apartment now seizes me like a fever.

※

Once outside, Wilús hauls the ham joyously behind him like a pet dog. It becomes flecked with motor oil, dirty snow and wood splinters from him bouncing it around as we make our way down the narrow alleys. No matter. I already have it carved up in my mind as prime barter. I'm eager to get us beyond Birkenau's fence before full daylight. A metallic gray sky and glowering clouds heavy with moisture are coming in fast from the east. The fallen snow is dense and resisted our steps, but we scurry through the barracks lanes as best we can—to the fence bordering the road. Beata had told us that the electrical barrier no longer worked and that the wire is torn open at various points.

We churn through the whitened avenues, beyond the main gate and the SS residences, and alongside the fence to find an opening. The food sack is weighty and Wilús and I drag it together. My foot kicks at something, and I stumbled over a long muzzle, sharp black ears upright, from under the snow's crust; a guard dog, his teeth bared in the rigors of his last bark before being shot. I don't want my cousin to see it, and thankfully he is already at the fence.

"How do we get out, Romek?" Wilús whines and rattles the wire, his gloves sticking to the ice particles. We're parallel to the railway line that must lead back to the city but which way? The wind starts pestering us as the day lengthens. A burnt and blackened *Kuebelwagen* (jeep) lies wheels up on the outer bank, having fractured its way clean through the barbed wire. I throw the food sack into the road, help Wilús to leap the frozen security ditch through this gap and we're out! We are free!

The main highway is a void stretching into a forest with a few scrubby bushes before us. My cousin yelps in delight, "We're going home!"

His announcement cues the arriving blizzard. The snow comes pelting down and, within a few minutes, we are adrift in a white haze with no visible boundaries anywhere! I bend and feel for the rail line; we keep to the right of it. The swirling white blast cakes the front of our coats, making the wool a hard ice shell. The far distance disappears and the weather beating down on us becomes yet another enemy to flog us. Wilús, who by now, has lost the blanket that Beata had given him, grabs on to my waist and starts to sob how cold he is, his cries are a screeching misery that competes with the bitch of a wind. He begs me to please, please take him inside, anywhere!

A Bitter Liberation

I'm scared, thinking how it's a bitter stupidity to escape the camp, only to freeze to death in this persecuting storm. In these moments, I feel tortured by far more than the weather. *What will happen to my seven-year-old cousin if I falter, if I can't live anymore?* I'm cleaved open from missing my father; I wish he were here, spurring us on. I'm weeping too, I can't reconcile the fact that I refused to go with Papa, that I had abandoned him. I imagine now that finding my mother will be a two-edged blade—she will certainly ask why I disobeyed my father.

How could I be so stupid as to stray with a small child into a thousand perils? The boy is screaming above the wind, "Let's go back, please, Romek!"

I lie to Wilús beautifully and tell him that we're not that far from a marvelous shelter made just for us. "Where? Where is it?" he shrieks. "I'm cold, I want my Mama! Please, Romek, I can't walk anymore."

"Dry your eyes. I promise we'll get there soon, then I'll cook up some hot chocolate for you."

I drag him and the food sack through the hounding blizzard and pray for even a stand of trees where I could stretch a blanket into a makeshift tent. Shadowy phantoms up ahead give way to plain telegraph poles and I count our steps between each one. My head aches, my clothes are wet to my skin. Then a different shape looms out of the stinging flakes. I'm afraid to trust my eyes, but there it was, a roof beam of a darker white, a chimney pinnacle, the double doors of a...blessed shelter, the electrical station. G-d, let the doors not be locked!

"Wilús!" I shout. "We're here!"

I run for the half-buried entrance and depress the latch hard; the doors scrape inward a little. I can see a dry interior. I claw back the snow just enough so we can fit the food sack and the two of us in through the opening. The doors give reluctantly and we enter. Wilús sobs and cheers at the same time as I brush the snow off him.

We are inside a sturdy brick structure with a defunct furnace, rows of winding pipes, and a small turbine engine enclosed in a steel cage. Along the front wall divided laterally by a wood panel one meter high is a rudimentary living area for the maintenance engineer, a small bed with thick quilts, a cast-iron stove, a desk and two chairs. In a cupboard, I find a supply of blankets, a few plates and cups, a large pot and a kettle. However, our most glorious discovery is a deep chute in the back of the place with an abundance of coal. I have matches sealed in a tobacco tin in my sack and soon have the stove blazing away. I put Wilús naked in the bed and hang up our wet clothes on the chairs to dry.

"Where are we?" he asks.

"Not far from the city," I fake.

"Will the soldiers come for us?" His cherubic face is raw from windburn.

"No, Wilús, there are no soldiers here."

"Make the hot chocolate, Romek. You promised."

I boil the mixture with sugar in the kettle and the kid drinks it down lustily. I lay out a bedroll with the blankets by the stove. Get some sleep, I tell him, but he's already snoring, embracing his ham as a teddy bear.

The granite walls of the station are thick enough to subdue the wind's roar. The coal hisses in the stove, its heat is tremendous, steaming up the windows. I lie down but can find no comfortable position; my knuckles are dried and cracked open from the cold. The light in the place reminds me of the sedate hues of a hospital, the windows skirled with ice on the outside, refract the day in muted tones. We could be anywhere in the world. I lie awake for a time, vigilant and plotting as to how we'll get out of here if we're surprised by any German military. I scratch a diagram with a spent match on the old reports lying on the desk. The soldiers might break open the front door, but the desk placed against it would give us a good ten minutes. Snatch up what we can and jump down into the coal chute. It led down to a deep cellar on the building's south side, where more coal is strewn along a conveyor belt that opens onto a ramp when the truck delivers the fuel. We could just about do it—and get away into the woods if the place wasn't surrounded.

The plan gives me relief, but not from the nagging desolation of our scattering. My mother and Hanka—I can hardly conjure their faces anymore. It is as if I see them through deep brown waters, me drowning beneath the weedy tumult and above their anxious gazes are searching but not finding me. My recall of Papa eludes me, save for the vision of a long line of ashen-faced marchers dragging themselves through some alien and scabrous ravine. He turns and looks back, waving for me to catch up. I come awake. Outside the wind has dropped and the night has already sealed us in. In the encompassing silence, I secretly ask my father if there can be a reckoning. What if Wilús and I get home to live along the distance of old men, how will that be? What about my father and I, when next we meet, how will we be?

❦

We camp out in the turbine house for two days, rested and ate well. On the third morning, the blizzard ceases. Wilús guffaws when I finally wedge open the doors to be faced down with a huge wall of snow taller than I was. Between the frozen barrier and the door lintel is barely a thin strip of brilliant, azure sky.

"How do we get out?" asks my cousin.

"We dig," I say.

There is a shovel by the coal chute with which we excavate a load of snow, heat it up in the pot and the kettle, and then pour the hot water on the ever-widening breach at the entrance. It is hard going as I work the shovel and

Wilús scrapes away at the frosty mass using a frying pan. It takes us two hours to stack up the snow and form a ramp beyond the doors.

It was close to noon when we leave to begin walking again. At first, Wilús kicks up a fuss, saying he likes it here. It's warm and safe. He petulantly declares he's staying put.

"You'll be all alone," I warn him.

"I don't care!"

"You'll freeze to death. You don't know how to light the stove."

"Yes, I do. I watched you do it."

"You'll burn the place down."

"Then I'll be warm."

"Not for long. Come on, get moving!"

"No! I want to stay in the bed. Leave me some food and go away!"

My first instincts are to snatch the rotten kid by the collar out into the blinding sunlight, but his eyes are breeding defiance. I sit down on the food sack, bury my face in my ragged gloves and pretend to sob how we have to get to Krakow to meet Papa, how my mother's hens need feeding, and if the soldiers return they'll shoot us both for stealing their coal. Wilús, with his feelings sliding about like loose beans in a jar, offers his wondrous response. He comes over and throws his arms around me, soothing me and saying, "Don't cry, Romek, please don't cry. I'll take you home. Come on, I'll show you the way. Let's go."

We clambered up and over our boy-made slope, and out into a blanched expanse of wind-tamped snow and raw blue sky. The rail line is totally submerged and the telegraph poles buried up to their haunches. Above us, metal cables are crusted with daggers of ice that cracked and dropped at dangerous, random intervals under the warming air. Uneven humps up ahead seem like they might be bushes, stunted trees, or even buried men. Even though the weather is benign for now, my fear of us being totally lost returns.

Wilús swings a glance to the left, then to the right, and brightly announces, "This way, Romek, come with me."

It doesn't matter if I bet to lose on the impulse of this seven-year-old; any direction is as good as another. He takes my hand and smiles sweetly. I let him tow me along, marveling that, at his age and with all that he has lost, he can summon such an easy grace to comfort my distress.

Tall white giants at some distance shed their ogre's appearance the closer we get and assume the lithe nature of spruce trees. They stood in frozen columns on either side of our route, a sure sign they're bordering the obscured highway. The snow weighed their boughs down and I tear one away as a long and sturdy rod. We jam it hard through the ice crust and it echoes the reassuring tap of concrete—the road indeed! I let Wilús do it again, as a merit for his path finding. "We're almost home, Romek," he laughs in delight. We crunch along for several more hours in the nourishing sun and the sharp, sweet air, our food sack furrowing a trail behind us.

The wind has become gentle, fluting our voices to a yelping clarity. It is pleasing where we walked, the heads of the trees a dark, shaggy green in the afternoon melt. Bolts of snow and ice cascade from their limbs, but it makes me nervous when the watery thud is heard behind us. We stop to listen frequently, fearing the slithering approach of a tank, the rumble of oncoming military vehicles.

"Wilús," I say. "If the soldiers show up, head into the trees. Leave the food and just run, OK?"

"That's no good. They'll find us, Romek."

The boy wheels about and points to our deep footprints and the trough of the food sack stretching far behind us. We may as well have mounted a neon arrow in our direction. There is also the line of betraying cans and other provisions strewn in our wake. The remains of the ham stick smartly out of the snow, as if dropped by some ancient hunter. One end of my sack is a grinning hole. I tie it off and we run to go get the dropped stuff. (This included my essentials: a can-opener, my tin of dry matches and a small fruit knife I had tied in a rag.)

Over our heads... a faint thunder, high in the air. "Look! Look, Romek, stars in the daytime!" squeals Wilús.

I follow his pointing finger to where a swathe of spangled orange lights cleaves the sky to the north of us. A plume of brown smoke appears in the far distance followed by a blazoned surge, magnificently red against the blue that punctuated the entire horizon in a line of fiery bursts. Cannonaded winds, more smoke and the drone of a bomber fleet above add to the din.

"Get off the road!" I shout, dropping the sack and grabbing Wilús by the sleeve.

"It's the war!" he chortles, pulling away from me. "I want to see!"

"No, no, you don't! Move!"

But he stands stock-still, staring up, his eyes mesmerized by a metallic thrashing low in the heavens. I pick him up bodily because I see swooping over the tree line the winged bulk of a low-flying aircraft coming our way! I run and dive with him in my arms. We are rolling over the edge of the snow bank, sputtering against the drift, rapidly spinning down into the mercy of the pines. The plane is so low, there's a sharp crack as it shears off branches and, from our white pit, I catch a glimpse of the pilot and his gunner. On the wings are markings I've never seen before. No bombs are spewed and the gun ports in the iron belly remain blessedly closed. The nose of the aircraft swings up to vertically meet the squadron far above, regrouping some kilometers away for another sortie.

A Bitter Liberation

The road becomes solidly quiet.

"Did they shoot our food?" asks Wilús.

I leave him back in the trees to rest and make a series of fast runs to grab the sack and some cans. From there on, we chart a course through the forest parallel to the snowy highway. It would be dark in a few hours and I was of two minds whether to cut some boughs and build us a makeshift shelter, or press on with the hope that we might find a barn or a shepherd's hut for the night.

Wilús is in good spirits, rattling on how he's now "seen the war," and it wasn't that great, "Just a lot of big bangs and noisy wings."

I'm still mulling the shelter problem when I hear the first strains of music, then distant voices. The trees are thinning out and we see brick chimneys, a cluster of buildings, and another wide fence shattered with huge holes.

"It's Krakow, we're home!" says Wilús.

"I don't think so."

"Yes, it is. There's music coming from the cafés. Listen."

Music yes, being played by three ragged fiddlers in striped uniforms, seated in the late afternoon sun by the open iron gates, above which arches the familiar sign, *"Arbeit Macht Frei"* (Work Makes You Free).

We have traveled for three days only to circle back to Auschwitz!

A man, also a prisoner by his dress, exits the guardhouse to stare at us. His uniform is surprisingly clean and impeccably starched, boots shined to reflection despite the slush he stands in. I recognize the carefully oiled crenellated hair and the purple triangle on his breast pocket. It's Milosz, the privileged prisoner, who once gave us soup when we were first inducted into the camp.

"Sir," I call to him. "Please can you help us? We're lost. Where are the soldiers?"

I ask because I expect us to be marched away to somewhere in the next instant. The three fiddlers wave to us and rack their bows into a Haydn minuet, in the triple time usually played for receiving wedding guests. Milosz grins at us amiably and I notice in fascination that his lips appear lightly rouged. Also, the purple triangle on his shirt is half torn away to reveal a pink one hidden beneath it, the insignia of men who romanced each other.

He saunters over, his arms open in welcome then all three of us are talking over each other.

"Dear boys, where are your parents?"

"We don't know. We walked from Birkenau."

"What brave little souls."

"Can you help us Sir? We have no place to live."

"Don't worry. We have a lot of accommodations."

"Where do we report?" I ask meekly.

"You don't have to, the war is finished. The Germans are no more. They're gone!"

"What day is it?"

"January 23rd. You both come with me. You look like you could use a good supper."

"Here, Sir," says Wilús politely. "We brought you a present."

He reaches into the sack and handed the man a can of yellow peas. Milosz seems startled. He ruffles my cousin's hair and looks like he might break into tears.

✻

While I can remember it, I have to take note of all the things we saw in the Auschwitz of its final days. I can only compare it to a circus in a madhouse. I was told that there were some seven thousand prisoners or more still alive and in residence. Clusters of inmates, long disabled from any independence, decision-making or freedom of movement, drifted about the place in dazed bewilderment. Many were looking for food and lost relatives. Although the Germans had burned down several of the warehouses, groups of prisoners went on daily looting rampages through the remaining stores. Some ate themselves literally to death. The place was also a sewage dump and littered with the frozen dead. The corpses of several German military swung in the wind from the gallows near Block 11 and were used for target practice by former members of the Polish and Jewish underground.

Wilús has an itchy skin condition from bad nutrition and a worrying cough. I insist that we are inseparable and Milosz arranges for us to bunk down in the infirmary. The man has taken a true maternal interest in me and my cousin and says we'll be better off with clean sheets, extra rations, and some nursing care. The clinic is the former facility for the soldiers, so the place is comfortable and well equipped. The prisoners of medical status—doctors and nurses—have been able to change their camp stripes for the white coats and the starched aprons of their professions.

Milosz is a compulsive gossip, and I suspect him of tall tales in his kind impulse to entertain us. He tells of a man who had taken a slew of new suits from the clothing storage, worn three at once to keep warm and to impress the wife he would soon return to, but he didn't have the will to leave the camp because he lacked a wheelbarrow to transport the remaining thirty-six outfits. Since male and female prisoners were now free to mingle, one woman became the sweetheart of three different widowers, two of them a father and his son. Others mocked her for her loose behavior but the quartet was very happy. "Each one has a ration of good love," said the Jezebel in question, "...and why not? I'm alive when several times I was selected for the gas."

There are more guests than patients in the infirmary and I know I can walk the camp safely and leave Wilús in the assured protection of the nurses. With his angelic looks and quirky affections, he's a boy that most females, young and old, are drawn to.

January 25th is my twelfth birthday and Milosz shows up with several chocolate bars for my cousin and me. "What else would please you, Roman, dear heart?" he asks. He brushes my hair gently with the same care as my mother would. I want my father, I tell him, that's what I would like, and I want to know where my Mama and sister are. Can you help me? I knew that he was a "fixer" and had access to every scheme that riddled the chaos that now passed for the camp's administration. I pester him to look among the German files, the endless lists, the records and names and locations of where they shipped people.

I get myself so worked up over my plea that I start to cry because it occurs to me that even if Milosz finds out any information, it's likely that my parents were dispatched to different lagers. Who would I seek out first and how? Besides, the management of the camp office had ordered many files to be destroyed or removed to Germany in the past few weeks, but it's my birthday and I am hoping that my parents, wherever they are, will kiss my memory. I have a hunger not to be forgotten.

Before Milosz can pay off the woman who can pay off the Polish clerk still working in the Auschwitz central files, my life is pitched into its next chapter, courtesy of Russia. I am playing soccer with some other boys with a real ball in the medical compound when Wilús comes streaking down the gravel path, wearing two coats over his pajamas, yelling, "Romek, the war, its back! The soldiers are here!" I grab him immediately but it's too late for us to hide.

A Voroshilov tank lumbers towards the camp's main gates. Tethered to its rear is a handsome young captain being towed along on skis, as relaxed as any winter sportsman on the peaks of Zakopane. He is followed by a huge contingent of Russian infantry, more tanks, and to my cousin's screeching delight, warriors on horseback!

The prisoners give a mighty cheer and throw open the gates. Shouts rise up in a sonorous blend of Polish, Yiddish, and other tongues all underscored by the musical rumble of Russian. The sturdy soldiers are mingling with the prisoners, hugging and shaking hands. "It's over, Comrade, you are free... free!" they chorus. Women battalions also come striding through the gates, some of them seasoned from fighting alongside their men on the front lines. I see my cousin hoisted joyously onto the shoulder of a pretty lady lieutenant and more women soldiers are kissing and hugging all the kids. "*Malchic, Malchic,* Little guy, little guy," they are calling, "All is well, we are here!"

My first reaction is one of sheer exhilaration. Wilús is whooping and calling to me from the perch of his Russian beauty, the color returning to his cheeks. The first wave of liberators is followed by supply trucks, ambulances and mobile medical units. A swarm of their nurses and doctors mingles with the internal medics, asking a host of questions in Polish regarding the health of the inmates.

More soldiers arrive by the hundreds. The Russian platoon's General is a thin bespectacled Marxist, all brisk efficiency. He enters the camp riding an excellent chestnut horse, directing many things to be done at once. There are cameras and news reporters shooting photographs and filming. One cameraman wants to film prisoners pouring joyously through the open gates and when we don't look delighted enough at this rare moment, he has us repeat the same actions several times until he too is overcome with happiness.

It is all tumultuous and overwhelming. We are truly free. While it is hard to take it all in, the effect is electrifying. I grab Wilús and say, "Get your stuff, we're going home, to Waska Street!"

"For real this time? Do you know the way?" asks my cousin.

I give him the tribute of that. "You said *you* did."

"I do," he declares brightly. "Home is over there," pointing a grubby finger towards the direction of Slovakia. I don't know the way either to our former city, which was at least a day's march on foot. After our previous hellish trek through the snow, it is time to find some grown-up help. We meet up with a Polish inmate named Vladek, an older man wearing the red triangle of political prisoners, a communist with a bicycle. He is going back to Krakow too and agrees to let us travel with him.

On the morning of January 28th, Vladek, Wilús and I walk out of Auschwitz on the final journey I had dreamed about for the past four years. Our new friend ropes our freshly refilled food sack across the handlebars of his bicycle and we set out along a highway thronged with former prisoners, Polish and Russian military, and displaced persons of all types, heading to the city and other points. The weather is still bad but our spirits were unstoppable. I feel buoyant and full of hope. Wilús is looking healthy and his slight frame has actually filled out a little.

At certain villages we journey through, residents still with an intact roof over their heads came to their gates and hedges to stare at us, some with guilt, some with disdain, some exhibiting the same curiosity as if a circus is passing by. Roosters crow, chickens peck in their snowy yards and their goats bray at us. It is an unreal feeling to see the plain trappings of life still holding fast.

The Russian soldiers we meet along the road are princes of boisterous concern and generosity, billeted in barns and local homes, their units well supplied with provisions. They would call to us, especially to Vladek, (who they assumed was our father). "Such beautiful children you have! Come, Comrade, eat with us, sit down and celebrate the new peace."

They stroke our hair and stare at Wilús and me in wonderment, taking off our striped prisoner's hats, throwing them into the fire, and replacing them with their army caps. Such fine brave boys, they would joyously pronounce and toast us, wishing us long lives as men and many kids of our own. Vladek told me they are so enamored of children because Russia had lost many millions of all ages in their struggle against the Germans.

We sit among them, listening to their laughter and deep-bass songs around the fire. Their celebration of us kids is evidence to me that it is a new world and we are free to walk in it. The spires of my city are coming closer and there arose in me such a soaring happiness tainted with the awful anxiety that the much-loved faces I hope to see will be waiting for us at the Waska Street apartment...or not.

Wilús, who in his undefeatable optimism, frequently believes that his parents are in New York, south of Heaven, says that we might find some nice grown-ups who will look after us until our folks show up, a temporary arrangement, because, as the Russians had declared, we are very fine boys... and we are finally going home!

22

The House on Dluga Street

I WILL SPEND MANY HOURS in my future life, now that it looks like I'll have one, tormenting myself with permanent bewilderments.

I've been locked up in four different places—all before the age of twelve—so I hardly dare trust this new liberty. (My Papa used to say that most people, when first relieved of harsh pain, feel lost without it, that our spirit's mechanism is still primed to enfold it.) But what truly nags at me is the ever-receding presence of my brother into the past. There is no sweetness in liberty or victory without Manek.

Although we have survived, in part, because of him, I wander through a maze of longing because he is not here to walk home with us. My brother was a man of fine intelligence and careful dignity. He would have most likely kept his life, had he never sought to buy privileges for his family in Plaszow and a place for us on Schindler's freedom list. He would have avoided the snarled web of the Chilowiczs and not have been punished to death by Amon Goeth. *Stay close to us, Manek*, I whisper to his absent spirit.

The long walk on the freezing highway reduces my cousin to a wild dybbuk of complaints. He has a bad notion that we're going back to the Ghetto and gives out a whining rotation of "I'm cold, I'm hungry, my feet hurt, carry me. I want to rest, I want to pee, to eat, to stay here, to go back. I don't like you, Romek!"

Thankfully, soon the city is upon us, rising out of the cold January afternoon. I see the tower of the old town hall, (which always leaned from the heavy wind that first swayed it two hundred years ago), the gothic walls of the Florianska Gate and the twin belfries of the Krakow basilica. I want to be excited and overflowing with hope but the walk to here has sapped me.

The buildings of the town are still intact but people seem to be camping in the streets, beggars, street hawkers, coffee-sellers, itinerant musicians, girls with consumptive faces selling single cigarettes, sausages roasting over fires composed of burning tires where the stench of rubber melded with sizzling pork. All the street life seems to exist mainly to court the liberators, the pink-faced Russian soldiers who stamp along the pavements in their heavy wool coats.

Vladek's apartment is close to the Wyspianskiego Park, now a corral for Russian horses and tanks under camouflage canvas. Wilús switches to his angelic boy mode at this information but we are dissuaded from any horse viewing because Vladek says his wife is waiting to meet us.

I stand, hand in hand, with my cousin in the courtyard of their multi-family tenement on Wiessa Street looking up at women in their athletics of stringing laundry on a rope from one window to the other. Many eyes from the balconies stare down at us but more so, at Vladek and his wife who collapses in his arms, sobbing and calling out praises at his survival. Wilús pulls at my sleeve and whispers, "Let's go inside, why don't we?"

"We have to wait until she finishes recognizing him," I say.

The wife sights the two of us over her husband's shoulder. In her stunned gaze, she points and asks, "Why are they here?"

In their apartment, there is a kitchen off a huge living room, a bedroom and another room in between, a kind of den where we would sleep. The home is scrupulously clean. Everything severely in place, there is no lived-in aura to it at all. In the short twelve hours we are under Vladek's roof, I never get to know the wife's first name. We call her "Pani Vladek" which is just as well because, despite having her husband alive and home again, her joy seems dimmed by our presence.

We sit at their table, eating a vegetable soup made gamey by old mustard greens floating on its greasy surface. Wilús slurps his meal, and smiles back and forth at the couple. (I had earlier washed his face and combed his brown curls. He was looking, from the neck-up, his picture-perfect self.) I catch his thoughts. *This is how it once was, a mother and father and children around a table, capped by lamplight, webbed in by affection.*

Wilús proudly declares to Vladek and his wife, "My Mama and Papa, they are coming for me soon and we will eat soup together." As he speaks, he places his small paw gently on the woman's arm, his gaze alight with happy expectation. The woman roughly pushes his hand away and doesn't look at him. My cousin holds out the offending limb and whirls around to me in helpless shock. He bites his lower lip to keep it from trembling. The soup comes back up in my throat.

I re-swallow and have to excuse him to the she-pig. "I'm sorry, Pani Vladek, Wilús is only seven and is still learning his table manners."

Vladek looks ashamed and starts in with noisy stories of our adventures on the road. His wife ignores him and us except to say that it's time for "them" to go to sleep. She practically tears the dishes off the table and walks outside to wash them under the water pump. I know this well, this raw unreasoning hostility. Still, it bewilders me. I have no idea of how to mend it.

Vladek strokes Wilús's hair and lays the boy down tenderly in the quilts, excusing his wife as being overwrought at their reunion. Once the oil lamp in the room is blown out, Wilús holds on to me tight, curling up squirrel-like into my chest. I hear the light rapid thud of his heart. His hands are damp on my neck.

"Is that lady going to hurt us?" he asks.

"No! She won't hurt us. Besides, it's my job to take care of you."

"She's not going to let us stay here, is she?"

"You wouldn't want to, would you?"

"Where will we live? Maybe we can go back to the camp place."

The pitch of his complaints drops to a whisper because I'm busy listening to other voices coming through the wall. Pani Vladek's poisonous hiss, "How could you bring that trash here! I'm not feeding those parasites! We've barely enough to keep body and soul together!"

Next, Vladek's spineless murmur, "Please, they're just kids, they have nobody."

"They're Jews! They *are* nobody! They should have burned with the rest!"

Wilús hears everything too and gets the shakes. "You see," he whispers, "she's planning to kill us, just like the witch in Hansel and Gretel—she'll cook us in an oven!"

(All this he mangles from Grimm's original story and us once passing by the crematoria at Auschwitz when I had to lie to him with another fairy tale. I had told him the ovens were for making bread.)

"Don't worry," I say. "There'll be no boys baking anywhere."

He raises his eyes to me. I see, even in the gloom, their glint full of old terrors.

"Can we go away from here, Romek? Please?"

"We will, first thing in the morning. I promise you."

※

Vladek had told us of how the Jewish Aid Society had opened a place of refuge on Dluga Street, especially for camp survivors. We make a secret escape from his house at first light but arrive at the refuge to find the doors locked and the place impenetrable.

The wind strikes up and Wilús starts to blubber that he's freezing and wants some bread and jam. I shout and bang on the doors until my knuckles hurt. Inside footsteps stomp across tiles and a man's voice grumbles to stop the damn racket and sod off, they don't open until nine!

I yell that I have a small child with me, please let us in. Another calmer voice arises, insisting that the doors be opened, then I sense more hesitation and hear argument. The voice that I would come to know as that of the night watchman says, "But Sir, it might be troublemakers, drunks or shits looking to break a few Jewish heads."

Next, comes a reply, "For the love of G-d, Ignacy, open the damn doors!"

A gap of a few meters and Wilús urgently pushes in ahead of me, his cheeks punished blue by the wind. He halts in fear at the sight of the ill-tempered watchman with a wooden club and behind him, an older man in a heavy brown suit. Both stare down at us for some minutes and then look beyond us into the chilly street, surveying north and south with keen eyes.

The Brown Suit returns and asks me, "Where are the others?"

The House on Dluga Street

"What others, Sir?"

"Your mother and father, your other relatives?"

"We have no others. It's just me and my cousin."

"Which camp have you come from?"

"Lager Auschwitz, Sir."

The men exchange swift glances. Ignacy, no longer severe and defensive, gathers my cousin up in his arms and jostles him cheerfully. Brown Suit says his name is Director Jakubowicz and that we can stay here in the hostel for as long as we like. He calls for a woman named Pani Mira who appears at once. She looks like the world's mother with her shiny red hair and heavy-set hips, as comfortable as any armchair.

Pani Mira takes us to a large room on the first floor decorated with flowery plasterwork and cherubs flying around the beading and the light fixtures. Once a formal salon of now desiccated grandeur, it serves as a dormitory. I see a row of mattresses on the floor and several boys sleeping under heavy blankets of Red Cross issue. A classic tiled stove in the corner sizzles out terrific warmth and a curtain segments a private area at the far end reserved for girls.

Mira beds Wilús down and says she'll go to the basement to get a mattress for me. At the room's north window is a huge oak armoire, rampant with carved oak leaves and bluebirds, as wide as a large bed. I can reach its top from the windowsill. I tell Mira that all I need is bedding and a pillow and I'll sleep aloft where I can survey the male section of the room and keep an eye on my cousin.

Wilús pines about joining me up on my roost but forgets the want when Mira brings us sweet hot cocoa from a pot on the stove and offers us some gingerbread. "I like it here, Romek," he says, grinning through cocoa-mashed cake. "Is it true, they'll let us stay?"

The next morning I stand before the desk of Director Jakubowicz and tell him I'm actually fifteen years old and would like to be employed. There are very few cooking facilities in the hostel, and other than some essentials, all the hot meals have to be brought in ready-made. I conjure a fine resume of untruths, of how I had worked with my mother in the kitchens of Plaszow, the prisoner commissary at Auschwitz, and that I'm available for work right now, Sir.

The man gives me a wry smile of disbelief and declares that the hostel is not a four-star restaurant but a strong, willing boy is always an asset. He says he has a job in mind for me and that Pani Mira will watch over Wilús, who is busy anyway charming two fourteen-year-old girls in our dormitory, also recent arrivals at the shelter.

I am to journey with a carriage driver named Majer Kucharski to a quasi-military kitchen across the river in Podgorze where an overflow of Russian and Red Cross supplies have bloomed into a generous pantry that supply the Jewish Aid hostel and other refugee settlements around town. This daily run was my kind of assignment, although I am apprehensive at touching down again on the streets of the former Ghetto. The work is made pleasant by Majer's good-natured humor and his young mare who wears a battered straw hat with holes cut out for her sharp ears, an engaging animal that added to the adventure. He placed several wooden crates on the seats of his open carriage to carry the food and we'd go clopping across the Vistula once a day to bring back kettles of hot soup, baked goods, stews, fruits and urns of tea.

I would sit in the back of the carriage and Majer, a jolly type, would laugh at me as I foolishly waved at passersby like a miniature duke. On the return journey, I would be squeezed in among the crates of piled up apples and pears, and with steam rising from the closed pots, as if I was perched on the slopes of a smoking volcano. These trips through the city afforded me visions of its spirit after the long occupation. The streets were thronged with returning residents, Jews and Christian Poles alike. In the eyes of these former refugees always a questing urgency, an uncertainty, are we truly home...at last?

However, for some, being free is not that different from being in the lager.

I sometimes ride the trolley car back when Majer's carriage is overflowing with supplies. On one such day, the old vehicle rattles down Starowislna Street and is delayed at the corner of Miodowa, blocked by a shouting crowd of onlookers. Something is happening in their core. From under the elbows of the other passengers, I see, as if watching frames of a movie slide by, a man half-fallen to the sidewalk, his head streaming blood. He tries to stagger forward grasping at thin air for help. A second runner, also bleeding, dashes into the scene and helps him up, just as a club came in from the right, held in a uniformed hand, and slams down hard across the rescuer's back.

A woman on the trolley car in front of me shakes her head, clucks her tongue in disgust, and asks loudly, "Is such awful conduct necessary?" The bludgeoned man might have agreed with her question. He stands protectively over the wounded victim and turns to argue with their assailant. You can tell by his calm stance and the eloquence of his hands that he's trying to add reason to the situation, but the street crowd is looming for a kill. They roil around the two injured men, pointing and insinuating, fixed in their righteous indignation. Then the endless chant, "Lousy Jews! Get rid of them, once and for all!"

I must be leaking terror because the ticket collector puts her arm gently across my shoulders and asks some other passengers to let me have a different seat. No young boy, she says to the other travelers, should have to witness such things. "There, child, sit and be well, you are safe along my route."

The House on Dluga Street

Life at the Dluga Street refuge is a pleasant interim. The staff is openhearted to the constant stream of former camp inmates who drift through their doors, beggarly, lice-ridden, disoriented, wrapped in tattered blankets, appearing like livid-eyed prophets in some winter desert. I help Pani Mira and the kitchen team serve meals in the dining hall, knowing that there will be extra rations for Wilús and me at the end of the evening, but more so I can question as many survivors as possible.

"Excuse me, do you know a family named Ferber? A man named Leon who speaks like a gentleman? You might recognize him from the face before you that asks? I resemble him, so Mama says. Please, Sir, have you heard anything of the prisoners they marched from Auschwitz to Germany?"

I draw a blank from most people, many obsessed with their own losses.

A gaunt woman eats her meal alone the way ravenous dogs chomp on a street kill, eyes roving left and right, chewing nervously. She seems to me to be extra hungry, so I go over and offer her a second helping of soup but try to disregard the lunacy in her gaze. She stares at me, drops her spoon and rises from the table, calling "Chaskel! Chaskel, is that you? Oh, my angel! My darling boy, where have you been?"

I have the pot of hot soup between her and me, so the skeletal arms actually embrace me by the head, spiny fingers gripping my cheeks.

"Chaskel, sweetheart, don't you believe them?" she whispers, "Those awful liars, I didn't abandon you. We went to the showers together. They pushed us women back and locked the doors...because the room was so full of children. They told us to wait our turn, and then they sent us away. Every day, I looked for you. Every day! Chaskel, say you forgive Mama?"

Her face is very close to mine, she stinks of cabbage and emanates despair, but she scans me intently through the soup steam, her mind careening down her longing. *Could it be him, my boy? Chaskel was taller? Chaskel?* Pani Mira is suddenly by us, lightly prying the woman off me, urging her gently, "Come, Gustawa, sit down and finish your dinner."

I'm polishing the banisters of the front hall one afternoon and half-listening to Director Jakubowicz and his secretary process the liberated wanderers who arrive in throngs prior to the dinner hour. I look up and observe a thick-necked man standing by the front desk, signing the register and offering his Auschwitz number. He's wearing a good wool coat over his inmate's stripes and expensive winter boots. Rolls of fat spill over his collar, the bulk of him is massive and all at once familiar. (No one could gather such weight in the camp without damning others—but who is asking?) His fingers are short and blunt, and their grip on the pen I recognize as once having wielded a bamboo cane across my back. They are the hands of the Kapo, Meilech Bronner.

I panic at the sight of him. "You can't let *him* in here!" My shout echoes off the staircase! The Director looks up and swings his head between the two of us. Bronner passes off the sting of my voice; I can see he remembers but dismisses me in solicitous tones. "Poor kid is obviously insane. They often come out of the gates totally deranged. It's only natural with the parents gone, all the gassings and the entire place a graveyard."

But I'm still yelling, "He beat other Jews! He stole their food and wrote them up for Block 11 to be flogged! Please, send him away. He'll hurt somebody. Look at him! Ask him how he got to be so fat. *Ask him!*"

There are murmurs of outrage in the line of waiting refugees. An emaciated elderly man steps out of the line and declares the boy here is speaking the truth! Bronner makes a run for the door, but Ignacy the watchman and two other men are on him before he's through it. Director Jakubowicz orders that he be locked in the cellar while they wait for the police and beckons me to come into his office at once.

There were several days of interrogations by Director Jakubowicz and Pani Mira.

At first, I am scared that somehow Bronner will go free and come at me for revenge. But I became a public mouth and cannot hold back the details once I have started. I tell them of so many others too, of our *Blockelteste* Stasiek, also a beater and a food robber, of the units in the guard towers and their shooting parties, contesting who could pick off the most kids in the wire alleys. Pani Mira shows me photographs of several high-ranking Nazis, "Uncle Pepi" among them, Karl Höcker, adjutant to the Auschwitz commandant, Richard Baer, and more rogue doctors, Eduard Wirths, Johann Kremer and Carl Clauberg.

"Roman, have you ever heard or seen these people? Have you heard others speak of them and what they did to prisoners?"

I try to help as best I can but am only able identify two or three.

❋

The supply kitchen in Podgorze is where I encounter Vassili Ivanov, a Russian Captain who is a Jew from Kirovskaya. Vassili is a man with a golden nature, compulsively generous toward children, and one of the kindest human beings I've ever met. He possesses a great and immediate energy, and can manage a dozen complex actions at once. He speaks Polish fluently, but in gilded and elaborate sentences, as if he's rehearsing a play. He had a wife back in Russia, but the war had gotten between them and any making of offspring.

On learning that all realities pointed to us being orphans, he takes an instant and protective interest in Wilús and me. One day when I am trying to haul one of the empty soup kettles across the floor of the supply kitchen with my sleeves rolled up, Vassili steps behind me and lifts the heavy cauldron as if it's a feather. He sets it on the stove and grabs my scrawny arm to examine my camp tattoo. He shakes his head and denounces the Germans as utterly debased and beyond all redemption.

"Good son," he asks, "how can a young boy like you live without parents?"

"I haven't much choice, Captain, Sir."

"Do you have any family at all?"

"Just my little cousin, he's at the refugee house."

"Bring him here and you'll both feast like the Czar's princes."

I make many such trips to Podgorze, often with other boys from the dormitory too and sometimes Wilús. Vassili makes a great fuss over both of us and feeds us until we have to undo the top button of our pants to breathe.

"Good son," he once pleaded, "you and that angel cousin must come home with me. Both of you will be like the flesh of my body and always be the children of my heart because I chose you above all others. My wife will agree and think herself blessed that I brought her two wonderful ready-made boys. We'll send you to the best schools and universities. You will forget all these bad times and have two parents and a hundred cousins who will love you. You will come to Russia?"

"Where in Russia?" I ask him.

"Deep in Russia, we live in a place of green forests and beautiful rivers. You will want for nothing, I promise you."

I thank him and say I that still belonged to my parents, whom I believe are alive. To go with him as his son, despite his generous affection, would be such a betrayal of them. I know they are under the same sky at night and Hanka too, somewhere in the darkness, still alive and thinking of me, even as I ache for them. Besides, I can't just give Wilús away for adoption. As wonderful as Vassili's promise of a home is, I long for my own family. I want to find them.

※

On a day when I have some free time, I make a journey that feels like walking on knives and go alone to our former apartment on Waska Street, under a sky of watered light that threatened a blizzard. My old neighborhood is now, mostly a deserted shadow land; scabrous, decimated, ashes were in every place that the snow had not reached. The burnt columns of synagogues still stand, in fragile hesitation of imminent collapse. The blasted windows of abandoned houses on Dajwor Street blow drifts of plaster dust and ice crystals into air when the wind charges through their barren rooms.

I hear whimpering coming from one dwelling, through a shattered door. I caught sight of a feral dog nursing her young under a stairwell. I have a second's thought of taking a puppy for Wilús, but the mongrel bitch snarls hellishly at me, dropping the pulpy red mess she'd been chewing on. She drags herself and her mewling brood into the shadows, and catches the tiny headless body in her teeth. A haunch of her coloring splinters under the bite.

So many hungers, nothing I can make right. I want very much to talk to someone in this moment, a human tinge to anchor me.

I pass the double doors of courtyards filled with rotting trash. Inner balconies torn from their moorings sway vertically from homes vandalized many times over. In one court, a cluster of dirty kids, much older than me, squat around a burning armchair. A foul-looking girl rises from the smoke and debris and points to me. She has no upper teeth, her mouth a gaping rebuke. "You," she slavers, "do you have any food?"

The others turn my way, their savage gaze ugly and territorial, hands reaching for makeshift clubs. I shake my head and run, away from their eager need to hurt. Their shouts and curses echo and I hide beneath the basement steps of a leaning house frame on Bartosza Street. The daylight is graying. Most of the streetlights have been stolen for scrap metal. I have a terror of being caught in the dusk here, where the chair burners might hunt me down. I slide along the walls and quickly around the corner to our place.

The main lobby doors of our apartment house have long been broken open and I'm in the front hall, made spacious now by the torn-down walls of the concierge's studio. Gisela Zaluski's calendar still hangs askew, dated 1939, on each page a dusty illustration of Our Lady of Czestochowa. I stand at the foot of the stairs and holler, "It's me! Roman! I'm home!" I call their names repeatedly. I don't walk to the third floor at first because the banister is missing from the entire staircase. I stop and listen. A desolate silence meets me.

On the stairs, I start my futile wishing. Please...please be here. Many of the dwellings gape open, making me afraid of their inner shadows. A large, ripped-up sofa blocks the entrance of one, wedged in by frustrated looters. A bread knife still suspended in the velvet upholstery, its horsehair stuffing surges up through the stabbed fabric. Above me, I hear a rustling and I think maybe it's my mother. "Mama?" I yell. "It's OK, it's only me, Roman, are you there? Is that you?"

My pleas loose a cascade of snow from the broken upper skylight. It slaps down on our landing and its missing floorboards. I leap the gaps into our former home.

Inside, it appears as if a room-to-room battle has been fought here. From the emanations of destruction, common objects echo the violence of their absence. The porcelain bathtub has been cleaved in half, faucets taken, the sink missing, as if ripped from the wall a minute ago by the slant of the twisted pipes. The kitchen must have been quite a haul: the water heater, the samovar, shelving, cupboards, and oven, all gone. The room is also wide open to the elements. Small humps of snow and ash intrude on the linoleum from the terrace. Balcony railings have been dug out, the doors hijacked. I recall my father had them custom-made with panes of finely etched glass. (They would have brought a healthy sum on the black market.) I have a wide view of Wawrzynca Street to the right and nothing remains of my mother's chicken coops or their inmates, not even a feather. Their grain bin has been lifted too.

My parent's bedroom is completely empty and I see a single set of male boot prints in the dust, much too big to belong to my father. By the onyx marble fireplace, a decaying bedroll is spread out to the windows, its quilting colonized by several months of green mold. The sleeper has long departed. In the fire grate itself, among the cold embers of burnt furniture, a blackened metal tube—one of my father's Pelikan fountain pens, the model 100N, and his favorite.

I spit on the barrel and rub away the soot; the engravings are still there. The 24-carat gold nib is missing, easily melted down. But the pen is of him! I polish it more and the mother of pearl barrel gleams. I put the item deep inside my shirt and am foolish enough to believe that this omen connects us.

I move into the living room, where a pyramid of crushed tiles is all that remains of the tall stove in whose heated belly I used to dry my shoes. Dust shadows on the wall, ghosts of the taken dresser—my father's favorite chair, his desk, our beds, and the mahogany dining table. The past presence of the raiders still lingers, such greedy phantoms. I feel them clawing at the fabric and surround of our lives. *The Jews have gone...forever...and what finery they've left for us! See, such excellent taste this family had. Be sure to leave nothing to chance, the Passover silver and good holiday linens sometimes they hide in the walls, or in a false draw in the closets. Look carefully. Bring the axes, the saws, and the shovels. Tear up the bricks and the floorboards if necessary.*

I don't care. I sob loudly to the empty wasted room. Have it all, take it! There are no real treasures to welcome me. They are not here. Not here! My legs give out from underneath me and I slump down among the spread of broken white tiles, dizzy and grieving until I actually vomit into the dust.

A slant of last afternoon sun spills in from the ransacked kitchen. I dare not be here when the night arrives; the vast loneliness of the building will bury me. I stagger up and out the shattered entrance. I stop for a brief minute at the former apartment of my good friend, Moniek Hocherman, where piles of debris block any real access. I add him to my list of lost comforts. The strange rustling motion from above reaches me again and I'm afraid some squatter with a murderous bent is waiting for me to trespass up one more level in the encroaching dark. I back down the staircase, picking up a heavy chair leg as I go. Whatever menace may be here will take nothing more from me!

✻

When I return to the refuge hostel, I lie to Wilús that the tank squads leveled our building long ago to construct a highway. I get a fibber's payback. Wilús, who had been given a toy bear on wheels by Pani Mira he likes to rumble all over the dorm room says, in tones meant to comfort, "Romek, your Mama and Uncle Leon have gone to stay in New York with my and papa. We need to get some things called passy ports and then we can go there too."

My whimsical little cousin, in his unshakeable fantasy that his parents were still alive, has churned up an idea in me. We have no adults to call our own at the time and no one is rushing with open arms to claim us. Despite the generous offer, Russia and life with the Ivanovs is out, but I recall my mother once saying that we had cousins in Baltimore and Brooklyn. Director Jakuobwicz advises me that for us to leave Poland without any guardian, we'd have to secure petitions from the "authorities" signed by our relatives in America, and we'd need some money to start our new life.

The Pelikan pen inside my shirt directs my intentions. It imprints a name on my determination—Bronek Persky, owner of a fancy stationary store on Franciskanska Street who had once been a steady client of my father's.

On our expulsion from the city in 1940, Papa had left his prize collection of rare and antique Pelikan pens—over three dozen of them in their velvet case—for safekeeping with Bronek. I can hear my father saying we'll not forget to retrieve them when all this mess is over. My mother had countered in her sharp circuitous fashion that even a starving dog would bite its own mother. Papa had argued, Bronek is an honorable Christian. His word is his bond. I find, however, that this is not true of his wife.

The Persky's business in its post-war state has become a seedy emporium of second-hand goods. Gone is the embossed linen stationary from Florence, the engraved business cards, the delicate notepaper for shy girls perfumed with essence of violets. Pani Katarina Persky now scours up items from abandoned properties and bargains with refugees for their last possessions: old leather satchels from destroyed schools, books from closed publishers, typesetter's drawers full of jumbled metal fonts, stacked boots for the disabled and club-footed. At any other time, I would be fascinated at by her stock, but I'm here for my father's pen collection.

The woman stares down at me from the cashier's grille of her high wooden counter, her eyes float large behind her bottle-thick glasses. "So you are Leon's boy," she murmurs in distraction, as if I was Leon's shoelace or something incidental to his unknown existence. "We don't have your father's property," she says, avoiding my gaze, and in the same indifferent breathy tones, tells me her husband Bronek lies upstairs, speechless and severely detoured from life by the war and a crippling stroke. "You see, young Romek, he would be the only one who knew whatever happened to Pan Ferber's pens."

I still have the wondrous charred Pelikan hidden in my undershirt. I contemplate showing it to her, but that she might soil my father's open trust with her skilled liar's ooze drives me into a rage. "Why don't you ask me, Pani Persky, if my Papa's still alive or if my missing mother is halfway to another concentration camp with my sister? Ask me about Manek blasted

The House on Dluga Street

into a no-name grave in Plaszow, or how I manage to be a twelve-year-old parent to a seven-year-old boy! Ask me about the never-ending, bloody road we've traveled, and how we are adrift with nothing to tie us to anyone or anywhere but our longing and memories!"

She stares at me for quite a few shocked minutes. I lower my head to avoid her gaze and start to shake, but I will not cry in front of her. I think of my father and resolve to be stoic. She rings open the cash register and slowly pushes several coins across the bald varnish of the counter, five zlotys in all. "There, Romek," she says, "treat yourself to some nice pastries, it's what you deserve."

23

The Secrets of Rabka Zdroj

I HAVE NEW CAPTORS; two young sirens in the refuge house have taken a shine to me and my cousin. Ludwina Lubasz, age sixteen, and her fourteen-year-old sister, Konstancya, are known around our refugee's dorm by the single title of "Luda-Konni" because of their instinct for paired mischief. The orphaned girls are the last survivors of a family of fifty-four members, formerly of the Lubasz apparel factory in Warsaw, now all gone to the gas, with one hoped-for exception. They believe their tailoring father is somewhere in a camp on the Finnish-Russian border, still sewing uniforms.

Luda-Konni seek me out whenever I'm unloading the food from Podgorze into the white-tiled pantries of the refuge house. In the quiet time, after supper, Pani Mira allows us to sit at the broad pinewood table and drink sweet black currant tea. "Just look at that, Romek," says Luda, opening the pantry door so we can take pleasure in the wooden bins overflowing with spring vegetables and tubs full of musky plums, green figs and golden-skinned pears. Speaking as a boy who, months before, had lifted heels of dry bread from the pockets of corpses in their barracks, stark hunger, once endured, is a strange taskmaster. Staring at the full pantry, I feel something akin to a holy wonder at this abundance before our eyes.

Konni Lubasz is sweet and warm and the first female to ever kiss me longingly on the mouth for giving her a tortoiseshell comb that I'd found on the street trolley. I like the idea of having a girl adore me, just to say I had one. However, I had no idea what women and girls were about at all. My two pillars of scant awareness have been Mama and Hanka and my fuzzy perception is that both women could be bossy, fearsome, sweet smelling and essential.

In fact, I am constantly miserable from missing my family, a wanting that rolls over me daily in the echo of their names. I remember my sister long ago reading me ghost stories that kept me awake half the night at the least shadow moving on the wall, but Manek would comfort me, saying we should have sympathy for the poor ghosts that clutch and howl to be part of the living. My loneliness proves to me that a person can become a phantom while still breathing in their skin. I continue to wander across Krakow to the places of my earlier childhood, as if I might dredge up more pleasant realities from little snippets of the past, but there are no familiar faces to anchor me. The game I used to play with Tadek Horowitz of becoming invisible has finally been achieved.

Nothingness has found me and rendered me as a vapor in rags.

The Secrets of Rabka Zdroj

❂

Wiluś has not been well. He cries a lot and complains that he can't walk straight because of severe pains in his ear. Director Jakubowicz says he will arrange for the doctor to come and treat him, but so far, only a nurse visits us. She binds up his head with a poultice and gives him a light narcotic. He's fast asleep late one evening on the mattress with Luda wrapped around him and several other young ones. Down on the floor I hear the scrape of a chair being moved. A slim figure full of shadow vaults lightly along the windowsill and Konni is instantly beside me.

"Move over, Romek, I'm cold."

"You shouldn't be here," I protest. "Pani Mira will be angry if she finds us together."

The girl throws back my quilt and is beneath it in a second. My face grows heated in the darkness. Konni is winding her arms—soft female tentacles—all over me, but her camp-fed bones have sharp points, not much woman in them at all. "I heard you crying before," she says. I deny it in a fierce whisper and consider pushing her to the floor. "You often cry in your sleep," she insists, "like a puppy down a well."

All my prisoner years I had slept in my clothes for warmth and to prevent them from being stolen. Now this wild insistent girl is calling me little husband and trying to wrench me out of my pants! I pulled part of the quilt around my waist and push her off. She relaxes and says, "Let's cuddle, OK?" She kisses my eyelids tenderly and rocks me against the emaciated fence of her ribs. I lay there, awkwardly, a downed tree of failed romance. I kiss her back on her ringworm scars and feel the muscles of her gaunt face tighten in a smile. It comes to me that, other than hugging Wiluś to me in the barracks bunk to fend off the cold, I have not held another person in a long time. The memory of the separation with my father collides with Konni stroking my hair and whispering endearments. I break in two and sob uncontrollably. The wasted angel in the dark says, "It's OK, I am here. Please don't cry. There is nothing bad anymore."

Oh, but there is. Misfortune is an endless road.

It arrives one morning at Dluga Street in the form of Dr. Pavlov Koeppen and his team of physicians and medics from the University Hospital, earnest hunters of scurvy, venereal conditions, tuberculosis, anemia, gastroenteritis and a host of other camp afflictions. They enter with uniformed ambulance drivers, stretcher-bearers, nurses in blue-and-white starched dresses, and a van full of pharmaceuticals. Among them is a pediatrician, a balding young man with sparse tufts of blond hair rising above his ears, named Karel Hirschberg.

The staff cordon off rooms for the examinations because every resident is to get a physical. Director Jakubowicz smiles and reassures us that this is to discern who is infectious and who needs to be hospitalized. "We are commencing, ladies and gentlemen," he declares, "with a program of recovering your health to its natural state."

The adults form lines by gender, screens are set up and the medical team begins their examinations, but there is something in the whole process that tips an avalanche of memory. It's sparked by a woman named Romeska Nordlinger and her two young brothers, who start up a racketing refusal to cooperate. Other faces around me shrivel before this band of well-intentioned healers—echoes of yelling, people in uniform, a recall of other medics in white coats who once butchered the unsuspecting. Luda and Konni recoil from the gentle touch of a soft-spoken nurse, pushing her away and protesting loudly. Mad Gustawa, who still thinks I'm her lost son, shrieks with a hellish terror that contaged everyone. Old men raise their hands as if held at gunpoint and backed up against the wall. The women grab onto each other in familiar fear, that any human hand that ever touched us in the camps (especially Auschwitz) most always delivered pain or worse.

These are the rebellions of the body provoked by the regimented nature of this medical morning. Silver scalpel visions surging out from recollections of former places of no mercy. The marble slabs of Block 10 with their bloody slots, swift cuts made without anesthesia, organs lifted at random from living flesh still pulsing, the naked sitting on Mengele's benches waiting for their turn to be hurt, wounds left unstitched that seeped to death or caused the infected to scream all night in their bunks.

Dr. Koeppen quickly reads all these terrors. He speaks to us calmly, orders the ambulance drivers to wait outside and urges his team to go slowly. Karel Hirschberg has the wisdom to remove his white coat, then his jacket, rolls up his sleeves and opens his medical kit. He brings out a stethoscope and a hand puppet shaped like a black bear and proceeds to press the scope to its breast with tender concern.

Curious, some of the children forget their fear and step out from behind their mothers. They begin to laugh easily and point at him. An old man snipes, *why send such a fool of a lad to do a physician's job?* Hirschberg sits down on the floor with his small bear. He smiles and asks who would like to listen to their own heart? The bear too asks in solemn tones (and later, we learn that the pediatrician has an uncle who is a skilled ventriloquist in Lublin). Wilús, his head still bandaged, tugs me forward by the hand and says to the wooly face, "My ear hurts a lot."

My cousin flinches when Dr. Hirschberg gently unwinds the dressing and shines a light (held by the bear puppet) into his ear, its exterior swollen to the size and color of a small dark plum. The physician gives me a dismaying look and declares to his nurse, "We have a severe mastoid case for the hospital." Wilús cries even louder at this news and stubbornly refuses to go until Luda comes and wraps him in her shawl and says to us that she will journey with him. Something like the sun erupts over my cousin's face and he enters happily into the girl's waiting arms.

The Secrets of Rabka Zdroj

Then it's my turn. I strip off to the waist; the bear doctor travels his stethoscope in a circular motion over my ribs. I'm not sick, I tell him. Hirschberg nods and says nothing. He pulls down my eyelids and declares me anemic. The bear then puts the scope in my ears, its detecting end on my heart, and I hear a loud slow whoosh, as if the ocean were rushing into a shoebox.

"It's a slight murmur," the doctor says, "but something to be monitored. We should make sure the heart muscles are strengthened as you grow."

"Do I need to take medicine?" I ask him.

He let the bear answer, "No, Romek, you need to take a vacation!"

✻

So it is that myself, two dozen other boys, and some girls, all deemed sickly, are commandeered by Drs. Hirschberg and Koeppen to be sent to the town of Rabka Zdroj, a spa resort cradled in a valley of the Beskid Wyspowy Mountains. "You will like it there, Romek," beamed Director Jakubowicz. However, his declaiming of the healing virtues of Rabka's boron brines and rehabilitation pools set off the second maniacal fit of the day among the residents.

No, we would *not* like it there, according to a loutish kid named Jerzy, who fires up a tale of how the Germans had once run a school for the SiPO (security police) in the town and forced local Jewish kids to run through streets so their sharpshooters could hone their target practice. Jerzy, who had previously lived rough but free in Krakow's back alleys throughout the war, threatens to flee the refuge house rather than suffer being transported to Rabka.

I am not thrilled either at the idea of leaving Krakow or Wilús, (although I would have never been allowed to visit him in the hospital because of my age). Besides, I hear from some of the resident inmates that many Jews of our transport are still at Schindler's Brinnlitz factory. I cling to the hope that Mama and Hanka can find their way back to the city and come looking for me.

"Give me letters," says Konni, "for your Mama and Pani Hanka. I promise I will present them if they show up, and I will be beautiful when I do."

My hasty scribbled notes, full of hesitant, stumbling words such *as I'm alive, I hope you are, please wait for me... please wait* are rolled up and tied in a scarf of Konni's. The next morning, as I climb into the truck, she kisses me boldly in front of everyone (which makes me squirm).

The journey to the mountains is a solemn one. In the truck's open bed, we are two rows of nervous kids still not trusting our destination's end. Some boys fake bravado; others tremble in wooden silence from entrenched memories of the selection trucks and the cattle car. The girls of our group have more courage, clustered together; they talk easily among themselves and ignore us.

As the vehicle climbs higher into the mountains and the fields fall away into a bright green mosaic below us, we breathe easier in the cool sweet air and the warming sun spilling over the valley along the silvered rivers of the Raba and Slonna. Such is the peace of this place that even Jerzy tones down his suspicions and rolls up several cigarettes to be shared. It is early June and the slopes of the lower hills are spangled with wildflowers, hedgerows dusted pink with the fallen blooms of ripening apple trees.

As the truck lurches ever upward, I see a farmer behind an old-style plough singing encouragement to a broad-chested horse; the man and animal surge harmoniously along the opening furrows. He waves to us and we boys holler back a greeting. The sharp contrasts of the world confuse me. I still hear the war roaring inside my brain—so do these others. We carry it as a sharp-fanged beast embedded in all our moments, and there's no reconciling it with this golden spring day where normalcy and sunlight wash over us. A slack-faced tubercular lad named Oren, who coughs a lot, chides us for our meager joy, saying, "C'mon, it's a vacation, what's not to like?"

The truck bowls its way through Rabka's tidy streets, past ancient buildings made of larch wood, past roadside shrines enclosing saints honored by fresh crocuses, by grandmothers knitting on stone benches and a man selling poppy seed bread and *oscypek*, the local smoked cheese. The first odors of the place that hit me are the overwhelming sulfurous blend of sour eggs and iodine issuing from the rich therapeutic springs that flow through and beneath the community. All along the town's Planty gardens, invalids, both ambulatory and in wheelchairs, are taking the mountain air escorted by their caretakers.

Our final stop is a former convent transformed decades ago into a sanatorium. We leap down from the truck to be greeted by several cute nurses, a plump medical director called Dr. Ostrowski, and the matron, a sturdy woman dressed in black, named Pani Rulka Metzger, who marches us along a marble hallway to our quarters. Beyond its length I see open glass doors leading to a broad patio and a well-tended orchard.

Two divides of the world run through Rabka; the sick and the hedonistic. The sanatorium had once been a haven of the touring rich and local gentry, and to some extent, it still is. Healing was promised from its molten pools so guests could overload their systems with expensive food and wine only to have their indulgences drained away the next day. During the few weeks of our stay, we encounter an array of local practitioners who offer magnetism, seaweed wraps, hypnosis, oily massages, herbal concoctions, thermal and even electrical cures for our wasted health. Pani Rulka is a great believer in solar therapy and advises us to sit semi-naked in the enclosed orchard at noon to let the June light bathe our skin (out of sight of the girl patients and young nurses, of course).

I become good friends with Jerzy and Oren plus two other boys, Galen and Henio. We five share a room with real beds and cotton sheets so laundered and pristine, I press my face into them to drink in the good scents of lavender and chamomile. After two weeks of lounging, reading, playing cards and constantly stuffing my face, my limbs fill out and I begin to feel that life might actually click back into place.

The sanatorium has a large upper porch overlooking the front garden, another sunny therapy area where the kids who are tubercular or asthmatic lie in deck chairs after ten in the morning, sipping fresh orange juice in their patched graying underwear and wearing goggles against the bright rays. Female patients have their own reserved area on the left side of the terrace. There, the girls sit shy and aloof with light sheets modestly wrapped around their limbs. We four join Oren in solidarity because the juice service is non-stop and we can flirt with the nurses. Since tobacco is strictly forbidden, we save our secret smoking sessions for the apple orchard in the late afternoons.

At sixteen, Oren looks like an under-developed twelve-year-old. His lungs are like paper after a long and ruinous detention in Majdenek, followed by weeks of hiding in the forest of Krepiec. Despite the loss of his entire family, he seems to be an innately happy youth and his serenity affected me for the better. "You know, Romek," he says, raising his face to the pine-studded mountains, "this is the place I want to be, I could stay here forever."

I am curious to ask him how he had survived living alone in the wilderness just a few kilometers from the Russian border but Jerzy, who was protective of Oren, advised not to remind him of all the bad things he'd endured.

My Rabka gang, as I call them, is an odd mix, vastly different from each other in temperament and instinct. Jerzy's history is many wars within the war. At fourteen, he is a Krakovian like me but barely socialized; an illiterate street rat, the only one among us who has never been a camp detainee. A person of savage reflexes, he eats with his hands, spits anywhere and thinks nothing of opening his pants and relieving himself on the sidewalk. He had been raised by an unscrupulous grandmother who once sold him to a childless couple, then schemed his kidnapping and kept the purchase money.

"I was six when she first sent me to beg in the square," he tells us, "she beat me if I came home with less than she expected. My back is deformed because of that bitch and her whip!" He lifts his shirt to reveal his scarred spine bowed to one side jutting through his skin.

I call him the sentimental gangster because he has spurts of sudden generosity and might hand you a fistful of zlotys, or shovel the untouched food off of his plate onto yours. Jerzy always has money and tobacco and I never question how he comes by them. He had lived in the sewers of Krakow, on riverbanks, in root cellars, and in abandoned vehicles. When his grandmother tried to pimp him at age eleven to a rich cleric who loved boys, he sold her out to the German garrison and told them she was hiding Jews.

"She should have killed me at birth," he says gleefully, "it would have been safer."

He'd danced for vengeful joy as he watched the soldiers drag her away. It didn't seem to matter to him that one oppressor had simply been replaced by another. He regarded her arrest as his real birthday. My mouth is agape in awe as he tells us these terrible things. I thought I was a tough survivalist until I met Jerzy.

Galen and Henio are the aristocrats of our quintet. Both cousins were born to wealthy professional parents. Henio had been a piano prodigy, and was still a virtuoso but with no instrument. He was the youngest son of an investment banker, arrested by the Gestapo and hung for allegedly damaging the finances of Christian society. Galen's father had been a famous archivist at the Jagellonian Library and as such had been maligned and arrested with other professors by Hans Frank on the flimsy excuse of housing subversive literature, including Mozart's autographs and the starry manuscripts of Copernicus. For many of the war years, Galen and his botanist mother had been hidden by various academics who had once served the Library well.

These two orphans wear the refinements of their upbringing. If Oren is the Rabbi of our group and Jerzy, the street urchin, these boys carry themselves like young lords. Their manners are exquisite; both are well read and speak English and French fluently. Galen had somehow survived part of the time by posing as a French Christian in Auschwitz—even in the latrines. Henio's luck came in being selected to give piano lessons to the children of the camp's Sturmbannführer, Richard Baer, who had forbidden anyone to damage the boy's hands. Galen was passionate about nature and had set his sights on being a biologist—once he could get into any university that would take Jews.

In the presence of these two well-bred youths, Jerzy is restrained and deferential. They are golden beings who touch him kindly. Henio will whistle to him and us Chopin's nocturnes right on key and Galen reads patiently to the feral teenager from some battered children's books we found in the sanatorium's recreation room. I decide to teach Jerzy how to write his name and some other literate feats. Soon he is able to scrawl a pretty good postcard greeting back to Pani Mira who is the first woman he has ever truly revered.

Friday nights after the candles are lit and the prayers and Shabbas meal are finished, Pani Rulka unlocks the main staff room, which, to Henio's delirious joy, holds an old upright piano. We refugees from Dluga Street, girls included, the nurses and the sanatorium's staff right down to the gardener, all congregate on opposite sides of the room until Henio lets loose on the keys, playing several polkas in succession. Gradually, shy boys in their fake toughness and cast-off clothing shuffle over to the nurses and girls and ask them to dance.

When the weather is blazing hot, we shelter in the cool gloom of the sanatorium's spacious treatment rooms. There is also a small marble chapel totally devoid of any sacred objects, just the shadow of a large cross and the outline in the far wall of where the altar had once sat. When I ask Pani Rulka what has happened to the furnishings and holy objects, she says that the fixtures had gone to the barracks in Zakopane so their priest could celebrate mass for the German platoons. Henio asks her why on earth such evil people would want a mass, since it seemed they were permanently unrepentant. She has no answer for him and walks away.

Down at the basement level of the sanatorium are several hot sulfur pools heated by ancient fires in the earth's belly. Four of us help Oren slide into the waters and I carry his spittoon and towel because the odorous steam would cause his lungs to bellow and cough. The walls of the therapy salons have been hewn from sheer rock and floating about in the briny heat and mist gives one the feeling of being hidden in a subterranean lair. One bathing pit here is nothing more than a basin of warm wet clay raked over daily, and which invites instant tomfoolery. We entertain Oren by dancing around in it, whooping, wrestling and slathering ourselves all over until we look like equatorial hunters with only the whites of our eyes showing.

※

One fine morning as the sun is still gentle, Pani Rulka sends a group of kids off on a nature walk, deep into the sharp clean air of the Beskid ranges. The five of us inevitably drift away from the main cluster to go adventuring on our own. I love this as much as mud-mashing. Here, Galen and Oren come into their own, pointing out the tracks of where a lynx or an alpine chamois has padded up the mountain trail before us. They know which mushrooms and berries we can snack on and which are lethal. We hike along dense bramble ledges and look down on the town and the four hundred-year-old larchwood church below. Often, it is necessary to slow our pace on these outings to allow Oren to steady his breath who, despite the steep slopes, is pink and charged with happiness at wandering in this paradise.

But the serpent glides silently where one least expects it.

We halt at a fast-running stream to drink and bathe our aching feet. Jerzy and I wander up stream to a small hillock for a cigarette to avoid our smoke affecting Oren. The two of us slump against the rise, fumbling tobacco and speculating on girls when I feel something hard pressing against my back. I shift and it moves too. I sit up, scrabble through the slick damp moss and free from the soil a dirty white bone, long and indented with animal bites.

Jerzy leaps away in immediate terror. "Don't touch that! Romek, put it down!" he cries. I drop the object at his harsh order and kick it into a patch of sunlight. Bewildered, I bend to pick it up again, but he grabs my arm.

"No! You mustn't," he orders.

"Why not?"

"It's not from an animal!" he hisses.

The slope from where I plucked the item has partially caved in from my tugging and I realize at once that, were we to search there, the partnering pieces of this femur would be found. Jerzy snatches up the bone and pitches it high into the trees.

"We should tell someone," I say.

"No! Not the others," he answers and jerks his head in the direction of our three friends. "What's the point? Leave it be, Romek, forget you ever saw it."

All the way back to town, the now-secret item weighs heavily on me. Jerzy, whose emotions always seemed fleeting and random, gets the others to sing randy songs as we descend down to the green trail to the sanatorium. He laughs heartily, slaps me on the back as we cross the lawn and say we should find some willing girls and go fool around in the mud pool.

I excuse myself, explaining that I need to pee but I want desperately to be alone. I sit for a long time in the disused chapel with the door fastened and pull the pale bone into memory. *You should be used to such things*, I tell myself, *all the thrown-away people you've seen stacked up in the camps, my relatives, slumped and bloody, on Plaszow's Appellplatz, the girl's corpse frozen under the waters of the Auschwitz conduits, the rotting dead who would never be liberated.*

I close my eyes. In the dark cool of this G-d-flown place that still smells of incense, the bone speaks a righteous chant. We are one and a multitude, innocent and unjust alike. Honor our nameless blood singing under these mountains. I think of my father, Mama and Hanka, of Manek, and how they might instruct me in this moment. I speculate on the identity of the remains now embraced by the green mercies of the forest. The dead live no more than within a whispering distance of us, on the other side of breath's mirror, they are always there. I hear their fervent rustle and can't go to bed for fear they will crowd my sleep with their grief and wanting.

Later, I walk out into the scented night of the garden and stare up at the impassive forest, a black fortress of trees. What mysteries feed their roots? I hear the efficient footfall of Pani Rulka arrive on the stone patio. She comes and stands next to me, asking kindly, "Are you not tired, little Romek? Don't you feel sleepy after all the fresh air you've had today?"

I turn to gaze at what seems to be an honorable woman and I ask the questions lying leaden in my chest.

"They are...here, aren't they?"

"Who is here?"

I sense she knows the answer already. A low wind ripples across the meadows beyond us, maybe a distant murmur in the earth itself. She waits and stares at me, then raises my chin to her eyes and says, "Child, you are very young and have a whole life before you. What good is this questioning? Are there not sorrows enough that you should want to retrieve those that are old and gone by?"

"Tell me, please, Pani Rulka, and I will stop asking."

The Secrets of Rabka Zdroj

She hesitates for some minutes and then speaks. "In 1941...Jews arrived here from other cities and towns to be kept safe by our own Jewish community," she explains. "We all lived peaceably together until senior military came from Germany. Wilhelm Rosenbaum, a man named Hans Kruger, and several others. They brought soldiers from the garrisons in Krakow and Zakopane and opened a school for the worst dregs of humanity."

"Why did they need a school?"

"It was an academy for brutes and butchers, Romek. There they trained members of the Security Services, the Polish police, Ukrainian security collaborators, Russian prisoners from internment centers, and many recruits from the SS camp at Trawniki. Rosenbaum, who was full of rage because he bore a Jewish name, unleashed Satan on our Jews not only from Rabka but on those in the surrounding districts, from Makov Podhalanski, Bely Rast, and many other places. These innocents, mainly mothers and children, were brought to the school and used as moving targets for the shooting range."

"And...the graves?"

"Everywhere, by the hundreds, in the forests, beside the streams, behind the houses, some ploughed into fields, G-d's holy wheat."

She bends her head and makes the sign of the cross. When she looks up, I can see by the patio's dim lamp that her eyes are moist, which makes me want to comfort her. We stand for a long time like this until she puts her arm around my shoulders and asks me, "Roman, have you ever seen our apple candles?"

"You mean candles stuck into fruit, like some shops make at Christmas time?"

"No, child, that which happens to our apple trees every summer. Look."

She spins me around to face the left aspect of the garden. At first, I can see nothing unusual, just the glowering dark from the pines leaning down the mountain to the fence. But leveling my gaze, I see what she's intended.

Almost every tree in the orchard is ablaze, shimmering with dots of light, the iridescent cast of a thousand glowworms in June.

❦

My sun-drenched days at Rabka with my new friends continue but there are no more forest exploits. I prefer to lounge in the orchard shade or bask in the sulfur pools. My gang of four and I are browned by the summer heat, boiled to a ruddy health by the mineral waters and muscled up from the endless supply of good meals. With the exception of Oren, who always keeps himself neat and orderly, we have the look of wild gypsies and our hair hung about our shoulders until Pani Rulka says to either go into town for haircuts or else she would personally take the scissors to us. Oren stays behind the afternoon the rest of us troop out together to visit the barber.

In Rabka, we make a small holiday with Jerzy's mystery money supply, noshing our way through the quaint avenues with post-haircut treats of lemonade, illicit beer and salted pretzels. On the way back through the country lanes to the sanatorium, we stroll along a trail bordering a field of high corn to cut our distance short. It's late afternoon and the sun is already dragging shadows across the hills. The broad curtain of green stalks shudders in a rising breeze. I stop to listen because I think I hear the pitch of male voices other than our own.

"What's wrong?" asks Jerzy.

Galen says, "We're not alone," and points as out of the corn fields, emerge six sour-faced lads, teenagers by the look of them. Their leader is a blond youth with heavy pimpled jowls. He carries a corn stalk in his hand the length of staff, which he whirls around his head. The others wield stripped down branches and empty vodka bottles, but one who looks older than all the rest pulls a sharpened ice axe from his belt, the kind mountaineers use to cut hand steps in glaciers. They all line up in a barrier before us and the blond bloat declares, "Look at this! The Jews are back!"

Jerzy's face darkens and he gestures for us to close ranks around him. He calls the blond a whore's abortion and a poxy shirtlifter whose face he'll break if they take one more step towards us. I, for one, have no courage at all about this threat.

"Let's go," says Galen, "we don't want any trouble."

"Too bad!" sneers one of the Poles. "You're trespassing, this is a Catholic field."

The blond leader whirls his cornstalk ever aggressively until Jerzy manages to grab it, leaps upwards and catches the boy hard in the face with a flying football kick. "I wished you hadn't done that," I manage to blurt out above the screams of his bleeding victim and the curses of the others now ready for revenge.

"Into the corn!" shouts Henio. "Split up, they'll never find us!"

We flee into the green curtain two by two; Jerzy and I go dashing down one row while Henio and Galen take off to our left. It is an escape of utter panic and comic terror. We round one avenue of plants only to meet one of the vodka drinkers head on. Both Jerzy and I hit him together, pounding him until he falls heavily, moaning in stark surprise. From various hidden points of the field, I hear Galen call and Henio shout triumphantly, followed by screams and a great crash as many stalks are flattened somewhere up ahead. "You wait, lousy Zyd!" come the threats. "We'll bury you with the rest of the shit!"

I hesitate in the endless dense greenery. *Which way!?*

The Secrets of Rabka Zdroj

"Straight ahead, Romek, keep moving!" Jerzy drags me by the sleeve.

I hear several of our attackers surging ever closer from behind and to our right. "Trap the bastards!" they're shouting. My foot catches in a pile of blighted corn ears. I pitch forward and become a yelling tangle of stalks, tassels, and dusty roots. My face lands next to something shiny, the gleaming salvation of the ice axe, its polished serrated edge shone wickedly. I see Jerzy get slammed to one side by a heavy fist and the blond avenger stomping him brutally in the ribs. I rose with the fearsome weapon in my hand, urging myself to act fast before my nerve deserts me. My head hums and I think it's coming from the swaying green leaves. I'm praying out loud to my missing father. Papa, please don't let me be a murderer, but all the while feeling that a quick kill could be a very good thing!

I holler like a fiend and charge at the two boys now tearing at each other. Jerzy, sprawled in the stalks, grins at me through his bleeding mouth. He darts up and his next blow hurled the Catholic marauder my way. I twist to the right, the axe flashing in the late sun, and next slicing through the defending forearm of the swine blondie. The boy lets out a terrible squeal. He staggers and his warm blood gushes over my shirtfront. I am sickened and horrified at the visible notion that I've cut through human flesh; his arm muscle is opened like a filleted steak. I stutter something futile, like, "Please, if you stop fighting, I'll bind up your arm."

Jerzy is shouting at me to finish him off. "Roman, get him in the eye! Do it! Do it, now!"

I can't do it because my enemy is sobbing pitifully and hobbling away, bleeding all over the corn stalks. Jerzy tries to grab the axe from me. "Give me that, you fucking Nancy pants!"

"No, Jerzy!"

His eyes are dancing crazily in his head, and it's a surety that my feral friend will actually commit murder unceasing here in this crop, to the disgrace of the long past dead who now nourish its ripening. I throw the tool high across the waving tassels and hear it drop softly among the roots. "Please, Jerzy, let's end this. Let's find the others and go home."

He shakes his head and regards me as if I'm mentally deficient. The sight of my blood-soaked shirt makes me gag and I vomit into the dust. This seems to drain Jerzy of his fury, he puts his arm around me and says, "It's OK, Romek, some people have to work their way up to a killing. I'm not sure you're ready for this kind of fight."

I don't remember how we made it to the road, but there we found Galen and Henio waiting, bruised but valiant, their humor restored on finding us alive and victorious. There was no trace of our attackers, just the wind soughing among the green stalks.

Of course, the incident gets ahead of us. Descending the hill to the sanatorium, we spot the local Politzei van parked in the driveway and Jerzy takes us to hide in the orchard until the two officers come out with Pani Rulka and drive away.

"You go in, Roman," Galen urges. "See what's happening."

I creep in through the kitchen and walk headlong into our matron and Dr. Ostrowski. He takes one look at my blood-soaked shirt, gasps and calls a nurse immediately. The good doctor grabs a towel and tells me not to bend forward. He makes me lie down on the kitchen table and asks with much concern how I have walked so far with such a serious chest wound and, gently lifting my shirt, he is shocked at *not* finding my lungs hanging in shreds.

The four of us are expelled that very evening from the Rabka sanatorium. This is done actually with much kindly embarrassment and urgency. We are the subject of rapid-fire local gossip because the swine blondie, now a local martyr, is being stitched up in the local hospital. There were mutters along the main street of Rabka about the return of the Christ-killers, and a man in a tavern made a vodka-soaked announcement that uppity Jews were stepping out of their graves and coming for revenge.

We are instructed to pack at once and to stay in our room until after dark and wait until the other kids and staff have gone to bed. Thereafter, Pani Rulka brings us silently down a back staircase and out to a side lane where Dr. Ostrowski waits in his car. Oren walks with as far as this point.

"Just when you think all the crap is over for good, it rises up again like a bad smell," he says ruefully.

"You won't come back with us?" I ask.

"No, Roman, I'm done with running. This is my last stop, I'm happy here."

We all embrace him. I give him a new pack of cards and Jerzy hands him a pornographic novel he has filched from somewhere but that he can't read.

Scanning back over sixty years, I can still see Oren on that night, his hand to his concave chest, his smile ethereal, waving goodbye by the orchard gate with the cape of glow worms slowly lighting up the apple trees behind him.

24

Graveyard Days and Reunions

SINCE KRAKOW'S MUNICIPAL POLICE CHIEF has been sniffing around the refugee center, Director Jakubowicz is less than overjoyed to see him and then us. He orders we four confined to the house for the next week until the fuss in Rabka has died down.

"Is it not enough that we have to endure new persecutions in the city?" he lectures angrily, "that you boys have to incite pogroms all over the countryside? These Poles never expected Jews to return. Your very survival is an affront to many of them."

Our confinement is not so hard for Henio and Galen—both boys are claimed within a few days by two wealthy perfumed aunts. These ladies come for them toting half-a-dozen elegant suitcases, new passports and four immigration visas for Argentina, who whisper to the two cousins the news of a recovered family fortune now stored in the Banco de Galicia y Buenos Aires. This event seems to eclipse our crime and is a cause for warm celebration among the other residents.

However, that life should be so transformed into well-financed liberation and instant affection sears Jerzy to his core, opening up in him the bitter wound that he has never, in all his fourteen years, belonged to anyone. He flees from me and locks himself in the bathroom to weep bitterly. Later, when the janitor comes to force the lavatory door open, the place is deserted, water flowed from the ripped up pipes and wind blew through the destroyed window. Jerzy had returned to the streets. I would never see or hear of him again.

The disappeared from my life at this time also include Luda and Konni. The Red Cross has repatriated their father, Ernst Lubasz, and the girls have happily departed with him back to Warsaw, where the family hoped to eventually regain their clothing business. Wilús is still confined to the hospital, with Pani Mira visiting him every few days. She assured me that he is making a good recovery and, as a darling of the children's ward, is being detained longer than medically necessary because of the shoals of brute force roaming the city seeking out unsuspecting Jews.

The departure of my friends is not the only change at Dluga Street.

Many of the earlier residents have moved on, some to traipse through the DP camps of Europe looking for surviving relatives, others to knit together some semblance of a life, believing in a restorative vision that what had been before the axe of war fell, could be repaired and made right again. Pani Mira tells me that not since ancient times has the world seen such a mass migration of listless wanderers.

One morning, I am called to the Director's office and quake to see a very tall uniformed police inspector, Klement Haldzinska, and another official person in a dark blue suit. Jakubowicz announce the men as being from the *Najwyszy Trybuna Narodowy,* (the Supreme National Tribunal). They stood close together with the Tribunal man holding a heavy sheaf of files under his arm. *This is the moment of my arrest*, I think, *for wreaking havoc on Christian souls in Rabka*. I am the only one of my gang left here and assume that a quadruple punishment is headed my way but actually the gavel is about to fall for a more superior evil.

I sit small and fearful in a hard wooden chair with the two men and the Director staring at me across a vast expanse of desk, but at least they all are smiling. For one second of feeble hope, I wait to hear that they have brought good news of my father, or any of my family, but no. Inspector Haldzinska explains that they are collecting evidence from former Auschwitz inmates for the war crimes trial of Meilech Bronner, and could I please tell them what I saw him do to boys like me in the camp?

The serious-faced blue suit, Emil Komarek, comes and sits down close to me and speaks softly, "You have no need to fear, Roman. You should know that we are the people who will send Amon Goeth to the gallows. Your brother, Manek, will be avenged."

The mention of my brother's name stings but I have no notion that Goeth is in jail. So many feelings collide, a longing for Manek suddenly surges up in me, anger at Goeth at having just one death to face plus a great joy for the blessed rope. I have this wanting to tell someone that I love about this, but am too ashamed to cry in front of these important men. The face I look into is reading me closely. Komarek gently pats my shoulder hair and says, "Help us and you help Poland, and boys like you everywhere."

Director Jakubowicz smiles maternally and pours me a glass of black currant tea while the men sit with their notebooks at the ready. I tell them all I had seen in Auschwitz. The way Bronner would slash at us with his bamboo cane, how he boasted of whipping his fellow Jews into the mud, never to rise again, and how he searched for twelve-year-old Catholic girls from the Kinderheim to sell them in the camp's brothels.

Towards the end of my statement, I become aware that the door has opened and there is another presence in the room.

A waft of rose water drifts up behind me. I turn to see a stylishly beautiful woman, well attired with a dashing red hat my Aunt Cyla could have made, sitting by the file cabinets. Inspector Haldzinksa introduces her as Ida Stepkiewicz, a highly regarded journalist from the Krakow radio station. She smiles radiantly through movie star scarlet lips, showing brilliant white teeth and stands up to display a shapely, athletic figure as to imply she must have spent the war at a spa. My mouth gapes open at this stunning vision. She smells like a garden on a warm summer morning. I am so beguiled by her perfection that I hear nothing but the smoky nuance of her voice when she asks me if I would accompany her to retell the Meilech Bronner story on her radio show.

Then, Jakubowicz is answering for me and ushering me out of the chair towards the door. (I think to this day she is the first adult woman that made me utterly stupid with desire and adoration—a reaction I learned to moderate, as I got older). She even takes the haunt out of me denouncing Bronner to the listening public and makes me brave for the task. In the police limousine riding to the studio between her tailored elegance and Inspector Haldzinska, she tells me how people should share their war stories. "Speak your truth to the world, Roman, so that people everywhere will know how Poland and its Jews have suffered."

The jaunt to Radio Krakow I count as my one moment of fame. Though I am only thirteen, I feel the heroic strength of a grown man at a vital task inspired by a dazzling woman. In the gap of these brief hours, I sense a feeling of goodness, glamour, and purpose that this is what life could be like if only the dark times would recede forever.

People at the radio station shake my hand warmly and Ida orders rare orange juice for me and some excellent pirogi, which we eat together in her office, all the while, she asking about my family in her friendly but detailed way. Our conversation continues at the broadcast console before a set of microphones as wide as dinner plates, but Ida guides me smoothly through my Bronner testimony with carefully directed questions. I feel I will be sad when it is over, but she sends me back to Dluga Street in the limousine with several bars of dark Swiss chocolate and the perfumed imprint of her lips on my cheek. I vow I will never wash my face again.

✻

In the kid's dormitory, I still sleep on top of the wardrobe, but I miss Wilús and Luda-Konni a lot. There were a few other girls, who have moved into the female sleeping section with younger siblings, but they mostly keep to themselves. I ache for someone to pal around with and enroll in my misadventures. I lay awake, feeling lonesome, fantasizing about the scarlet-lipped smile of Ida and wonder if, at twenty-seven, she would wait until I was at least eighteen and could stand shoulder-to-shoulder with her as the man of her life.

In the immensity of a single night, when I am warm and secure in my reverie of her and her red hat, there comes a distant but urgent murmur drifting up the stairs, as if a stadium crowd is approaching the refuge house from several kilometers away. I hear a ring of metal hitting concrete and harsh laughter. The ceiling above me is striped by light from the street lamp that is suddenly extinguished. I turn over to recapture the image of Ida and decide to think about us at a beach. In my fantasy, it's a sultry July day and her gymnast's form strides along in a sleek swimsuit, her hair lifted provocatively by the wind, tanned legs churning up bright water.

However, the murmuring grows louder and my beach moment is struck down by a piercing scream from Pani Mira, who erupts into the dormitory yelling at top volume that all the kids have to get to the basement immediately!

There's a great hammering coming from the front hall, breaking glass, shouting men, ugly obscenities. I'm in my shoes and coat instantly, dressed from my camp habit of sleeping fully clothed. Pani Mira is shaking and ordering me to hide, "You must, Roman, at once!"

I speed out to the landing and down below I see Director Jakubowicz, Ignacy the janitor, and several male inmates piling furniture up against the front door. Outside rises a brute chorus of "We've come to finish the job the Germans started!" The door panels seem to be bowing inwards under the hideous blows of the fury without. Ignacy sights me and shouts, "Hide or die! The Jew baiters are here!"

I am gone on his last words, fast along the corridor to the men's bathroom where the window destroyed by Jerzy is blocked by a temporary piece of plywood. I'm running on legs of cotton and fear I will collapse but better to flee than be confined here and laid siege to. *Too many enclosures where the herding begins, the ghetto walls, the camp gates, the electrified wire, too easy to pick off the corralled, this is how it works, don't get fenced in anymore, it won't do, I won't do...it.*

The wood tears away easily from the splintered window frame and I sight Jerzy's route, a three-meter drop, but the water pipe running down the length of the wall will help. It's very dark, but I clamber down the pipe and hit the surface of the kitchen roof with both feet, next onto the coal bins, and then into the alley. I can hear the terror howling on Dluga Street's frontage. *Must run, must get away before they see me.* I'm good at this, still the artful practitioner of invisibility. I know how to dart into basements and glide noiselessly beneath wide sills, cross deserted courtyards, moving from shadow to shadow, unseen even by dogs.

Intending to head for the Planty and make a route through its sheltering trees, I turn the corner into Bastowa Street and pull myself into a doorway because there's a car on fire a few meters away, and men standing around it, applauding the blaze. A mighty noise blasts from the other side of Dluga, an explosion that lifts the fiery debris of gas lines high into the night sky. The knot of rioters swivels in its direction. I start across the street, but halfway, I am seen by two other men who suddenly emerge from a house on the corner. They wave a loud greeting to me but then halt. One grabs the arm of his companion and mutters to him. He is pointing straight at me, and the gesture speaks he's not one of us, not him!

They start to run in my direction and shout something I have no time to hear. I tear into the Planty shrubbery, weaving into the darkness, keeping my breathing low, my steps soundless. They're pounding after me and shouting. I have no idea of what time it is or where I'm headed. I can't hide in the sewers by the river—too many rats and the night traffic of johns looking for girls selling themselves along the wharf. Plunging into the water could take me unseen to the Podgorze side, but the Vistula's currents are swift for drowning. I can't go back to Waska Street either, and risk the feral kids living in the ruins of my old neighborhood. Then it comes to me—the Miodowa Street Cemetery! Who looks for the living among the dead?

I find myself on the far side of the Rynek Glowny, the city's main square, and it's a short run into the Kazimierz. I speed across Starowislna Street and on to the cemetery. I don't need to leap its ancient wall; the Germans have blown holes the size of gateways in its bricks and made away with many of the *matzeivas* (headstones) for building materials. Once a good ways in, I find an empty sarcophagus dumped over on its side like an open box. No dead inhabit it. It's dry and deep enough for me to sit up and lie down in. I drag some other gravestones and push them in front to wall myself off from any searching eyes.

The noise of the human tumult is now very far away, overlaid by church bells and distant traffic. Here there is nothing but the light rustle of birches, black thorns stirred by a hesitant wind and the thrum in my ears is my terror subsiding. Tomorrow I'll tug branches down from the trees and create an extra layer of fake shrubbery. I make a pillow of my jacket and settle into my marble bed.

Thus, I visit the grave for the first time and chuckle to myself—I'm a living corpse but at least I'm in good company with so many famous Jews buried around me. I remember Papa saying that this site gave final rest to Kalonimus Epstein, founder of the first Hassidic prayer house in Krakow, the painter Maurycy Gottlieb is here too, and my brother's hero, the Zionist, Rabbi Ozjasz Thon.

I fall into a heavy sleep in the middle of planning what to do next. Got to get Wilús out of the hospital, can't take the kid back to Dluga Street, the pogrom shits would take pleasure in hurting him, where to go? I have to find something to eat when the morning comes, another place to live, and continue to look for family. I slowly swim down into dreams of Manek and Papa, mine the only heart still beating in the Miodowa Street Cemetery.

I awaken to find my face sopping wet but it's not raining and I yell in shock at being poked at by a dark leathery snout and two black eyes staring into mine! I back up in terror—but the eager brown dachshund keeps licking my face and whining a morning greeting. His tubular head just fits through the narrow opening of stones. Beyond his sharp bark and frantic paws, I see the hem of an old tattered raincoat; a woman's legs encased in cheap boots and smell the home-rolled cigarette in her fingers. A female voice says, "I'm glad you're not a ghost! If you come out, I'll find you something to eat."

I'm hesitant to move. I don't know if she's one of Jew-beaters but the dog prompts me—he looks shiny, well fed and relentlessly happy. She must treat him well. Why not a lost boy? I roll out of my tomb and stand up to see a heavy-set woman of about thirty, full lips above badly stained teeth, smiling down at me. Her hair is acid blonde with the roots showing a better shade of natural mahogany. I stand up at once. The small dog sits between us, swinging his sleek head from one to the other. She pulls hard on the cigarette and regards me curiously, her breathing leathered by nicotine.

"Waiting for a funeral?" she queries.

"No. Are you alone?" I ask her.

"During the day—pretty much" she says. "What's your name, son?"

"Roman. Are you going to tell people I'm here?" I back away from her politely, in case I have to run. I have already sighted an escape route off to her left.

"I'm not in the betraying business. Besides, you look like no one owns you."

Her last words shame me and she sees that at once. "I don't like to eat breakfast without company," she says warmly.

We exchange more pleasantries and I mention the food she'd promised and ask her could she please turn around for a minute because I have to pee very badly. Her name is Zelina; the dog is called Beppo. She says she has some part-time work scrubbing floors and cleaning the house of a priest. Her husband had disappeared at the Russian front in 1943 and she now lived with a boyfriend named Silosz, a manic drunk who runs a coal barge twelve hours a day along the Vistula. She has some choice curse words for him in that awful mixture of rough love and disgust that, as my mother would say, bad compromises aroused in some women.

It doesn't help to hear that her man is a rabid anti-Semite. "Such a fuss he makes," she says, "over a few scarecrow Jews." She flicks her cigarette stub into the trees. "Some men can no more find their reasoning than they can locate their prick in a dark cellar."

She knows what I am and I don't dare risk her kind interest by asking about *her* faith, but the mention of her bigoted lover is troublesome. She scratches her plump neck; there are bruises behind her ear and a blue thumb mark at the base of her throat, and I know instinctually that he had inflicted them. She catches me staring at her punishments and raises her coat collar. "Silosz loves Beppo," she defends, "as a mother loves her newborn. I've seen him sob at the very notion that the animal should be ill."

But you're not a dog, I think. "Is he going to be your husband?" I query, truly meaning if he isn't...can he be removed?

"He's already someone else's," Zelina declares tartly. "He likes her money and she pays him to be gone. When you grow to be a man, remember to behave well around good women and G-d will remember what you do."

"Does it work the other way too?" I ask, "For boys who are hungry?"

For the next two weeks, Zelina is my lifeline. I am allowed to go to her apartment once a day, usually in the mornings when she is alone, where she feeds me barley and honey warmed with milk, and hands me a package of boiled eggs, black bread, and cheese whenever she has it. She fills several empty beer bottles with fresh water I can take and store in my tomb refuge and once in while she allows me to wash in her kitchen sink.

Her apartment is two slummy rooms with a shared toilet in the hallway in a building that had long been a dump before the war. The roof sags dangerously over the street as if exhausted and the masonry betrays decades of neglect. Scabrous bubbles of mold swell from the hallway ceilings and the staircase stinks of urine and cigarette smoke. Zelina's living space doubles as a kitchen with a tiny bedroom beyond. The place is furnished entirely with worn upholstery and other mismatched items Silosz has bargained for with second-hand *shonnickers* (peddlers) along the river. If it happens that her man is too hung-over to go to work, she hangs a bright shawl from the apartment balcony and I know then to meet her in the graveyard by the funeral house. The times that her priest employer has meat for his table, she enlarges her regular raids of it to include me.

"Father Hieronymus hates fish, so he stocks up before Friday," she reveals.

We eat with our hands, two pagans giggling and moaning satisfaction, our cheeks stained by the juice from Catholic lamb chops. Before us, fresh from her stove, more lamb racks lay steaming in rosemary resins and Zelina says there will be a buttery raisin kugel later. Food like this moves me to tears, makes me want to live indoors again with little Beppo and this blowsy generous woman.

On certain days, when she has taken too much of a beating from the barge man, she forbids me to visit her at all and leaves the food wrapped in newspaper on the grave of Dr. Thon. I stare up at her apartment and sometimes hear harsh shouting and then her crying. Silosz has made for Zelina a concentration camp of one, and put her in as much daily terror as any former prisoner. I feel ashamed for her and frightened for myself that her mate could maybe take the life from her, and her nourishment from me. She never seems bitter about her bruises, claiming that if you remove his unending disappointments and fists out of the equation, Silosz is really a meadow of expansive love. She reminds me of a stalwart field beast determined to withstand the blows of a depraved farmer, patient and enduring, whose strength will not be stemmed.

"But you can leave him, you can escape anytime," I say to her.

"And go where, with what?" she argues, the small dog grinning on her lap.

"Then kill him!" I urge, overlaying the blunt jaw of Silosz with the image of Amon Goeth, dissolving into a portrait of Meilech Bronner, all the same lineage of destroyers—here is murder utterly validated. Why not? Let the world throw them away, there is no human stamp on them. "People would understand," I reason.

"That's fine advice from a young boy like you. Did your people kill their captors?"

Her words silence me. *No, we couldn't*, I want to say. We were gathered up too soon, too fast, bewildered and frozen by such overwhelming and unknowable malevolence. We were people of the bad dream from which there was no awakening. Their weapon was our massive grieving—from robbing us and bleeding us of what we loved, so ruinous to courage, the innocent shot casually at the ghetto wall shrank us into easy submission. Still the predator clips at our heels, robbing me of the wonderful if temporary sensation at Dluga Street that I might be safe at last.

I'm only thirteen but I know, if it isn't for the fact that I would disgrace my father and shame my family, I could easily wait for Silosz in the dark, with the rusting scythe I'd found by the Cemetery's wall. I sharpened it against a granite headstone in a new understanding of how useful death can be.

Zelina keeps her vow not to inform on me and gathers news from her visits to the Dluga Street settlement that the place is still under threat and that some residents have fled to other safe houses. Jakubowicz and Pani Mira have arranged with the Matron of the Children's Hospital for Wilús to stay there while the persecutions continue. They tell Zelina that she should send me back at once. However, she declares to me that I should return only of my free will. I say I'll take my chances out here in the open. For people like me, life only offers a limited number of escapes and I need to save up the dwindling allowance that remains.

In my graveyard community, I sleep a lot or am able to find distraction in the summer afternoons by strolling along the avenues of burial sites and reading the names of the departed. Some had memorials of a cryptic nature such as that of Julius Begleiter, who was buried with his two wives, Nela and Chaja, beneath an epigram from the book of Jeremiah, *"The heart is deceitful above all things and beyond cure. Who can understand it?"* (Jer. 17:9)

I watch for anyone walking along the paths, and hide instantly rather than risk any stranger's interrogations. Once, I encountered a very elderly man, well dressed but so shrunken and racked with age that, if there had been an open grave, he would have lain down in it. He was davening before a headstone bearing the paired lions of Judah holding a crown. He saw me before I could hide and snarled at me cruelly, that I did not belong here, that this was not a playground for young louts! I tried to fake politely that I had come to look after the graves of relatives, but he said I looked like a dirty Christian beggar, and not to soil the rest of respectable Jews with my filthy presence. He seemed incandescent with hate and I wanted to hit him for his arrogance, for mixing delicate prayers with such obscene disregard for one brought so low. I backed away from him and made myself invisible in the trees.

He didn't intimidate me half as much as the gangs of teenagers who hold beer-drinking sessions in the cemetery and urinate on the graves, or the clusters of rough men supping at jugs of cheap vodka and methylated spirits, cajoling their ragged women to lie down against the headstones while they grunt with lust over them. It's August and daylight stubbornly lingers into a pastel dusk, too much illumination to frame goatish pleasures.

I cannot afford to be seen by such demons. I map out several routes of escape and alternate hiding places. I take to carving long staves from tree branches, using the scythe, making their points a stabbing force if I am ever cornered. These weapons I conceal in several places along the avenues. The scythe and my staves are also my sleeping companions.

I feel my most isolated at night, particularly when I see the lights go out in Zelina's apartment window. I am not afraid of the dead, but the darkness pressing in on me keeps my nerves taut. Coiled in a blanket that the woman has given me, I lie at an angle in the sarcophagus, my spears by my side, boxed in by the wall of stones, but with enough space to see out along the path.

Often I yearn for a cheerful graveside fire, a lulling comfort to stare into, but it would signal my hideout too much. Fire is not for the invisible; it deadens the craft. Besides, my unlit nights are fulsome enough, crackling with secrets; wings rustling through leaves, the intent glide of garter snakes pushing aside gravel, and once the ribbed silhouette of a feral Doberman that growled at my hidden scent but kept on padding his way to the gate. In these endless and solitary hours, fear makes my listening so acute I can detect the light scrabble of a rat in the undergrowth in the same second as that of a distant pebble kicked over by a human step.

Two things that hound me most are rain and the full moon.

Luna's watery light blurs the edges of shadows, swaying them in a rootless threatening motion. It silences the city beyond the cemetery and causes me to see forms that could be men or other dangers rising up as sinister columns of implacable darkness. Moonlight gives the birches a soft liquid presence and elongate what grave stones remained standing, white sentinels of lost worlds, voiceless histories, remnants of ancestors, and always the mulched smell of earth nourished by the giving-out bones. It's on their long-forgotten grace that I sleep.

Rain is another matter entirely.

A ferocious electrical storm sends a howling downpour swirling across the Cemetery, it bludgeons branches, causing them to lash at each other or break away as if they had been axed. Somewhere beyond my refuge I hear the slow groan of a larch submitting to a destroying wind and it falls to be caught in the fork of a black thorn tree. The grass around me becomes a bog and a mercurial shift in the slant of rain unleashes a torrent of water into my shelter, filling it like a bathtub. I roll out before I drown, grab what possessions I had and run for the half-exposed apex of two juxtaposed tombstones. This shallow "porch" barely keeps me dry. I huddle beneath it, sodden and cold. The storm waters pelt down and cut me like many fine needle points. There is no sleep tonight, just a low-level stupor accorded by rainfall.

Zelina and Beppo come out extra early the next morning, the little dog bouncing along the muddy paths with eager canine purpose, barking a greeting even in the persistent drizzle. "I couldn't rest for the storm," Zelina says, "thinking of you out here."

She takes me quickly to the apartment, strips off my sodden clothes and fills a tin bathtub with hot water. She laughs kindly because I have kept hold of my grubby shorts, turning sideways to her, clutching them at the waist, and blushing as I step into the welcoming soapy heat. "Keep them on if you must, Romek," she says, "But we'll have to find you another pair before the fleas dance away with them. Make sure you wash your private self with this. I won't look."

Zelina hands me a bottle of delousing liquid to comb thru my hair and to spread its stinging therapy in the meager thatch growing between my legs. When I am dried off, she has me dress in a change of cast-off clothes Pani Mira has given her for me. We breakfast on several bowls of comforting soup, after which I lie down on her rug, which smells of coal dust and boiled cabbage while she covers me with quilts and shawls so I can sleep away the afternoon indoors. Beppo comes to lie at my head, his alert eyes small olives of wariness. We already have a plan if Silosz returns to the apartment unexpected.

The front door of the building would often jam and he always pounds on it like an enemy. She would hear his impatience and fly down the stairs to offer him a sensuous delaying greeting while I am to zoom up to the next landing above their place and wait up near the attic for her to urge him inside. The glasses and the vodka would be ready on the kitchen table along with a bowl of his favorite cold potatoes rolled in sea salt. Beppo is to be locked in the bedroom throughout this ritual so he doesn't whine his detection of me. A click of the bolt in the apartment door is my signal to hurtle down the stairs, out into the street and back to my grave.

I once asked Zelina why couldn't she just simply introduce me to Silosz and have them let me sleep by the stove until I could find another place to be. I would even do any kind of work for him. Maybe he could use a lad like me on his coal barge. She pointed at my crotch and said, "Romek, the moment you open your pants to pee, he would know what you are. Those men throwing paving stones and horse shit through the windows of the house on Dluga Street, they're his heroes."

It is after the episode of the feral Dobermans that a gift of leaving came to me. I awoke in my tomb place one night to a hideous bustle, the clip-clip of claws on stones, panting rotten meat breath, the dark-on-dark of animal muzzles against which white teeth lay open and eager. There is no moon to deceive me but I might fare better by its shape-shifting light. Something is pissing against my marble barrier, I catch the hot ammonia stench, and the sensation of my hideaway being scrabbled at and dug out somewhere down by my knees. I raise my head to look out but pulled back just seconds before marauding jaws snap shut against the air!

Graveyard Days and Reunions

I yell loudly, grab one of my staves and pound it against the wall of the sarcophagus because I have no courage or heart to pierce the starving hide of the animals outside. A great pacing and circling, then a howling chorus all around me to intensify their hunt, the Doberman had brought his mate. We battle in a rhythm for about a half an hour with me trapped inside the marble tomb, they determined to excavate my shelter and have at me. I shriek aggressively above their barking, shouting Zelina's name, hoping she might hear me, sleeping beside her own brute. This would quiet the dogs for a time, and then I realize that my cries are muted by my stone box. I hear the dogs grunt and circle and then the digging and snarling start up once more. If I fall asleep, it would be over—so much for my vow of never being enclosed ever again. I have to get out and beyond them.

I yell out my plan, give them Zelina's brisket wrapped in wax paper, hidden in the jacket under my head, open one small stone, poke at them to drive them off, and throw the meat as far as I can from a sitting position across the cemetery. Bad idea—throwing arm and propulsion limited. I have only one chance to win—I had once seen the male Doberman trotting through the grave avenues, a writhing cat still alive but bloody and mutilated in his jaws. There's no doubt he could do me a lot of damage.

I pull myself into a crouching position and burst out of the grave roaring and lunging at the two dogs. They startle and whine, skittering back like puppies with a ball thrown. They track the package of hurled brisket that sailed high over the wall into Miodowa Street. When they leap to follow it, I grab my blanket and run for the nearby blackthorn, to scale it and rest high and safe on its cracked bark. From the street, I hear the two dogs snarling over their prize and wedge myself tighter into the tree's sturdy fork. I eventually fell into an uneasy sleep lulled by traffic humming far away in the city's center.

❋

A child's reedy voice drifts across my slumped awareness, the coaxing murmur of adults following it. I'm balanced face down in the tree fork and ants are parading along my cheek. It's very early on a benign August morning. Plumes of hesitant light spill along the avenues, gilding the white *matzeivas*, (headstones) perches now for noisy crows gathering to heat their open wings with the coming day. They are my sentinels. Crows basking easily means no Dobermans. My limbs ache from sleeping contorted like a pretzel in this tree, but I'm weary for more rest and can barely move. I pull the blanket over my head and drift off in the woolen gloom.

The child's shrill tones rise up again, a miniature cantor sifting through my sleep and then a man's gentle intonations of caution. The child's words, a small boy's stubborn bleating reaches me. "He's here. I know he is! Pani Mira said so."

A woman is saying my name and it's not Zelina! Another calls beyond her, it's the man, then the child, all of them off key shouting "Roman! Roman!"

My heart slams against my ribs and I pray this isn't a dream, make it real, dear G-d, let it be so! I'm awake in a second and yelling back, "I'm here! I'm here."

I sit up too quickly and smash my head against a branch, but never feel it because the impatient glee of Wilús is shrilling wondrously all over the cemetery. "Romek! It's us, Romek, where are you? I can't see you!"

But I see him! Hurtling through the brambles, curls bobbing, small hands raised against falling. I'm struggling down from the tree shouting with joy. It's so definitely my sweet Wilús, healthy and a little plump, prancing sturdily beneath the blackthorn, but the morning's abundance doesn't stop giving. Beyond him I catch the swing of a woman's summer dress, a delicate flower print, a pair of leather sandals and the finally the girl herself—my sister, Hanka! Alive and in full bloom!

For one moment, my emotions lurch because the face of my mother is not among them. Behind Hanka is her love, Joe (Juzek) Lipschutz. This is no shift of sleep into craziness. This is real! I'm fully awake and they're all standing below my tree bed. My sister is laughing although tears stream along her cheeks. Wilús is shouting that he wants to climb the tree too, and Joe is reaching up eagerly with his broad arms saying, "Jump, Romek, jump. I won't let you fall."

This is how it was on that gift of a morning. Everyone is speaking at once yet somehow we still hear each other. Wilús asks to be lifted into the tree. I haul him up to a branch and the fresh kid grimaces and tells me I stink. Hanka keeps hugging me, saying, "I don't care—you smell wonderful!" She bears a pleasant odor of peppermint soap and her flowered dress of rice starch. I'm ashamed of pressing my dirty self next to her but I can't let go.

They have a thousand questions: Are you hungry? Are you hurt? Are you ill? Why are you sleeping in this bone yard? Did you know how we knew you were alive? We heard you on the radio! "We went there," Joe is explaining, "to the radio station and Pani Stepkiewicz told us you were at Dluga Street and the people there said you were hiding here. We would have turned over the entire city looking for you!"

I'm feeling faint, I stagger and my sister makes me sit down in the leaf mulch because I'm hollowed out to have to listen to my own questions in case the answers break me—but they must be asked, "Mama? She is alive?"

Both he and Hanka smile with joy. "Alive! And safe and waiting so much to see you," says my sister. I stare beyond her, beyond them all, hoping to see Mama coming down the avenue.

"No, no, Roman, she's not here," explains Joe. "But she is safe and at a place for freed prisoners, a very nice place, at least it is now. I waited at Schindler's factory for Mama and Hanka but when they didn't show up after the liberation, the Jewish Aid people and the Red Cross tracked them to Bergen Belsen."

"Where's that?"

"In Germany," says Hanka, and she might have said that my mother had recently moved to Mars for the complexities of yawning distance that suddenly depressed me, as did my next question. "And Papa? Where is my Papa?"

Wilús is humming to himself and digging grubs out of a birch's bark. Hanka and Joe exchange those dismaying glances that adults make when they have to decide how they're going to explain things to a kid.

Hanka kneels down beside me and says gently, "Papa we are still searching for, but it takes time, Roman. There are people...with camp records... but we will find him, just as we found you. The most important thing is that we get the family together, or at least you and Mama in the same place then Papa will know where he will be welcomed and that you will be waiting for him."

25

The Journey to My Mother

I WALK OUT OF THE MIODOWA STREET CEMETERY between Hanka and Joe, my dirt-encrusted hands resting in their soft palms. As grimy as I am, I raise Hanka's fingers to my nose several times to catch the faint violet oil my sister has dabbed at her wrists. The perfume is a signifier, of everything lovely and civilized restored to her, and, by their presence, bestowed to me.

"When can I see Mama?" I ask my sister.

"It will take some days to travel to her in Germany,"

"But they hate us there?" I protest.

"They can't afford to hate us anymore, Romek," says Joe. "The British and the Americans have become their jailers."

"When do we leave?" I ask, half-hoping it would be now.

"In about three days," declares Hanka. "I want you to rest a while; our first stop will be Prague."

Wilús rides on Joe's broad shoulders, pointing at everything in the cemetery lanes and demanding me to produce Beppo, because Hanka has promised him a dog one day if he behaved, and he is under the impression that the little dachshund I have talked about is mine. I look back only once in the direction of Zelina's windows, the morning sun rendering them opaque, bright and sightless. I send her a silent thanks—she had crossed my life and kept me alive among the departed. I vow not to forget her.

We spend exactly two hours at Dluga Street while I bath and change into the new clothes that Hanka and Joe have brought for me, issued from a small suitcase that has a leather tag with my name on it. Director Jakubowicz greets me as if I have only been absent for a moment, but I think he is relieved to be getting rid of my cousin and me forever. He hands off some papers to Hanka for her signature and advises that now that I belong to my family again, I have no need to be tearing around the city's streets living like a gypsy.

We say our goodbyes with much handshaking, but I am eager to get away. The future is already here and it has kick-started an intense impatience in me—I want everything I might be destined for to happen now! The four of us head out into the sunny afternoon, walking together as a family. I have to declare it because the feeling has echoes of long ago, yet it is so novel. "We are walking together!" I say loudly. "Together!"

Wilús picks up on it and begins chanting as he skips along, "Walking! Walking! Good-looking boys are walking!" that causes the adults to guffaw and made other people on the sidewalk turn their heads and smile.

The Journey to My Mother

I glance to get the complete vision of my reclaimed clan as we pass the shop window of a locksmith. The boy who stares back at me is reasonably tall, hair washed and finally lice-free, his face wind-burnt from living outdoors but looking immaculate in a crisp blue shirt framed by a gray wool jacket with dark pants. The new black leather shoes I am wearing squeak as my calloused feet press against their hand-stitched welts. I feel awkward and awesome all at once and realize that for the first time in five years I am wearing clothes that actually fit me, not cast-offs from dead people.

"These clothes are not haunted," I tell Hanka, "They are mine, they are of me."

We stop at a café on Franciscanska Street recently reopened a few weeks previous. I sit at the table, at first like a mute animal, as one having to relearn how to navigate the expanse of a white linen cloth set with fine china and flatware bootlegged from a Warsaw hotel, which is now a brick pile. The owner, a reedy energetic man named Piotr Kukascy, apologizes for his limited choice of pastries, with sugar and flour still hard to come by. However, the menu to me reads like a scroll from Eden. There is a fine pear tart with a base of almond paste, macaroons oozing apricot jam, and small delicate muffins embedded with dark plums.

Wilús nags for one of everything, but with enough angelic charm that Hanka orders a huge plate of these mixed delights. I want to drink hot chocolate until I float away in it. "Romek, you deserve whatever your heart desires," says Joe and asks Piotr for our steaming mugs of the fragrant drink to be slathered with whipped cream and grated walnuts. It is ecstasy in a cup!

To most people, such commonplace things might seem pleasant but unremarkable. For me they carry, in this moment, a whole spectrum of feelings from rank anxiety that some awful force might rip these moments away from me to happiness so profound as to be dreamlike. My thoughts are running in many directions, from the worn cogs of operating against terror to dormant stirrings of sitting with people I love, seeing them strong, free and whole again. My sister seems to catch the whirring disorder inside me and put her arm around me.

"Are you OK, Romek?" she asks discreetly.

"More than OK," I say and nestle into her.

I look over at Wilús; his chin is spread with custard and macaroon crumbs and he's giggling through the mess. He scoops his spoon into a huge dollop of cream and offers it to me, his eyes shining with eager generosity.

"You have to eat this, Romek," he says. "It's good for you."

Joe has fixed it so we can stay for a brief time in the abandoned apartment of one of his colleagues who had long ago fled to the USA. It had a very large bedroom, a decent size kitchen, and a living room with a mattress and two dilapidated armchairs. Hanka takes the bedroom while we men, as Joe called us, would camp in the living room. Despite its limited furnishings, the place is spotlessly clean and sunny. A small, well-appointed bathroom has Wilús whooping with delight. He locks himself in and flushed the toilet numerous times as if it is the finest game on earth. It's only when Joe bangs on the door and threatens that he would see no more pastries this week if he doesn't come out at once, that the quirky kid finally emerges, his hair suspiciously wet.

Joe has endless patience with Wilús. "He's making up for lost time, Roman," he comments. "We should let him carouse and romp like a young foal."

※

More journeying but this time I'm not worried about being moved on.

I will travel as a free citizen, each day closer to seeing my mother. Besides, I've come to believe there's some odd sort of safety in constant motion. Hanka orders us to have our clothes packed and to be ready. Joe shows up on the third evening, driving a second-hand car he's promised to take across the Czech border to deliver it to a garage in Budziejowice, in Southern Bohemia. We have no passports, just each a document naming us as Polish-born citizens but displaced persons.

Joe has been teaching Wilús to read, telling the child for sanity's sake that "DP" after his name is a great honor, something that sounds like a knighthood but not so much. I ride in the back of the car with my cousin stretched across me like a log. I stare from the window at my city and ache with the intuition that I will not see Krakow again, perhaps for a very long time.

At the station in Budziejowice, we board the night train for Prague. Joe argues skillfully with the conductor to allow us one sleeping cabin at a group rate so we can conserve some of the travel coupons issued to us by the Jewish Rehabilitation agency. The conductor strides away, thrusting a packet of French cigarettes into his pocket. Joe's bartering means that Wilús and I will sleep on a lower berth wedged together like sardines. I take him to the toilet, a narrow cabinet on the train no more than a bare hole in floor, the tracks visible beneath us. I hear the conductor call out that we now are beyond Polish territory. Wilús urinates as the engine screeches and picks up speed entering Czechoslovakia. "Look, Romek," giggles my smart-assed cousin. "I'm peeing in another country!"

Later, the rocking of the train lulls my thoughts. In the narrow frame of a window, the stars are reduced to ribbons of passing light; the squat hulk of a white barn appears for a few seconds, the distant shoulders of mountains proving their darker mass against the night. Cows shocked awake by the bellowing train, rise up and stagger away into a waiting forest. Wilús is asleep on top of me, a warm puppy of a boy against my chest. I'm wide awake, thinking of how I'm going to explain to my mother that I had abandoned my father in Auschwitz, that I had disobeyed him because of my own crazy phantasms of disaster. Now that fear and hiding are no longer my first instincts, I have a greater clarity for thinking, seeing both past and present as a seamless whole.

"I'm so sorry, Papa," I whisper to the clacking darkness. I will find him, and we will talk like men, like equals together. I will make him see how the road I've traveled has given me wisdom. How I tried to get his pens back, helped bring a brutal Kapo to justice, and foraged successfully for my cousin and me. I imagine he will smile at the robust child who is now Wilús, noisy with life, old terrors like this landscape receding far behind us. The list of what I will say to him grows in pleasant extent. He will listen patiently, nodding approval here and there, and I will see the quiet pride in his eyes. I *will* find him.

The train hurtles its way through a small rural station and its lights illumined the faces of my beloved sleepers. Their slumbering makes me lonely. I wish Joe were awake so we could talk. I shift my mind from the choking guilt to positive thoughts of my father and the stories he would tell me of his pen-selling travels. He once had many clients in Prague, several banks that would buy his pens customized with their directors' names.

"Romek, you would like Prague," I recalled him saying. "Jews have left their mark there since the ninth century. Great men of the Talmud: Yehuda Loew, the Maharal, who created the Golem to protect his flock from persecution, David Ganz, a mathematician who wove sacred calculations from the many names of G-d, and Jacob Bassevi, knighted by the Hapsburg king. Such gifts they offered: scholars, astronomers, historians, and philosophers. When the Church slammed the door in their faces, they took to the books, the quiet refuge of the mind, so make sure you do likewise, little Rabbi."

※

In Prague, we stay for several nights in a Jewish refuge house not unlike the one on Dluga Street while Joe goes out to try to buy us places on a train that can take us to Germany. This is a time when much normal travel has been disrupted. The Russians have pretty much commandeered the rail system connecting several liberated nations to move huge numbers of troops and armaments.

Our temporary residence, according to the harried desk clerk improbably named Arpat Gotthammer, had once been a former sixteenth-century brewery. As the sun dapples through its diamond-paned windows, I can see the dust motes floating up from its broad oak planking. Several decades of hops and yeast have soaked every timber with sour ferment that gives me a headache and leads Wilús to argue for camping out in the lush overgrown garden because it is patrolled by homeless cats. He takes to running at these snarling creatures, squealing with delight, with an immediate and fetching love, his arms outstretched despite their arched backs and bared fangs. My cousin's high-octane energy rattles Hanka. "Romek, this boy has gone too long without any toys," she says, "without any playtime at all. Can't you amuse him?"

The next night, it's a different train, a slum on wheels, a coal-powered zoo.

Its compartments and corridors are jammed with loud-mouthed Slovakian and Russian soldiers, multi-national refugees, a few Jews trying not to appear conspicuous, black marketers scrounging to cheat travelers of their meager valuables, communist pamphleteers, women looking to hook up with a protector, and several families traveling with weary hollowed-eyed children. The carriage is rife with odors: cigarette smoke, unwashed bodies, sweat and engine oil, cheap vodka, and some distant miasma of boiled vegetables.

I am curious and eager to wander among all these characters but Hanka shoots me her severe do-as-I-say look and orders me to sleep because by morning we will have crossed the border into Germany.

The next day, as we walk from Munich's Central Station, we emerge into bright sunlight and a great devastation. I see an entire landscape of tall brick towers piercing the sky—street after street. However, they're not really towers but the single walls of buildings that have been sheared away. I see the bare frames of houses and bombed-out municipal buildings, a forest of destruction continuing to the horizon. The blackened front of a church presents only its Gothic façade, the structure behind it, completely obliterated. The former nave is a pyramid of shattered timbers, stone and glass. It reminds me of a book of architectural cutouts I had when I was six. A huge marble lion projects out of the pile as if he had just awakened to roar at the disorder.

The long avenues of wrecked masonry give the streets a spectral quality. Packs of stray dogs, scarred, emaciated and wild-eyed—standing with hesitant supremacy on the pinnacles of brick heaps, stare down at us with not even the strength to bark. We round a corner to see clusters of men and women clawing through mountains of rubble to lift out a single shoe, a battered pot, a bicycle almost bent in half, some torn clothing, a chair with no legs. They seize on these items and argue over them, as if they have discovered the rarest treasures.

There are small encampments of people in the ruins, boiling water in tin cans balanced over small fire pits and one man was roasting something dark and bloody on a stick over open flames. Several dirty children with sores on their faces and a ragged woman sit before a hut fashioned from sheets of corrugated metal and cardboard boxes. The kids seem listless, sealed up in themselves. Wilús waved and shouted something friendly to them but they shrink closer to their mother. "They can't understand you," says Hanka, "They're not Polish."

The only Germans I had ever known had been military, selection squads and camp guards who certainly deserved to be sent to hell. However, what I am looking at now are kids just like me sitting in bombed-out places, waiting for hunger to find them.

"We can't stay here," I say. "Not in all this mess."

The Journey to My Mother

I stare around at the blasted cityscape, willing us to not to be guests of the rubble dwellers and their homemade grills. Joe catches my rising distress and puts a hand on my shoulder. "Come, Roman, we have a ways to walk, to a good place with real food."

It takes us an hour to find the UNRRA center (the United Nations Relief and Rehabilitation Administration) where Hanka says we can rest and be fed. Along the way, we come upon the fragments of the University's buildings, its many books floating in water-filled craters. Next, an elegant bishop's palace and an army of Catholic clerics carefully lining up the stones of destroyed walls along the garden walk and numbering them, as if to remember where they had once fitted. A line of carved statues of saints stands watching in the gray-dusted grass, a crowd of wood no longer open to the prayerful pleas of Munich's residents to protect them from the firebombing that rained down on them in the final days of the war.

The UNRAA DP processing center is part of a severe-looking ministerial building with several American Quonset huts added as feeding and sleeping facilities to replace its north wing that had been bombed to smithereens. The wide avenue before it is crowded with jeeps and trucks, US flags flying from their radio antennae. There I see a flash of red metal and gleaming chrome, a vision so startling it makes my breath catch with a sudden rush of memory. Grace built from Detroit steel, a wide-winged bright scarlet Cadillac, the car of Tadek Horowitz's dreams! "It's here, Tadek!" I say to his long absence. "It's here!" I shout so loud it made everyone in my group halt. "Must be a General's car," Joe says. We have to pass it to gain the entrance to the security desk.

A young American corporal, all rude health and a winning smile, is inside wiping down the upholstery. He waves at us. I run my hand over the shining fins and the broad headlights and I remember Tadek in this moment, not with pain but in exultation, with a closeness in the loop of time.

"Romek, ask the nice man if he'll let us ride in it?" says Wilús, who is busy rattling the handle of the driver's door.

Hanka pries his fingers away and she and Joe hurry us all inside the center. Two white-gloved military police direct us towards a huge dark paneled meeting room that looks like a vast library. Through its double doors I hear a strident clamor, shouts, arguments and even tearful pleas. I see several large oak desks, with queues of hundreds of people streaming out from them. More refugees are wearily propped against the wall clutching sheaves of papers in their hands, waiting for the opportunity to stand in line at any of the desks. Harried clerks type furiously on long-paged documents or patiently explain in a babble of different languages why the face or the family that stands before them cannot be repatriated at this time, nor would they be emigrating all that soon either.

A notice on the wall instructs: *The quotas for Australian visas and for the USA are exhausted for the week—please return on Monday for new visa opportunities for America and the Commonwealth nations. Some open emigration slots maybe available for Canada if applicants submit their requests tomorrow at window number five by at 10:30 a.m.*

A lone thin Jew, looking quite elderly, is incensed at this news. His voice trembles as he declares, "Madam!" to a headliner of an American blond with a warm smile, "I'm compelled to be in Germany by misfortune, but I have no wish to end my days here and left to rot in the soil of my enemy!"

I watch as she reaches out and gently touches his arm, answering him fluently in his own Yiddish. Her capacity for the tongue astonishes and then calms him. He grips his hat nervously, but forces a slow grin of wonder when she says next, "Mr. Bernstein, a representative from the Jewish Immigrant Aid Society from Montreal will be here tomorrow. Since you are a skilled furrier, you will have preferred status for residency and a labor permit. I know you've been waiting many weeks, but I promise you, I will place your application in his hands myself and personally supervise the processing of your visa. You will soon be under sail."

The blond officer stamps his documents loudly, a little drumming of freedom, and hands him a copy. Nathan Bernstein stares at the approved application in awe, hardly believing his luck. He's so used to protesting the blunt wall of being nowhere, but I sense fear retreating from him. She's the one, I think, the yellow-haired angel at the gate who can get things done. Now I see Bernstein positively glowing with joy and notice that what I thought was advanced age is actually a much younger man marked by the deprivations of imprisonment. He thanks the woman of endless patience, and bends over to lightly kiss the hand that will deliver him to a new life across the Atlantic. His wasted forearm bears the Auschwitz tattoo, several earlier denominations prior to my own number, most likely from the intake of 1943.

Along the walls are several notice boards where refugees have posted messages (in several languages) seeking family should they happen by. One board was completely covered in photographs with the request posted above them in German, Polish and English, "*If any of these persons are identifiable, please make their names and whereabouts known to the UNRRA Search Department.*"

"Let's look there," I say to Hanka and run over to it, hoping the one face that would emerge would be Papa. I dart from one side of the board to the other, but my sister halts me when Wilús asks me if he can see a photo of his parents?

"Your family is right here with you, sweetheart," she says and scoops up the boy in her arms. He is immediately distracted by her affection and lets her carry him off to a bin of used toys available to absorb the waiting of displaced young ones while their parents upgrade their status from stateless to hopeful.

The Journey to My Mother

Joe says to me he will ask the duty Lieutenant about my father and will leave a detailed description of him, as he has in many such centers between Munich and Krakow.

"It may take a while to locate him, Romek," he advises.

I see a barrel-chested American officer with lively blue eyes moving through the crowd with easy authority and Joe pushes his way to meet him. The soldier answers his greeting in perfect Polish, in a garrulous, highly charged manner. "Hi, I'm Lieutenant Mitch Wolkowski, from Green Bay, Wisconsin." Joe's grips his arm as if they have been friends forever. Wolkowski keeps their conversation going while barking orders left and right to his adjutant and several office staff in English and in German. Between these linguistic acrobatics, his Polish flows like that of a native.

He raises his cap to Hanka and turns his broad grin to Wilús and me. "Hey, sprouts, you look hungry" and presses into our hands the first Hershey bars we ever taste. Although I cannot understand the English label at the time, Hanka reads it slowly "US Army...Field Ration D." Wolkowski tells us that he is a second generation American with grandparents from Katowice who once made the best *Wiejska* sausage in the region. In between descriptions of his grandfather's delicatessen and its provisions, he quickly sifts through all the documents Joe hands him with grunts of approval interspersed with loud praises for *Kiełbasa Lisiecka* and its pork-filled cousins.

He beckons to a female sergeant, winks at her, and pulls a bunch of chits from a file she's holding. He hands one to each of us. "Take these kids to commissary. They look like they could use some solid chow. I'll fix a ride for the boy with the Brits." he says with a concerned glance at me. "You folks can billet the family here tonight. We just shipped out three hundred Greeks back to Salonika, so we got plenty of free bunks."

In the UNRRA commissary, we are allowed to eat from the hot table line as much as we could handle. The food temporarily distracts me from questioning Joe on why Wolkowski is fixing a ride for me "with the Brits." Through the kitchen doors, I can see a vast storeroom with giant cans of corned beef, beans, coffee, and sacks of various fresh vegetables resting beneath racks of newly baked loaves. The warm bread in my mouth is a revelation, true bread with no weird or ersatz fillers! Sweet crunchy grains so fulsome and comforting, and real butter, rich and smooth, gold in grease form. If this is American abundance, I ask my sister, can't we go to New York or the Green Bay place, and pick up Mama on the way?

"Romek," she says cryptically, "how would you like to be with Mama in the next twenty-four hours?"

I am so astonished at the offer that I choke and blow crumbs across the table. Joe taps my back and assures me such a trip is more than possible. As my sister explains it, Joe, Hanka, and Wilús would continue onto Linz in Austria, where Joe has a cousin with a house with many rooms. They would stay there with Wilús while Hanka and Joe filed the papers with a family judge who would rule for them as his guardians. Technically, Wilús couldn't attend a school, or emigrate anywhere, until Joe and Hanka straighten out his legalities. Right now, they could easily pose as his parents but not forever. Nor do they want to draw the attention of any Jewish legal aid zealots who might send him to an orphanage.

Wilús, of course, is as changeable as the wind and starts to carry on that we all have to go everywhere together forever and forever! I can see the growing uncertainty spread across his elfin features, his lower lip pursed, which was always a short trip to panic and a tearful outburst. "Make him understand, Romek, please," whispers Hanka, "that we will all see each other again very soon.

"We have spoken to the lawyer in Linz," she explains, "who must physically see the child as evidence that what we're doing is legal."

Besides, their process could take several weeks, and would delay me in getting to Mama.

Later my sister would tell me that Bergen-Belsen still holds many terrors for her, of her being in a deep typhoid fever in the latter days of the war while trying to nurse Mama in a barracks rife with disease. "You have to understand, Roman, there were no bunks, and we slept on the floor. There was no help, no food, and no warmth. The dead rested, bloated and festering, next to the living for days on end, until those who had any strength left could drag the corpses to the nearest ditch. "

"By April," she says, "we overheard talk of Ernst Kaltenbrunner, a General of the Waffen-SS, ordering Josef Kramer to execute every prisoner still living rather than abandon the place to the Reich's enemies."

My mother and sister and other inmates were saved because of the gastric afflictions of Himmler, who was persuaded by his physical therapist, Felix Kersten, to reverse the order.

Hanka and Mama were eventually nursed back to health by a medical team led by Brigadier Hugh Llewellyn Glyn Hughes, a British military physician, and Dr. Hadassah Bimko, a 32-year-old Jewish dentist from Sosnowiec, all traveling with the British 11th Armored Division and the Royal Artillery 63rd Anti-Tank Regiment, who took command of the camp.

"Mama understands that we may go to Austria with Wilús," she goes on, "but Roman, what she doesn't know is that we've found you! The sooner you reach her, the better for her joy it will be."

"What about Papa?"

"We won't stop looking for him, I promise you," Joe assures me.

"So I go to meet Mama by myself? How do I get there?' I demand, a little hurt that we'd have to separate temporarily but with the rising and secret excitement of a potential adventure in the offing. Hanka promises they would follow me to Bergen-Belsen in a couple of weeks.

The Journey to My Mother

"You don't have to journey alone, Roman," Joe explains. "Lieutenant Wolkowski has arranged for you to travel with a unit of the British army leaving for Hanover tomorrow morning. You'll be embracing your mother by tomorrow night. G-d knows that lady is way overdue for a miracle."

We are assigned to a double-winged Quonset hut that serves as overnight accommodation for DPs in transit. From outside, the unit looks like a small aircraft hangar, but inside the UNRRA planners have made it humanely comfortable with brightly tiled walkways and linen curtains. The dormitory is divided into male and female sleeping quarters by a narrow hallway on whose walls orders are posted prohibiting the use of alcohol, cigarettes, loud conversation, and fraternizing between the sexes. Joe and I have camp beds on either side of Wilús. I have to explain to him that I am going away for a short time to see his Aunt Malia while he takes a short vacation in the Austrian mountains with the others.

"You'll come back?" he asks, his small voice full of doubt.

"Yes! I promise. And Hanka and Joe will bring you to see us."

He swings his head to Joe, who he now calls *Papa Joe*.

"There'll be no bad people there, Papa Joe? No bad soldiers where Romek's going?"

"No bad soldiers. It's a very nice place," Joe assures him, "With other kids your age.

"Are there animals, Romek? Will Aunt Malia have a dog?"

"Maybe we can find you one when you get there."

And I swear in my heart that after the tumult that is likely to be my meeting with Mama, I will grab the first stray mutt I can get my hands on, hopefully in scale with Wilús's small frame, and place the creature in his arms personally.

※

The next morning Joe wakes me before it is light so I can quickly bathe, dress and be gone before Wilús is awake. He embraces me, holding my face between his hands, his eyes fierce on mine. "Roman, you are no longer alone, you have a family, now go claim your mother. Hurry, Wolkowski is waiting for you in the lobby."

When I meet up with the American lieutenant, he is speaking in English to a tall, aristocratic-looking officer, Captain Bramwell Harcourt of the British Army on the Rhine units. Harcourt is as lean as a tree, bony-faced, with several insignia bars and stripes on his uniform, career-military all the way. He's a regal-looking man and under his hawkish nose rested a reddish, elegantly waxed mustache. He eyes me with the scrutiny of a severe schoolmaster that makes me pray that my forthcoming journey will be a short one. "This is the lad?" he asks of Wolkowski. "Have him in the lorry in ten minutes."

The Captain marches away with a clipped stride as if he is on the parade ground. Wolkowski and I follow him out to the street, where the American explains to me in Polish that the Captain, a Sandhurst officer, might appear to have a rod up his backside, but is the father of three kids around my age, and could be softened up at the right moment.

"Listen, sprout, there'll be a bunch of Tommies on the convoy, great guys to a man. Ask for a Sergeant Lawrence Murphy, an Irish gunner. Studied Baltic history at Cambridge. He speaks some Polish, might help you out in a pinch. Here, take this with you and enjoy."

The Lieutenant hands me a heavy knapsack, US army issue. Inside, I see several fresh chicken sandwiches wrapped in wax paper, apples, oranges, more Hershey bars, and two bottles of the brown drink called Coca-Cola with my very own bottle opener.

"Your friend Joe filed search papers for your dad," he says. "As soon as we find him, the UNRRA folks will contact you where you're going. Be safe, OK?"

He shakes my hand and pats my shoulder several times.

Harcourt is standing by a canvas-covered truck, the lead vehicle of a convoy of six, all flying the Union Jack from their radio antennae. He salutes me stiffly. I instinctively raise my hand to my forehead too, not wishing the officer to think me disrespectful. It seems to be the right gesture because I catch the ghost of a smile as he turns and announces to the dozen men seated in the back of the truck something about a new recruit and to make space for me. The men shout a hearty greeting in their yowling English vowels that I don't understand, extend their hands and haul me up into the truck bed. Harcourt takes his position in the cab by the driver, cracks an order and the entire convoy pulls out into the ruined city.

For the next six hours, I am somewhat lost, in the midst of these foreigners, ruddy-faced English soldiers, with bad teeth and sunny natures. A young man with a dark complexion, black hair, and amazing green eyes, says a friendly good-morning to me in the most musical Polish I've ever heard, he's the history-loving Irishman, Sergeant Murphy. He asks if I've ever studied the subject at school. I tell him I haven't sat at a desk since 1940. "Jesus, laddie, you'll have some catching up to do," he says kindly. "Bergen-Belsen has a school now. I'm sure your parents will enroll you in it."

The men watch me curiously, nudge Murphy with their elbow, and by the gesture I guess they are saying, "Ask the poor little bugger how he made it this far?" Murphy does ask and I condense my past into a few sentences. There's a short silence when I mention Auschwitz, and the men exchange solemn glances with one another. One man takes off his corporal's cap and rams it on my head and smiles broadly. Murphy translates, "Oakshott here says you'd make a fine soldier. Maybe you should bring your Mum and family to Blighty, learn English and take up a trade in London. We've already got the Polish Government over there, and some twenty thousand Polish airmen and soldiers who fought on that side of the channel."

The Journey to My Mother

But I want to know about them. The whole unit is made up of seasoned warriors, many of whom fought their way to shore at Gold and Sword beach on D-day. Murphy is a reconnaissance strategist, a great map-reader, and a forward gunner. "I have a good memory for monuments," he explains. Oakshott, a window-cleaner from a place called Tunbridge Wells, is known for working covert bombing raids against German army camps. He has an ambition to start a fish-and-chips shop once discharged, and says his wife Alice was saving their business funds in a vase under the stairs. A small, pinched-faced man, Geraint Thomas, is a former church organist from a village in North Wales and delights us all by singing a majestic hymn with a rich and nuanced tenor voice.

I notice he speaks English as if he is waltzing the language over a hilly terrain, with swoops of emphasis and rising inflections on the end of his sentences. Although I can't follow what he is saying, his manner of speech is very pleasant to my ears.

He explains via Murphy that he had been in a British prison as a conscientious objector and very much against the war at the outset, until the London blitz when the Germans bombed the life out of the capital for fifty-seven consecutive days. "Well, after that," says Thomas, "I just couldn't stand by and do nothing. Not that I wish to teach a young boy that it's a bad thing to have principles and then change your mind, but sometimes you have to make choices pressed by the circumstances you find yourself in. I joined the army my first day out of Holloway prison."

Soon, via my learned Irishman, I have the life story of every man in the truck. They break out their rations, insisting that I share theirs and keep the provisions Wolkowski gave me to hand along to my mother. Oakshott also gives me a pair of nylons as a gift for Mama, one of a dozen pairs he was intending to send to his Alice. "Not every day a bloke finds his missing Mum," he says cheerily. "Be like Christmas in July."

Soon the conversation lulls into a smoking session among the men. "We'd offer you one, young Roman," says Murphy, "but Harcourt is a stickler for discipline. He'd have us in the stockade for corrupting a child or some such shite!"

I don't mind. I am watching the signs of the passing towns, Celle, Winsen, then suddenly the sign for the Bergen-Belsen camp emerges along the highway, and in a few minutes, we are at the main gate. However, I am fearful of seeing the stark barracks, the burial ditches and funeral pyres, now cold and ashen. Murphy gently assures me that the old prisoner quarters are now destroyed and the DPs are housed in the camp sector where the former billets of the German army are located.

Through the truck canvas, I see people strolling along paved avenues bordered by lush flowerbeds in bloom. There is a playing field with kids kicking a soccer ball; young women sprawled on lawns, and elderly men reading on wrought iron benches under shady trees. If the camp's notorious past had remained unknown, any stranger passing by would have thought they were looking at the well-kept grounds of an upscale sanatorium.

Oakshott lowers me down to the tarmac and Harcourt walks me to the duty guard, beckoning Murphy to come with us to translate for me. He says a few words to the guard who nods in understanding. Then the Captain shakes my hand, and through Murphy, declares, "Young man, I want you to know that if my children show half as much fortitude as I can see in you, I would be proud of them forever. Be well and be happy." He tucks his regimental baton under his arm, salutes me once and strides away. Murphy gives me a smile and a wink, "Maybe I'll see you again one day, on my side of the pond. Good luck, boyo, to you and your Mammy."

The convoy pulls away and I hear the men singing raucously a tune my Aunt Cyla taught me about the English hanging their washing on the Siegfried line, a song that she always said would drive Goebbels into a fury, whenever the BBC penetrated the German airwaves.

They are gone and I'm left with the duty guard, a somber Polish Jew whose name badge announces him as Dov Bozniacka. Although I'm back in my mother tongue, his gloomy demeanor is all too familiar, that haunted, post-war deprived look that makes me miss the spirited brightness of the British unit. Bozniacka barely looks at my DP papers and indicates sourly that I should go with him.

He walks ahead which gives me a chance to look around. I see families walking together, a trio of Hassids in earnest argument, a man gathering tomatoes from a row of healthy vines, and a woman outside a newly painted barracks pinning wet laundry to a clothesline. Bozniacka calls out to her. I see her reach up to pin a sheet, she has a shock of white hair, she turns around…a breeze flaps a pillow case, half-hiding her eyes, then I see…she has the face of my mother!

The next few minutes make mayhem of time. Fragments of long months that have been broken, are seamed together of their own volition where minutes became shards of seconds. The world appears to tumble around me, invert then right itself. I feel an exhausting confusion, as if I might faint. I cannot quite believe the woman hurrying towards me is my parent, sobbing and screaming my name. She has her hands on my face and is kissing me hysterically.

"Roman! Roman!" she shouts to a gathering crowd, "This is my son, Roman! This is my son who has lived!"

Epilogue: Bergen Belsen

AT THIRTEEN, I FEEL LIKE the world's oldest living child. Just as ancient beasts evolved their forms through primal swamps, volcanic embers and the drift of ice plates and unending winters, I am burnished and reshaped by my fiery wartime road.

On the day I reunited with my mother in Bergen Belsen, she does not let go of me for several hours. Even as she cooks the first meal we would share together in a long time, she has me stand next to her with my arm around her waist. "I have to make sure, Romek, this is real," she says, "that you are not some phantom boy who will disappear the moment my back is turned."

When I asked her about my father, she says, "Later, Romek, you must eat."

This answer implies news of him has arrived and brings with it instant foreboding. She buzzes with secrets of the most damaging kind. The food tastes like a lie in my gullet. There are no formalities, no dignified messenger with the calm utterance, "We regret to inform you, Roman, that your father, etc., etc."—only the dull bone of grief sharpened by my mother's dry sobs when I eagerly press her for more details.

"He is...not alive anymore, Roman," she says simply, her voice husky, struggling to lessen the impact. Dead in Flossenburg camp just a few days before the US army arrived at its gates in April 1945. The circle between my refusal to walk with him out of Auschwitz and my arrival here was finally closed by an injection of phenol to his heart.

I like to think that my father's last view of this world was the Bavarian mountains beginning to green at the first hint of spring. The apology that I have carried for him these hundreds of kilometers with every hope of his loving forgiveness now brands me for all time.

The expectation that he's survived can be cast away from me but not the wanting of him. Too late, I am too late to explain, to plead for his easy tolerance, for the nod of his head as he thoughtfully absorbs without judgment the impetuous actions of a stubborn boy. *I did it, Papa,* my mind utters silently, *so Wilús and I could live, I made us live, don't you see?* I feel like the prodigal eternal and my father's presence will walk with me as much as Manek's always does. Just as I had uttered private comforts to my missing brother along the road, I now add Papa to my secret conversations whispered across the unmapped terrain where this life junctions into eternity.

※

I am alive in a new century with the receding corridor of decades spinning out behind me. The war is long past but, for most survivors, there is no escaping its distant echoes; they are perpetually embedded in their every fiber. I know of camp compatriots that, in the pristine safety of a New Jersey suburb, still flinch at the sound of a car backfiring. Their hands tremble as they rake the first spatter of orange leaves across the withered grass, expecting cordite smoke on the air and the shouted command, above the racket of kids in the street playing stickball. The textbooks and psychotherapists may define it as part of survivor syndrome but ruts worn in the soul by war, systemic violence and constant danger are part of a larger call for the universe to right itself and uphold the intent of life that we only truly flourish where love dwells.

Such thoughts are not mine originally. I hear my father's voice again in his simple beliefs of kindness, honor and right conduct. *These are jewels of the soul, that which makes a man his best human self, little Rabbi,* he is telling me. My only answer to the bleak emptiness that follows his loving presence is, "I did not forget you."

Frequently in the afternoon quiet of a winter day or in the muted dark, just before the daylight widens, my consciousness is populated by figures from the past. They are all around the edges of my life: Manek, Papa, Moniek Hocherman, Tadek Horowitz, Pinie Koza, Tadeusz Pankiewicz, Oskar Schindler, my infant cousin, Lonius, an innocent lamb for the fires of Auschwitz and many more too numerous to name.

How gently they clamor at me, each face asking for memoriam, for an assurance that, despite all the years that have passed, I will not allow any evidence to be erased that they once had a voice and a vital place in this world.

Postscript

On Columbus Day, 1949, Malia Ferber and her then 16-year-old son, Roman arrived in the USA to start a new life.

They settled in New Jersey and were soon joined by Hanka and Joe Lipschutz (who had married in Bergen-Belsen), to be followed by Wilús Schnitzer and Victor Lewis and his wife.

Many years later, Roman met and married Maxine Singer and went on to have two sons and a daughter.

At the time this book was completed, he had five granddaughters. He returns to Poland frequently, and always to the Remuh Synagogue in Krakow to say Kaddish for those family members and good friends lost in the Shoah.

Made in the USA
Columbia, SC
15 April 2019